ASSAULT ON AN ABBEY

THOMAS O.P. SWEENEY

Printed in the United States of America

Print ISBN: 9781735448503
E-Book ISBN: 9781735448510

**Canoe Tree
Press**

4697 Main Street
Manchester Center, VT 05255

Canoe Tree Press is a division of DartFrog Books.

TABLE OF CONTENTS

CHARACTERS

Cedrik Balthazar	Warrior
Eric	Warrior
Leif	Warrior
Alexander	Warrior
Suleiman	Warrior
Barney	Demon 2nd Class
Boss (female)	Satan
Boss (male)	Satan
Polina	Demon 2nd Class
Abigail (Abby) Williams	Clerk in a medical practice near Philadelphia
Margret Preston	Friend of Abigail's father
Faiza	Ali's chief wife
Adeela	Daughter of Omar the shepherd

Ali	Taliban Head of the Tareen tribe in the village
Mohammed	Taliban Head of the Akakhel tribe in the village
Bahri	Itinerant Trader in Afghanistan
William Stanton MD	Oncologist
James Lucas MD	Oncologist
Charles Barr MD	Oncologist
Marguerite Camp	Office Manager for Stanton, Lucas and Barr
Nancy Simpson MD	Member of **The Group of Five**
Diana Chan	Television reporter for the local CNB station
Ellen Spalone	Friend of Diana Chan and Dr. Jones' Office Manager
Alice McKenzie	Mother of two boys with Autism
Francine Burke	Mother involved in hospital melee
Chad Mitchell	Republican Senator from Wisconsin
Mary Chase	Democratic Senator from Rhode Island
James Delaney	Democratic Senator from Illinois
Kathy Burns	Republican Senator from California
Rev. Raymond Curtis	Pastor of Rejecting Sodom Church

Raphael Melek	DC Lobbyist
Mike Angelo	Pizzeria Owner from Brooklyn
Angelina Gabriella	Employee at Halvorson's in Portsmouth, NH
Lucius Diamond	President of the United States
Tommy Sullivan	Agent
Douglas Keenan	Producer and promoter
Lorena Mason	Assistant to Tommy Sullivan
Father Buchanan	Abbot of the Monastery
Father Jubal	Individual Retreat Master
Sven Sorenson	Captain of the *Soul Searcher*
Olaf Karlsson	First Officer of the *Soul Searcher*
Hans Fischer	Engineering Officer of the *Soul Searcher*
Richard	Boson of the *Soul Searcher*
Bruce	Deckhand
Monica	Executive chef
Suzette	Sous chef and Head of Guest Services
Brittany	Stewardess
Tiffany	Stewardess

Janice	Stewardess
Lionel Simms	Hedge Fund Manager
Dorothy Simms	Wife of Lionel Simms and philanthropist
Sylvester Berkshire	Ne'er-do-well son of Presidential Candidate James Berkshire
Dexter van Allen	NYC Real Estate investor
Phyllis Greenfield	CEO of a Fortune 500 computer hardware manufacturing company
Rebecca Wagoner	Managing Partner of large Wall Street law firm
Antonio Spiga	Singer, actor and film producer
Darby Clark	Star of show in Atlantic City
Major General Tillis	Commanding General of Walter Reed Medical Center
Dr. Spencer	Physician at Walter Reed Medical Center
Sergeant Murphy	Paralyzed patient at Walter Reed Medical Center
Dr. Marks	Chief attending physician on the Spinal Injury Ward
Janelle	French nurse in Loala
Claudette	French nurse in Loala
Francois Obutu	President of Kilnmari

Frankie Obutu   Son of Francois and Annette

Joshua Weinschenk   Head of Israeli legation in Loalaville

Terrence Ngao   President of Loala

Marie Justine Obutu   Obutu's lesser wife

Annette Obutu   Obutu's primary wife

LCDR Trevor Dawson   Commander of the extraction team

AUTHOR'S NOTE

First of all, this book is a work of pure fiction. All of the events are the product of my imagination. Some of the locations mentioned are obviously real, but the events the book describes happening in and around them are not real. The same is true of the characters in the book.

I really wish that there was such a person as Abigail. On second thought, there are people like her, many people. I'm not talking about her mysterious magical powers. I'm talking about her innate kindness, goodness and generosity. She is by no means perfect, and she knows this. She tries her best to put others first and to consider the effects that her actions have on others. She is a kind, gentle soul we can all try to emulate.

As I was about two-thirds of the way writing this work, the Coronavirus struck. I did not sidetrack Abigail by asking her to chase it down. I allowed her to focus on the mission I had already set for her. I think my representation of the panic and violence that could occur when people get desperate is pretty accurate.

ACKNOWLEDGEMENTS

I wish to thank my wife, Jennifer, for reading the pages as I wrote them, offering comments, corrections, and support all along the way.

I also want to thank Colette Dennison from Collette Tours. Colette was our tour guide on our visit to the Emerald Isle and did a masterful job of bringing the magic and the history of Ireland to life. On this tour, I visited Innisfallen Abbey outside of Killarney on Lough Leane. This site provided the inspiration for the abbey in the opening part of the book.

My dear friend, Terry Shields, deserves a special nod of thanks. Terry read the multiple drafts of the manuscript. His comments and corrections were invaluable.

A special thank you goes to Brigitte Werts. Brigitte edited the manuscript, and I think she did a masterful job. Among other things, Brigitte is a fiend for commas. One can never have too many of them.

First, foremost and always, this book is dedicated to my wife, Jennifer. She is my rock. God only knows where I would be without her, but I'll wager it would not be a pretty sight.

I also want to dedicate this to my son, Tom Jr., and my daughter, Christina. Tom is a wonderful son, a loving husband, and an outstanding father. I am very proud of him. Christina passed away in 2017 after a brave fight with Lupus. Her mother and I miss Christina every day. Requiescat in pace my dearest daughter

Finally, this book is dedicated to the United States of America, the land of the free and the home of the brave. May God preserve it from all enemies both foreign and domestic.

IRELAND 9TH CENTURY

S omewhere in the southwestern part of the island is a very beautiful and usually tranquil lake. The lake and the surrounding area at that time were in the territory ruled by the O'Reilly clan. The beauty of the lake and the land was surpassed only by the harshness of life for the inhabitants, the serfs. These serfs were tied to the land and the O'Reilly's. In years of good harvest, life was good, people were well-fed, and taxes were paid to the O'Reilly's. In years of poor harvest, life became a struggle to survive, people starved to death, and taxes were paid to the O'Reilly's.

To make life more challenging, Ireland was the target of frequent raids by bands of marauders from Scandinavia and the continent. The raiders were brutal. Killing, raping, and plundering were the norms. Villages were completely burned to the ground, crops were destroyed, people starved, and taxes were paid to the O'Reilly's.

In the center of the lake was an island. Upon the island, a group of monks built a small monastery and set about doing what monks did in those days. The monastery started small, but soon buildings with stone walls appeared. There was a building with small individual cells for the monks; a building with a kitchen and refectory; a building for copying manuscripts, studying and readings; and a chapel where services were held three times a day. Eventually, a school was opened for sons of the nobility to attend. Since the monastery was on an island, it was not easily accessible for the common folk on the mainland. Occasionally, members of the O'Reilly clan would row or sail over to the island for Mass or to remind the monks that the monastery existed through the good graces of the O'Reilly's.

In the summer of 857, a band of raiders from Scandinavia attacked the area. They laid siege to the fortress the O'Reilly's had built for defense. Local serfs sought refuge in the fortress and were initially welcomed by the O'Reilly's. As the siege went on, food supplies began to be exhausted. As the food was depleted, the O'Reilly's began expelling serfs from the keep to the mercy or lack thereof of the marauders.

Amid the siege, the chieftain of the raiders turned his sights on the monastery. He was sure they would have chalices, candlesticks, and other accouterments of sacred services made from gold and silver and was confident that they were his for the taking. The monks had built walls for defense, but they were peaceful men of God who had no in-depth knowledge of the finer points of warfare. They also did not have weapons to speak of. A few knives, hatchets, and a sword or two was the full extent of their weaponry. The raiders counted the monastery as low-hanging fruit.

A fleet of about half a dozen small boats was amassed to carry the invasion force of about 20 men. They planned to attack from the southeast shore of the lake. The day of the invasion was cold and blustery which caused white caps to form on the lake. The raiders were all experienced seamen, so rough water on a lake was not a concern.

The landing spot they selected was one of the few on the island without steep ledges and rocks. While not exactly a sandy beach, the spot included a gentle slope to the upper level. It featured a rather narrow path that initially was not wide enough for two men to stand side by side. There were fairly steep hills on either side of the path, so transit to the top of the hill mandated taking the path. As the path ascended the hill, it increasingly got wider. If viewed from above, it would look like a funnel.

As the force approached the island, they saw the monks cowering behind windows and walls. It did not appear that the landing would be contested. Just as they were ready to disembark, their gaze fell upon five men who looked and acted like warriors. These men had shields with the scars of previous battles upon them. They each carried broadswords and wore helmets. Two also were equipped with maces[1]. They wore no badges or outward sign of their allegiance or nationality. They just stood at the top of the rise where the funnel started to widen and dared the invaders to step onto the island. The apparent leader of the group was a young man with light brown hair and a beard that had not fully grown in. He could not have been older than 20 years old. At first glance, he was not an imposing or threatening figure.

The leader of the raiding party took one look at the five figures on the hill and thought himself fortunate indeed. He was leading a force of 20 battle-hardened warriors against a boy and four others. He liked the four-to-one advantage, and he really liked the prospects of gaining honor and glory from his chieftain, not to mention a large split from the booty they would return with. Life was good. The only way he thought that it could improve was if there were nuns or other women on the island with whom they could pleasure themselves. Nuns were preferred since they always put up fierce resistance, but, he thought, beggars can't be choosers.

---

1. A heavy medieval war club with a spiked or flanged metal head, used to crush armor.

He barked out several orders to the other boats and ordered his vessel in first. Upon jumping from the boat into the water, he found it to be about chest high and incredibly cold. No big deal, a little action with the sword would warm him up considerably. The terrain dictated that they progress up the hill in a single file since the path was so narrow. It was not what the leader would have drawn up, but he did not consider it a major impediment. In a short time, all of the boats had disembarked their warriors and remained near the shore.

Two of the invaders preceded the leader up the slope. The first was met at the top where the funnel starts to widen by three of the defenders, one of whom swung a mace. It landed and cracked the skull of the hapless warrior who crumbled to the ground. The second invader tried to step over his fallen comrade but was speared through his chest by a broadsword. The leader yelled for the remainder of his men to rush the hill. The five defenders took turns servicing the invaders so that none became exhausted. The leader watched as his men were cut down and found himself facing the boy who led the defenders. He figured if he could kill this boy, his men would be able to break through and fight on open land where, with their numbers, they would surely prevail.

He charged his opponent with wild thrusts and was truly amazed by the boy's skill with the broadsword. Most grown warriors had to use two hands to heft and control the blade. Not this lad. He spun it like a twig. The leader's thrusts were met with skillful parries. It was like the boy was toying with him. The leader looked desperately around to see who might be able to come to his assistance. To his astonishment and anger, he saw 12 of his men lying dead on the ground and 7 more in the water trying to get to the boats. That was the last thing the leader of the raiders saw. A well-aimed swing of the boy's broadsword freed his head from his body. A severed head is basically a ball, and it bounced down the path into the water. The five victors watched its progress down the slope and cheered mightily when it finally sunk beneath the surface of the lake. All five of the warriors looked as if they had merely taken a leisurely stroll around the village.

The abbot of the abbey came out from one of the buildings followed by the rest of the monks and the schoolboys who were enrolled there.

"Sir, who are you? How can we thank you? We owe you everything," said the abbot.

The 'boy' replied, "No thanks are necessary. You owe us nothing. And to answer your first question last, my name is Cedrik of Balthazar. Farewell, good Abbot, we must be off. Pax vobiscum." And with that, the five turned around and went to the far side of the island where they were never seen or heard of again.

The siege of the O'Reilly's keep lasted only another day or two. The seven survivors reported to the chieftain upon their return from the island that they had been defeated by a huge army that was, even as they spoke, preparing to cross over the lake and destroy the raiders. The chieftain was a wise man. He knew when to raise and when to call and when to fold. He had little to gain by continuing the siege and ordered a retreat to the coast. Along the way, they burned everything they saw and tried to rape anything that moved. That is why to this very day the sheep in this part of Ireland all have the same shocked look on their faces.

For their part, the monks recorded the story of the attack on their abbey in a history they were painstakingly compiling for future generations. The story was also verbally passed down to novices as they began their journey of faith. Over the centuries that followed, the monastery prospered and grew, as did the legend of Cedrik of Balthazar and his four companions. There were hard times to be sure, but overall it was successful. The final assault on the abbey was complements of the Tudors, Henry and Elizabeth, when they suppressed the Roman Church. The English royals confiscated the Church's property and dispersed the monks. The precious documents were lost. Thankfully the verbal legend remained alive and well.

PROLOGUE

I t has not been a good period for the boss and his band of merry demons. Barney, typically one of his most dependable demons, recently lost his perspective, misplaced his priorities, and made a mess of the boss's hold on the U.S. Congress. In a fit of rage, the boss shipped Barney off to Afghanistan to live as a human among the tribes near the Khyber Pass. Barney always prided himself as being an urbane sophisticate. He was always the epitome of style and grace, a true metrosexual in every respect. A Maserati was Barney's preferred method of conveyance. Now he is riding a burro and wearing filthy, dusty, ragged clothes. He is badly in need of a shave and a bath. Barney is not a happy camper and neither is the boss.

Boss has always prided himself on being resilient. He is like a Timex watch. He can 'take a licking and keep on ticking.' He is confident he will make a comeback. The only questions are where, when, and what the comeback will look like. The possibilities are endless as he looks around the world.

More genocide in Central Africa? Too easy.

Revolution in Venezuela? Possible. Make sure to file it away for future use.

Something involving the Vatican? That is always fun. Clergy scandal? Too blasé. Another scandal with the Vatican Bank or the Curia? Interesting. Worth looking into.

Get something brewing in the Middle East? It is always fun to see the Muslims tear each other to pieces. It is easy to start and, once started, it lasts almost forever with little or no maintenance. A lot to recommend this one.

Something with Israel? High reward, but incredibly high risk. Not worth the potential loss.

How about the European Union? Don't really need to do anything there. Brexit will provide entertainment for years.

Do something to get back in the saddle in Washington? That moron, Barney, did a number there. Eventually will have to re-engage. Why wait? Congress? The upcoming elections? Opioids and other drugs? Gun violence? Impeachment? Collusion? Tampering with US elections? The list is endless.

As the boss mulled over all of these potential pearls, he developed a headache. Evil was supposed to be fun, but lately, it had become more like work. What could he do to get things back on track?

Just then, Boss experienced a transformation. Gone was the fashionably dressed male of about 45 years old with green eyes, medium length, neatly combed brown hair, no facial hair, and a nice smile. In his place stood an incredibly beautiful woman. She had shoulder-length auburn hair with red highlights, a gorgeous tan, and a figure that Playboy Playmates would kill for. She had striking green eyes, lustrous and glimmering like sparkling, shimmering pools. She was wearing a low-cut silk blouse, a short, tight skirt and stiletto heels. To herself, she said, "I can blame Barney all I want, but in the final analysis, he just got beat by a better team. Barney focused on a pawn, Bob Wallace, and was unaware that his real opponent was that damn order of monks in Georgia. If I take them out, who knows what mischief will ensue? Taking them out won't be easy. They are bright and talented, but worst of all, they are motivated by idealism. Doing good! Making the world a better place! What a bunch of crap. I'll show them who is boss."

Suddenly, another demon appeared. This one had a female form and was named Polina. Polina was a tall blond woman who appeared to be in her early twenties, although, as with all of the boss's assistants, age is meaningless. Polina was incredibly thin and looked very much like a runway model for some chic design house in New York or Paris. She had medium length hair and looked like she just stepped off of the boat from St. Petersburg. She spoke with traces of a Russian accent. With a worried look, she said, "Something is going on in the United States, and I think you need to be made aware of it. I'm not sure if you want to get involved or not."

The boss replied in a very snarky tone, "Polina, dear, why don't you tell me what's going on and then I can decide what to do?"

Polina looked terrified. She knew this form of the boss was a monster who would rip someone's head off and laugh while she did it. As she composed her answer, another transformation occurred and the male form of the boss was back. Polina breathed a sigh of relief. This form was every bit as evil, but on the surface, at least, he was more rational and less likely to lash out indiscriminately. "Boss, there is a woman in a small town outside of Philadelphia. She was somehow granted magical powers and can cure sick people. She is not even aware of it yet."

The boss replied, "Then, Polina, how is it that you are aware of these powers?"

"Boss, I was at a hospital in Philadelphia the other day and saw her in action. I am the only one who took notice. She wasn't even aware that she did anything. She walked by an older man who had cancer. Within five minutes, the cancer was gone. The doctors just discovered this today during a routine exam and are dumbfounded. They don't know what to make of it."

The boss looked perplexed. "Why should I care about something like this? It seems to me that it is just a minor aberration. Why waste time and effort with it?"

Polina answered, "What happens, if and when, this girl, as well as other people, become aware of her powers? Think of the public outcry. There will be riots trying to get close to her. Don't you think it might be wise to get ahead of the situation so we can better manage it?"

The boss thought for a few seconds and ordered Polina to go back and keep an eye on things and learn everything she possibly could about this girl.

THE INVISIBLE GIRL

Abigail Williams was as plain as vanilla ice cream. She was quiet to a fault. Self-confidence was nonexistent. She had no friends and very few acquaintances. She had the unenviable ability to walk into a room and no one would notice. The opposite was also true. She could leave a room and no one would notice.

Abigail grew up in a middle-class family in a suburb of Philadelphia. Her father worked as a sales representative for a large chemical company. He was very successful and made a good salary. He had a vast territory to cover: from Maine to Delaware and as far west as the Indiana/Ohio line, and spent almost all of his time on the road. He would typically leave on Monday morning and return around noon on Friday, spending the remainder of Friday and usually part of the weekend working on expense reports, contact reports, and other sales-related paperwork. He adored his daughter though he spent almost no time with her, claiming he was too busy at work.

Abigail's mother was overbearing and very critical of her daughter when she was sober, which wasn't often. She was a drunk, a mean drunk. When she wasn't climbing into the bottle for booze, she was popping pills. Abigail learned very early to give her mother a wide berth. They were not in the least bit close and barely spoke to each other. She had no brothers and sisters, and the house her family lived in was in an older neighborhood that had no children living nearby. She was isolated. Most girls had toys and dolls to play with. Not Abigail. She had a few coloring books and jigsaw puzzles, and that was it. Her mother did not care, and her father was too busy to notice. Her parents lived each of their lives isolated from their family and thus condemned Abigail to do the same.

On weekends her father would try to spend time with Abigail, or Abby, as he called her. Unfortunately, he had chores to do around the house, grass to cut, groceries to buy, and bills to pay. These activities severely limited the time he had available for Abby. Her father would occasionally take her shopping for clothes. He was generous to a fault but had absolutely no sense of fashion or style. Since she had no female to mentor her, she and her father floundered when they went shopping for clothes.

When Abigail was 12, her mother and father got into a terrible fight. Her mother accused her father of having an affair. She went on and on about how good she had been to him and Abigail and kept asking how he could do this to her. There was no physical abuse, but the emotional violence was devastating to Abigail. It ended with her father slamming the door and leaving. He stayed away for two weeks.

About a month after the fight, Abigail went home and found her mother dead on the floor. No one was sure if it was accidental or suicide, but a combination of alcohol and drugs was the official cause of death. When Abigail found the body, she had no discernable outward emotion, but secretly she was elated. She didn't expect her mother's death to be a game-changer, but the source of conflict, shame, and guilt was gone. She felt relief.

Her mother's funeral brought some surprises. Aside from her father's bosses, a few co-workers, and several neighbors, no one else attended. No one, that is, except for a very attractive woman, exquisitely dressed with perfect make-up. She had a wonderful smile and a gentle voice. She was the antithesis of Abigail's mother. Abigail sensed immediately that this was the 'other woman' and that her dad was crazy about her.

The pretty lady that Abigail saw at her mother's funeral was indeed a 'friend' of her father's. She lived in Pittsburgh, which is on the opposite side of the state from Philadelphia. As if it were possible, Abigail saw less of her father than when her mother was alive. His business trips carried over for two weeks about half of the time, instead of the usual four-and-a-half days. His lady friend made frequent trips on the weekends he was home to visit them in Philadelphia. She stayed in the spare bedroom while visiting. When Abigail did the laundry, she noticed that the sheets on the bed there looked as fresh as the day she made the bed several weeks previously.

The lady's name was Margret Preston. When visiting Philadelphia, Margret would make a valiant effort to engage Abigail. She would take her shopping at the mall, and they would have lunch at nice restaurants. Margret was very fond of Abigail's father, and she was lonely. However, she did not love him, and she was sure he felt the same towards her. Their relationship was a pleasant diversion from their humdrum existences. Margret felt sorry for Abigail and tried to help her. Abigail had absolutely no sense of fashion and her hair, that she cut herself, was usually unkempt. She owned absolutely no make-up. Margret diplomatically tried to show Abby that there were pretty clothes to wear and that a few hours in a beauty salon could do wonders for a girl. Over a few months, Margret could tell she was beginning to make progress. Then it happened. One rainy night a drunk driver ended up in the wrong lanes of the Parkway near Squirrel Hill in Pittsburgh and plowed his car right into Margret's. Margret never knew what hit her. Her death was quick. Abigail also never knew what hit her. She got a phone call from her father late one evening telling her that Margret was dead. Margret was the first person who ever noticed Abby; the first person other than her father who ever cared about her; her first friend.

Abigail's metamorphous from extreme introvert to something else was aborted before it could ever take off. She was devastated and was inconsolable for weeks. She quickly returned to the warmth and security of her isolated cocoon.

School was more of the same. She had no friends, and her teachers were barely aware that she was there. When she raised her hand to answer or ask a question, she was usually overlooked. She faithfully did her homework and got good grades, but if her teachers were asked about her, they would all have to pause and try to picture her.

She made it out of grade school relatively unscathed, but not so middle school. Kids can be cruel, especially pre-teen girls. Abigail was teased unmercifully. The slights, the insults, the scornful looks were incessant. She had no refuge at school, and she certainly had none at home.

High school was a variation on the same theme. When it was time to change classrooms at the end of a period, the corridors turned into a gauntlet that Abigail was forced to run five or six times a day. It was mostly the girls who were responsible. The boys usually turned away and did their best to ignore the torture being inflicted on Abigail by the other girls.

There was one notable exception. His name was Craig. He was a mean son-of-a-bitch. He had a terrible inferiority complex. Like many who feel inferior, he turned into a bully. He was always careful to go after the small, the weak, those who were unable to defend themselves. He was quick to try to ingratiate himself with teachers and members of the 'in-crowd,' but most were able to see right through him. His modus operandi, when he spied her in the hallways, was to follow her while loudly calling her name along with some very derogatory adjectives.

On one momentous day, Abigail was enduring the gauntlet as she moved from History class to Algebra at the end of the first period. The hallway was very congested and the herd of students moved at an excruciatingly slow pace. Craig spotted Abigail in the crowd and pushed his way towards her. He got right behind her and loudly began his litany. There was no place for Abigail to go. She had to stand there and silently endure the moron's wrath. Eventually, small tears started down her cheeks. Craig was emboldened. The tears were like throwing gasoline on a fire. As Abigail shrunk smaller, Craig expanded his attack.

Suddenly a thunderous voice boomed, "**HEY NUMB NUTS, KNOCK IT OFF.**"

There was total silence in the hallway for a few seconds. Finally, Craig figured that the voice was addressing someone else and continued his harangue.

"**DAMN IT, I SAID KNOCK IT OFF! I'M TALKING TO YOU, ASSHOLE!**"

Craig looked around uneasily. As the crowd started to back off, he saw a young man about his size storming towards him. The young man had a rugged face and light brown hair. He was cleanly shaven and wore a neat shirt and chinos with loafers. He looked very 'preppy'. Craig saw that anyone who was in this guy's way, girl or boy, big or small, was roughly pushed aside. The young man came up to Craig and stuck his nose about an inch from Craig's. In a very threatening voice, he said, "You slimeball! You maggot! You pimple on the ass of the world! Who do you think you are?" Craig was silent.

"I'M WAITING! I WANT AN ANSWER AND I WANT AN ANSWER NOW! WHO DO YOU THINK YOU ARE?"

It was apparent to all that Craig was out of his element. He had been called out and had no idea what to say or do. He started to walk away, which turned out to be a terrible idea. The young man grabbed his arm, spun him around, and threw him into the wall. Then he got back into Craig's face, but this time he was less than an inch away. Craig barely whispered, "I was only having some fun."

The young man took that to be the wrong answer! **"WHAT DO YOU MEAN YOU WERE JUST HAVING SOME FUN? I DIDN'T SEE ANYTHING FUNNY."** He looked around at the crowd of students and asked, **"DID ANY OF YOU SEE ANYTHING FUNNY?"** His question was met with total silence. **"THAT'S WHAT I THOUGHT."**

Then the young man turned to Abigail. He took her hand in one of his and with the other, he brushed the tears away. "Don't cry, honey. This bastard isn't worth it. You go to class now. I still have some unfinished business with this loser."

Abigail looked at him and gave him a shy smile, then turned and started to walk away. Her schoolmates started to disperse. The young man said, "I was speaking to Abigail, not to you all. You all stay where you are."

When Abigail disappeared, the young man turned on the crowd. After calling them a bunch of gutless cowards and a few other colorful phrases, he admonished them for their insensitivity and their behavior. He was particularly harsh with the females. Few, if any, in the crowd could make eye contact with him. When he was finished with them, they hung their heads and proceeded slowly to their assigned classes.

Just about every student was late for their next class. Abigail was an exception. She was on time. Craig was also an exception. He was very late for his class and looked like he had fallen down some stairs when he finally arrived. At the end of the day, the subject of discussion in the teachers' lounge was about what a strange day it had been. How quiet and subdued the students were and how they were all late to second-period class. None of the teachers were able to get a satisfactory answer as to what occurred, although some made valiant efforts to do so. The cone of silence had descended on the high school.

Abigail spent the rest of the day thinking about the nice young man who had come to her rescue. No one had ever done anything like that for her before. When she changed classes after the second period, no one did anything mean or malicious. In fact, most of the students, while not overtly friendly, were at least courteous. She passed Craig, who was a mess. He looked away from her and hurried down the hall. Maybe things were going to get better.

She had never seen her knight in shining armor before that morning and did not have a clue to his identity. Over the next week or so, she searched the crowds of students in the halls, the cafeteria, and assemblies looking for him without success. One day she passed Craig in the hallway. She looked him directly in the eyes and asked Craig if he knew the identity of her savior. Craig looked like he was ready to faint. He looked wildly around in every direction as if he feared for his life. Finally, Craig muttered in a voice not much louder than a whisper that he had no idea who the young man was. As soon as he answered, he averted his gaze and hurried away.

Abigail continued to search for the young man without success. After a while, she filed him away in her memory bank as a pleasant memory. Her memory bank was not overly crowded with pleasant memories, so she cherished this one.

After graduating from high school, Abigail enrolled at the local community college. She received an Associates' Degree in

Accounting and landed a job as a clerk for a group of Oncologists practicing in Philadelphia. She was a very conscientious and reliable employee. Marguerite Camp, the office manager, relied on her, but the three doctors in the practice didn't even know her name. If they referred to her at all, it was "that girl." She was content to go into her little cubicle every day and lose herself in medical records, billing issues, and other paperwork.

Occasionally, Marguerite would ask her to take something to one of the doctors who was making rounds at one of the many fine hospitals in Philadelphia. Abigail never refused to go, but she dreaded the chore. Leaving the security of her cubicle to catch a train or a cab was a necessary evil. If she happened to have her car with her, she had to drive through crowded streets, find a parking spot, and then track down the doctor in the hospital. That meant she had to engage others in conversation, which left her open to ridicule and scorn. When she found the doctor, she knew she had to give him a little time to recognize her. One time she had to remind the doctor that she was one of his employees.

On one particular rainy, blustery day, she was sent to deliver papers to Dr. William Stanton. She learned that he was currently on the 7th floor. She exited the elevator to see the nurses' station with a crowd around it. There were nurses and orderlies in scrubs, as well as Dr. Stanton and another doctor Abigail had never seen before in their white coats. The doctors were speaking to a couple who was obviously in distress. The woman wailed pitifully as her husband tried to keep a stiff upper lip. He was failing miserably. A man in a Roman collar had his hands on each of their shoulders. The family kept motioning to a nearby room with glass windows blocked by closed curtains. As usual, no one noticed Abigail. For some reason, she felt compelled to enter the room and was appalled by what she saw. A young boy of six or seven was lying in the bed in obvious agony. He had tubes going into each arm, an oxygen mask on his nose, and wires attached to just about every other part of his body. Monitors and other instruments displayed sine waves, graphs, and an array of numbers. The boy was struggling for every breath and looked to be in pain. Abigail's heart went out to the lad. She walked over to the bed and gently reached out and stroked his forehead. His eyes popped open and he stared at her. She smiled and whispered that things would be all right. She took one of his small hands in hers, gave it a gentle squeeze, and exited the room. No one noticed her. She took a deep breath and approached Dr. Stanton. As unobtrusively as possible, she silently handed him the papers and headed to the elevators. He did not acknowledge her. He was not even aware she had given him a file.

When the elevator doors opened, Abigail saw that she would have fellow travelers. An orderly was pushing an older man in a wheelchair. The patient's hands were restrained and he was babbling nonsense. Abigail had spent her entire life being ignored and she was damned if she would do it to others, no matter what the circumstances. She looked directly at the old man and smiled. Presently the elevator reached the ground floor and all three passengers exited. As they did, a patient on a gurney pushed by two nurses rushed by. Abigail heard something about a stroke. She shook her head and silently wished the patient well.

Abigail returned to the office and the security of her cubicle. She worked alone with no disruption until noon. She always brought her lunch and usually ate it alone at her desk, and this day was no exception. When she finished her meal, she went out to use the ladies' room and stretch her legs. She passed by the three doctors who ran the practice standing in the hall holding a conversation. Dr. Stanton was speaking animatedly. "I'm telling you I have never experienced a day like this. First there was the Miller boy. He was on his last legs. Cancer had metastasized all over his body, his vitals were almost nonexistent, and the pain meds were not working. He was in store for a horrible death. I was at the nurses' station with the family and a priest telling them that the end was close. I told them we were doing our best to make him comfortable. You know, the usual spiel. All of a sudden one of the nurses grabbed my arm and took us to the boy's room, where we found him sitting up in bed despite the IV's and wires. He was groggy, but he was smiling. I checked his vitals, and they were perfect. I ordered lab work, and you know what? They came back negative for cancer. There was no trace of it."

Dr. James Lucas said, "How is that possible? He had gone beyond the point of no return."

Dr. Stanton replied, "You're telling me? I asked the boy what he remembered, and he said that a lady came into the room and told him everything would be all right. Then she left. He said he started feeling better right away. He said nothing else happened. I haven't signed a release order yet. I want to keep him around for observation for a few days."

Stanton paused for a moment then continued, "But that's not all. An orderly was moving an Alzheimer's patient in a wheelchair. This guy was in the advanced stages of Alzheimer's and would probably be permanently bedridden in a week or so. All of a sudden, the old guy becomes perfectly coherent. He remembers everything that ever happened in his life. Hell, his memory is better than the three of ours combined."

Dr. Charles Barr was incredulous. "Did the orderly have anything to say?"

Dr. Stanton replied, "Not really. He was transporting the patient in the elevator. The elevator stopped at a floor and someone got on. He didn't pay much attention to the person. He's not even sure if it was a man or woman. He's not even sure what floor it stopped on. He said that they got to the ground floor and everyone got off. The person went one way, they went another. He said that they hadn't gone far at all when the patient started to converse normally. He said that the old guy said he didn't need his hands tied up. He took him back to the ward. I understand that the neurologists are going crazy. They can't explain it and are at a loss. They have no idea if it is safe to discharge him because they don't know if this is temporary or not. The patient is demanding to see his lawyer and is threatening to take both the neurologists and the hospital to court if he is not released. I'll tell you, I'm glad I didn't want to be a neurologist."

This elicited a chuckle from the other two doctors. Dr. Stanton went on, "Just as I was getting ready to leave to come here, I heard about a lady who had a very severe stroke. They brought her in, put her on a crash cart, and rushed her to the OR. By the time they got there, guess what? No stroke. The paramedics and ER docs swear that she was in a world of hurt, but all of a sudden it goes away. Go figure."

Dr. Barr remarked, "That's three unexplained occurrences at the same place. I wonder why? It's one heck of a coincidence."

AFGHANISTAN

A village was built on the side of a hill not far from the border with Pakistan. By Afghan standards, the rural village was quite large with about 500 inhabitants, 3 dozen or so mud-brick structures with tin roofs, and scores of chickens, sheep, goats, donkeys, and horses. Most of the population there was engaged in raising and tending the animals or farming. A handful owned small stores and provided some small measure of commerce to the villagers. Life in the first half of the 21st century was pretty much like it had been in the 20th century, the 19th century, all the way back to the 14th century.

In the very center of the village was a mosque. The villagers practiced a fundamentalist form of Sunni Islam. They did so, not out of strong faith, but because this was what had always been done. Anyone who dared question the norm was usually put to death in a public spectacle.

This village was the center of a dispute between two rival Taliban chieftains. The tribe was the dominant source of allegiance among the Afghans. First came the tribe, then Allah, then the family and, somewhere way down the line, came allegiance to country. In most cases, country never even made the list. This particular village was a mix of two tribes who somehow over the centuries came to tolerate each other. The village was near the path that traders and caravans had for centuries traversed with their goods destined for far distant lands. Money makes for strange bedfellows. In this case, two tribes, the Tareen and the Akakhel, lived in one village to share the bounty of the trade.

Tolerate does not necessarily translate to trust, and it certainly did not in this village. As a result, each tribe patronized the small stores belonging to members of their particular tribe and shunned merchants from the other tribe. The two Taliban chieftains were from different tribes and each considered the village to belong to him. Armed fighters routinely strolled through the village and terrorized the villagers from the rival tribe. Every male in the village owned one or more automatic weapons, and the AK-47 was the weapon of choice. These were plentiful thanks to the carelessness of the Soviet Army when it occupied the area and then hurriedly retreated from Afghanistan. Since the inhabitants were roughly equally divided between the two tribes, neither chieftain was able to prevail.

That was the case until Ali, the chieftain from the Tareen tribe, noticed a beautiful young girl crossing the square to draw water for her family. It is not clear what attracted Ali to her since she was covered head to toe in fabric. She looked like a laundry basket with two feet. Ali already had three wives. Four was the maximum allowed by Islam. Ali could barely stand the bedlam and bickering caused by three females living under the same roof, not to mention the children that naturally ensued. Nevertheless, Ali was genuinely smitten and wanted her badly. He asked an aide who she was and then resolved to ask her father for her hand in marriage. That meant that he was in store for a torrent of caterwauling the likes of which he could barely fathom from his three current wives.

Under Islamic law, all wives are created equal. The husband is required to treat all of his wives the same. In practice, this is rarely the case. One of the females will try to become dominant. Ali's chief wife was a mean-spirited woman in her mid-forties named Faiza. Her father had arranged her marriage to Ali when she was 14 years old. They had been married for about 30 years. During that time, she had seen wives come and go, yet she retained the preeminent spot among the wives. At this point in her life, she was very content with Ali's other two wives. They both knew their places and, most importantly, they both knew Faiza's place.

As the chief wife, Faiza was permitted a small degree of freedom. For example, she was able to go to the market if accompanied by one of Ali's other wives as opposed to a male relative. While visiting the market one morning, she ran into an itinerant trader named Bahri. Bahri was a successful trader. He had a donkey for his personal transport, as well as two others to carry his merchandise. Bahri traveled from village to village bringing goods that were not manufactured in the villages. He also brought gossip and news from the outside world. His arrival in a village was always welcomed by the locals. Bahri was a charming rogue. Words rolled off his tongue like honey. In addition to his charm, he was considered by most women to be extremely good looking. He had a beard that was turning gray, as well as some gray beginning to show in his dark hair. Afghan men are not known for their sartorial splendor and Bahri was no exception. His dress was very plain. He did not stand out in a crowd.

Encounters between members of the opposite sex were strongly discouraged by the mores in that section of Afghanistan, but sometimes they were unavoidable. Faiza approached Bahri in the market square one morning, followed at a discreet distance by wife number three. They greeted each other formally and correctly, neither making eye contact with the other.

Bahri opened the conversation by asking, "What is it that I might show you today, revered lady?"

Faiza replied, "I am looking for a new saucepan. The lesser wives have made my current one almost unusable. They have no idea what to do in a kitchen."

Bahri nodded his head knowingly and clicked his tongue several times. "I have several that I will be happy to show you." He went to a bag still strapped to a donkey and pulled out two pans. Faiza examined them closely and finally chose one. "A very wise choice, revered lady."

Now began the entertaining and interesting part of the conversation: negotiating a price. "How much are you charging for a pan of such low quality?" Faiza began. Bahri quoted an outlandishly high price. He knew it, but he had to start somewhere. Faiza laughed and said, "Are you mad?" Thus began the contest. It was like watching two very skilled swordsmen fencing. Thrust/parry. Thrust/parry/counter thrust. For the next five minutes or so the contest went on. Bahri kept lowering his asking price. He could afford to since he started so high. Faiza on the other hand barely came off her original bid. She made even the most modest concession seem like it was tearing at her insides. Bahri finally reached his last and best offer, and Faiza was quick to recognize it for what it was. With a curse, she accepted it. "You dog. You are a pirate. You dare humiliate me in front of my exalted husband's lowly third wife?" She paused just a second and took a deep sigh, 'But I have no choice. I agree to your unreasonable and insulting offer." Bahri bowed and smiled. "You are a most wise, understanding, and generous person. It is always a pleasure doing business with you."

Wife number three watched the exchange with fascination. She was astute enough to realize she had just witnessed a life lesson taught by two master teachers, and she appreciated it.

Faiza brought her back to reality when she barked, "Well, don't just stand there. Pay the man." The third wife pulled the money out of her bag, gave it to Bahri, and took possession of the pan. Then the two women turned to go.

Before they could go, Bahri said in a low voice, "A word, revered lady?" He took Faiza a few steps away and said, "I saw your husband, Ali, the other day by the well. Adeela, the daughter of Omar, the shepherd, was also there drawing water for her family. The way Ali looked at her was more than a passing glance. I think he is smitten with her. Just a word of warning." With that, he bowed and walked away.

Not for the first time. Faiza was grateful for the burqa and niqab she was forced to wear. She hated it, but sometimes it was useful. This was one of those times. Her garments prevented anyone from seeing the look of terror and hatred that came over her face. If Ali were to marry Adeela, the balance of power at home could be radically altered. All she knew was that Ali was a mean, vindictive, selfish son-of-a-bitch. His needs and wants were the only things he cared about. She felt her position as the first wife was secure since first wives rarely were replaced, although they frequently fell out of favor. She was comfortable with both of Ali's other wives. While she didn't exactly like them, she was able to tolerate them and be cordial to them as long as they showed her the proper deference and respect. There were many other women and girls of whom this could not be said. At this stage of her life, she was not receptive to dramatic changes. She resolved to handle the matter quickly and efficiently and permanently.

The very next day, Ali and Faiza were alone in their home. The other two wives and the children were outside playing and enjoying the weather. Very matter-of-factly, Faiza said, "Some of the women were talking at the well this morning. They had some shocking news. Evidently, Adeela, the daughter of Omar, the shepherd, was seen being more than friendly with Ahmet, the son of the cloth merchant. They said he had his hands all over her, even inside of her clothes. She was moaning disgustingly." She paused for a moment to weigh the degree of shock on her husband's face. She was delighted with the results. He was livid. Not wanting to miss a chance of fanning the flames, she continued, "I guess I am not surprised. Omar is, after all, from the Akakhel tribe, and they are all descended from sheep stealers. His daughter is a cheap tramp. You know how I hate sharing this village with those unwashed scum. They are so far beneath us of the Tareen tribe, yet they go around as if they were our equals."

Her husband did not utter a sound, but several veins in his neck bulged. Faiza knew he was beside himself with anger, and she inwardly smiled. She had won. She had fortified her position in the household.

What she did not know was that Ali had visited Adeela's father, Omar, earlier that day to propose marriage. Even though they were from different tribes, Omar was honored to have a Taliban chieftain propose marriage to his daughter. His family's standing in the village would rise dramatically. Omar agreed to Ali's proposal and promised to approach Mohammed, the leader of the Akakhel tribe, the following day to secure his approval. Omar was uncertain what Mohammed would say about an intertribal marriage, so he had his arguments ready about how such a union would help bring the village together.

Without uttering a sound, Ali glared at Faiza, turned on his heel, and went directly to his bed. He would sleep alone that night. The next morning, Ali summoned four of his men and all five, armed with AK-47 rifles, crossed the village to Mohammed's house. They were met at the door by one of Mohammed's bodyguards and made to wait outside while he announced their presence to Mohammed.

Presently they were permitted to enter and found Mohammed in a room with four of his men. All were armed. Tension in the room was high. Mohammed looked quizzically at Ali and inclined his head for Ali to state his business.

Without any of the usual niceties, Ali got right to the point. "As you know, I have three wives. The Quran allows a man to have four wives. Several days ago, I saw a female who I thought might be suitable as a wife. I inquired about her and found that she was Adeela, daughter of Omar, the shepherd, from the Akakhel tribe. I went to Omar and proposed marriage to his daughter. He agreed and promised to approach you. It has just been brought to my attention that Adeela is a whore. She committed adultery with Ahmet, the son of the cloth merchant, who is from my tribe."

Mohammed was quite serious in his reply. "Are you formally accusing Adeela of adultery? I know you are aware of the seriousness of the charge."

Ali replied, "Of course, I am aware of how serious this is. The Quran specifically forbids this kind of behavior. It must be stopped and punished before it spreads. We cannot tolerate it in our village. The honor of the Tareen tribe is at stake."

Mohammed scoffed, "So this is about the pride of the Tareen. You ask that I order a young girl stoned to death on the say-so of a rumor and the pride of your tribe?"

"No, not just my tribe. I have been personally humiliated. At this point, whether she did it or did not do it is immaterial. I am open to ridicule, and I know you do understand that I cannot permit that."

Mohammed sighed and nodded his head. "Yes, I do understand. However, she will not be stoned. She will be shot." He summoned one of his bodyguards to fetch Omar and his daughter. Then he turned to Ali, "What about Ahmet? Where is he? I assume he will face the same punishment. After all, he is one of yours, the scurvy dog."

"You let me worry about Ahmet. Be assured he will be punished when we find him. It seems that he fled into the night. No one is sure where he went or even when. He just disappeared. We have severely questioned the cloth merchant, his father, without results. Please do not worry yourself. We will find him and when we do..."

"I will hold you to that. Now, as for the girl. She will be shot outside the village tomorrow at first light. One of my men will do it. She will be kept here in a room by herself until it is time."

Ali replied, "Honorable Mohammed, you must realize the Tareen cannot allow that an insult to one of us to be handled by another tribe. It is a matter of honor."

Mohammed grew visibly angry. "Do you think I will allow the Tareen or any outside agency to punish one of our own? No, I will not permit it."

Ali thought for a moment then proposed, "We will do it together. One of your fighters will accompany you, and one of my fighters will accompany me. Each fighter will have eight rounds of ammunition and will fire all eight of them into her. I propose that since this will be a very explosive and emotional event that we forbid any men from our tribes to bring weapons. We need no intertribal violence in such a confined area."

Mohammed thought for a moment and could not find any fault with Ali's proposal. Certainly, it was distasteful, but it was fair to both tribes, if not the girl." He nodded and said, "So be it. I agree."

Shortly thereafter, Omar arrived with Adeela. She was covered head to toe in a burka and her face was covered with the niqab. Only her eyes were visible and they clearly showed the terror she felt. Without greeting or preamble, Mohammed said in a clear, emotionless voice, "Ali from the Tareen tribe has accused your daughter of committing adultery with Ahmet. The law specifies stoning, but in this case, I have decided to show mercy. Adeela will be shot tomorrow immediately after sunrise"

Adeela screamed and Omar looked as if he would faint. He muttered "This cannot be true. Adeela is a good girl and never would do such a thing."

Adeela cried, "I am innocent. I have never been with a man. Please believe me."

Mohammed was clearly uncomfortable and wanted the scene to be over with quickly. "I have made my decision. The matter is closed." He nodded to two of his men who came and grabbed Adeela by her arms before either she or her father could react. They quickly escorted her out of the room. Her pitiful wails echoed off the walls until she was outside.

Omar looked around the room at each of the men present. None met his eyes. Ali and Mohammed both turned their backs to him. He knew he was beaten and quickly left the house.

News travels fast in a small village. Bad news travels even faster. Within minutes just about everyone heard about Adeela and Ahmet. Faiza smiled contentedly at the news. Her plan worked better than she could have hoped.

Upon hearing the news, Bahri showed no reaction. His face was impassive. He did, however, pack up his three donkeys and quickly leave the village. He had to travel 10 or so miles to a slightly larger village and meet a man. The man he was looking for was a CIA operative named Osman. Osman had been plying his craft for the CIA in Afghanistan and Pakistan for 20 years. Osman's birthplace was Columbus, Ohio. He was educated at Ohio State and was recruited by the Agency right before graduation. Bahri found him at a small café having coffee. He approached Osman and the two exchanged formal greetings. Then Osman bid Bahri take a seat. Bahri related the news about Adeela, as well as the fact that she was to be executed in public right outside the village the following morning. Osman thanked Bahri for the news and handed him 8,000 Afghan Afghi (about $100 US). He instructed Bahri to return to the village and observe the execution. He warned Bahri to pick a spot well out of the way where he could observe and not be seen. Osman did not explain to Bahri why he wanted him out of the way, but he implied it was important. Bahri stood and the two men exchanged the ritualistic farewells.

Bahri did not rush. Based on Osman's warnings, he figured he would find a safe hideout close to the village and spend the night there. Sleeping outside in Afghanistan is the epitome of danger. Some would call it foolhardy, but Bahri was no fool. He was a clever and enterprising individual. He had a location that he had used before and knew it to be perfectly safe.

After Bahri left, Osman placed some currency on the table and left for his home. He was not married and lived alone. Many of the villagers thought this strange, but none openly questioned it. Osman closed and locked his door and went into a room with no windows where he took a small powerful radio set from a secure hiding place. He turned it on to the desired frequency and in unaccented English relayed everything that Bahri told him. He placed particular emphasis on the fact the Adeela was to be shot in public and that all observing the execution would be unarmed. The voice on the other side of the transmission responded, "Roger. Understand. We'll take it from here. Out."

Three hours later, a US Army special ops UH-60 Blackhawk helicopter took off from Bagram Air Base and headed in the general direction of the Khyber Pass. On board were two sergeants first class from the Army's Delta force, as well as a staff sergeant. The two SFC's were elite snipers. The SSG was a linguist from the Army's Special Forces who would also serve as the team's spotter.

Several hours later, the chopper deposited the three men on a mountain top about five miles from Ali and Mohammed's village. The three men loaded their gear on their backs and proceeded to maneuver over the rugged and dangerous terrain, ever mindful of encountering locals who would most certainly report their presence to the Taliban or one of the other militia groups in the area. The team carried a supply of plastic restraints, gags, and blindfolds to contain any indigenous personnel they encountered. By nightfall, they were in place on a hilltop overlooking the hillside and open area adjacent to the village.

The weather the following day was totally appropriate for the events that were about to unfold. It was a gray, overcast, gloomy day in the area of Afghanistan near the Khyber Pass. About half an hour before sunrise, male villagers began making their way out of the village to the hillside adjacent to the village. They came individually and in groups of two or three. There was no merriment or laughter. Every one of them was deadly serious. Not one of them was armed, at least not openly. Although there were no signs posted, men from the Tareen tribe took seats on the hillside closest to the village. The Akakhel men sat farther along the hillside. The temperature was cool, and the men bundled in their coats to stay warm.

At last, Adeela made her entrance. She walked unsteadily from the village to the far side of the path that leads to the village directly opposite the hillside now crowded with the males of her village. One member each of Ali's and Mohammed's tribes walked on either side of her. Each man was armed with an AK-47 rifle. When they decided they had gone far enough, one of the escorts shouted for her to stop. The other then pushed her roughly to her knees with her back facing the hillside.

This entire spectacle was witnessed from the hilltop overlooking the village by the three Special Operations NCO's from the US Army.

The two snipers, SFC Jeremy Hastings and SFC Charles Tessmer, had their M24A3 sniper rifles with scopes set up and ready. These weapons fired a .338 Lapua cartridge and had a maximum stated range of 1,500 meters. In actuality, both soldiers had killed targets in excess of 2,000 meters. The shots they would be taking this morning were in the 1,200-meter range, shots that would be impossible for mere men, but barely a challenge for these decorated warriors. Each of the three soldiers wore headsets that connected them by radio to each other, as well as several other parties on the net. Sergeant Hastings keyed his headset and reported, "This is Knife 1. The girl is in place. She looks like a bundle of laundry someone dropped on the ground. There are two goons with weapons next to her. The rest are sitting on the hillside about 50 meters away. None appear to be armed. Over."

"Roger, Knife. This is Ike Leader. We are in position and waiting for your signal. Out."

Adeela knelt there in silence, interrupted only by her sobs. She was shaking uncontrollably. Finally, from the village strode Ali and Mohammed. The two tribal leaders walked side by side as a sign of solidarity. The expressions on their faces conveyed two very different messages. Ali's face showed peace, contentment, and satisfaction. He had been humiliated and now he had his revenge. Mohammed's exhibited loathing, anger, and hatred. He was not sure if the girl was guilty or not. He was forced into this vile deed in order to keep peace in the village.

"This is Knife 1. Looks like the brass has arrived. Two guys just left the village and are walking towards the girl. Won't be long now. Out."

"This is Ike Leader. We are about a minute out. Standing by. Out."

Ali and Mohammed walked up to their respective gunmen and nodded. Each of the gunmen raised his rifle and looked to Mohammed for the final signal. Just then, both of the gunmen's heads simultaneously exploded in a splash of crimson. Before anyone had time to process what happened, let alone react, the heads of the tribal leaders also exploded. Adeela heard the thump of bodies hitting the ground behind her but was too scared to do anything or make any movement. Those on the hillside just stared in shock.

At the first crack of the shots, SSG Reilly, the linguist/spotter/Green Beret, keyed his headset, "This is Knife 3. Execute! I say again, execute! Over."

"Roger Knife 3. Beginning first pass now. Out."

Just as the men on the hillside processed what had happened, the sound of a helicopter punctuated their hearing. They looked in the direction of the village to see an AH-64 Apache racing in at low level with its M230 chain guns blazing. To their horror, they saw two more Apaches close behind getting ready to open fire. The M230 delivers approximately 600 rounds of 30 mm ammunition per minute. The noise the gun makes while firing sounds like a loud zipper. Every fifth round is a tracer that has the effect of making the helicopter look as if it was spewing a very straight red rope. Ike 1 finished his first pass and veered off to the right to prepare to circle back. Ike 2 and Ike 3 also made their passes. Instead of firing its chain gun, Ike 2 dropped bomblets. The first pass of the three helicopters was devastating to the men of the village.

To make matters even worse for the villagers, right after the choppers' first pass a voice came on the US radio net, "Ike elements. This is Scoundrel 6. We are a flight of two F-16's loaded with napalm[2]. Our original target is socked in, so we had to abort. I don't like landing heavy with that stuff on board. We monitored your transmissions. May we offer our services?"

---

2. Napalm is gasoline in gelatinous form. It is highly flammable and is used in bombs.

"This is Ike Leader, Roger Scoundrel 6. Glad to have you. Use the edge of the village as your starting point and drop along the hillside. Do not, repeat, do not drop on the village."

"Roger Ike. Scoundrel elements rolling in hot now."

Suddenly the roar of the two US Air Force F-16 Fighting Falcons filled the air. The planes came in over the village and dropped their load of man-made-hell perfectly on the hillside. The flames and smell were breathtaking. The three soldiers of the Knife detachment on top of the distant hill could feel the heat of the blast. Sergeants Hastings, Tessmer, and Reilly exchanged glances. Each had seen napalm delivered many times, and each time produced the same reaction of shock and awe. Almost in unison, these battle-hardened warriors each muttered his own expletive: "Wow!" "Jesus!" "Oh my God!"

"Scoundrel 6, this is Ike Leader. Good job. Thanks for the help. Over."

"This is Scoundrel 6, no problem. Out." With that, the two jets climbed and took a northwesterly course away from the village.

"Ike elements, this is Ike 1, let's make a couple of more passes." Passes two and three were anticlimactic. Not one man left the hillside without severe wounds and or burns, and there were only three of those so fortunate. The remainder lay dead on the slope. As Ike 3 completed his third pass, the three gunships formed up for their flight back to base.

On the hilltop, the sniper team reported what they had observed. When the report was finished and acknowledged, a new voice came in over the net, "Roger Knife. This is Salesman 6. Understand estimated 200 killed, and the Taliban totally eradicated from the village. Great job to all. Salesman 6 out." Just as the three soldiers finished packing their gear and policing the four spent shell casings, a Blackhawk appeared and took the team back to home base.

As the three gunships left the scene, Bahri came out of hiding on the far side of the road and ran as fast as he could to Adeela. She was flat on the ground in a state of shock and had no idea what had transpired behind her. She heard the zipper-like sound of the chain guns, the roar of the helicopters and jets, and the explosions from the bomblets. She felt the heat of the napalm. Thankfully, she was far enough away so as not to be burned. Bahri grabbed her and pulled her to her feet. "You are unhurt. You will be safe. Trust me and come with me."

She numbly allowed herself to be led away from the hillside and its carnage. She didn't glance down at the bodies of the two Taliban leaders or those of her-would be executioners. She just followed Bahri as he led the way to his three donkeys. He helped her mount one and they quickly headed in the direction of the village where Osman lived. When they arrived late in the afternoon, she had somewhat recovered her composure. Along the way, Bahri told her that he did not see her father leave the village with the others to witness the execution. He probably stayed behind with her mother to try to console each other. This made her feel better. Osman immediately took her to a center for displaced persons and told her they would help her. He had explained her situation to the staff and they were very compassionate. They deliberately stayed far away from religion or politics. Their sole mission was to help those in perilous situations.

Bahri took his leave of Osman and rounded up his three donkeys. As he did so, a woman approached him. She wore the burka and niqab. Only her eyes were visible. Bahri was immediately suspicious. Women in this part of Afghanistan did not approach strange men under any circumstances. Also, almost none had striking blue eyes. She got close to Bahri and pulled her niqab aside.

Bahri could only gasp, "Polina!"

Polina laughed and said, "How're you doing, Barney? Long time no see. Boy, do you need a bath. You stink."

"What are you doing here? Slumming?"

Polina gave a short, wicked laugh, "Nope. I've come to fetch you. The boss wants to see you."

PHILADELPHIA

The next thing Barney/Bahri knew, he was sitting in a very well-appointed office some place far, far away from Afghanistan. He was wearing his own expensive clothes and felt clean. A look in the mirror confirmed that the old Barney was indeed back. He had a very pleasant face. He looked to be about 5' 10', early fifties with medium-length brown hair that was going gray. He had a well-trimmed beard and mustache, again brown with traces of gray. His eyes were gray, and he wore wire-rim glasses. He had an average build and wasn't thin or heavy. He wasn't a jock. He was....average.

Polina sat on the couch across from him. "Well, how does it feel to be back in the asphalt jungle, away from donkeys, horses, camels, guns, and religious fanatics? At least here they have cars, drunk drivers, guns, and religious fanatics."

"Polina, dearest, it feels great. The tribal infighting was wearing me down. Every time I thought I was making progress, someone would insult someone from a different tribe and off they would go. Everything is a matter of sacred honor over there."

Several days passed, and Barney and Polina were again sitting in the office. They were idly chatting when the door to the office opened. In walked the boss. She was wearing a very nice dress, pearl necklace, and heels. Her hair was pulled back in a ponytail, and she presented the image of a very attractive, confident female. The over-sexed predator was nowhere to be seen. She came over to Barney and gave him a warm embrace. "Barney, it is so good to see you. Welcome back. That was great work you did in Afghanistan."

"Thanks, Boss. But what did I do that was so great? Every time I tried something, one of the natives would do something idiotic and off they would go shooting and killing each other. No rhyme or reason. Just something to do."

The boss smiled and said, "You don't know, do you? When you set up the execution of that girl and informed the CIA, you created a perfect storm. Two Taliban leaders were taken out. Both of those guys were also tribal leaders. That airstrike that came in killed just about every male in the village. So you have a village claimed by two warring tribes with no males to run it. That village is right on one of the world's oldest and busiest trade routes. You created a vacuum. Well, nature abhors a vacuum, and so do the tribes of Afghanistan. Both tribes sent armed members from other villages to re-establish control of the village. And, oh, by the way, three or four other tribes thought that the village would make a great addition and sent fighters to it. They had one heck of a battle. The women in the village are beside themselves. As you know, it is the duty of male relatives to marry the widows of deceased family members. Barney, you effectively created a plethora of widows. The system is overwhelmed. Who knows what will happen to them? It is total chaos over there. I surreptitiously arranged to have Faiza identified as the cause of this disaster. Once the other widows found out that she instigated the entire affair by inciting Ali, she was doomed. A mob of outraged women from the Akakhel tribe attacked Ali's house. They beat Faiza and then beheaded her. The other two wives were merely beaten. Widows from Faiza's tribe, the Tareen, just stood by and watched. Quite a few even cheered and urged the Akakhel women to hit harder." She laughed a wicked laugh and said, "I understand that the doctors are saying that the two surviving wives may be able to eat solid food in about six months."

She paused for a moment, smiled contentedly, then went on, "To make this wonderful story even better, somehow the media found out about the airstrike. They are calling it a massacre and a violation of the rules of land warfare. They smell blood and are calling for heads to roll. How can the US military kill so many unarmed, peaceful civilians? It was bad enough that they used helicopter gunships, but the use of napalm was over the top. I personally think it was a very nice touch.

"It doesn't matter that all of those guys were members of the Taliban. Both the Senate and House are calling for investigations. Iran's ambassador to the UN delivered a scathing denunciation of the 'barbaric, great Satan'. It's on every channel and all over the net. I love it. Barney, you did one heck of a job."

Just then, there was another transformation and the male form of the boss appeared. "Well, I didn't call you back here to pat you on the back or build up your already overly inflated ego. There's work to be done. Polina stumbled upon a fascinating young lady. It seems she has the power to cure people. I am not sure where she got this gift or even how powerful it is. It appears that she doesn't even know she has it. Polina, why don't you take it from here?"

"I first saw her at a hospital in downtown Philly. She passed a man who had terminal cancer and almost immediately the cancer disappeared. I followed her around for several days. One day, she went to a hospital to deliver a file to one of her employers. She works as a record clerk for a group of oncologists. Well, she went into a room where a young boy was on his last breaths from cancer. When she left the room, the boy was alert, in no pain, and acting like a very frightened young man with all of the IV's, wires, and tubes all over his body. She then runs into an old man with Alzheimer's while riding the elevator. By the time the ride was over, the man showed no sign of Alzheimer's. She gets off the elevator just as OR personnel are rushing a woman stroke victim to surgery but, upon arrival to the OR there is no sign of a stroke. The people in the hospital have no answers. At first, they were chalking it up to a series of happy coincidences. Then rumblings started surfacing from all over the area about so-called miracle cures. Mind you, not a huge number, but anything over one or two a year is abnormal. Here we have close to a dozen in less than a week. Thus far, no one has linked these cures together. The physicians involved are treating the cases they see as isolated, one-off events."

Barney asked, "How do you know it's this girl performing the miracles?"

Polina answered, "I've been following her. I have seen every one of these cures. It is so low key that no one is aware of it until she has gone by. Word is spreading among the medical community. Next thing, some reporter will start to snoop and the story will be all over TV. It's inevitable."

Barney looked bored and replied, "OK. So what? I don't see what the big deal is."

Polina snapped, "Barney, pull your head out and think for a minute. Can't you see it? It goes viral. Miracle cures are happening in Philadelphia. 'Come to Philly for a cure and a cheesesteak.' The place will be mobbed. No one is sure what they are looking for, just that Philly is the place to be, the City of Brotherly Love. Eventually, it has to happen that this girl will surface as the source of the cures."

Barney shrugged his shoulders, "I still don't know what the big deal is."

"Barney, what happened to you in Afghanistan? Did you get hit in the head? Think, man. Think."

"OK, Polina, tell me about this girl."

Polina then proceeded to describe Abigail Williams in great detail. She described her childhood, her relationship with her mother, her complete lack of social skills, her shyness, and her insecurity. She related that Ms. Williams lived by herself in a row house she rents in Upper Darby, and even though she has a car, she takes the train into Philadelphia most days. She said that Abigail has several acquaintances, but no real friends.

Polina and Barney took their leave of the boss, promising him they would not disappoint. The boss replied in a very sinister tone, "You had better not. Barney, there are worse assignments than Afghanistan. I hope you understand that."

Threat made. Threat received. Barney could not imagine a worse assignment than the one he just completed, but he was confident that the boss could. His fear transferred to Polina and she vowed to herself that she would not fail. Together they left the building, climbed into Barney's Maserati Gran Turismo Sport. It was Rosso Trionfale (metallic red) and had a black leather interior with rosso stitching. Barney loved this beauty and relished the way it made him feel. In almost no time, they navigated the streets of downtown Philadelphia and found a parking garage less than a block away from Abigail's workplace. They walked down to the corner and saw a young couple holding a baby right outside the entrance to the building.

Barney and his colleagues can have one of two classes of assignments. Both Barney and Polina currently work in the At Large Division, also known as the ALD. That means they come and go as they see fit. They usually don't have a specific territory. They may be given an assignment such as the girl in Philadelphia, or they can freelance. Those in the other division are assigned to a specific area. They move into a place and live like the inhabitants. That was Barney's assignment in Afghanistan. It is inconceivable, but one day he just appeared. Every one of his neighbors and associates would swear that they always knew him. No one can remember a time without him being there. His mission was to do whatever it took to blend in even if it meant taking a job.

Those in the ALD are not fettered with the same rules that humans have. They can transport themselves at will from place to place and from one dimension to another. Some, like Barney, prefer to have a physical conveyance from time to time. Few, however, have a Maserati or Ferrari. Most settle for a Mercedes, BMW, or even a Porsche. Barney and his ALD colleagues have the ability to be visible or invisible. They can appear to someone, carry on a conversation with him, and yet be invisible to everyone else. When the conversation is over, Barney and his colleagues may allow the person they spoke with to recall it in detail or think of it as an amorphous occurrence. As Polina and Barney approached the couple standing on the corner with a baby, they were invisible.

The couple was standing close to each other in front of the oncologist office where Abigail worked, and both were crying inconsolably. The woman held the baby tightly. Just then, a girl in her early to mid-twenties turned the corner and headed down the street. She barely glanced over at the little family holding itself together on the corner. Neither the man nor woman was aware that anyone had passed by. Barney and Polina watched the scene play out. About 100 feet down the block, the young woman opened what appeared to be some sort of service entrance and entered the building. Just as the door closed, the baby uttered a shrill wail and began fidgeting. The man and woman looked at each other in shock and then at the baby. "Honey, she seems to be hungry," the woman exclaimed.

"How can that be?" asked the man. "The doctor said she would probably never ask for food and that it would be up to us to try to get her to drink milk."

The woman snapped, "I know what he said, but it sure looks like he was wrong. Come on. We are going back inside and show him." They entered the building, followed by the invisible Polina and Barney.

They marched right up to the receptionist, a dour-looking woman who had mastered the sneer that the powerful used with the powerless. The man breathlessly said, "We just left here, and something has come up. We need to see Dr. Barr right away."

Her majesty peered over her reading glasses at the young couple. "I'm sure you do. Dr. Barr is with a patient." Without even looking at the PC screen or any kind of record, she went on to volunteer that Dr. Barr's schedule was booked solid for the rest of the day.

The young man lost it. He bent over the counter and, in a low, menacing voice said, "You listen to me and you listen well. I want to see Dr. Barr and I want to see him now. You had better go and fetch him, or I promise you I will climb over this counter and you and get him myself. Do I make myself clear?"

Her majesty was not impressed. She had been threatened by bigger, meaner, and scarier men before. She was impervious. The young woman holding the crying baby leaned over the counter, looked her straight in the eye, and said, "Just do it!" The receptionist experienced real fear and immediately got up to do the woman's bidding. One just doesn't mess with mama bear while she is protecting her cub. In less than a minute, a very harried looking Dr. Charles Barr entered. He took one look at the couple, and with real concern in his voice, asked, "You just left. Is everything all right?"

He escorted the couple and the baby back to an exam room and listened to their story. They told him that they were standing on the street corner after just receiving the news that their daughter probably only had a few days to live. They were holding each other and crying their eyes out. All of a sudden, the baby started wailing like a banshee. This sound emanated from a baby with healthy lungs and not a baby standing at death's door. Dr. Barr took the baby, called in his nurse, and started his examination. The more he examined, the more perplexed he appeared. The same was true of the nurse. The color had drained from her face. He finally stopped, ordered some blood work, and looked at the parents. "I'm not sure what is going on, but your daughter appears to be healthy and normal. Hungry for sure, but otherwise healthy and normal. Feed her, and while you do, I am going to consult with the other doctors here." He left the room and the young mother pressed one of her breasts to the baby.

In no time at all, the baby was content and being rocked by her father. Dr. Barr knocked and re-entered the room, accompanied by his two colleagues, Drs. Stanton and Lucas, as well as his nurse. The nurse took the baby and laid her on the examination table. Stanton and Lucas began their exam and Barr started questioning the parents. "Let me get this straight. After we had our discussion about the prognosis not looking good, the two of you left this building with your daughter. You paused on the corner to try to gather yourselves together. Suddenly your daughter starts crying and acting like any other hungry baby. Just like that?"

The young man and women both nodded their heads. Barr went on, "Did anyone come by, or stop, or speak?"

The woman replied, "Not that I can remember. Oh sure, there was traffic going by on the street, but no one stopped or took notice of us. I certainly didn't take any notice of anyone or anything."

"Wait," said her husband. "I seem to recall someone walking by us. I didn't pay any attention to them. I can't say if it was a man or a woman or where they went. I just sensed that someone walked by."

Drs. Stanton and Lucas completed their examinations. Lucas proclaimed, "Well, I agree. This baby is perfectly healthy. She is showing no signs of cancer or of ever having had cancer. I'd say this little lady is ready to go out and meet the world head-on." Stanton smiled and nodded his head enthusiastically.

Polina and Barney watched the scene unfold with great interest. They watched the young couple gratefully shake hands and thank the three doctors and the nurse. They watched them walk out into the waiting area, where they both smiled at the receptionist, who somehow managed to give them a very brief smile in return. They turned their attention back to the three doctors and the nurse. The four of them were huddled together, asking each other what the heck was happening. Polina poked Barney on his shoulder and nodded to where Abigail was sitting at her desk with an ear cocked towards the impromptu meeting. Polina said, "Barney, that is the famous Abigail Williams."

Barney replied, "She sure doesn't look like much. I wasn't expecting much, but this sure isn't it." He paused for a second, then exclaimed, "Wait, I've seen her before. As we were crossing the street from the parking garage, she walked by the couple with the baby. She didn't say a word to them. It looked like she barely was aware of their presence. Are you implying that she cured that baby?"

"Barney, I'm not implying anything. Thus far, there are three facts: a baby is dying, she walks by, and the baby is suddenly completely healed. Draw your own conclusions."

They walked over to Abby's desk so they could examine her more closely. Barney was amazed at how plain, ordinary, and forgettable she was. "I wish I had a camera," he joked. "I'm not sure I could describe her or even recognize her without a picture."

THE PRACTICE

Once each month, a group of the most highly respected and qualified physicians practicing in and around Philadelphia meet for a luncheon. Attendance at the luncheon is by invitation only, and these are issued by **The Group of Five**. These are the most senior and influential doctors in the greater Philadelphia area. Physicians are invited regardless of their specialties. Surgeons, OBGYN specialists, psychiatrists, urologists, and oncologists are just a small sample of the specialties invited. Usually, once a physician is invited, the invitation turns evergreen. Those who receive these invites prize them and make every effort to clear their schedules so that they may attend. The 'unofficial' name for this group is **The Practice**.

The locale for the luncheons varies every month but is always held in one of Philadelphia's most exclusive and expensive restaurants. During its heyday, The Original Bookbinders was a favorite meeting place. Now restaurants such as Lacroix Restaurant at the Rittenhouse and Barclay Prime host the monthly meetings. Physicians typically start arriving around noon and then spend an hour or so networking with colleagues. The topics during this open networking were usually the same: new advances in procedures or medications, new assignments at the various hospitals in the area, the upcoming crop of talented doctors, golf and tennis stories, and, of course, just good old-fashioned gossip. It was very informal, but a prodigious amount of information was typically exchanged during that hour.

The meeting this month was attended by Drs. Barr, Lucas, and Stanton. Normally only one or two would attend the luncheon with at least one remaining to attend to the practice. This month they decided to close their practice for an afternoon, given all of the strange events they believe occurred. They wanted to see if any of the other physicians were aware of 'miracle cures' in the area.

Seats are assigned at every meeting by **The Group of Five**. They, or more likely one of their office managers, ensure that no one sits with the same persons for at least three or four meetings. That way, everyone has an opportunity to meet and form opinions and alliances amongst the entire group. Closed cliques were explicitly not a byproduct of these meetings.

When the three doctors arrived at Barclay Prime, they split up, mingled with their peers, and listened attentively for any mention of unexplained cures. There was none. Finally, in a group of four or five other physicians, William Stanton told the story of his young patient who appeared to be minutes or hours away from death when suddenly he was completely cured. Stanton related that the boy returned to school, acts like a normal seven-year-old and is completely cancer-free. He added the stories of the stroke victim and Alzheimer's patient who were suddenly cured within minutes of the Miller boy's cure. "Have any of you heard of anything strange going on?" he asked.

One of the other doctors replied, "Now that you mention it, Jim Saunders has a patient who had dangerously high blood pressure, diabetes, and kidney failure. This guy had so much going on that Jim didn't have much hope. One day the guy comes in and he is a poster boy for healthy living. His kidneys are fine. There is no more diabetes and his BP is normal. All this with no medication. The guy said his meds were making him ill, so he stopped taking them. Jim is at a loss to explain it. His patient says it just happened. He didn't do anything special. It just happened."

Another added, "Mary Phillips has a patient she treated at the VA hospital. This guy had a spinal cord injury and was paralyzed, confined to a wheelchair, and had no feeling from the chest down. He went through in-patient therapy at the VA and was finally released. Mary saw him every other month. Well, he came in one day, and guess what? He was walking normally. There was no muscle atrophy. He told her that he was sitting in a park on a sunny day getting some air. Suddenly he started getting sensation in his legs. He looked down and he could move his feet. At first, he didn't tell anyone. After several days of moving his legs, he figured he might be cured. He called his brother, who came and spotted for him while he tried to stand up. Not only did he stand up, but he was able to walk without any assistance, a walker, or a cane. Mary took x-rays of his back and there is no sign that he had ever been injured. She is at a loss."

A cardiovascular surgeon spoke up. "I have a patient who desperately needed a heart transplant. He has a rare blood type and things looked pretty ominous. Well, he came in for an exam and now has the heart of a healthy 20-year-old. He can't explain it. He says all of a sudden he could breathe normally, has the energy level of a five-year-old, and has never felt this good." He shakes his head. "I thought I was the only one to have this happen. Looks like I was wrong."

What started as a small group of four or five physicians soon grew to 20 or more as other doctors overheard the discussion and joined in. One of the doctors who listened to the discussion was a member of **The Group of Five**.

Once all the doctors in attendance were seated in their assigned seats, an eminent and respected physician tapped on her glass for silence and stood up. Dr. Nancy Simpson delivered a very brief welcome and then began. "I listened to a group of doctors just now exchanging stories of unexplained cures. In the very brief time I was listening, I counted 12 or so from a group of 20 doctors. If we are seeing 12 cures from such a small sample population, what is to say that there are no more? I wonder if these cures are limited to Philadelphia or if other regions are also seeing it. I think that we need to determine if what we are witnessing is just a very happy coincidence with no underlying common thread or if something else is going on. I hate to do this to you, but Bill Stanton, can you and your folks coordinate the effort? To everyone else here present, will you contact every physician and health care provider you know to see if they have noticed any cases out of the ordinary? Please funnel the information in as much detail to Bill's office. We need the date, time, location, and details of the case. I volunteer my practice to contact medical boards in all 50 states. Also, please activate your 'old boy' networks throughout the country and see what they have to report. Finally, and this is important, please try to keep this as confidential as possible. I think we can all agree that rumors of miracle cures could foment and incite all kinds of trouble and mass hysteria." After lunch was over, most of the doctors returned to their practices to start making phone calls instead of taking the afternoon off, which was their common practice.

THE INVISIBLE GIRL

When the three doctors returned from their luncheon at Barclay Prime, they immediately went into the conference room with Marguerite Camp, the office manager, and closed the door. This threw the nurses, aides and office staff into a tizzy. The doctors weren't expected back until the next day. They always took the afternoon following the luncheon off, a respite the staff always looked forward to. This break gave the staff a very short window to catch up on the minor and trivial things that had been left dangling. With this unexpected appearance of the doctors, whispers and rumors started flying around the office like wildfire. Of course, Abigail heard the rumblings at a distance but did not participate. She had learned long ago that most things were out of her control. When they finally came to fruition, they invariably had a very unpleasant effect on her. Some folks are meant to walk, and some are meant to be walked on. She was sure she was in the latter category.

Finally, the office door opened and Marguerite motioned for Abigail to come in. That got the tongues wagging. "Were they finally going to get rid of her?" "What does she do around here anyway?" "No one likes her!" "Good riddance!" "You know, she really wasn't that bad."

Abigail meekly got to her feet and entered the conference room. She was expecting the worse and was already trying to figure out where to send her resume. The conference room was windowless with several pleasant prints on the walls, some artificial plants, and a medium-size conference table with 10 comfortable rolling chairs around it. Stanton was seated at the head of the table with Barr and Lucas sitting on either side. The office manager had a seat near the opposite end of the table. Stanton smiled and said, "Have a seat, Ms. ...

"Williams," Marguerite quickly interjected.

Stanton coughed and said, "Yes. Ms. Williams. May I call you ...?"

"Abigail," interjected the office manager again.

"Ah, yes, Abigail."

Abby took a deep breath, smiled, and nodded.

"Well, Abigail, we have a situation," Stanton intoned.

"Here it comes. I'm being laid off," Abby thought to herself.

Stanton continued, "There have been some strange and unexplainable occurrences in the local area recently. A lot of doctors here are baffled. We don't know the extent of them, how many, if just this area is involved, or if they are related. In short, we know nothing. We need data. All of the doctors who attended **The Practice's** luncheon today have been charged with canvassing all of the remaining doctors and health care providers in the area to see if any of their patients experienced miraculous cures."

Abigail interrupted, "Do you mean like that baby girl the other day?"

"Yes, that's exactly what I mean. As scientists, we are taught to believe that there is an explanation for everything, but as human beings, we know that some things cannot be explained. Call them phenomena or miracles or whatever; they are there. What we are trying to determine here is what we are looking at. Does that make sense?"

Abigail nodded and waited for the other shoe to drop.

"I have been tasked with being the data collector for **The Practice**. As doctors become aware of an unexplained cure, they will funnel the information to our office. Marguerite has sung your praises to the rafters and has recommended that you be our data collector. If you accept, we will let all the health care providers know that you are the point of contact. It's a big job, but we are sure you are up to it. What do you say?"

Abigail was shocked and said in a low voice, "Does this mean that I am not being fired?"

The other four in the room looked at each other with amazed expressions on their faces. Then they began to chuckle and finally to laugh. Charles Barr said, "Of course you are not being fired. Whatever gave you that idea? You are a valued member of this team. You are getting a promotion."

Marguerite picked up the conversation, "Abby, what do you say? Will you do it? With your organizational skills and attention to details, you are the person for the job. What do you say? By the way, it comes with a 15% pay raise."

Abby became light-headed. She was shocked. She smiled and whispered, "Of course I'll do it. How can I thank you all?"

All four came around to Abby to shake her hand and congratulate her. Then Marguerite went out and asked all the staff to come into the conference room. When everyone was in the room, Dr. Lucas stood up and told the staff about the unexplained cures that were seemingly happening in the Philadelphia area. He said he would not go into specifics at this time, other than that one of the cures was the baby with cancer from the other day. After explaining the canvassing effort to collect data from all health care providers, he told them that this practice was appointed as the central data collection point, and to expect incoming calls, e-mails, and faxes with reports.

Further, he explained that if they were to receive any communication about the cures, they were to forward it immediately to Abigail Williams, who, he was pleased to announce, was just promoted to this new role. He noted the shocked expressions of all gathered when he announced Abigail's promotion and wondered about it. He ended by requesting that the staff keep the story about the cures confidential, although he was confident this was a waste of breath. He would bet money that word would be on the street the second the meeting was over. He concluded the meeting by publicly congratulating Abigail, expressing confidence in her ability, and asking if there were any questions. There are always questions. Some people are incapable of restraining themselves from asking questions, no matter how dumb or inane. When the last question was finally asked, the meeting broke up. Several co-workers smiled and nodded congratulations to Abigail as they exited, but most hurried out of the room to their desks.

Polina and Barney had been invisibly standing in a corner for the entire meeting. They looked at each other and began laughing uncontrollably. The person causing the ruckus was the person appointed to keep track of it. Talk about bizarre. They could not wait to tell the boss.

THE REPORTER

Diana Chan was an investigative reporter for the local CNB TV affiliate. She had the three B's: built, beautiful and brilliant. She was also a person of great humanity, compassion, integrity, and principles. Diana was of Asian/ American descent and was very proud of that fact. Unlike almost everyone else in the media, she did not have an agenda. She was careful to craft her reporting, so it stood straight up and did not tilt to the left or right. If something was wrong, she said so. If something was right, she said so. Unfortunately, in today's world, there were many more of the former stories than the latter. She was uncompromising in her principles, much to the chagrin of management. Several of her stories were either killed by her supervisors or given to other 'journalists' to present on-screen. While Diana deeply resented this, she refused to back down. She soon had a reputation in the broadcast industry as a woman who was talented but difficult to work with, someone who was not a team player. This reputation was a considerable deterrent to executives of other networks who would otherwise have actively pursued her. She was a pariah in the industry. Not so with the viewing public. She was almost universally adored. For this reason, and this reason alone, the station could not touch her.

Diana fully understood her position. While she did not like it, she accepted it. She refused to change. She refused to be a mouthpiece for the 'suits' in New York and Los Angeles. She became very adept at watching her back.

Her life revolved around her work. She was unmarried, which gave rise to some nasty rumors and speculation about her sexual orientation. She shrugged them off. She was definitely straight. She loved men. In fact, she preferred being with a group of guys rather than a group of girls. She just had not met Mr. Right, and since work kept her busy, she didn't spend a lot of time looking for him.

She had a lot of friends of both sexes, good friends with whom she frequently met for dinner and or drinks. Several days after **The Practice's** luncheon, she met several girlfriends for drinks after work. The bar was lively and crowded, but the five friends were able to find a table where they could talk. After the usual banter about their love lives or lack thereof, discussions turned to their jobs. All five of these ladies worked in downtown Philadelphia. In addition to Diana, one worked in a bank, two others were attorneys, and the fifth was the office manager for a well-known group of neurosurgeons. None of the ladies had any spectacular news to report, including Diana. She told the group she was looking into careless spending by a local township's school board, which did not excite anyone. Finally, Ellen Spalone, the office manager said, "You know, I think there might be something going on. Dr. Jones came back from **The Practice's** monthly luncheon and called me in. He gave me a list of doctors and asked me to contact them. I was supposed to ask if they have had any unusual cases lately. You know, like patients who experienced sudden, unexplained cures. If any did have such a case, I was supposed to get as much detail as possible, inform Dr. Jones and then send a report to Dr. William Stanton's office. Evidently, Stanton is pulling everything together. I'll tell you, I felt really strange calling up doctors who I had never heard of and asking them if they were aware of any miracle cures. By the way, none of the doctors I spoke with were aware of any directly. Some had heard rumors, but nothing that they would stand behind as being factual. What was odd was that several told me I was not the first to call asking them the same question. Just as I said, something's going on."

Diana's antennae were tingling. She could smell a story. "Dr. Jones didn't go into any details?"

"No, nothing more than what I just said," Ellen replied.

"Do you know who the point of contact is at Dr. Stanton's office?"

Ellen nodded her head and said, "It is a girl by the name of Abigail Williams. She is a clerk in the office who handles records and billing. I guess Stanton figured this would be right up her alley."

The conversation then moved to the Eagles, Phillies, 76er's, and Flyers. Just because they were female didn't mean they couldn't be rude, crude, and socially unacceptable. Thus, they were very loud and boisterous. After all, there was the sacred tradition of the Philadelphia sports fan to uphold.

When the group broke up and the Cowboys, Cardinals, Celtics, and Blackhawks had been cussed to oblivion, Diana walked the short distance to her apartment. She was captivated by Ellen's story of prominent physicians canvassing colleagues about unexplained cures. She made a mental note to follow up on it. She had the wasteful school board story to finish and could not wait to get it done. She was convinced that there was no malice by anyone on the board. It was just a series of honest mistakes committed by amateurs. Besides which, the total amount of money involved was inconsequential. She hoped to have it done in a day or so and move on to something more substantial.

Several days passed and the school board story was ready to present. Station management was so unimpressed and bored by it that they killed it immediately. Diana was happy and relieved. She hated the story. Now that she was unfettered, she told her producer that she had a lead on a potentially major story and asked for permission to track it down. She said she didn't want to go into details, but hopefully, she would have an outline in several days. The producer was skeptical but agreed to give her three days to investigate.

Diana went back to her desk and looked up the number for Dr. Stanton's practice. She endured the mandatory torture of the automated answering system and finally was able to speak to a real human being. She asked to speak with Abigail Williams and was told that personal calls were not permitted. She tried to explain that this was not a personal call, but the receptionist cut her off and put her on hold. After five minutes of cooling her heels, the receptionist was back. "Look," Diana said, "I want to speak to Ms. Williams about the mysterious cures that are happening."

The receptionist asked, "Are you calling from a medical provider's office to report one?"

Diana barely got two words in. "No, I…"

The receptionist snapped, "I'm sorry, we are not authorized to discuss this or any other confidential medical issue. Have a nice day." and hung up. Diana just stared at her phone. These doctors must be good to have rude morons like that on staff and still have patients.

Not to be deterred, Diana called back and finally got the bitchy receptionist on the line. "I'm calling from the office of Dr. Jones. I have a report to make and was told to contact Abigail Williams at this number."

In a professional voice, her majesty replied, "Just a minute, please. I will transfer you."

"This is Abigail Williams," a soft voice said.

"Ms. Williams, my name is Diana Chan. I am a reporter for CNB Channel 14. I would like to ask you some questions if that is all right."

"Ms. Chan, I enjoy watching you on TV. You are one of my favorites."

"Thank you. Is it OK if I ask you some questions?"

Abigail replied, "I'm awfully sorry, but there is nothing I can say."

Diana smelled blood, "Ms. Williams, I haven't told you what I wanted to ask you about."

"Uh, I just assumed."

"Assumed what?" questioned Diana,

Abby replied, "Oh, nothing."

Diana had her opening and took it. "What do you know about sick people in this area who suddenly find themselves cured? I have heard that over 20 unexplained cases have surfaced so far."

The trap was set and into it walked Abigail with her eyes wide open. "That number is way too high. I only know of six." Silence. "I mean I really can't talk about it. I don't know anything for sure."

"Got ya!" thought Diana. "Come now, Ms. Williams. By the way, do you mind if I call you Abigail? Ms. Williams sounds too formal."

"I'm sorry, Ms. Chan, but I have to go. Have a nice day." Without waiting for an answer, Abigail hung up.

Diana smiled a big smile. She was on to something big. She knew from experience that secrets are hard to keep, and the difficulty increased exponentially as the number sharing the secret increases. She had to move quickly to beat the rumor mill.

THE NEWS BREAKS

Diana spent the better part of the afternoon calling the offices of physicians she knew to be members of **The Practice**. She ran into the proverbial brick wall. Some denied any knowledge of 'miracle' cures or effort to identify them. Others just refused to make any comment. Undeterred, at about 3:00 p.m., Diana went to the nearest office of one of the members, a dermatologist. She entered the office, told the receptionist she was waiting for a friend to arrive and sat down, pretending to read a magazine. She took close mental note of the receptionist and the nurses who came to call patients, as well as anyone else who looked like an employee. Since most were female and wore surgical scrubs, she was readily able to eliminate the patients. After 45 minutes she made a show of checking her watch and muttered loud enough to be heard, "I guess she is not coming." She left and found a seat in an outside lobby near the elevators. Starting around 5:00 p.m., the elevators began discharging many passengers wearing scrubs. She spied several from the dermatologist's office, but they were in groups. Finally, out stepped one of the employees walking alone who Diana recognized. She approached the woman and introduced herself. "Hello, my name is Diana Chan. I am a reporter for Channel 14. I'd like to ask you a few questions, if I could."

The young lady looked shocked and stammered, "I really don't have the time. I'm in a hurry."

"I understand. Look, this will only take a few minutes. I only have a few questions. Can we go someplace and talk? I promise it will be brief." Diana reached out and touched her arm in a friendly gesture.

The woman hesitated a moment, then smiled. "I guess I can spare a few minutes. Why don't you walk me to my car? It's in the garage across the street. By the way, my name is Gloria."

The two ladies shook hands and walked side by side to the garage. During that short walk, Diana learned that Gloria had worked in the medical office for three years and considered it a good place to work with everyone being supportive of each other. The four doctors who ran the practice were "gems" in Gloria's opinion. The only unexplained cure she knew of was a middle-aged man who had pre-cancerous lesions. He was an avid golfer and had damage caused by the sun. The doctors tried burning the lesions off with liquid nitrogen, but that treatment was not successful and the patient had been scheduled for blue light treatment to try to eradicate the lesions. At the scheduled time and day, the patient showed up with no trace of any lesions or sun damage. In fact, one of the doctors noted that his skin looked like that of a young child. This information was not earth-shattering but did fit into the unexplained category. Gloria emphatically told Diana that she could not and absolutely would not divulge the patient's name. "That would be illegal."

Diana asked, "Do you know if the office reported this to Dr. Stanton?"

"I don't know for sure, but I would bet money that we did."

"Have you heard of any other unexplained cases in this area?

"I'm sorry, I haven't. Do me a favor, if you run a story about this, please don't use my name. We were told to keep all we see or hear confidential."

Curious at this request, Diana asked, "Do you know why they told you to keep things quiet."

"The doctors didn't give an official reason, but the office manager told us they are worried about the public's reaction if word gets out about miraculous cures in Philadelphia."

The two parted ways leaving Diana to ponder whether this was what she was looking for or not. She told herself that getting information this way was hard yardage, but unless and until she could put names to the cases and try to discern a pattern, this was what she was left with. "Oh well," she thought, "more phone calls and offices tomorrow."

The more she fished, the more she was convinced that a really big one was out there somewhere. Her supervisor at the station complained that she was spending too much time on a phantom story with nothing to show for it. Diana was passionate in her defense of the story, and with great reluctance on the part of her supervisor, was allowed to continue. The station assigned her several stories to present on-air as a 'talking head.' These did not take a lot of time as someone else had put them together. All Diana had to do was look pretty, speak slowly, and with authority like she knew what she was talking about, look into the camera, and smile.

For the next week, Diana continued making phone calls and visiting doctor's offices. She would get nibbles on the line, but the big fish kept eluding her.

On a bright sunny day, Diana decided to go to Abigail Williams' place of work and confront her. On that very same day, Abigail chose to walk across the street to the small park there and eat her lunch while enjoying nature. Polina and Barney decided to join her. They found her sitting on a bench, relaxing, and eating a sandwich. They smiled at her, and Barney asked if she minded if they take an adjacent bench. Abby nodded and murmured that she didn't mind. Polina and Barney sat down and went through the motions of two co-workers taking a break and talking shop while they did it. Abby pretty much ignored the chatter and kept to herself. Finally, Polina looked over and spoke, "It's a beautiful day. We don't come here often, but it is too nice a day to pass up."

Abigail offered a tentative smile, "I know what you mean. It feels so good to be out in the fresh air."

Polina responded, "Barney, here, and I work in that tall building down the street. Our offices have windows, but the view we have is of the building next door. We could see it was a really nice day and were going stir crazy. We had to escape. What about you, where do you work?"

Abigail pointed across the street. "I work in that doctor's office there."

Barney smiled and turned his charm on her full blast. "My name is Barney and this is Polina."

Abby shyly smiled and replied, "I'm Abigail." That was all that was needed to start a conversation. Barney and Polina could schmooze with anyone about anything. They could discuss quantum physics, mid-16th century Czech literature, the latest developments in medicine, or who was going to win the World Series, as well as the ramifications of the latest Supreme Court ruling. They could also discuss mundane things such as the weather, the price of gas, and how inefficient local government was. Abby could not. She was mildly in shock that anyone was having a conversation with her. That seldom happened. These folks appeared to be interested in her, in what she thought and in what she felt. Granted, the conversation was stiff and formal and lacked any intimacy at all, but it was conversation, and Abby savored it.

As this was going on, Diana walked into the medical practice of Drs. Stanton, Barr, and Lucas. The young lady behind the counter was very affable and courteous. The usual receptionist was on her lunch break and this girl, who was normally in the billing department, was filling in. Diana breathed a sigh of relief. She was in no mood to confront 'Attila the Honey.' "I'd like to see Abigail Williams if she is available," said Diana.

The receptionist replied, "She's not here just now. I saw her leave the building for lunch. She was carrying it in a bag, so I'll bet she is across the street in the park. She goes there sometimes on nice days."

Diana smiled and thanked her. She left the building and crossed the street to the park. As she crossed the street, she saw a man and a woman sitting on a bench chatting with another woman who was sitting on an adjacent bench. She also spied a young woman holding the hands of two children, both of whom appeared to be less than five years old. The children were there, but they weren't. They were lethargic and they seemed to be in their own little worlds. The three walkers passed by the three people sitting on the benches, and Diana's attention became focused on the two children. They suddenly became animated and fully tuned in to their surroundings. One suddenly hugged his mother. The other started pointing to several birds flying by. For her part, the mother looked shocked. Tears came to her eyes. Diana couldn't take her eyes off of the scene. Somehow, she felt as if she was witnessing something special.

Barney and Polina also saw what was unfolding. They, however, knew exactly what they were observing. They quickly told Abigail that the time had gotten away from them because they were enjoying their conversation so much and said goodbye. Abigail was very pleased with the compliment and then turned her attention to the mother and her children. For their part, Barney and Polina disappeared. They became invisible but remained in the park, observing everything.

Diana strode purposefully towards the mother. "Ma'am, is everything all right? You look upset."

The woman smiled and said, "This is the first time my two sons have showed any interest in the outside world. They have severe cases of autism. Right now, they are acting like any other two-and four-year-old boys. They have never done this before."

Diana replied, "I was crossing the street to go to the park and I saw what happened. You were walking with them, holding their hands, when all of a sudden, just as you passed those three people on the benches, the kids became animated. I didn't think anything of it until you became upset." Diana turned to gesture to the three on the benches, but, to her surprise, there now was only the single female. The couple had left, and the young lady on the bench was in the process of putting the remnants of her lunch into the bag in preparation to return to work. Diana said to the mother, "Would you mind waiting for just a second? I really would like to speak with you about what just happened, but I need to say something to that girl over there." The mother nodded her approval.

Diana turned and caught Abigail just as she started to walk away. "Excuse me. Are you Abigail Williams?"

Abby was startled and a little frightened. She never had people just come up to her before. "Yes, I am. Do I know you?'

"No, we have never met. I am Diana Chan. I am a reporter for Channel 14. We spoke briefly on the phone the other day."

"Oh, yes, I remember. Look, I really am in a hurry. I have to get back to work. I don't have time to talk,"

Diana replied, "It's really important. I know something is going on, and I think you know a lot about it. Now, I can go on air and tell a story about hundreds of miracle cures in Philadelphia. I can mention that your office is in the center of these cures. I can then report what is happening when mobs of sick people descend on this park right here looking for a miracle. Trust me, I can and I will sensationalize the entire thing, OR, you and I can have a quiet conversation, discuss the facts, and I'll put out the real story. It's entirely up to you."

Abigail thought for a moment and finally said, "OK, I'll talk to you. I really do have to get back to work. Let's meet some-place later, and we can talk."

Diana smiled inwardly and said, "Do you see that bar across the street? Let's meet there. Say 5:30 this afternoon?"

Abby nodded and left. Diana turned to the mother and her two children. With a big smile on her face, she put out her hand and said, "Hi, my name is Diana Chan. I'm a reporter with Channel 14. Thanks for waiting. And your name is...?"

"I'm Alice McKenzie," said the woman. "These are my two sons, Jason and Jacob."

Diana put a concerned look on her face and, in a solicitous voice, said, "I couldn't help but notice that you seemed traumatized just now. Can you tell me why? I don't want to be nosey, but you seemed shaken."

Alice replied, "As I told you earlier, we were walking along, and suddenly, out of the blue, both boys started acting like normal kids."

Diana asked, "Did you see anything? Hear anything? You're saying that this just suddenly happened?"

"No, I didn't notice anything. We were walking along, and we passed that couple sitting on the bench, and suddenly the boys were normal."

"What about the woman on the other bench?"

Alice looked baffled, "What woman? I didn't see any woman."

Puzzled, Diana said, "The woman that I just went back and spoke with." She turned and pointed at Abigail's retreating back. "Her."

Alice replied, "I never noticed her. Was she sitting on one of the benches?"

At this point, Diana was starting to get flustered. How could this woman not notice a woman sitting on a bench right in front of her? Then it hit her. Diana asked herself what Abigail looked like. She thought about it and thought about it, but she was not able to picture Abigail in her mind. She was totally unable to describe her. Diana finally gave up and turned her attention to the situation at hand.

That afternoon at 5:45, Diana was sitting in the bar where Abigail had agreed to meet her. She was sitting by herself in a booth that offered a clear view of the door. There was no sign of Abigail, and Diana was asking herself if she might have been stood up. She told herself that she would leave at 6 o'clock or when the whiskey sour she was sipping was gone, whichever came first. As she was making that decision, the door to the bar opened and a young woman walked in. Diana looked and looked and finally decided that this must be Abigail Williams, even though she was not 100% sure. She waved her hand and was rewarded with a tentative smile and a returned wave from Abigail. She approached the booth and sat down. "Sorry I'm late." Then she paused for a second and then blurted, "I'll be honest with you, I almost didn't come. I'm not comfortable speaking with strangers, and I don't think I should be talking to a reporter about what you want to discuss."

Diana took a sip of her drink and gestured to the waitress. Looking at Abby, she said, "What would you like to drink? My treat."

"Thanks, but I am not a drinker. In fact, I have never had alcohol."

Diana looked somewhat surprised. "Really? Is it a religious thing?"

Abby laughed and said, "No, not at all. It's just that I never go out and socialize. I know some of the kids in high school were drinking. Same in college. I was never part of that scene. I never had the opportunity and was never tempted."

"I am having a whiskey sour. It's got a nice taste, not strong or anything like that. Want to try one?"

Abby hesitated and finally smiled, "Sure. Why not? You only live once."

The waitress approached and Diana ordered two whiskey sours. She turned her attention to Abby. "Remember today when we ran into each other in the park?" Abby nodded. "Did you notice that lady with the two young boys?" Again, Abby nodded. "Did you notice anything strange or unusual?" This time Abby shook her head. "Well, let me tell you what happened."

Diana began her story, "It seems that the woman, Alice McKenzie, has two sons, both born with profound autism. They haven't related to anyone or anything since they were born. They live in their own little worlds. It is heartbreaking. The McKenzie family lives in a high-rise apartment building not far from here. Her husband is a very successful lawyer whose income is more than enough to provide for the family. Although she is a former teacher who would love to get back into the classroom, from an economic standpoint, she does not have to. She can stay home and take care of the boys. She said she often takes them for walks in the park. Occasionally, she will drive them to Fairmount Park, but this park is close and convenient and gets them outdoors into the fresh air.

"She told me that today they walked past you and that other couple in the park."

Abby interjected, "What other couple? I was alone."

Diana was stunned. "Are you telling me no one was in the park near you today? I saw a couple sitting on the bench across from you, and you all appeared to be having a conversation."

Abby looked at her quizzically and said, "No, you must be mistaken. I was alone."

Diana shrugged and continued, "Well, they walked by you and, as they did, the boys suddenly became alive, if you will. They started communicating, showing emotion, noticing things around them, and doing things normal kids do. That is why Mrs. McKenzie became emotional. I went over to offer assistance. Once she told me what happened, I suggested that she take the boys right away to their doctor. They see a pediatric neurologist not far from Rittenhouse Square. I told her I was a reporter and would like to accompany them to offer assistance and tell the doctor what I observed. We got to the office and she told the receptionist what happened. I have never seen anything like it. The receptionist immediately brought us back to a treatment room and the doctor and his nurse were there in seconds. Alice told them what happened and I confirmed her story and added a few things she omitted. The doctor paged his associates, who came running. They examined both boys, and then the nurses took them for some testing. In a little over an hour, the doctors returned with the boys. Everyone was smiling. The neurologist said that both boys tested in the top five percentile for their age group in verbal, cognitive, physical, and coordination skills. The older boy, Jason, was using words that some high school kids wouldn't understand. The doctors then began questioning both of us, and I'll tell you, they were pretty intense. We kept repeating what we had seen. Finally, her doctor asked that Mrs. McKenzie make an appointment to see him in a week, which she did. He said he had to report this as an unexplained cure, but for her not to worry. She just needed to be thankful that her sons appeared to be cured."

Abigail smiled and nodded. "I heard about that late this afternoon. I think you know or have surmised that I am like a scorekeeper at the office. When something unexplainable happens in the Philadelphia area, something like this, all the health care providers have been asked to report it to our office. We are the central record-keeper."

Diana quickly said, "That's what I heard, and that's what I want to talk to you about."

"I'm sorry, but I really can't say more or go into any details. There is patient confidentiality, and the doctors I work for are trying to keep this low key. They don't want to start a panic."

Diana replied, "I understand. No names. That's fine. You understand that things are happening, and eventually they will get out. People talk. That nurse in a surgeon's office talks with her sister who works for an oncologist who talks with her next-door neighbor, and guess what? A rumor begins. The next-door neighbor calls her sister in New York who has cancer and tells her that miracle cures are happening every day in Philly. That same day the sister is on the next train to Philadelphia."

Diana paused and finished her drink. She noticed that Abigail's glass was almost empty. She raised her eyebrow and pointed at Abby's glass. "Another?"

Abby said, "I really shouldn't, but it did taste good. Sure, why not?"

Diana signaled the waitress, then continued, "Ms. Williams, let's see if we can come to some sort of understanding. I don't expect you to give me names. I understand privacy laws. Can you at least describe the extent of these cures? All I'm interested in right now is number and types of cures."

The waitress returned with the drinks and departed. Both ladies took a sip, then Abby said, "I can't remember them all off of the top of my head. There have been over 20 in less than 2 weeks. The types of cures cover just about every kind of specialty." She went on to recount the spinal cord injury, various cancer cures, several Alzheimer's cures, several stoke cures, a couple of heart and diabetes cures, and ended with the two boys in the park this afternoon. "More reports coming in every day. The three doctors for whom I work are in shock. They want to use the term miracle but are too professional for that."

Diana was impressed. "Is there any pattern to where these occur?"

"Not really. Most are first noticed in doctors' offices, which is no surprise. Some happened in hospitals and others happened out on the street, like today in the park." She paused for a second and said, "Come to think about it, a couple happened right here, outside near the park."

Diana was as classy a journalist as could be found on earth. She would never get someone drunk and then pump her for information. She always wanted to be able to look at herself in the mirror and not be ashamed. "Ms. Williams, it's getting late. Look, neither of us have eaten. What say we grab my car and go to Jimmy G's Cheesesteaks? They have the best cheesesteaks in Philly. It's not too far. I'll drive you back here after we have eaten to get your car. OK?

The next morning, Abigail and Diana Chan were seated in the conference room across from Drs. Stanton. Lucas and Barr. Marguerite Camp sat at the end of the table. As the two agreed the previous evening over cheesesteaks, Diana would come to the office around 11 o'clock. Abigail would have already briefed her employers about the purpose of her visit so they would be prepared. Diana announced herself to Her Majesty, the receptionist, who oozed nothing but charm. She obviously had been briefed and had probably been threatened to be on her best behavior or else. She escorted Diana to the conference room, where everyone was already waiting.

After introductions were made and the mandatory small talk was completed, Diana took over. She told them that she learned about the mysterious cures that were occurring from a friend. A little digging on her part unearthed the fact that there was a story. She was not aware of the proportions of it, and she doubted anyone knew how big it was. She also allowed that the entire thing could be nothing more than an aberration. She said that word was already getting out. She called the Philadelphia Visitors Bureau before coming to this meeting. An official there said that occupancy in local hotels and motels had spiked unexpectedly over the past few days. There were no special events in the city which would explain the spike. A call to police headquarters confirmed that there was an unusually large number of pedestrians out and about. No trouble had yet been reported, but the police were watching closely. She told them that she planned to go ahead with her story. She outlined what she was planning and told the doctors that they were free to comment. Charles Barr asked that Dr. Simpson from **The Group of Five** be informed since she was instrumental in trying to quantify the phenomenon. The other doctors concurred and Diana had no objection. Barr placed a call to Dr. Simpson, who joined the discussion on a speaker-phone. None of the doctors liked the idea of going public, but they knew there was little that they could do. Dr. Lucas remarked that perhaps this was the wise thing to do, defuse the hysteria before it began. Consensus was reached, and Diana Chan said she thought she would have the story ready to air in two days.

SHOWTIME

Channel 14's 7:00 p.m. newscast opened as usual with the two smiling, very good-looking and very well-dressed anchors looking directly at the camera. Bobbie, the brunette female, started by saying, "The Philadelphia area has recently been the scene for numerous mystery cures. The story was uncovered by Diana Chan, who is reporting live from outside Independence Hall."

The screen changed to show Diana, microphone in hand, standing outside of the famed Philadelphia landmark. In a low key and unemotional tone, Diana told the story of how over 20 people with various diseases had suddenly been cured. Some of these people had been in critical condition. Some had what the doctors described as permanent conditions. Finally, other patients had less severe treatable conditions that suddenly disappeared. The local medical community was investigating, but so far had not reached any conclusions. She cut away to show her interview with the McKenzie family. The interview had been shot in the spacious living room of their apartment. Alice and her husband were sitting together on the couch, while the two boys did what two active little boys do. They made their parents very nervous.

Before the cameras started rolling, Diana told them not to worry. Two very active boys made the story even more touching. Alice's husband held her hand as she recounted the very minute that her boys were cured and her reaction to it. Diana inserted that she happened to be in the area and witnessed the entire event. Alice went on to say she had no idea how it happened, but that she and her husband are eternally grateful. The scene went back to Diana, who closed the live report by reminding everyone it was a breaking story, and she was still developing leads. She asked for the public's help by notifying the station if any of them were aware of or experienced a sudden and unexplainable cure of any kind of ailment, injury, or disease. She went on to say she would provide on-air updates as she found and verified them. Then she turned the program back to the anchors. Jack, the male anchor, thanked her profusely for her hard and diligent work, made an inane comment about how good news tended to spring from Philadelphia and then broke for commercial.

Abigail watched the show intently. She thought Diana had presented a fair and balanced account, and she wondered where it would all go from there.

The next day, Dr. Lucas asked Abby to accompany him to Children's Hospital of Philadelphia. He had several patients he wanted to see and meet with their parents. He was also going to pick up some documents and wanted Abigail to take them back to the office. He drove since he was allowed to park in a covered area reserved for physicians. The only drawback was that this parking area was located near the emergency room waiting area. As they entered the building, he said, "I hate coming in this door. Too many sick people." He looked down at Abigail, who was staring incredulously at him. "It's a joke. Man, you really need to lighten up. Don't take everything so seriously."

They passed the ER and walked down the corridor towards the main lobby and the elevators. Abby felt a presence behind her. She turned and saw a crowd of people rushing after them. Before they got to the lobby, the crowd surged around them, encircling them in a mass of humanity. There was crying. There was yelling and screaming. There were pleadings. People were pushing their children at Dr. Lucas. For his part, he was looking wildly around, trying to make sense of what was happening. People were grabbing at him, ripping his suit, and trying to touch him. It reminded Abigail of some of the scenes she had seen on television when screaming fans surround a rock star. The big difference was that the fans just wanted to be near 'greatness' while these folks were desperate. There was real fear and desperation in their actions. They were all intent on getting to Lucas no matter what.

Abigail was engulfed with people and would have fallen except that the crowd was packed so densely that there was no place to go. Abigail was roughly pushed to the edge of the crowd and, thankfully, saw a janitor's closet. She took refuge in it and huddled in the darkness shivering with fear. Just like Dr. Lucas, she had no idea what happened, or more importantly, why. The big difference between the two now was that she was safe while he was in peril from a ruthless mob.

The commotion raged beyond the closet door for what seemed to be hours, but in reality, was less than 10 minutes. When the noise finally subsided, Abigail cracked the closet door open and carefully peered out. The corridor was deserted. She took a deep breath and made a dash for the lobby and the front doors. She ran into the street and hailed a taxi. She gave the driver the address of the office and asked him to step on it. While sitting in the cab, she noticed that her left forearm was bleeding. The driver noticed it, too. "Are you OK, lady? Do you want me to take you to a hospital?"

"No, just drive me to my office. It's a medical practice. They can take care of me there." Abby pulled out a handkerchief and pressed it over the cut, grit her teeth and tried not to cry.

Back at the hospital, James Lucas was sitting in a doctor's lounge sipping coffee and was still in a state of shock. He was surrounded by a crowd of other doctors, hospital security, and Philadelphia police. The CEO, CFO, Chief Legal Counsel, and the Public Information Director for the hospital were also in attendance. The police took the lead in questioning Dr. Lucas. He repeated over and over that he had no idea why he was attacked. It came as a complete surprise to him. He repeated the story five or six times, and then a thought struck him. "I was accompanied by an employee from my office. I lost track of her just as the mob attacked. I don't know what happened to her."

One of the police investigators scowled at him, "This event occurred 45 minutes ago, and you are just now realizing that one of your employees is missing? You have got to be kidding me."

Lucas stammered in reply, "No, it's not like that. You have to believe me. I was and still am in shock. All I could think about was that these people were somehow angry with me and wanted to hurt me."

Another police officer said, "Tell us about this employee."

"Well, she works in the records and billing section. I asked her to accompany me so I could give her some files I needed to be brought back to the office as soon as I was finished with them."

The second officer said, "Tell us her name and we'll try to find her. She's probably all right, but we need to make sure."

Lucas looked dazed. He finally said, "I think her name is Audrey or something like that. I believe it starts with an 'A.'"

Before anyone could react, another officer who had witnessed the interrogation came forward while putting his cell phone away and said, "I just called your office. No one there has seen or heard from her. By the way, they told me her name is Abigail, not Audrey."

Lucas just sat there, sipping coffee with his eyes closed.

On television sets around the Philadelphia area, all of the stations broke into their regular programming with breaking news. On Channel 14, Diana Chan stood with a mike in her hand. She had been driving to work when the station manager called her and told her to get to Children's Hospital ASAP. A van with a crew, camera and antenna would be there shortly. Diana hated to go into a broadcast cold, and this one was freezing. All she knew was that some kind of riot broke out on the ground floor of Children's Hospital of Philadelphia. A hospital spokesperson was getting ready to give a preliminary briefing. Diana told the Channel 14 audience that the briefing was about to start and she would be back at its conclusion. She entered the auditorium with her cameraman and listened.

The spokeswoman was an attractive person of color in her early 30's. She appeared somewhat rattled. "Thank you for being here. I will relate the facts as we now know them. Keep in mind that this is a fluid situation that keeps changing as new information is uncovered. Here is what we know thus far. At approximately 10:00 a.m., Dr. James Lucas, a well-respected oncologist, and a female employee of his entered the hospital via the entrance near the emergency room waiting area. As they walked down the corridor towards the main lobby and its banks of elevators, a crowd rushed after them. It seems that they were attempting to get close to Dr. Lucas. Many were carrying their children with them and were demanding that he heal them. This entire situation caught Dr. Lucas by surprise. He reported that he was afraid for his life. He thought the crowd might kill him. They kept grabbing him, ripping his clothes and some even threw punches to get him to stop. He described the crowd as being totally irrational."

She took a sip of water and continued, "The female employee is missing at this time. We presume she was able to get out of the way of the crowd and is either in hiding or has left the hospital. We are reviewing the surveillance videos now to determine what happened to her."

She paused and took a deep breath. Then she resumed, "There were several injuries sustained by people in the melee. Several children sustained bruises. Several more sustained broken bones. Evidently, some of the adults got into altercations with each other and also sustained bruises, bloody noses, and an assortment of other minor injuries. Dr. Lucas, fortunately, sustained no serious injuries, just an assortment of cuts and bruises. We currently do not have any information regarding the status of his employee."

The spokesperson concluded, "Look, I know you have a million questions. So do we. Unfortunately, you now know as much as we do. We are just beginning our investigation. As more information becomes available, I will let you know. I am not in a position to take questions at this time. Thank you."

There were howls of protest from the assembled media representatives, but not from Diana. As the spokeswoman was winding down her briefing, Diana and her cameraman left the room. She called her station and told them to have the anchors do the closing and sign off. She had a lead and wanted to follow it immediately. Leaving her crew and microphone behind, she went into the ER waiting room. It was easy to determine who had participated in the mob just by looking at the appearance of the people sitting there. There were several police officers getting statements and taking names of the witnesses for furthers questioning. Diana walked around the room, identified herself, and asked several different people to describe what happened. Law enforcement and attorneys often complain that eye-witness testimony is highly unreliable. Diana was amazed that the stories she heard were almost word for word the same. She asked one lady if she would be willing to be interviewed on TV. This woman was star struck and readily agreed.

Diana smiled at the camera and said, "I am live from Children's Hospital. I have Francine Burke with me. Ms. Burke was in the ER when the crowd action occurred. She has kindly agreed to an interview." The camera focused on Francine Burke and Diana asked, "Ms. Burke, could you tell us in your own words what happened?"

Francine Burke smiled her best smile and said, "I was sitting right here with my son, Bobby, waiting to be called. Bobby has been running a fever for some days now, and I thought it best to have it checked out. We don't have health insurance, so we use the ER. They are real nice here. All of a sudden, we heard a breeze blow through the room and down the hallway following a man. I think there might have been a woman beside him, but I can't be sure. After they passed the waiting room, all those closest to the corridor were cured. Not just the kids, but everyone. Fevers were gone. Kids were suddenly active. Broken bones were mended. One little boy had burned his hand pretty bad. It was healed. Same with the parents. Those who were wearing glasses had to take them off. They could see perfectly without them. There was a lady on crutches; well, she didn't need them anymore. I'm not sure why she had them in the first place, but she didn't use them after this man walked by. Another guy had one of those portable oxygen things. All of a sudden, he was breathing normally. He no longer needed it. When those of us who were sitting away from the corridor saw what happened, well, we wanted to be cured. There was a mass stampede after this guy. I think we took him by surprise. He kept trying to get away. The more he tried, the more we pressed him to cure our kids and us. I have no idea how long it lasted. Finally, hospital security and some police officers were able to stop it and sort things out. You know, looking back, it was pretty stupid of me to take my kid and rush into a mob like that. He could have been hurt."

Diana followed up, "He looks unharmed to me. Did he get hurt, and did he get cured?"

Ms. Burke sadly shook her head, "No to both questions. Maybe I was just imagining things about that man curing people. It sure looked real. I guess I was wrong. It looks like we were all wrong."

Diana smiled at the lady and said, "Thanks for your time, Ms. Burke." Then to the camera, she said, "Ms. Burke's story is almost the same as every other person I interviewed here today. I will be here the rest for of the day following this story. Now back to our regular programming." Once the cameraman gave the all clear-signal, Diana thanked Ms. Burke again and dialed the station on her phone. The station manager took the call and praised her reporting. She was the first reporter to get a story about the riot on the air. No other station appeared to be close to filing anything other than a regurgitation of the press briefing. Diana told him she was going to hang out here for a while, but there was another lead she may follow up later. The manager said he would send another crew to the hospital if she decided to go elsewhere.

At the office of Drs. Stanton, Lucas, and Barr, an employee was in the breakroom getting coffee. The TV was turned on and suddenly there was an alert about breaking news. She listened to it for just a few seconds then ran to get Marguerite Camp, the doctors and anyone else she saw. They all crowded around the TV and watched as the surveillance video played the mob scene in the corridor. One lady said, "There's Dr. Lucas. Where is Abigail?" They all searched the screen frantically and someone finally blurted, "There she is on the far right. Looks like they have her pinned up against the wall." The scene then flashed to Diana Chan giving the introduction for the press briefing she attended. The folks in the office just stared at the TV with incredulous looks on their faces. This sort of thing doesn't happen in Children's Hospital, and it certainly doesn't happen to people they know.

While everyone was watching the briefing, the taxi deposited Abigail at the front door of the office. She didn't feel like going around to the side door and fiddling with the lock. She paid the driver and entered the building. There were several patients in the waiting room. The receptionist was sitting on her throne and did not notice her. She hurried past everyone and gratefully sank into the security of her cubicle. She put her hands over her face and forced herself not to cry.

Once the interview with Francine Burke was concluded and regular programming resumed, the group that had gathered in front of the TV started to disperse. There was a lot of head-shaking going on and several conversations about poor Dr. Lucas and what on earth could have happened to Abigail Williams. They hoped she was all right. The girl who had the cubicle adjacent to Abigail's passed by and saw her sitting at her desk. The girl was startled and blurted out in a very loud voice, "Oh my God! You're here!" Marguerite and several others of the office staff hurried over. They all were peppering Abigail with questions, giving her absolutely no opportunity to answer. Finally, Marguerite was able to take control and took Abigail to the conference room. She told the others that she would call them in once Abigail had a chance to compose herself. She asked one of the girls to fetch Drs. Stanton and Barr.

Abigail was shown a chair at the head of the table and Marguerite sat beside her. The two doctors arrived and quickly determined that Abigail was not far from going into shock. Dr. Stanton noticed the wound on her arm and immediately got up and left the room. He came back a few minutes later with his nurse, who was carrying dressings, antiseptics, and other items necessary to protect the wound. He examined her arm and pronounced that she did not require stitches. His nurse assisted him in cleaning the wound and putting a dressing and bandages on it. He then gave her a tetanus shot.

Abigail detested being the center of attention. It had happened so infrequently in her life that she had no idea what to do. Unfortunately, when she had been the center of attention, it involved the likes of Craig in high school.

Dr. Barr spoke to her in a very quiet and soothing voice. He told her everything was fine. She was safe here. They would protect her. Stanton's nurse left the room and came back shortly after that with a cup of steaming tea and a few cookies. Dr. Barr thanked the nurse, gave the tea to Abigail, and said, "Take this, dear. It will do you good. Just sit and relax. When you feel like it, tell us what happened. Dr. Lucas called a little while ago. He is worried about you. He said that he was fine, but he lost track of you." Stanton looked at him quizzically. Barr subtly shook his head and rolled his eyes. That was so farfetched that it was almost unbelievable. Lucas would never do such a thing. For her part, Abigail closed her eyes. She could not remember the last time someone worried about her. It felt good.

After she finished the tea, Abigail felt better. She began describing the scene at the hospital, how they were walking past the ER waiting area heading to the main lobby when she had a sensation, turned her head, and saw the crowd. She described being hit and pushed and elbowed. She finally was pushed to the edge of the crowd, where she found refuge in the janitor's closet. She told them about waiting until the coast was clear and then running out of the hospital and catching the cab to bring her here. She had no idea how she got the cut on her arm. She first noticed it in the cab.

Dr. Barr: "Were they trying to hurt you?"

Abigail: "No, I don't think so. They seemed to want to get past me to get to Dr. Lucas."

Dr. Stanton: "Why? Were they mad at Lucas?"

Abigail: "I don't think so. I think I heard some of the people call out calls about cures, but I can't be sure. If they were talking about cures, I certainly don't know what they meant."

Dr. Stanton looked at Abigail and smiled. "We are all very pleased you made it through this relatively unscathed. If it's OK with you, I'd like you to tell your story to everyone else here in the office. They are all dying of curiosity. After that, we are going to put you in a cab and send you home. Today is Wednesday, I don't want to see you back here until Monday. Understand? Marguerite will get someone to take over the cure reports while you are out."

Marguerite put Abby in the cab and paid the driver in advance. She then went back into the office. By this time, things were really backed up. Neither of the doctors had seen a patient in well over an hour and the waiting room was getting crowded. Many patients were verbally voicing their displeasure, and Her Majesty, sitting on her imperial throne, merely sneered and quoted trite phases about how hard the doctors were working and that they should just be patient.

Once the doctors started seeing patients after Abigail had left, they were in for three shocks. The three patients who were in the waiting room when Abby arrived back from the hospital were suffering from the late stages of lung cancer, pancreatic cancer, and liver cancer. Barr saw the lung cancer patient. "Mrs. Peabody, how are you today?"

The senior citizen replied that she was really feeling much better. Barr mechanically said that that was fine. It was good news. He examined her, looked at the x-rays that were taken just before he came to examine her, and then he abruptly left the room. He grabbed Stanton and asked him to come into the treatment room and verify what he was seeing. Stanton looked harried and replied he was with a patient who had been there for several hours. The look on Barr's face caused him to change his mind. Stanton performed a brief examination and studied the x-rays. He turned pale and his eyes widened. Barr told the woman that they needed to confer with each other, and the two doctors left the room. Stanton said, "Are you kidding me? There is no trace of cancer."

Barr replied, "I know. Based on the progression I had previously observed, I thought she was down to her last few months. Now it appears that she is not sick at all. I'm going to send her to The University of Pennsylvania's Med Center and run a battery of tests. I think they will come back negative."

Stanton concurred. He went back into another treatment room where the pancreatic patient waited and experienced a sense of déjà vu. The middle-aged man was feeling fine. He was energetic and active. Stanton left and got Dr. Barr. After Barr examined the patient, they went out into the hallway. Barr said, "Maybe this guy can catch a ride with the lung patient or maybe they can split the cab fare." The doctors had a chuckle and went back to work.

Dr. Stanton went into the room where a very irritated liver cancer patient fumed at the wait. Within 10 minutes, this patient was also driving to the UPA Med Center.

Dr. Lucas finally arrived around 1:00 p.m. The other two doctors expressed perfunctory concern for his welfare and then proceeded to regale him with the stories of the three miracle cures. The other patients seen by the two doctors that morning were all exactly what they expected. They all had cancer and were battling it with different degrees of success. There were no more miracles that day. It was a routine day at the office.

The next day, the three doctors were together in the conference room discussing the previous day's occurrences. Lucas didn't have anything to add about his experiences, other than he was terrified.

He didn't get the feeling that the mob wanted to hurt him, per se. He thought they were driven by something else. They kept saying that they wanted a cure or to be cured. He wasn't sure. At any rate, it was over his head. He said that he lost track of that girl from the office who was going to take the files back. "I can never remember her name. Is she all right? Did she get out OK?" The other two doctors just looked at each other and shook their heads. Lucas' only saving grace was that he was absolutely brilliant, one of the finest physicians to ever walk the earth. As a human being, he was a total failure. He was on his third trophy wife, each one younger than her predecessor. He had six children equally divided between the three wives. All were in boarding schools, three of them in schools in Europe.

Dr. Barr said that the report on TV included an interview with a lady who was in the mob. "She said that when you and....Audrey walked by, people near the corridor were cured. Do you recall hearing that?"

"I think I might have heard something along those lines, but it didn't make any sense to me then," Lucas replied. Then he said, "Let's talk about what happened here."

Stanton started, "We got a late start. We were all watching the reports from Children's on TV. We were wondering what happened to, I think her name is Amy. After the report ended on TV, we all went back to work. Marguerite found Amy at her desk. She was shaken. We got her calmed down and I told her to take the rest of the week off."

"With pay?" asked Lucas.

"You cheap bastard. Yes, with pay." The three doctors got a chuckle over that. Then Lucas got serious. The three who were cured, were they really cured?"

"We requested UPA to step on the testing, and yes. It appears that they are not only not in remission, but there is also no sign of them ever having had cancer." Barr replied.

Lucas asked, "What made them special? One cure would have been unlikely but possibly believable, but three in a row? Did they come in contact with something or someone?"

Stanton answered, "All three live in different sections of the area. One lives in King of Prussia, another in Springfield, and the third in Paoli. The only common spot is right here."

Barr surmised, "That brings us back to square one. Everyone here was watching TV except for Mary at the reception desk, and it's safe to say she wasn't doing any curing." Then he added, "Why do we keep her around? She tends to make people sick."

"Shhh," whispered Stanton. "She is my wife's niece. My wife's sister is a real BITCH. Mary is just keeping up the family tradition." The doctors had another chuckle then set out to meet the day.

THE SENATE COMMITTEE

The following Monday, Abigail arrived at work. She entered by the side entrance as she almost always did and made her way to her cubicle. Reviewing the log of miracle cures, she was astounded to see that it was close to 500. She checked the dates and saw that some were three years old. Almost all of these reports were verified by physicians. Just then, Marguerite Camp came by. "Abigail, good morning. How are you doing, Honey? Have you recovered?"

Abigail replied, "Good morning, Marguerite. I'm doing OK."

Marguerite pulled up a chair and sat down. "Listen, it hit me on Wednesday when we didn't know where you were that we don't have your cell phone number. I had everyone in the office, including the doctors, exchange cell phone numbers on Thursday. Let me have your number, and I'll add it to the list. I'll send out the complete list later this afternoon. You should load all of them into your contact list."

Abigail looked surprised. "I don't have a contact list."

"Of course you do. Every cell phone comes with one. Let me see yours."

Abigail pulled out a flip phone. Marguerite asked, "How old is that, Honey? It looks like it should be in the Smithsonian."

Abigail answered, "I bought it years ago. I really never use it. I don't have anyone to call and no one calls me. I don't even know why I still have it."

Marguerite shook her head. She mentioned the cure log and how it suddenly grew. The growth probably was a function of the stories coming out of Children's Hospital. They discussed it for a brief time, then Marguerite left. She headed straight to Dr. Stanton's office and told him the story of Abigail and her cell phone. She told him she wanted to go out over the noon hour and get her a state of the art phone. Before Stanton could comment, she told him she was planning to charge the phone and the contract to the office. She would not have a repeat of Wednesday morning. Stanton knew resistance was hopeless and gracefully surrendered.

Over the next week or so as reports of cures increased, the number of people arriving in Philadelphia multiplied daily. The nearest available hotel rooms were in Delaware and central New Jersey, and these were at a premium. Hotels in Easton, Bethlehem, Allentown, and Harrisburg, PA were preparing for the onslaught. Such was also the case with hotels in Baltimore and DC.

Parking downtown was non-existent. The city ground to a crawl and was headed to collapse. Public transport and taxis were running full out. Extra buses and trains were put in service, but they could not begin to keep up. The city tried to set up remote parking with a shuttle service to move people into the city, but the already overextended public transportation system ground to a halt.

Grocery stores struggled to put food on the shelves, but between the crowded roads making deliveries almost impossible and the increased demand, they too fell behind. To exacerbate this situation, independent over the road truck drivers refused loads into the area. They only make money when they are driving. Sitting in traffic while burning fuel is a recipe for bankruptcy. Restaurants, both five-star and fast food, initially made a fortune. Then their supplies dried up and they had to close. Gas stations also went dry, and with them the vehicles they serviced. As the vehicles ran out of fuel, their drivers abandoned them where they sat. Roadways were impassable.

Basic necessities such as toilets became priceless. The city brought in portable toilets as fast as they could, but they, too, became overloaded. The trucks that serviced them could not get into the city. The porta-potties became cesspools on the landscape. Restaurants, gas stations, movie theaters, anything ordinarily open to the public started to charge for their facilities. The cost of using them skyrocketed. Then the supply of toilet tissue evaporated, and they were forced to lock their doors.

The people roamed the streets, looking for the cure. These were desperate people who were at the end of their ropes. As might be expected, tempers flared, fights broke out, shots were fired, and people were wounded and killed. It was the scene from *Dante's Inferno* that all people knew might happen, but prayed they would never see. The city had hit the bottom rung of *Maslow's Needs Hierarchy*: basic survival.

The governor mobilized the National Guard to keep order and try to clear the streets. All roads into Philadelphia were closed within a radius of 50 miles to all non-essential vehicles. The airport was closed to all flights except resupply missions. Dover Air Force Base also was called upon to handle the logistical load.

As almost always happens in a crisis, that lovable gang of miscreants in Washington, also known as the Congress of the United States, decided to conduct hearings to determine what was going on. The Senate Committee on Health, Education, Labor, and

Pensions (HELP) issued a subpoena for Dr. James Lucas to appear in front of them. Dr. Lucas was selected because he was at the center of the riots at Children's Hospital, his office was responsible for tabulating the cures, and several of the cures occurred near his office. When Dr. Lucas received the summons, he was beside himself in anger and frustration. Aside from having to pay for a suite at the Hay Adams Hotel for himself and his current trophy wife, he had to pay for a suite for his attorney plus attorney's fees. Since he needed an assistant, he had to pay for a room at a budget hotel for what's her name. Since the airports and roads were closed, Dr. Lucas' attorney asked for and received from the HELP Committee permission to hire a helicopter to transport them to DC. The chopper would pick them up at Penn's Landing Heliport located adjacent to the Delaware River and land them at a small civil airport near Alexandria. He booked a limo to take them to the Hay Adams. Abigail would take a cab to her hotel.

Abigail had mixed emotions when she was told she was going to Washington. She had never been there and was excited to see the sights. On the other hand, she dreaded leaving the security of her little world. Who knew what she might encounter?

The hearing was scheduled for Tuesday. Lucas decided to go down on Sunday so he could get settled in the Hotel and discuss with his attorney what might be expected at the hearing. It was unclear to all exactly why he was being called to testify, and it is always best to be prepared for anything that might come up.

On Sunday morning, Abigail left her home early to head for the heliport. With the congestion in the city, even short trips could take hours. She made good time and arrived a little early. Her four traveling companions arrived shortly thereafter, and in no time, they were airborne heading for DC. This was Abigail's first time flying either in an airplane or helicopter, and she was excited.

The pilot noticed this and gave her a set of headphones to wear. He pointed out the sights they flew over and she was enthralled. Flying was old hat to the others who just sat back, relaxed, and occasionally glanced out the windows. To Abigail, it seemed just seconds before they were landing near Alexandria. The limo was waiting. The pilot had called ahead and requested that the airport manager have a taxi standing by, and it was. Once everyone had retrieved their luggage, Lucas, his attorney, and their two wives boarded the limo and headed to the Hay Adams. Abigail climbed into the cab for the ride to Motel 7 in Arlington.

The motel was basic in its amenities, but it was clean, the bed was comfortable, and it was located in a safe area of town. There were several restaurants, cafés and fast food places nearby. Abby very much wanted to see the sights in Washington. The desk clerk at the motel told her about Hop-On Hop-Off bus tours. There was a stop a short distance from the motel, and Abby decided to try it. She got off near the Lincoln Memorial and was moved by its majesty and message. While walking along, she passed a lady in a wheelchair. Shortly after that, she heard a shriek. Turning, she saw the lady standing up and crying like a baby. Abigail had no idea what happened, but the lady seemed very happy. The Vietnam Memorial unleashed strong emotions. Its stark simplicity and powerful message brought tears to Abby's eyes. She went to the registers that index the names of the fallen and their places on the walls. She passed by a man who had been severely burned. His face and arms were severely disfigured. As she prepared to leave to go back to the bus stop, she passed him again. His skin was perfect. He kept staring at his hands and touching the smooth skin of his face. Tears were streaming down his cheeks, and he seemed not to notice or to care.

Abigail had a wonderful afternoon touring the big attractions. She noted where the Capitol Building was and realized that she would be going inside of it on Tuesday. On Monday, she planned to visit Arlington National Cemetery and the Tomb of the Unknowns, The Smithsonian and, if time permitted, the Marine Corps Memorial. She was completely unaware of what she had left in her wake during her Sunday excursion. Numerous people no longer required glasses or hearing aids. A couple of people who were deaf from birth could hear clearly. A child who was born blind could suddenly see. A large number of people all of a sudden started to feel better. Many had colds and coughs, several more had heart problems, and others had various types of cancer. When they went for their next doctors' appointments, they were in for the shock of their lives.

Monday was more of the same. Abigail thoroughly enjoyed visiting the sights. She had read about these places, and now she saw them firsthand. And just like yesterday, Abby radically changed the lives of literally hundreds of people for the better. She was like a wisp of wind. By the time people realized that they had been healed, she was gone or lost in a crowd. Word spread quickly throughout the city. The local CNB affiliate got wind of the cures but decided to wait before running the story. They wanted to avoid another Philadelphia if at all possible.

On Tuesday morning, Abigail awoke to a beautiful, sunny day. She had breakfast in a small café with outdoor seating and, when she finished, caught a cab to the Capitol. She asked a Capitol policeman for directions to the hearing room. She was one of the first to arrive, so she had the opportunity to look around the great room. She noted where the Senators would sit and the row of chairs behind them for their aides. She saw the table facing the Senators that had the name-plate "Dr. James Lucas" printed upon it. There were two chairs at the table. She presumed that they were for Dr. Lucas and his attorney. She was unsure where she was supposed to sit or do, so she just stood near the back of the room.

As ten o'clock approached, the room began to fill. Dr. Lucas and his attorney arrived. Both men were wearing what appeared to be $1,000 suits with carefully coordinated ties and highly polished shoes. They truly looked the part of two very successful men. Lucas saw Abigail and walked over to her and handed her several very full file folders. "I'm not sure what to expect today. What I'd like you to do is sit right here, and if I need the folders, I'll motion you." He smiled a quick smile and asked, "Any questions?" Abby shook her head no, and he returned to the witness chair.

Senators and their aides began to wander in. The chairman of the committee was Senator Chad Mitchell, a Republican from Wisconsin, who was just beginning his third term. He narrowly defeated his Democratic challenger in the previous election. It was typical of most elections in the modern era, full of accusations of corruption, greed, and wrongdoing on both sides. Both candidates came away smeared in mud, with their good names gone and reputations ruined. However, Mitchell won, so all was good in the world.

A tall, thin man, who appeared to be in his mid-forties, entered. He was cleanly shaven, wore a well-pressed suit, wire-rim glasses, and carried a well-used leather briefcase. He gave her a nod and a smile. "Do you mind if I take this seat?" he asked, motioning to the empty chair next to her.

Abigail hated to be near other people, but there was little she could do in this case. He had the right to sit there if she wasn't saving the chair. She nodded and said, "This chair is not taken."

The man smiled and sat down. He said, "Thanks. I have some time to kill and thought I would watch the action here. Evidently, they are looking into those miracle cures in Philadelphia. Can you believe that's happening?"

Abigail just smiled and shrugged her shoulders.

The man continued, "My name is Raphael Melek. I am an attorney and lobbyist. I have a small practice in Georgetown. My lobbying efforts are for the liberal causes, you know, the environment, higher minimum wages, things like that. I am here today to watch the proceedings of the House Armed Services Committee. They are looking into that incident in Afghanistan where we got the drop on an entire village of Taliban fighters. Some of the Democrats are trying to hang the CIA agent who called it in, as well as the team leader of the attack helicopters. I'm a liberal, but I value justice more. I think they are off base here." Changing the subject, he said, "How about you? Where are you from?"

At this point, Abigail was utterly flustered and nervous. Talking to strange men was definitely not her forte. She stammered a little and was finally able to say, "Philadelphia."

"Philadelphia? Are you connected to this hearing?"

She nodded and quietly said, "The man I work for is the primary witness today, Dr. James Lucas."

"I'll be darned. Is it true what the news is reporting about Philly, that the town is basically shut down by gridlock?"

She nodded again and said, "I'm afraid so. It's pretty bad up there. It's almost impossible to move, to get to work, to go shopping. With all of the crowds, there isn't much to shop for. We have no idea what brought this on or when it will go away." She paused for a second, then changed the subject. "I'm Abigail Williams. I'm pleased to meet you." She offered her hand and he shook it. Then she said, "I have never heard the name Melek before. Where is it from?"

Melek laughed, "Believe it or not, it's Turkish. It means 'angel.'"

Senator Mitchell called the room to order, explaining that the committee was looking into the events currently going on in Philadelphia. He said that this was a fact-finding hearing; its purpose was not to lay any blame or point fingers. "Our witness today is

Dr. James Lucas, a highly respected oncologist with a practice in downtown Philadelphia. The reason we asked Dr. Lukas to testify was that he was caught in the disturbance at Children's Hospital last week. We wanted to get his impressions of what happened. His practice has also been tasked by the local medical establishment to be the central data collection point for all of the reports about unexplained cures. I see Dr. Lucas is accompanied by counsel. Welcome, Sir. Now, Dr. Lucas, if you would rise, I will administer the oath."

Lucas stood up and Mitchell administered the oath. The senator then invited Lucas to describe in his own words the events that occurred at Children's Hospital. Lucas did so and repeatedly stressed that he had no idea why the crowd stormed him. He failed to mention Abigail. He did say that he heard reports afterward of several people in the ER waiting room experience cures of some sort, but he couldn't report on the validity of the stories at this time.

Once the Children's Hospital saga was presented, Mitchell turned to the big picture, the reports of unexplained cures coming in citywide. Lucas turned to Abigail and motioned for her to bring the files up. She did so. He nodded perfunctorily at her and she started to return to her seat. Mitchell said, "Doctor, what is that woman's name?"

Lucas looked bewildered. "Her name is Amber."

Mitchell called out, "Amber." There was no response from the retreating figure. He called the name out several more times, again to no response. As she approached her seat. Raphael whispered something to her and pointed to the dais. She turned around to see Senator Mitchell motioning to her to come towards him. As she did, she noticed that Raphael got up and followed her at a distance. When she got near the witness table, Mitchell asked, "Didn't you hear me call your name?"

Abigail replied, "No, sir, I heard you call someone named Amber. That is not my name."

"Well, what is your name?"

"Sir, my name is Abigail, Abigail Williams."

Just about everyone in the room turned towards Lucas, who had shriveled up into a humanoid of about three inches tall. Mitchell asked, "How long have you worked for Dr. Lucas?"

She replied, "For about three years now." Again everyone's attention turned to Lucas, who was now about one-and-a-half inches tall.

Mitchell shook his head and asked, "I'd like to ask you some questions since you work with Dr. Lucas. Maybe you have a different perspective to bring to the subject. Is that all right with you?"

Before Abby could answer, Raphael spoke up, "Senator. I'd like to have a word with my client."

Abigail looked shocked. Lucas' attorney stood and said, I will act as this lady's counsel."

Melek replied, "You represent her employer. If you were also to represent her, there may be a conflict of interest."

Lucas' attorney said, "Her employer will pay my fees. I don't think she is in a position financially to afford an attorney."

Melek's answer was, "I'm happy to offer my services pro bono." He then looked at Abigail, who smiled meekly and nodded her head.

Mitchell said, "I guess that's settled. Go ahead and have a word with Ms. Williams." As Raphael turned towards Abigail, Mitchell said, "I didn't catch your name." He paused a second, "You look very familiar. Have we ever met?"

"Yes, Senator, we have met. My name is Raphael Melek. I represented Robert Wallace a year or so ago in front of the subcommittee you were chairing. If you recall, Mr. Wallace had a lasting effect upon the Senate. He helped provide three of your former colleagues with the same type of retirement plan the State of Illinois offers to its former governors. I'm sure you remember Mary Chase. She is presently residing in the Hazelton, WV Federal Penitentiary, and is reportedly enjoying the fresh air and daily strip searches. James Delaney is basking in the sunshine at the Federal Prison in Atlanta and is having a wonderful experience learning about the many rewards of being a child molester. Kathy Burns is back in California at the California Institution for Women in Corona. Although the name implies a place of higher learning, it most definitely is not. She is, however, getting a different kind of education which she would probably not classify as higher."

"Mr. Melek, are you trying to mock this proceeding?"

"No, Senator. I am not. I was merely trying to respond fully to your question of 'Have we ever met?' He paused for just a few seconds then said, "I'll just be a minute conferring with my client."

He turned to Abigail and smiled a reassuring smile. "Don't worry. These people are like some dogs, they bark a lot but normally they don't bite. Answer their questions directly and honestly. Don't volunteer anything. If they don't ask, don't volunteer anything. If they ask and you know the answer, answer it. If you don't know the answer, say so. Guessing will just get you in trouble. If you are unsure what to do or say, I'll be right next to you. I'll be there to help you. OK?"

They both turned to face the dais. Mitchell asked Abigail to state her name and place of employment. Then he swore her in. What followed next was a repeat of Lucas' testimony. She described the chaos at Children's Hospital, her function in data collection, the fact that she collected the data and did not analyze it, and finally, what recent life was like in Philadelphia. She received questions from just about all of the Senators on the committee and answered each with confidence and sincerity. To those questions she was not 100% sure about, she truthfully said she did not know. When asked to guess or surmise, she politely declined. Her examination took a little less than half an hour. Finally, Mitchell thanked her and said she was free to go or stay as she pleased. She gestured to Lucas that she was going to leave. He nodded and gave her a little smile.

As they were leaving the room, Raphael touched her shoulder and motioned her aside. "Look, I have a feeling that things are going to get wild around here shortly." He handed her a sealed envelope and said, "This has $1,000 cash inside of it. It is not a gift; it's a loan. I know you will repay it. I want you to leave this building as quickly as possible, grab a taxi, and take it to your hotel. Tell him to wait for you. Go inside, pack your things quickly, check out, and have him drive you as near to Philadelphia as he can get. I believe Dr. Lucas put your room on his credit card, so this money is for a cab to get you to Philly. Do you understand what I am telling you?"

Abigail looked shocked. There was fear on her face. She nodded. "I don't understand why."

Melek said, "Listen, stories are floating around about miracle cures in DC. The Senate holds a hearing about it. What do you think will happen if and when people find out you were part of those hearings? What happened at Children's will look like a summer breeze in comparison to this tornado. I'll be in touch. Just go now." He surprised her by giving her a warm embrace and a gentle push to go.

Back in the hearing room, strange things were happening. Senators, aides, staffers, spectators, anyone who wore glasses or hearing aids removed them. A few muttered that the glasses were beginning to give them headaches. Others said that their hearing aids were suddenly too loud. One very elderly Senator who used a walker for mobility stood up and started walking like a healthy 15-year-old boy. People in the room started looking around at each other, and then the truth hit home. Those who needed it were suddenly cured, and the cures coincided with the appearance of that Williams woman. Several in the room stood up and raced for the door. Senator Mitchell pounded his gavel calling for order. He was totally ignored. He finally declared the hearing adjourned, which prompted a mad stampede out the doors looking for that woman.

'That woman' was heading rapidly for an exit. Along her way, she passed groups of people clustered together, getting ready to lobby Congressmen and Senators about their causes. One group consisted of people afflicted with Parkinson's disease; another group had first responders; disabled veterans composed the third group. As Abigail hurried passed them, many noted that they had suddenly been cured. Bedlam broke out. There were cries and screams throughout the building. The Capitol police had no idea what to do. No threat had been discovered. Reporters from all of the networks and wire services that cover Congress and the Capitol were babbling into their microphones. Since they knew nothing, what came out was jumbled junk, not dissimilar from their regular reporting.

Just seconds before the building went into lockdown mode, Abigail exited it into the fresh air. She flagged a cab on First Street NE and negotiated with the driver to take her to Arlington and then to her father's house in Springfield, PA. Her dad recently retired and did a lot of traveling. He currently was on an around the world cruise with a 'lady friend' and would be gone for several more months. She knew he would not mind her using his place temporarily. She was probably the only other person in the world who had a key. She also knew the codes to the garage door opener and burglar alarm. She would be OK.

Springfield is a suburb of Philadelphia located about 10 miles west of the city. Abigail grew up here and thus was familiar with some of the back roads leading into town. It normally is an easy three-hour drive from DC to Springfield. This day the cab covered the 150 miles in 5 hours. Traffic was brutal and detours numerous, but the driver pretended not to mind. He was getting one heck of a payday. Abigail didn't mind either. She had a chance to relax and catch her breath. About an hour into the trip, her cell phone announced that a text message had arrived. She was surprised to see it was from Dr. Lucas. He was worried about her. That was a first. She texted she was fine and that she had left the city to go to her father's house for a while. He told her that he was relieved and for her to stay put there for a while until they could get things ironed out. Abby stared at the phone as if it grew a head. This was totally out of character for Lucas. Maybe he actually was a human being.

Abby convinced the driver to stop a supermarket near Dover, DE. They had full shelves there, and she stocked up on groceries. She was confident that the stores around Philadelphia were not stocked nearly as well.

REVRAY

The period that followed the pandemonium in DC was the calm before the storm. There were no new reports of miracle cures in either DC or Philadelphia. The news agencies gradually and reluctantly gave the story less coverage. And then a shock jock on a radio station took a wild guess and associated Abigail Williams with the cures. He located her residence in Upper Darby, but after several days of stalking it, decided she was hiding somewhere else. A little research unearthed her childhood home in Springfield. He placed the house under surveillance, and it did not take long for him to determine that it was, in fact, occupied. He was smart enough to know that knocking on the door and asking to speak to an Abigail Williams would be an exercise in futility. He had to think of something more definitive and more creative. Something with shock value that he could parlay into something big. Then it came to him, an inspiration like no other. He found two blind people and hired them to knock on the door. He instructed them to claim that they were soliciting donations for the Blind People's Association. If they got a donation, fine, they thank the donor, pocket the money and disappear. If they didn't get a donation, they should just leave. He paid them well just to knock on the door.

At ten the next morning, the shock jock watched from a distance as the two blind people with their white canes made their way up to the door of the split level home. They rang the bell. A lady warily answered and listened to their appeal. She closed the door and returned in a moment and handed one of the pair some cash. A few words were exchanged. The door shut and the pair turned around. As they did, they both got excited. They wildly moved their heads in all directions. One pointed to something and said something. His partner vehemently nodded his head. They quickly made their way down the walk, carrying but not using, their canes. They approached the shock jock's car and excitedly said, "We can see!"

BINGO! He knew he had just hit a home run. He promised the pair a small fortune if they would allow him to interview them the next day. They agreed upon and a time and place to meet the following morning. He then made arrangements to get his mobile unit to be stationed on-site near the house at 8:00 the next morning so he could broadcast live. He had a cast of 30 or 40 stooges who would do his bidding at a moment's notice, and put the word out for them to also be there at 8:00 a.m. Finally, he called his office and told them to have signs prepared and delivered the next morning. He was ready to roll.

At eight the next morning, he went live. He announced he was in Springfield, PA, in front of 'miracle girl's' home, where a crowd had gathered to get the cure. He put the two blind people on and asked them to describe what happened. One of the men had been blind since birth. The other lost his sight in an industrial accident. The men recounted how they rang the bell, asked for, and received a donation, and as they were leaving, they could suddenly see. Both men went to ophthalmologists, who examined their eyes and found them to be free of all defects or diseases. Both men's vision was measured at 20/20. The crowd of stooges started cheering and waving signs that read, "Cure Me" and "We want the cure."

The 'radio personality' never mentioned Abigail's name on the air. 'Miracle girl' was much more sensational.

Eventually, the local police arrived to try to disperse the crowd. The stooges made a show of refusing to leave since they were on public property. Before long, more people arrived who had heard the radio broadcast and were either curious or more probably hoping to be cured. Television crews arrived, and before long, the news was out in Philadelphia that the 'miracle girl' was in Springfield. From there, the national networks put out the word, and the makings of a perfect storm were on hand. The anchors of all of the major network TV shows came to Springfield and broadcast their evening news shows from in front of Abigail's family home. For her part, Abigail had the curtains drawn and the doors locked. She would occasionally peer out of the corner of a window to verify that the crowd was still there. To her increasing horror, every time she peered out, Abby saw that the crowd was increasing in size. She did not have a clue as to why they were there and why more people kept coming.

The reporters canvassed the neighborhood interviewing neighbors. The answers they received from the residents were remarkably similar. The house belonged to John Williams. He was a very nice but quiet man. His wife passed away several years ago. He kept to himself but was always cordial to whomever he met. Some thought he might have a child, but they were not certain if it was a boy or a girl. Others were not sure if he had children or not. None of the neighbors could remember ever having seen child there.

When Diana Chan's story first broke and the national news outlets sent it out across the nation, one person who listened to it with passing interest was Reverend Ray Curtis. Raymond Curtis was born in a small town in Appalachia. It had less than 200 inhabitants. Curtis spent his entire life there except for the five years he spent in the state penitentiary for aggravated assault and attempted robbery. As he was beating a clerk at the convenience store senseless, he failed to notice the store's manager come out from a back office with a loaded shotgun.

Raymond Curtis was a small man in almost every sense of the word. He had a very low IQ with limited cognitive ability. He refused to take responsibility for anything, including his four children with four different women, none of whom he married. The time he spent in prison was the fault of the four African Americans who sat on the jury. They tainted the judgment of the other eight white jurors. He was truly a professional victim.

In prison, he found the lord, or more accurately, he found a scam. He was assimilated into a white supremacist hate group with ties to the Aryan Nation. He covered his body with tattoos of swastikas and other symbols of hate and intolerance. He was a loud-mouth and learned the sort of backwoods oratory style typical of hate mongers: high emotions; hate-filled words and phrases; appeals to the very lowest common denominator of his audience; and rejection of the law, authority, and order. He took a correspondence course, paid his money, and received a piece of paper ordaining him as a minister in a Christian Church no one had ever heard of before. A number of his white supremacist group also were duly ordained.

After his release, he returned to his little town in the middle of nowhere and converted the shack in which he lived into the Rejecting Sodom Church. Of course, he was the pastor. The closest church affiliated with one of the main-stream religions was in a town 25 miles away. The roads in this part of the country were not up to the standards enjoyed by the rest of the state, so a journey to a church 25 miles away was not something to be taken lightly. Besides, the choice ultimately came down to buying gas for the trip or buying moonshine for a different sort of journey. When Raymond Curtis declared himself to be the Reverend Ray Curtis and proclaimed that the Rejecting Sodom Church was open for business, a good number of locals decided to give it a try. Ray's sermons were fire and brimstone, with virulent expletives directed outward at the establishment that conspired to keep his flock enslaved in poverty. The people loved it. His reputation grew as did attendance at his services. Oh, by the way, the weekly collections also grew. His flock started calling him Revray, and he loved it.

The town in which Revray lived was so small it did not have a gas station or any kind of grocery store. The townspeople had to travel to the next town, about five miles away, for gas and groceries. The groceries were sold in an old place that was both a café as well as a general store. The gas station was owned by the same man as the café/general store and was located right next door. Revray needed gas and some basic groceries and drove his old pickup truck to the small town. He had a few minutes to spare, so he decided to get a cup of coffee and maybe a slice of pie at the café. He parked his truck and noticed a car the likes of which he had never seen. He walked over to it and saw that it was Maserati Gran Turismo Sport. It was Rosso Trionfale (metallic red) and had a black leather interior with rosso stitching. The license plate read LU-C-4. He shook his head derisively and assumed that there must be a Yankee in the area. He entered the café and saw that there was an open seat at the counter and he took it. He tried to catch the eye of the waitress, but she proved to be very adept at ignoring him.

"You from around here?" the man sitting next to him asked.

Revray was surprised. Most people don't speak to strangers in these parts. He replied, "I live in the next town over."

The stranger nodded and said, "I'm just passing through. I'm heading to either Philadelphia or Washington. I'll go wherever they find that 'miracle girl.' You see, I have a heart condition and I'm hoping she can cure me."

The waitress walked by and Revray tried to get her attention. She was a tall, thin, blond girl with a haughty air about her. Her uniform was too small and had the top five buttons undone. "No doubt an attempt to get more in the way of tips," Revray thought. "God knows her service won't get her any." Her name tag said 'Polina.' She continued past Revray, ignoring his call and raised hand.

Revray was getting impatient, and the stranger said, "You can't find good help nowadays, can you?"

Revray started to say something rude in reply, then he stopped himself. This guy had mentioned a 'miracle girl.' He wondered what that was about. "What did you say about a 'miracle girl' in Washington or Philadelphia?"

"You mean you haven't heard?" The man then recounted the story of the mysterious cures that happened in both Philadelphia and Washington. He said all of the TV networks were carrying the story. He told her about the mob at the Capitol and how the girl just disappeared. It was presumed that she was in hiding. He ended by saying he had to run and then extended his hand, "By the way, my name is Barney. It was a pleasure talking with you."

Revray took his hand and replied, "Raymond Curtis is my name. I am the pastor of the church in town. Good luck on your trip."

The man stood and exited the building. The next thing Revray became conscious of was the sharp twang of a female voice asking, "Well, you gonna order or what?" Revray focused his attention on the voice. It did not belong to the tall, blond waitress who was nowhere to be seen. It emanated from a short, pudgy woman with gray hair who was probably in her mid-50s.

Startled, Revray said, "What happened to the other waitress, the blond girl?"

The woman replied, "What are you talking about? Blond girl? There is no blond girl. I'm the only one here."

"Wait, I came in, sat down next to a stranger, and tried to order coffee and pie from that tall waitress. Her name tag said 'Polina.' She just ignored me."

The waitress snapped, "Mister, what are you talking about? I have never heard of a Polina. Besides, there was no one else here when you came in. You are the only person to come here in the last hour. You came in, sat down, and just started staring into space. I left you alone because you seemed like you were deep in thought. After a while, I said to myself, "Enough is enough. We don't rent seats by the hour. And that's where we are. You going to order or not?"

Revray's head began to hurt. He knew he was not going crazy, yet the waitress surely was not making it up. What was happening? He went ahead and ordered pie and coffee. He gulped the food down and hurried back to his little church.

Even though Revray's town was remote and poverty was rampant, everyone in the town owned at least one television. Satellite dishes were seen on most of the roofs in town. He turned on the CBN network and listened intently to the story of miracle cures in Philadelphia and DC. When Revray saw the crowds gathered in Springfield, he knew he had a rare opportunity. He called his fellow graduates in Theology from the Wadsworth ~~Penitentiary~~ Seminary and enlisted them in his plan. He then called an emergency parish meeting for that evening.

Women in the parish learned long ago that parish meetings were no place for them. Whiskey flowed like water. Fights were commonplace. Words that had never been uttered or even contemplated before were bantered about freely. Any that attended did so at their own peril. As a result, it was definitely a stag affair.

The few men in the parish who possessed average cognitive ability also feared to attend, but they did attend only out of fear of Revray. Revray was vicious and vindictive. Nothing was off-limits when it came to him achieving his goals. He would ruin someone's reputation and good name without compunction. In a small closed-in community, that could mean a man would be shunned and ostracized, and more importantly, so would his family.

Revray was in rare form this evening. He stood at the pulpit and railed against the work of the devil that was happening in Philadelphia and Washington. One of the demon's whores was curing people. She was not curing them in the name of Jesus but was using her powers to spread Satan's lies. He stoked the congregation into a virtual lynch mob. There were about 60 men at the meeting. He divided them into groups of four and assigned each group a vehicle for the 15-hour drive to Springfield. They were all to meet back at the church at 4 o'clock that morning. They were all to bring firearms (pistols and rifles were preferred) as well as personal items for a week. Those who had Confederate and Nazi flags were told to bring them. He then sent them home to pack and rest with the message that they were going to be doing God's work and would restore the white race to its proper place. Uppity blacks, Jews, Muslims, Asians, Catholics, gays, and women's libbers had better watch out. Justice was finally going to come.

At 4:00 the next morning, Revray's avengers began to assemble. On a good day, these boys were not punctual. On an early morning with hangovers, they were pathetic. Eventually, all were accounted for, and the convoy departed for the green fields of Pennsylvania. Revray had agreed to meet his fellow ministers and their flocks at Parking Lot 17 of Ridley Creek State Park, a wooded area not far from Springfield. Revray and his entourage arrived around 8:30 p.m. The lot was already crowded, but there was still plenty of parking available. Revray went immediately to confer with the other members of the clergy. It was good to reunite with his former cellmate and the other graduates from Wadsworth. Other groups continued to arrive, and by midnight all were present.

The leaders did not want to get caught in rush hour, so they delayed their departure from the state park until after 9:00 a.m. Abigail's home was in a relatively large subdivision, so the drivers were able to park away from the main streets. When all of the men were assembled with their flags waving and the signs raised, they proceeded to march down the center of the street towards Abigail's home. The total distance was about eight blocks. Residents watched the procession from the safety of their homes with fear and trepidation. Several made calls to 9-1-1, so word reached the police and the press that this rabble was descending upon the scene. The police compelled those already gathered who were hoping to be cured to move to one side of the street. They opened an area on the other side where they intended to herd the other group. Their number one goal was to keep the groups separated.

The 'church-goers' descended upon Abigail's sanctuary like a swarm of locusts. They were truly like the plague in the Bible. They proudly carried dozens of flags bearing the Stars and Bars as well as Nazi flags emblazed with swastikas. They chanted slogans such as **'God is the Only Cure,' 'Whore of Satan,'** and **'Burn the Witch.'** The signs they carried were even more hateful and virulent. This was a perfect representation of the worst in mankind.

The Springfield police were grossly outnumbered. Calls were made to the State Police and neighboring communities for reinforcements. The police set up a cordon in front of Abigail's property and motioned and gestured for the mob to assemble across the street. Not wishing to start the festivities too soon, Revray and his fellow clergy directed their followers to comply.

Battle lines were drawn. Stretched out on the sidewalk on Abigail's side of the street for at least a block were those seeking a cure. They were a peaceful group of men, women, and children.

Their list of infirmities, sicknesses, and diseases was almost infinite. They had absolutely no interest in a fight.

The neo-Nazis were lined up on the opposite sidewalk. The police were strictly enforcing the no-trespass ordinance on both groups. 'Stay on the public sidewalks, or else.'

Lined up in the center of the street were Springfield's finest. They were stretched thin, but they put up a brave front.

What neither the police nor the people on Abigail's side of the street knew was that Revray had unloaded four or five of his followers close to Abigail's side street before heading to the assembly area with the main force. These men dispersed and went to different parts of the crowd. They were very polite to the people standing next to them. They were so unobtrusive that they were almost invisible. Later, witnesses could not describe them.

After a decent amount of time to let the police get used to their presence and perhaps get comfortable with or at least less suspicious of their intentions, Revray took off his ball cap and vigorously rubbed his head. This was the signal. From his men planted in the crowd came loud calls: **"Nazi Scum," "Southern Trash," "Go Back and Screw Your Sisters,"** and **"Hitler's Stooges."** Revray's forces visibly stiffened. The police braced for real trouble. The reinforcements still had not arrived, although sirens could be heard in the distance. Then one of the plants threw a rock. The other plants followed suit. A volley of rocks rained down on Revray's boys. They knew it was coming and easily moved aside. No one was hit, but the fuse was lit. No bugler was needed to sound *Charge*. The 'church-goers' rushed across the street to the crowd of men, women, and children with hatred in their eyes. The police tried valiantly to stem the attack but were brushed aside like tumbleweeds in the wind. The invaders indiscriminately pummeled and beat the innocent. The men tried their best to protect the women and children. Mothers tried to shield their kids. From the safety of their vans, the cameras rolled, recording the carnage for posterity. The reporters voiced their horrified narrations to the world. Many had seen horrific sights during their careers, but none compared with this.

After what seemed like an eternity, but was only several minutes, the cavalry arrived. The State Police barreled down the street, assessed the situation, and immediately called for reinforcements, drew their batons and charged. Police from the neighboring communities began arriving and joined the fray. The police had little difficulty differentiating the cure seekers from the 'church-goers.' The mode of dress of the two groups made it obvious. So too did the injuries of the cure seekers and lack thereof of the other group. In short order, calm was restored.

Revray and his fellow clergy immediately started pointing fingers. They claimed that the other group instigated the trouble and even threw rocks at them as they assembled peacefully across the street to pray for the poor girl who was bewitched by Satan. The media ate it up. Revray's interview was played all over the world. During his five years in the "seminary," Revray had the opportunity, as do most cons, to become familiar with the law. He reminded all listeners that the First Amendment covered his right for assembly, free speech, and religion. The dastardly persons who threw the rocks tried to violate those protected rights and should be punished.

Ambulances started to arrive to tend to the wounded. Before the medics could get organized, something magical happened. The door to Abigail's residence opened and she came very tentatively out into the open. People stopped what they were doing and stared at her. The TV cameras rolled. For once, the talking heads of the media were silent. She was dressed in a very plain brown dress and brown casual shoes. She walked slowly down the walkway, and then she walked into the crowd that was on her side of the street. As she did so, shrieks and cries of surprise and even laughter marked her progress through the crowd. The injuries these folks sustained at the hands of the 'church-goers' were completely gone. In addition, the cures that these people so desperately wanted began to manifest themselves. Pain was gone. People could hear. Alzheimer's patients regained their memory and their lives. One man who was paralyzed by a stroke was cured. The list went on and on. Everyone on that street watched in disbelief. So too did those watching on TV. One reporter started to speak, but her producer wisely hit the mute button to spare the viewing audience from her mindless and meaningless babble.

When Abby had traveled through the crowds on both sides of the street, she turned and silently strode back towards her house. She kept her head high and looked straight ahead. Occasionally a child would catch her attention, and she would reward the child with a very sweet and gentle smile. She projected an air of dignity that was unmistakable. Later one reporter noted that as she was walking through the 'church-goers', every one of them took his ball cap off out of respect, including Revray.

BREAKOUT

When Abby returned to the safety of her father's home, she shut and locked the door and leaned her back against it with her eyes closed. She had done it. Earlier she had watched the TV news which reported that the 'miracle girl' was in Springfield. She shrugged her shoulders and watched with indifference until the screen changed to a shot of the front yard of her father's home. She bolted forward and turned up the volume. Up to this point, as far as she was concerned, her only involvement with the 'miracle girl' was as a scorekeeper and data collector. She had nothing to do with curing people. That was preposterous.

Then she watched in horror as the riot and fighting broke out, and people who were already hurting from injuries, sickness, and disease were beaten by that other group. She had lived her entire life in the shadows. It was all she ever knew, and she was comforted by her obscurity. However, she could not allow people to suffer if she had the power to stop the pain. She had no idea if she had any power or not, but, as a human being, she had to try. She told herself that if she tried and failed, it was no big deal. No harm, no foul, so to speak.

It also meant that the crowd would probably get tired and disperse.

Her heart was beating dangerously fast as she exited the house. She could feel the crowd's attention turn to her and noted that an unnatural silence permeated the scene like a dense fog. She walked resolutely down the path and into the crowd. The people parted as she approached, so her travel was unimpeded. For the most part, she stared straight ahead with no expression on the face. Occasionally she would see a child or someone who seemed to need a friend, and she would give them a small smile, a nod of her head, or a wink. She could feel something akin to a rustling going on behind her as she passed. She turned once and saw that, indeed, people were getting better before her eyes. Bruises from the riot disappeared as she watched. One person in a wheelchair stood up and started walking. Then, to everyone's astonishment, he jumped up and down several times then ran about 10 yards. People started cheering for him as he danced around with a massive grin on his face. She continued until she had passed closely by everyone on her side of the street. Then she did something that shocked the police, those on her side of the road and especially the 'church-goers.' She crossed the street and walked among the symbols of hate curing those who had been injured in the melee. As she passed by, those carrying the hateful signs and flags rolled them up so they were no longer visible. Before any of the 'church-goers' could approach her, she crossed the street and traveled the walkway to the house.

As Abby leaned against the locked door, trying to catch her breath and get her emotions under control, she felt a real sense of peace descend upon her. She felt good about herself for once in her life. She had accomplished something significant.

She turned the television on and saw that she was not the only one who recognized what she had done. The talking heads were praising her in ways she had never before imagined. The police commander on the scene reported that the leaders of the different groups had all been arrested and were in custody. He mentioned that they were all former inmates at the Wadsworth Penitentiary, a state institution where they all somehow got ordained as ministers. He quipped that he expected that they would have a reunion shortly at a Federal Prison where they would be able to get advanced degrees in Theology.

She had been in the house for about 10 minutes when she heard a commotion outside, the likes of which she had never heard before. She peered out one of the windows to witness a scene of pure bedlam.

In a quiet suburban neighborhood with limited access and egress, multiple forces were coming into a violent and cataclysmic collision. The police were trying to leave the area with their prisoners; those who were cured were streaming out trying to find their cars; and finally, a hoard of desperate people were flooding into the area seeking help.

The traffic was snarled. People were getting frustrated. People were parking in other people's driveways. All parking spots at commercial establishments were taken. The sides of the roads and streets all had cars parked. Drivers abandoned their cars in the middle of the streets and decided to hike to the house when they were not able to find parking anywhere. The situation was spiraling out of control. More and more sick and desperate people were pouring in. It was a sea of humanity at high tide.

The police were powerless. These were not bad people. They were people at the end of their ropes and trying desperately not to fall into the abyss. The use of force would be cruel. Tear gas would be counter-productive. The mission of the police soon became one of trying to protect the people from each other.

The closer to Abigail's father's home one got, the higher the levels of frustration, anger, and impatience. Fights broke out. People were hurt. Ambulances could not get near. Medics were carrying whatever kits they could, but numbers were against them.

Abigail was emotionally drained from her first venture out into the crowd. She was unable to repeat the performance. She huddled near the window, weeping like a baby, helpless and unable to move. The sound of the doorbell shocked her and terrified her. Who was able to get through the cordon? Were they going to harm her? Slowly she crawled to the door and barely cracked it. Standing there, smiling like nothing was wrong with the world, was that couple she had met in the park near her office that fine, sunny day when she decided to eat outside. Their names escaped her at first. Then she remembered the woman's name. It was Polina. She tried to remember the man's name. She thought it began with a 'B.' Then it suddenly came to her, Barney. That's it! Polina and Barney.

Polina smiled and said, "Abigail? Hi, I don't know if you remember us. We met at that little park near where we work. You were having lunch, and Barney and I were out to get a breath of air."

Abigail replied, "I remember. Your name is Polina, right?"

"That's right. Say, do you mind if we come in? We feel exposed out here."

Without a word, Abby opened the door just wide enough for them to enter, then quickly shut it. She led them into the living room and motioned for them to sit down. It was a comfortable room, but it was apparent that a professional decorator had never set foot inside of it. None of the furniture matched, but it was all very comfortable and of the highest quality. There were several tasteful paintings and prints on the walls. There was a framed picture of an awkward looking Abigail and a smiling older man. Polina sat on the couch and Barney in an easy chair. Abigail sat in a recliner. Polina asked, "Is that a picture of you and your father?"

"Yes, it is. It was taken a couple of years ago."

"It's a lovely picture. Your father is a handsome man."

"Thank you. I think he is very handsome."

Barney then spoke for the first time, "That's some scene going on outside. We saw what you did earlier. That was very brave of you. I don't think I could have done it."

Abigail blushed and said, "It was no big deal. Those people needed help, and I knew that I could do it, or at least I thought I could."

Barney replied, "I think it was a big deal. I'm sure those folks out there thought it was a big deal also. ALL of them. Did you see the way that those Nazis took their hats off to you as you walked by? I'm telling you, you made an impression today, and it was carried live across the country on TV. You are going to be a rock star."

More blushing, "Oh, I hope not. I don't like being the center of anything. The only times it has happened to me before was when kids were picking on me. I prefer to stay to the side."

Polina interjected, "Oh baby, it's too late for that now. People need you. People want to like you. The world is your oyster."

Abigail's eyes began to glisten with tears. "What do you suppose is going to happen here? I am so afraid."

In a very soft and soothing voice, Barney said, "I don't think there is anything to be afraid of. The police need to get you out of here very quickly. People will keep flooding the area as long as you are here. The police will figure out a way to move you to a secret location. From there, they will come up with some sort of interim solution to stabilize things. Wait and see. It won't be long before someone contacts you with a plan." He smiled and continued, "Polina and I just wanted to check in on you. You know, make sure you were OK. We wanted you to know you weren't alone."

He stood up and Polina followed suit. She said, "We'll be going now. We are on your side. This will pass pretty soon. Just wait and you'll see. No need to walk us to the door. We'll let ourselves out."

Abigail nodded and smiled a sweet smile of thanks. The pair moved to the door. She turned on the TV as she heard the door open and close. The picture on her screen was a live shot of the front of the house. She looked closely at it expecting to see Polina and Barney walking down the walk. They weren't there. She ran to the window and looked out. She thought she could see their backs as they disappeared into the crowd, but she couldn't be sure. It was almost like they vanished into thin air.

Abigail returned to the living room and the sound of her cell phone buzzing. The caller ID said that William Stanton MD was calling. She had not had contact with the office since her escape from Washington. She did not even know if she still had a job. That's all she needed: to be the scourge of Philadelphia and unemployed as well. With trepidation, she answered the phone. She was grateful it was Stanton who was calling. At least he had a soul, unlike Lucas. "Hello."

"Abigail, thank God! This is Dr. Stanton. How are you doing? We are all so worried about you. You did well getting out of DC when you did. Is this a good time? Can you talk?"

Abigail answered, "Hi, Dr. Stanton. Yes, now is a good time to talk. What can I do for you?"

"We all saw you on TV this morning. We are so proud of you. What you did was remarkable."

Abby stammered, "You mean you aren't mad at me? I was afraid you were calling to fire me for not coming to work."

Stanton actually laughed, "Fire you? Don't be silly; you are a member of the team. I'm calling to make sure you are OK. We know you need to lay low until this blows over. Don't worry about your job. It will be here when you are able to come back. In the meantime, we'll continue to keep you on salary. We'll review your status from time to time, but for now, no worries."

He continued, "Your attorney, Raphael Melek, called. He wants to get in touch with you. From the way he spoke, I think he intends to go to Springfield. I have no idea if they will let him through or not, but don't be surprised if he knocks on your door. I gave him your cell number. Let me give you his."

Abby wrote down the number and said, "I really don't know him. The first time I met him was at the Senate hearing. He was the one who got me out of town and back here. In fact, I owe him $1,000."

"Well, I don't think he is worried about it. He's only worried about you, as are we. Don't fret; all of this should be ending soon. In the meantime, stay in touch and keep us in the loop, OK?"

They hung up, and Abby just stared at her phone. "Could he be right? Will this all be ending soon? How did all of this start?" Questions and more questions, but unfortunately, no answers. She suddenly felt exhausted. She could not remember the last time she got any sleep. She turned off the TV and laid down on the couch. In seconds, she was fast asleep.

Her deep and relaxing slumber was rudely disturbed by the incessant ringing of her cell phone. She looked at a clock and saw she had been asleep just under an hour and a half. She felt better for having had the sleep. Another eight hours would have been perfect, but it was not to be. She looked at the caller ID but did not recognize the number. She hesitated then went ahead and answered it. "Hello?"

"Abigail, this is Raphael Melek. I represented you in Washington at the Senate hearing. I hope you remember me."

"Do I ever remember you? How could I ever forget you? You were a lifesaver. You got me out of Washington unharmed. I really owe you and much more than the $1,000 you lent me. By the way, I will pay you back."

"Oh, I'm not the least bit worried about the money. I am, however, very worried about you. You could be in danger. Just look outside your window. No one means to harm you, but some of these people are desperate. They or their loved ones are sick or dying, and you are their last and best hope. They will do anything to get near you. We need to move you."

Abigail shuddered and said, "How are you going to do that?"

Melek's reply was immediate, "In about 10 minutes, some State Police motorcycles will escort an unmarked black police car to the front of your house. A man will get out and knock on your door. Let him in. He will explain the plan to you. OK?"

Abigail whispered, "I'll be waiting. Should I pack a bag?"

"No, we don't want people to know you are leaving for good. It's best if we keep them guessing. We'll buy you anything you need once we get you out of there. Talk soon."

After hanging up, Abby grabbed her purse and loaded her phone charger and a couple of pairs of underwear into it. There was no telling what tomorrow would bring.

She went to the window and waited, watching the street and the crowd ever increasing in size. About 10 minutes later, a plain black sedan with four motorcycle cops in the front and the back pulled up with sirens blaring. The rear door of the car opened and out climbed the largest human being Abigail had ever seen. Silence fell over the crowd as Goliath ambled to the front door and rang the bell. With trepidation, Abby opened it.

The giant gave her a warm, friendly smile and said, "Hi, I'm Mike Angelo. Raphael asked me to come and get you. I hope he called you."

Abby just stared in awe at Mr. Angelo. Finally, she said, "Yes, he did. Please come in."

Mike said, "I am an old friend of Raphael's. I'm from Brooklyn if you can't tell from my accent. I run the best pizzeria in the tri-state area. I'm in Philly, helping my wife's cousin start his own place."

Abigail judged him to be of Italian descent, not that she could differentiate an Italian from an Irishman from a Jew from anyone else. She had seen Italians in movies and the stereotype seemed to fit here. He had black hair, but with Italians, that does not mean much. A lot never turn gray. Just looking at him, she judged him to be in his mid-fifties, but he could have been anywhere from forty to eighty. He looked like he could have just walked off the set of *The Godfather*, *Goodfellas*, or *The Sopranos*. He had on a black shirt with the top several buttons unbuttoned and wore a heavy gold chain around his neck. He had such an affable manner that Abigail like him at once.

He became very businesslike, "OK, listen up! Here's the plan. You and I are going to walk out of here together. You'll lock the door, and then we get in the car and drive away. Those motorcycle cops will make sure no one bothers us. Once we get to Philly, Rafi has a plan to get us out of the city without anyone's knowledge. It's pretty simple, so it should work without a hitch. Ready?"

Abigail grabbed her purse and nodded. Once outside, she locked the door, and they headed down the path. When the crowd saw her, they surged forward a bit, but the combined police forces on the ground held them in check. As they were approaching the car, Abby saw a very young mother holding a toddler. The child looked pitiful. Abby said to Mike, "Wait a minute." Then she walked over to where they were standing and smiled. The child recovered on the spot. Then Abby did the unthinkable; she went back into the crowd. Again, people parted in front of her as she approached. She probably spent 20 minutes walking through the multitude of people under the watchful gaze of Michael Angelo. No one in the crowd dared to irritate the big man. The network TV coverage recorded the cures for the world to see, and the world was watching.

After Abby had made herself available to all of the people in front of the house, she turned to the car. Michael followed. When they were safely inside, the big man said, "What was that all about? Don't you realize you could have been hurt?"

"The mother holding that young child was pathetic. Who am I to deny hope or, if possible, healing? That was the question I asked myself. When I could not come up with an acceptable answer, I knew I had to at least try. Who am I? I'm nothing. I have never been anything and probably never will be anything. So I ask again, 'Who am I to deny hope to anyone?' Listen, I don't understand what is going on or why. Until I can figure things out, I'm going to try to do the best that I can knowing that I am flying blind."

Michael reached out and gently patted her arm to reassure her. "Listen. You keep telling yourself you are nothing. I hope you realize that you are lying to yourself. You are an incredibly strong young woman who is just beginning to flower into her potential. Trust me. I know something about this subject. I've been around a long time and have seen the good, the bad, and the ugly. And lady, you are the best of the best."

Abigail looked into his eyes and gave a shy smile. "OK, if you say so."

As the small motorcade proceeded to downtown Philadelphia, Mike explained the plan. There was a covered parking garage on North 10th Street, about four blocks from police headquarters. The PPD had already secured the entrances to the building. No one could enter. On the third level, there were three identical unmarked black police cars. There were also three identical white Genesis G90 sedans. Once their vehicle arrived on the third level and unloaded the two of them, another couple would take their place in the back seat. All four of the black cars would then emerge from the garage together and then scatter to the four directions. They would drive for at least four hours and then head back. Raphael was already in one of the white cars. Mike and Abby would join him. About 45 minutes after the police cars departed the garage, the three white Genesis sedans would depart and scatter. Their car would be under constant surveillance. If no one was following them, they would proceed to a large gated estate directly across the Hudson River from West Point near the tiny village of Garrison, NY.

This estate belonged to a Jimmy Halvorson, a very close friend of one of Raphael's other clients. A while back, Jimmy's company had a design flaw on an electronic component for a revolutionary new technology. Jimmy had bet the bank on this new technology and was facing ruin if it did not work. Long story short, this client, an engineer by trade, came to Jimmy's manufacturing facility in Portsmouth, NH, and solved the design glitch in four days. All of Jimmy's initial orders were filled on time, and he soon became seriously back-ordered. He had to rapidly expand the size of his company, which he did, and now its stock had more than quadrupled in value. Out of pure gratitude, Jimmy was more than willing to lend his estate to Raphael and his friends when he was asked to do so by the client.

Unbeknownst to Raphael, Michael, or Abby, another major player had an interest in this situation. Raphael had to involve the Philadelphia Police Department for help in evacuating Abigail from Pennsylvania safely and in secret. The Police Commissioner had a fraternity brother who happened to be the current resident of 1600 Pennsylvania Avenue, Washington DC. President Lucius Diamond was a political animal. He had no idea what to make of 'miracle girl', but he was damned sure he would have first dibs on any favorable political fallout and the right of first denial on any unfavorable fallout. When the Philly PC called him on his private number, the president's first reaction was to ensure the safety of the girl. He was certain she would or could be of value to him in the future, but only if she were alive.

The president summoned the Director of National Intelligence, the heads of the FBI and Homeland Security, the Secretary of Defense, and the Director of the CIA. He explained that the 'miracle girl' would be hiding at a secluded estate across the river from West Point near Dicks Castle. He wanted the estate watched unobtrusively. He told those assembled to put their heads together and get back to him with a plan. He emphasized again that he wanted the surveillance to be invisible. He went on to say that if a threat were discovered, contingency plans needed to be in place to eliminate it.

Once the black unmarked police car arrived at the third floor of the parking garage in Philadelphia, Abigail and Michael quickly got out and entered a white Genesis G90, which was parked nearby with its back doors open. Abigail noticed a man and a woman emerge from another vehicle and enter the unmarked police car, which along with the other three black cars, headed down the ramp to the exit.

Abigail immediately saw Raphael sitting in the front passenger seat. He smiled at her and shook her hand, "I'm so glad to see you again. I see you survived Springfield. I watched it on TV. You, lady, are impressive. It took guts to walk into that crowd. You were magnificent."

Abigail noticed a young woman a few years older than she sitting in the driver's seat. Raphael said, "Abigail Williams meet Angelina Gabriella. Angelina works for the gentleman who is loaning us the house in New York you will be staying at until things settle down."

Raphael explained that Angelina was in charge of opening up foreign markets for Mr. Halvorson's company. He went on to describe her background. She was fluent in five languages and conversant in several more. She was originally from Spain, where her father was in the diplomatic corps. She traveled all over the world with her family before taking a degree in International Economics at the Sorbonne in Paris. She followed this with a master's in marketing degree from the London School of Economics. Abby noted that she appeared to be in her mid-thirties. She was stunning with dark hair and dark eyes, about 5' 5" and was just slightly overweight.

Angelina chimed in, "I watched with Rafi on TV. I agree, you were impressive."

The signal was finally given for the Genesis sedans to depart the garage. Angelina eased the big car down the ramp and into downtown Philadelphia traffic and headed to New Jersey and I-95. The 3-hour trip was uneventful with Abby, Angelina, and Rafi engaged in casual conversation. Mike took a nap and his snoring made the car shudder. Rafi joked that they should all be wearing noise-canceling earphones. They finally crossed over the Hudson River on the Bear Mountain Bridge. The view along the river was fabulous. Shortly thereafter, they pulled up to a very large house surrounded by a high fence with a gate that was controlled by a keypad. Angelina punched in a code, and the gate swung open.

The house itself was a two-story Tudor with two wings and a separate three-car garage. Inside the house, the furnishings looked like an interior designer for *Town and Country* had carte blanch with a credit card. Everything was just so. Abby was afraid to touch anything for fear of breaking it. Angelina noticed this and said, "Abigail, just relax. Jimmy believes this house is meant to be lived in. If something spills or breaks, so what? It can be cleaned or replaced. I know him. He would want you to be yourself and enjoy the place." She paused and continued, "Why don't I show you around the place? The view is to die for."

As Angelina took her around the property, Abigail was

astounded more and more by the beauty of the setting. Looking north, the Hudson rolled passed the grounds of the United States Military Academy. The lush greens and stately granite buildings were spectacular. Towering over all of this work of nature stood the majestic heights of Storm King Mountain. Abby felt she would never tire of this view.

Angelina brought her back to reality. The mansion had a married couple employed as a combination of cook, housekeeper, gardener, and handyman. They would do the grocery shopping and take care of the place. Angelina reminded Abby that she had no clothes. Since no one felt comfortable with her going shopping, Angelina proposed that she would go to the Nanuet Mall and buy her some clothes, makeup, and toilet items. Angelina told her she had a good eye for sizes and was confident that she would be able to get her acceptable clothing. Abigail said she had no money with her since she left her wallet at the house in the rush to leave Springfield. Angelina smiled and showed her a credit card. "As I told you earlier, Jimmy Halvorson is very grateful. He insists that I take good care of you.

Michael came into the room and said to Angelina, "Ready to go?" Then to Abigail, he said, "I'm going with her to make sure she returns. There is something about malls that makes women lose all sense of time."

Angelina stuck her tongue out at him and said, "You're no fun. OK, let's go."

They left the room just as Raphael came in. He smiled at Abby and sat down opposite her in a comfortable chair. He was not a prepossessing person. He had a humble demeanor that belied his world-class intellect. Abigail was comfortable around him and trusted him unconditionally. "We need to talk about your future. You obviously cannot stay here forever. I'm sure you wouldn't want to." He looked at her and received a slight nod of agreement in return. "You have been given a miraculous power. I'd call it a gift, but in time you might call it a curse. No one knows how you received this power or how long it will last." Again, he received a nod. "You have heard the phrase 'strike while the iron is hot'?" Another nod. "What I would propose in general terms is to make an immediate impact; go out and show the world Abigail Williams is here. Get out of her way. She is going to make an impact." As he said this his voice filled with emotion much like a football coach's halftime pep talk. She looked at him expectantly.

"There are children's hospitals in every big city. There are Veteran's hospitals everywhere. There is that world-famous hospital in Memphis that specializes in children's cancer cases. What I am proposing is somehow getting funding and you visiting as many of these places as you can in a short period of time. Once we get the full measure of what it is you can do, we can come up with a long-term plan. How does that sound?"

In a very soft, meek voice, Abigail replied, "I guess it sounds OK." She paused and then continued, "Look, Mr. Melek, I am so afraid. I feel like the world is crashing down on me. I need to do something."

"I've got an idea. Let's contact the doctors who employ you. Let's see if they can come here and help with a plan. What do you think?"

"It's worth a try," Abigail said in a soft voice.

She made the call on her cell phone. She called Marguerite Camp's cell phone. When Marguerite answered, Abby began to cry. Marguerite calmed her down and inquired about how she was doing. After some small talk, Abby asked if Marguerite and at least one of the doctors could come to New York and discuss the future. Abby said she preferred Dr. Stanton or Barr, and Marguerite knowingly concurred with the choice. She said she would discuss it with the doctors and get back to her before the end of the day.

At about 5 o'clock, Abigail's phone rang. It was Marguerite with

Drs. Stanton, Barr, and Lucas on a speaker. Pleasantries were exchanged, and then Raphael introduced himself. Lucas remarked that he remembered him from the Senate hearing. Raphael explained what they wanted to try and asked if one or more of them was available to come to New York to flesh out the plan. Lucas immediately said he was too busy to leave the practice. Stanton and Barr agreed to come tomorrow, as did Marguerite. They said they would arrive tomorrow before noon.

A couple of hours later, Angelina and Michael returned. Angelina carried a small bag while Mike was loaded down like a pack mule. She was all smiles and excitement. She had conquered the mall. Mike, on the other hand, was not smiling. His feet were tired. He was tired of nodding and saying, "It looks good to me," or "I'm sure she will like it." He was, in other words, completely defeated by the mall.

Angelina grabbed Abigail and together they took all of the bags and packages and ran up the stairs to Abigail's room. They were gone for about an hour, then the fashion show began. Abigail came down in a variety of outfits including cutoff jean shorts, jeans with a hole in them, nice slacks, skirts, dresses for work, dresses for going out on the town, and finally a business suit. Of course, shirts, blouses, and shoes were included. The funniest part of the show was when Abby tried to walk down the stairs in a pair of high heels. Angelina explained to the men that she had never worn heels before and needed to practice. All in all, spirits were high and everyone had fun.

HOSPITALS

The next morning the four of them awoke to the smell of bacon frying and cinnamon rolls baking. The cook was preparing a full breakfast. Like zombies sleepwalking, the four of them followed their noses into the breakfast nook, grabbed coffee and juice, and sat down. When breakfast was served, they all dug into it. The other three were careful to stay out of Mike's feeding zone. People were known to lose one or more of their fingers if they got too close.

After breakfast, the four of them climbed the stairs for showers and to dress. When they returned downstairs, there was fresh coffee waiting. They all thought that life was pretty good. At 11 o'clock the speaker at the front gate was activated. The caller identified himself as Dr. William Stanton and two others. He said they were expected. The male staffer pressed the button to open the gate. A minute or two later, the doorbell rang.

After introductions were made, everyone came into the main living room and made themselves comfortable. Raphael outlined his rough plan. Everyone understood that if word got out that Abigail was going to be at a specific hospital, the place would be besieged. He went on to explain that neither he nor Abigail were in positions to differentiate who was and who wasn't deserving of being cured. Right now, they wanted to choose a specific locale with a high number of patients and see what she could do. The two doctors and Marguerite nodded their understanding.

Raphael continued by stating these hospitals were enormous. The longer Abigail spent in one, the greater the chance that she would be discovered. The trick is to get her secretly into the hospital, devise a way for her to cover as much ground as fast as she possibly could, come in contact with all if not most of the patients, and finally, extricate her secretly from the building before being discovered. Dr. Stanton said that they were most familiar with Children's Hospital of Philadelphia. They knew the layout and the people who operated it. He recommended that Children's be used as the test site. All agreed with the choice.

For the next several hours, the seven of them put together a plan of action. Late in the afternoon, Dr. Barr and Marguerite departed to return to Philadelphia. Stanton stayed at the house to act as liaison. Before he left, Dr. Barr called the Chief of Medicine of the hospital and asked him to set up a highly confidential meeting tomorrow morning with himself and all of the various department heads as well as the head of security and the Public Information Officer.

Two days later, Abigail and Dr. Stanton were driven to Stewart International Airport in Newburgh, NY. Waiting for them was a medivac helicopter. Once aboard, Abigail climbed into orange coveralls with the medivac company's logo on them. She also donned an orange flight helmet, which almost completely obscured her face. The helicopter departed and less than an hour later landed on the roof of Children's Hospital. The onboard medic motioned for Abigail and Dr. Stanton to depart and stay near him. He pulled a gurney with a plastic dummy strapped to it from the chopper and, while ducking under the whirling blades, hurried to the building's roof entrance, followed by Abigail and Stanton. Once inside, the Chief of Medicine and several of his staff greeted them. He introduced a very young doctor who he said would be Abigail's guide in the hospital. He, Dr. Stanton, and the others would proceed to his office and monitor their progress on the hospital's closed-circuit TV system.

Chad, the young doctor turned tour guide produced two Segway transporters. Abigail had never ridden one before, but as Chad promised, it was very easy to use. Chad put on a headset placing him in radio contact with each of the nurse's stations, and the two of them headed to the elevators. They got off of the elevator on the ground floor. To Abigail's surprise, there was a crowd of people close to the lobby elevators. Chad explained that the nurses were directed to move as many patients as possible and practical to the elevators. That way, Abigail would be able to quickly see patients without a lot of running around. The hospital had announced an emergency drill an hour before she arrived on the helicopter requiring all patients to return to their rooms and stay there until further notice. No details were given about the drill, but few questions were asked. It was, after all, just a drill. Once on the ground floor, they made their way through the crowd and then to the ER area. It took about 15 minutes on the Segways to cover the floor. This process was repeated on every floor as they made their way up to the roof: a crowd by the elevators, then a sprint to the rooms where the patients were too ill to move. The floor nurses crossed off each room-bound patient as they were visited by Abby.

Finally, a little more than five hours after landing on the roof, they were back at the landing pad. Abigail was physically and mentally exhausted, as was Chad. Dr. Stanton was there beaming. The Chief of Medicine had a dazed look on his face. He put both of his hands on Abigail's shoulders and kept saying, "Thank you, Thank

You, Thank you." As she was preparing to put on her helmet, Chad went up to her and gave her the warmest hug she had ever received. He had tears streaming down his face as he whispered, "I'll never forget this." He released her and the medic escorted her back to the chopper. An hour later, she was back in the car at Stewart Field.

Late that evening, Dr. Stanton called. He was still at the hospital. He was beside himself with joy. The hospital estimated that in the five hours she was on the premises, she had come in contact with over 95% of the hospitals' patients. Of those patients, over 90% experienced total and verifiable cures. The total inpatient cures approached 500. Outpatient cures were over and above these. Stanton said that the staff was working overtime on patients' releases. He figured the place would be empty in a day or so.

It was inevitable that the media would pick up the story. Stanton said that the calls to his practice were nonstop. The fact that Barr pretended ignorance and Lucas did not have details about what occurred just fueled the fire. He went on to say that the receptionist was so flustered that she threatened to quit.

Angelina and Michael were leaving the next morning. She to go to Portsmouth and Mike back to Philadelphia to continue helping his wife's cousin with his new pizzeria. They would be leaving early, so they said their goodbyes. They each hugged Abigail, and Angelina joked that they needed to go shopping together when all of this drama was behind them. She suggested that Paris might be nice. She went on to suggest that big Mike could accompany them on the trip. Both women had a good laugh. Michael just scowled.

The next morning all of the news shows headlined the 'Miracle at Children's Hospital.' The hospital's PIO issued a written statement saying that a mass healing event occurred at the hospital yesterday. The hospital was not prepared to and would not go into details about the event. It stated that there were over 500 total cures. It concluded by asking everyone to be grateful for what happened and not to fuel strong public reaction by speculating and spreading wild guesses.

While the official hospital's position was silence, no one expected that to hold, and it did not. Patients and staff became media darlings, granting interviews and generally embellishing their roles in the event. The media ate it up. Sensationalized stories flooded the airwaves. Philadelphia had already made headlines as the city of cures. This only added to the fanfare.

Safe in the mansion across the Hudson from West Point, Abigail sat with Raphael watching the TV coverage. "Raphael, you should have seen the faces on those kids when the pain went away; when they could walk; when they could see; when they could breathe. It was like nothing I could ever have imagined. I want to do it again."

"I know Abigail, but you have to be careful. Look what happened in Springfield and Philadelphia. If the crowds can't be controlled, then people will get hurt, and you may do more harm than good. Let's try a couple more hospitals and see what we can come up with. OK?"

Abigail called Dr. Stanton on his cell. He picked up immediately. He said he was with a patient and would call her back as soon as he was finished. Half an hour later, her phone rang. Abigail told him she wanted to go to another hospital and do it again. She gushed how happy it made her feel. Stanton fully realized the import of the situation and wanted to help. "Abigail, what do you think of this? There are two children's hospitals in St. Louis. They are only about three miles apart, and both are world-class. What would you think of hitting one, then flying to the second, and then exiting the city? If I can set it up, it will have a heck of an impact. Besides, no one knows you in St. Louis. Speed and secrecy are the keys. Let me get back to you."

Early the following morning, Stanton called back. The directors of both hospitals were thrilled at the opportunity. They developed a plan where Abigail would fly to St. Louis Downton Airport and then drive to Cardinal Glennon Children's Hospital in an ambulance. She would be met in the ER by a team similar to the Philadelphia team. A doctor would guide her throughout the hospital, starting in the ER and work their way up to the helipad on the roof. They would both be riding Segways, and those patients capable of congregating would cluster together on each floor. Those who were not able would receive individual visits in their rooms. Once on the roof, they would fly to St. Louis Children's Hospital, where the same protocol would be followed, except this would be top to bottom. Once they were finished, a car with police escort would be waiting at the ER's exit to take her to MidAmerica Airport, where a private jet would carry her back to Stewart Field. Both hospitals would be on lockdown starting an hour before her scheduled arrival time.

A week later, the trip to St. Louis took place. It went as smooth as glass. Everything Dr. Stanton promised from the chartered airplane to the ambulance to the police escort worked perfectly. When she returned to New York, Abigail was buoyed up. Her spirits were soaring. The looks on the children's and their families' faces were unforgettable. She couldn't wait for the next hospital visit.

The press found out about the visit after Abigail was safely back in New York. They excitedly reported the details of the visit, as well as interviews with those present in the hospitals. The interviews with parents of children who had little or no hope for survival before the visit were especially moving. The gratitude they expressed was genuine and deep.

Three days later, Stanton was on the phone with a proposal for a third trip. This one was to Ohio. There are several excellent children's hospitals in Ohio, and he chose one headed by a classmate from medical school. Stanton said that the basics of the visit would be the same as the visit to Children's Hospital of Philadelphia. A medivac helicopter would meet her at the airport and transport her to the helipad on the roof. The ETA was 9 o'clock. She and her escort would ride the elevator to the ground floor and work their way back to the roof where the helicopter would carry her back to the airport.

The day before the visit, Dr. Stanton's classmate did exactly what the other hospital heads did. She called in all of the department heads, briefed them on what would transpire the following day. She emphasized the need for confidentiality as everyone could well imagine what would happen if the public became aware of the 'miracle girl's' visit. After her meeting ended, the department heads, in turn, met with their direct reports and announced the plan for each of the floors and departments. Each department head emphasized the need for confidentiality.

As soon as the Oncology Department's meeting was over, one of the nurses in attendance went into an empty patient room and called her sister. She explained she would be in serious trouble if anyone discovered she made this call, but.......

Her sister had a child with a severe speech impediment. The poor little girl was bullied unmercifully at school. The sister listened intently. She said she would arrive at the hospital at 8 a.m., well before it went on lockdown. She promised that she would not utter a word about this to a soul. No sooner had this call ended, than the sister called a friend who had a bad stomach ulcer. After that call ended, the sister called another friend who was almost crippled by arthritis. The sister made several more calls, as did each of the friends. Before long, word of the upcoming visit had spread to four counties.

At 7:30 a.m. the next day, people began to casually arrive at the hospital. Soon, all of the ground floor waiting rooms were full and folks started going to waiting rooms on the second and third floors. By 8 a.m., there was a crowd outside of the hospital trying to enter the building. Police were summoned to try to bring order, but the people outside the hospital were determined and rushed the doors. A riot broke out. Several of the local TV stations had heard rumors about the visit and had camera crews on the scene. The police were totally engulfed and carried away by a human tsunami. More police arrived. The hospital tried closing and locking all of the ground floor doors even though this was a serious violation of the fire codes. The crowd ripped the doors down, broke out the glass picture windows, and entered the building en masse. Hospital security quickly assessed the situation and their first move was to disable all of the elevators. The hospital's first floor was a boiling sea of humanity that could not accommodate another person. The crowd spilled into the stairwells and started moving to the upper floors. Back on the ground level, the pushing and shoving bared already frayed emotions. Punches were thrown and fights broke out. It was pure chaos. Casualties began to mount inside and outside of the hospital. Ambulances and paramedics from neighboring hospitals arrived to offer help wherever possible.

On board the Learjet 75, Abigail snuggled into the plush seat and sipped a cup of hot chocolate oblivious of the maelstrom into which she was flying. The cabin attendant came back to her and told her that they were returning to Stewart Field. She said there was some sort of disturbance near the hospital, and it was not safe for Abigail to go there. The cabin attendant saw the curious look and disappointment on Abby's face. She told her that Dr. Stanton is the one who called to have the flight diverted. She told Abigail that they could get Stanton on the phone if she wished to speak directly to him. A few minutes later, a stunned Ms. Williams hung up the phone. Dr. Stanton did not go into the gory details about the events at the hospital. He merely said that word had evidently gotten out that she was coming there for a healing event and a large crowd had gathered inside and outside of the hospital. All of the local authorities, as well as the management of the hospital, agreed that it was in everyone's best interest to cancel the visit.

When Abigail returned to the mansion across from West Point, she was met by a shaken Raphael Melek. He met her at the front door and gave her a big hug. He escorted her into the den where a television vividly displayed images of the carnage. A reporter described the scene as something right out of Bagdad. Abigail sat down and watched with incredulity. She kept repeating, "What have I done?"

Raphael was wise enough to know that she was so upset that nothing he could say would make the situation better. He just sat there and held her hand as she watched the set.

Thanks in large part to the 24-hour news cycle and the short attention span of the American public, the story was short-lived. The TV stations returned to their regularly scheduled programming, allowing Abigail and Raphael time to reflect on the debacle in Ohio. The only possible explanation was that somehow word of her visit leaked and spread like wildfire. A short while later, Dr. Stanton called. His med school classmate confirmed that there was a leak at her hospital. Her staff traced the leak to a nurse in the Oncology Department. The media was demanding information and Stanton's classmate had to face them. Stanton said that they needed to re-assess the hospital visits in light of Ohio. He suggested that Abigail remain in seclusion for a while, and asked Raphael to stop by Philadelphia on his way back to Washington. A face-to-face meeting would be more productive than trying to do business over the phone. Raphael agreed and told Stanton that he would leave New York tomorrow morning and drive to the doctor's office in Philadelphia.

LIMITS

Abigail stood at the door and watched Melek drive away in a rental car. He told her he was unsure when he would be returning since he had his practice in Washington to take care of. She was beginning to feel lonely, but she knew she always had the couple who took care of the place for company if she desired it. She went into the kitchen and poured herself a cup of coffee. She picked up the *New York Times* and saw that the Ohio incident, while still on the first page, was located beneath the fold. It was slowly dying out. She skimmed the paper for other news then decided to take a walk around the property. It was such a lovely day that it would be a shame to spend it indoors. Besides, the chances that anyone would see her or recognize her were non-existent.

There was a wooden bench, as well as a swing, located near a copse of trees offering an unimpeded view of the river, the Military Academy and its grounds, and all of the points north. She sat on the swing and lost herself in thought. She had no idea where the magical power came from or even when it first manifested itself. She led such a sheltered life in Philadelphia that she probably came in contact with less than 50 people in a week. How many people were cured by coming into contact with her early on was an unknown. Now she was a celebrity. Riots broke out whenever she was recognized. She never craved the limelight, and now that she had it thrust upon her, she hated it.

She sat there deep in thought for a couple of hours. Whenever a boat sailed by, she tried to imagine where it was heading and what the people on board were like. She started to get hungry and headed back to the house for lunch. Thus far, the cook had had a very nice lunch prepared every day. Just as she reached the front door, she heard a car honking its horn. She turned and saw a metallic red Maserati Gran Turismo Sport at the gate. She had never seen one before and thought it was absolutely gorgeous. Standing next to it was the couple she had last seen in Springfield, Polina and Barney. They were both smiling and waving. She waved back and asked the gardener to open the gate for them. A few minutes later, they were inside sitting on comfortable chairs in the living room. The cook asked them if they cared for lunch and both declined with thanks. They said they were in the area and thought it might be nice to visit Abigail again. Barney noted that every previous encounter with Abigail had provided excitement, so who knew what this visit would bring? Everyone laughed.

Barney mentioned that they had been following the stories of the hospital visits with great interest. He thought it was truly remarkable and magnanimous of Abigail to put herself in potential danger for the sole benefit of strangers who were hurting.

Polina concurred. "Remember what she did in Pennsylvania, Barney? She walked into the riot, not once but twice. Talk about brave and unselfish."

Abbey smiled and shrugged her shoulders. "It was no big deal. I loved doing it, particularly the hospitals. I wouldn't trade the looks on those kids' and their parents' faces for a million dollars." At this, Barney and

Polina exchanged pointed glances. Abigail continued, "I feel horrible about Ohio. Not just because of all the people who were injured, but also because I probably won't be allowed to do any more hospital visits. I don't see any way they can secure the hospitals. Of course, they are a lot smarter than I." She did not specify who 'they' were.

Polina said, "What if we could figure out a way to make you available to huge crowds in an orderly and controlled setting? Is that something you might be willing to consider?"

"I loved helping people. It gave me a feeling of satisfaction and accomplishment that I have never felt before. I would hate not to be able to continue."

Barney looked at Polina and said, "I think I know where you are heading with this. It's a great idea. Are you thinking Douglas Keenan?"

"You got it." Polina turned her attention to Abigail. "Doug Keenan is a big-time producer and promoter. He can put together something like this from soup to nuts. I'll bet that he would do it for free or at a reduced rate since this is such a good cause."

"Excuse me. Something like what?"

Polina smiled sheepishly, "Oh, sorry. I got carried away. If Doug can get a stadium or other big facility, he can control the crowds and ensure your security and safety. Think about a football game or baseball game. Everyone has to pass through security checkpoints before they can enter the stadium."

"Excuse me," Abigail said again. "I have never been to a baseball or football game. I'm not sure I have ever watched a complete game on TV."

This elicited a laugh from both of her visitors. Barney spoke up, "Do you have any idea when your friends will return?"

"No, Rafi didn't know for sure. The other two never said if they would be back or not. Why?"

"Oh, no reason in particular. I was just curious."

Polina stood up and said that they needed to run. She promised that they would contact Douglas Keenan and get back to her if he thought that they could put a plan together. Abigail walked with them to the car. She told Barney how beautiful it was. He beamed with pride and asked her if she would like to sit in it. She jumped at the chance. She sat behind the wheel, grinning like a little kid. When she got out, she noticed the license plate, LU-C-4 . "I've never seen that on a license plate before," she remarked.

Barney laughed, "Oh, it's just a joke. Driving this car makes me want to go like the devil." With that, he and Polina got into the car and drove away. Today he felt like driving, so he did not go into transport mode.

Two hours later, Barney had the Maserati parked in a service area on the New Jersey Turnpike, and he was on his cell phone with Douglas Keenan. Keenan had followed the 'miracle girl' story and was amazed when Barney told him that he just left her. Barney described Abigail as incredibly shy, incredibly naïve, and incredibly sweet. He told Keenen that she wanted to try to find a different, safer forum to help people. He and Polina were kicking around the idea of holding a healing event in a stadium of some kind, and what did Doug think of that?

Doug at first didn't have a reply to that. It had never occurred to him. The more he thought about it, the more he liked it. He would have to find a stadium, book it, hire security personnel, coordinate with and get permits from the city, come up with a publicity campaign, and the list kept growing longer. After a few moments of silence, he told Barney that the idea had possibilities. "Would it be possible to meet with the girl? By the way, what is her name?"

A short while later, the call ended. Doug just sat at his desk gazing, at his cell phone. From the chair across the desk, Tommy Sullivan asked, "What's up? Everything OK?"

Doug played college football for Villanova. He was a large man whose features have the stamp of Ireland imprinted on them. He looked like one of the male models in print ads for Ireland. His personality was as big as the rest of him. He was totally lacking in guile. Without any dissenting votes, he was universally considered to be a nice guy.

The one word to describe Tommy Sullivan was elegant. His features, his manners, his dress, everything about him screamed elegance. He stood about six-foot tall with a normal build. He looked like a tennis or racquetball player, which he was. He was also a scratch golfer. Tommy was an agent. He represented athletes, movie stars, and many of the movers and shakers in the world. He was astoundingly successful. He had never been married but had a whole stable of beautiful women at his beck and call.

Doug briefly recounted the conversation with Barney for Tommy. "Evidently, this girl, Abigail Williams, is as fresh as newly fallen snow. She is totally innocent. She wants to help people, to cure them. We've both seen what happens just about every time she tries. People get desperate and try to bull their way in to get cured. Tommy, what do you think of trying to help her? We both know how the game is played. Hell, you perfected it. I'll work on getting a secure venue for her if you will work on protecting her from sharks, her adoring public, and herself. What do you say?"

Tommy shrugged his shoulders, "I won't say 'yes' and I won't say 'no.' I'll be happy to speak with her and size her up. I have never been accused of being a Boy Scout, but I have also never been accused of being a sleaze-ball. If you can set up a meeting, I'll go there with you. Fair enough?"

Doug smiled to himself. Tommy was hooked. Later that day, Doug made arrangements for the two of them to visit Abigail early the next afternoon.

Doug worked in Manhattan and lived in New Rochelle. Tommy's office was also in Manhattan, but he lived in White Plains. Doug called Tommy and told him that he would swing by and pick him up the following day around 11 o'clock. They'd grab a bite to eat and then drive up along the east bank of the Hudson to the mansion where Ms. Williams was staying. Tommy readily agreed. He liked Doug's company, and he could work from home for a few hours in the morning. The drive up the Hudson was scenic and beautiful. All in all, it sounded like a very pleasant day.

The weather the following day was something the Chamber of Commerce could only dream about. Doug had a late model Corvette that he loved to drive. He picked Tommy up on schedule with the convertible's top down, and the two friends enjoyed the freedom that the drive presented to them. All too soon, they turned into the driveway of the mansion and rang the bell. After identifying themselves to the man on the intercom, the gate swung open, and they entered the property. Both men were used to opulent residences. Usually, they were garish and overstated, screaming nouveau riche. This home was the antithesis of that. It was elegant and understated. The architect used the natural beauty of the surroundings to embellish and embrace the mansion as a natural component. This place was breathtaking for all of the right reasons.

A man was waiting for them at the open door. They introduced themselves and he led them into a very comfortable living room where they found a young lady sitting on a sofa. The first thing about this girl that they both noticed was how unremarkable she was. She was dressed in a gray sweater and slacks. She wore no jewelry, not even earrings. She did not rise when they came into the room but greeted them with a shy smile. "I'm Abigail Williams. Please have a seat and make yourselves comfortable. Would you like some coffee or something else to drink?"

"Nothing for me, thanks," said Keenan.

"I'm fine, thank you," replied Sullivan. "Now, what can we do for you?"

For the next hour or so, Abigail recounted what the past few weeks were like. Her face positively shone when she described the feeling she got curing people. She described their reactions, their shock, their joy, and in most cases, their gratitude. Parents with sick children provided the most satisfaction. She also described the riots she encountered. She said she wasn't frightened in Springfield. These were people who were hurting and she could help. Instead of hysterical crowd violence, sanity and reason took over. The people were respectful of her and showed it. The two incidents in the hospitals were different. The one in Philadelphia was caused, in her opinion, by surprise. People were suddenly cured and it spooked the crowd. The hospital in Ohio was a display of desperation. Desperate people were trying to push their way into the building when the access was closed.

The two men just sat there in silence, occasionally exchanging glances. God knows she didn't look like it, but this girl was special. In the course of their careers, both men had encountered the vain, the selfish, and the greedy many times. Sometimes it seemed to them that this was more often than not the case. This girl was a breath of fresh air. Finally, Keenan said, "I might be able to help. I know some people who own or control some of the larger sporting venues in Philadelphia. I might be able to stage an event at one of them. What about this power you have? How close do you need to be to the people for them to be cured? What I'm getting at is if we filled a football stadium with people, and you walked out into the middle of it, would the folks in the upper levels get cured? If not, then we need to come up with a different approach."

"I have no idea," replied Abigail. As far as I know, I have been relatively close to the people I've helped. Is there some way to test it out?"

Tommy interjected, "I have an idea. West Point is right across the river. I'll bet if we could get an appointment with the Superintendent, he just may let us use the football stadium there as a test. I believe it is called Michie Stadium. It can hold 38,000 people, so it is nowhere close to the 69,000 that Lincoln Financial Field can hold, but it's a good place to start testing boundaries."

Doug said, "Are you suggesting that we just waltz in and ask the guy who runs West Point if we can bring in nearly 40,000 people as a test?"

"No, of course not. What I'm suggesting is getting a hundred or so people with problems and spreading them out throughout the stadium. We bring Abigail in and see what her range is. It will be very low-key, and he may even let us do it for free. You know, as a public service."

"You know, Tommy, sometimes you are smarter than you look." Doug paused and then added, "You would have to be. No one could be that dumb." All three of them had a good laugh at that.

Tommy had a former client, an actor who ran for Congress and now sits on the House Armed Services Committee. Tommy called him, outlined his request for an appointment and the reason for it, and of the absolute need for secrecy. The Congressman said he would make a phone call or two and get back to him as soon as possible.

It was getting late in the day, and Sullivan and Keenan took their leave of Abigail for the drive back to White Plains and New Rochelle. They promised they would contact her as soon as they found anything out.

Three days later, Sullivan called Keenan at his office. He just heard from the Congressman. The Superintendent agreed to a meeting. Tommy called the number the Congressman gave him and talked to the general's secretary. The general had some free time the following morning if that would work. Sullivan booked the appointment.

The meeting the next day was a success. The general readily agreed to let them bring some people and spread them throughout the stadium. He admitted he had an ulterior motive. The starting quarterback on the Army football team had injured his ACL during the Army-Navy Game at the end of last season, and it had not healed as well as everyone hoped. Other athletes from hockey, lacrosse, and basketball could use some help, as well. The general wanted them included in the test. The general also wanted to witness the event in person. He mentioned that the Commandant of Cadets and the Dean and possibly several other senior officers would probably also like to watch. Sullivan and Keenan readily agreed. West Point has a large hospital located on its grounds. Fortunately, the clientele that it serves are generally healthy, but not always. They invited the general to include any and all from the West Point community who might be able to benefit from Abigail's power the opportunity to do so.

They left the general's office in high spirits and drove across the Hudson via the Bear Mountain Bridge to Abigail's mansion. They told her what they had accomplished. Now all they needed to do was figure out where the remaining patients would come from. Abigail suggested that they contact Dr. Stanton.

When Stanton heard the news, he was elated. He and his fellow doctors in Philadelphia were devastated by the Ohio debacle. This sounded so promising. He immediately offered to call the head of Memorial Sloan Kettering Cancer Center in Manhattan to see if he would be willing to send three or four busloads of patients to West Point for the trial.

Less than 30 minutes later, Stanton called back. The head of the cancer center was thrilled with the opportunity. He said he would provide four busloads of very sick patients. Stanton said that he discussed the need for absolute confidentiality with the doctor in New York. He was very familiar with the incident in Ohio and promised there would not be a repeat.

The coordination of the event was smoother than anyone could have hoped. The Superintendent assigned his aide-de-camp as his point of contact. The director of the cancer center appointed his chief-of-staff as his point man. Doug Keenan was the producer.

A little over a week from when they had the meeting at West Point with the Superintendent, a small convoy of four buses and four ambulances passed through Thayer Gate and climbed the hill to Michie Stadium. The Commandant assigned a full cadet company to assist the patients from Memorial Sloan Kettering, as well as the West Point Hospital. Before the buses arrived, Keenan met with the cadet company commander and selected the spots in the stadium where he wanted the patients placed. As the patients arrived, cadets escorted those who were ambulatory to their locations and pushed those confined to wheel-chairs to their places. The ambulances carried critically sick patients who were going to meet with Abigail right on the field.

Once everyone was in position, Abigail, accompanied by Tommy and Dr. Stanton, entered through the players' tunnel. She looked around in awe, as she had never been in such a place as this. She walked directly to the center of the field, where the critical patients were massed. Walking close by each one, she gave a word of encouragement and a warm smile. Everyone present held their collective breaths. Nothing happened for about a minute and looks of concern started to appear on faces. Then first one patient, then another, and finally all were trying to sit up. Their color had returned. Their vital signs were back in the normal range. The doctors and nurses who accompanied them on the journey were wiping tears from their eyes. These folks were going to make it.

Doug directed Abigail to walk around the field to see how far her power carried. There were people placed at various levels from the top row of the stadium to the first row. Abigail walked slowly around, making eye contact with those on the bottom rows. Nothing.

Doug then directed the cadets to escort their patients to the field. Two parallel white lines had been drawn about 20 feet apart. The cadets lined up the patients on the two lines, and Abigail walked up and down between the lines like an inspecting officer. The big difference was that she was smiling at each person. Nothing.

Doug then directed the patients to move forward until they were about 10 feet apart. Abigail repeated her walk. About a third of the patients started smiling. There was something going on. The quarterback started flexing his knee. Then he dropped his crutches and jogged a few steps, ran about 20 yards, then turned and ran to Abigail. He picked her up and planted a huge kiss on her cheek. Abigail was flustered. She was not used to public attention. Everyone else was laughing, including the Superintendent. He said in a loud voice, "Mister, put that young lady down." The cadet, still smiling, gave her another kiss and then complied with the order.

Doug shouted, "OK! We know it works for some cases at 10 feet. Let's see what it takes to get everyone. Please move forward a few steps until you are seven feet apart."

The patients did as directed, and Abigail repeated her walk. She smiled constantly and occasionally held out her arm to touch someone. Jubilation erupted. All of those present started laughing, hugging, crying, and in some cases, collapsing. It was total bedlam. It was also a victory. After the celebration and everyone started to calm down, the Superintendent surprised the visitors by inviting them to join the Corps of Cadets for lunch in Washington Hall.

Washington Hall is a huge dining hall in which all 4,000 cadets can sit down at one time for meals. The place looked to be filled when the visitors arrived. Somehow the cadet escorts managed to chaperone them to empty seats throughout the hall at tables with vacancies. This way, the visitors had an opportunity to share the cadet experience of a meal at Washington Hall. The First Captain ordered everyone to take their seats. Then he introduced the Superintendent. The 'Supe' was all smiles as he described what just occurred at Michie Stadium. The Corps stood and cheered. He brought out the injured athletes. The Corps really cheered. Then he brought out Abigail. The Corps erupted. The applause lasted for what seemed to be an eternity to Abigail.

After the meal was over and the cadets departed for afternoon classes, everyone thanked the Superintendent and his staff for their efforts and hospitality. The patients mobbed Abigail, thanking her and blessing her before getting back on the buses for the return trip to Manhattan. And finally, with Tommy driving, Abigail and Doug relaxed in his Audi SUV for the short ride back to the mansion.

All three of them were in high spirits when they returned to the mansion. Now they knew the parameters in which they were working, somewhere less than 10 feet proximity was required. The closer to the patient, the better. They also knew that security, both of the patients and Abigail, was critical. Now the question was how to proceed.

They batted ideas around for the next couple of hours. The ideas ranged from erecting barriers inside stadiums to keep the crowds in check to somehow blocking off a city street like Constitution Avenue in Washington and having Abigail drive up and down it in a Segway or a vehicle like the Popemobile. The stadium idea seemed to be the most viable, but it would require a lot more planning before it was ready. At five o'clock, both men took their leave and headed back to their homes. They felt like they had accomplished a lot. They made no commitment to Abigail as to when they would return. Both had to get back to their businesses.

After watching them drive out of sight, Abigail walked back into the house and asked the cook for a cup of tea. She turned on the television and saw a report on the evening news from Memorial Sloan Kettering Cancer Center. Several of the cancer patients who had traveled to West Point and their families were holding a news conference. They described what had occurred accurately and fairly. They heaped praise on West Point, the Superintendent and his staff, and the cadets. Then they got to Abigail. The tears of joy and gratitude flowed like the Hudson River. The former patients and their families kept thanking her and praising her. The questions from the press were predictable. Some were pertinent and germane. More than a few were inane, superficial, and ridiculous. They were an embarrassment to journalism as a whole. This is an amazing accomplishment in a profession where standards, morals, and ethics are so low that shame is not even in the vernacular of most of the members.

Abigail smiled sadly and sighed. She was feeling alone. She had spent most of her life alone and, before all of this, was happy and content. She bothered no one, and no one bothered (with) her. She had a job and a routine. Then suddenly, she was thrust into the spotlight. She absolutely hated the attention, but she liked the company of most of the people she had met. Raphael was an angel in her opinion. Michael and Angelina were open, caring, and warm. Doug and Tommy were all business but were honorable, honest, and generous. She loved being around all of them. Now they were gone. She knew they would return, but not knowing exactly when was troubling. The other two, Polina and Barney, just come and go. They didn't add or subtract to her life. They just showed up, said a few words, and left. They were like leaves blowing in the wind.

The next morning Abigail was sitting in the kitchen having breakfast and talking with the cook. It was just conversation, nothing of any importance, just talk. Suddenly the bell rang. Cook went to the intercom and answered. Sure enough, it was Barney. He and Polina just happened to be taking a scenic drive to Poughkeepsie on Route 9 and thought that they would drop in and see how she was doing. Abigail shrugged her shoulders and motioned for the cook to open the gate for them.

The two visitors joined Abigail at the kitchen table but declined the cook's offer of breakfast and coffee. They were just passing through.

"You'll have to excuse my appearance," said Abigail. "I wasn't expecting visitors, and as you can see, I'm still in my robe."

"Don't be silly, dear," replied Polina. "I told Barney it's not fair to just drop in on someone unannounced, but he wouldn't listen."

Barney said, "Hey, don't be silly. You look great. Looks like you had quite a time yesterday at West Point. The news shows are still agog about it. I'll tell you it is a good thing you have this hideaway. They would rip you to shreds if they could find you. He paused for a moment then said, "What's your plan now? Do you know how long you can stay here?"

Abigail shook her head. "No. Angelina said that Mr. Halvorson, the owner, doesn't need it just yet. She didn't know for sure how long I can stay."

Polina interjected, "That's very generous of him. By the way, what are you doing for money?"

"I have a little saved up in my savings account. Right now, I am still on salary from my job, but I don't know how long that can last. They can't afford to keep paying someone who isn't there. The good news is that my expenses are low. I'll make my rent and utility payments for my place outside of Philadelphia, but they are about my only real expenses. My car is paid off. Mr. Halvorson is providing food. I should be OK for a little while after my salary stops."

Barney and Polina exchanged glances. Barney asked, "Have you thought about charging for curing people? You could make a fortune.

"Oh no, I couldn't do that. That wouldn't be right. These people need help."

Barney replied, "I admire you, Abigail. I really do, but if I may say so, you need to be practical. So far as anyone knows, you are the only person on earth with the power to heal others just by being near them. You are a unique resource and need to be guarded and conserved. You've seen what happens when people have unfettered access to you. You don't want that. If you were to put a price on your services, that would restrict access somewhat depending on what you were to charge. It would also make you independent. You wouldn't be dependent on the good graces of Jimmy Halvorson or anyone else. It's something to think about."

"I agree with Barney on this," said Polina. "You need to look out for number one. I'd say you need to get away. Take some time for yourself. Get grounded, as it were. You have had a heck of a time in the last month or so. It must be overwhelming."

"Promise me that you will think about it, OK? If you do decide to get away for a breather, Polina and I might be able to help. We have a friend who owns a boat. I'm sure he would be happy to help. I'll call him if you like."

Abigail answered, "Thanks for the offer, Barney. I promise I will think about it. It might be nice to get away for a week or so. I'll sleep on it."

After they departed, Abigail took a nap awakened later by the ring tone of her cell phone. It was Tommy Sullivan calling. He said he wanted to come up the next day to talk to her. He was going to bring along his assistant if that was OK with Abigail. He said that they could get Stanton or one of the other doctors on the line along with Melek, Keenan, or whomever else was needed. Abigail had no objections, so they agreed to meet at the mansion at noon the next day. Abigail that she would have the cook prepare lunch for three.

Tommy's Audi SUVU arrived at the main gate late the following morning. His assistant turned out to be a very pretty lady named Lorena Mason. She was well dressed in slacks and sweater with an understated necklace and matching earrings. She had brown eyes and shoulder-length light brown hair. She flashed a friendly smile and followed it up with a firm handshake. All in all, she made a very favorable first impression. As they entered the house, Tommy explained that Lorena was the force behind his success. "In my line of work, I meet a lot of people who I need to keep straight in my mind. Sometimes events happen so fast I can barely keep up. That's where she comes in. She has a photographic memory. She is like a human video camera. It's scary the way that she misses nothing and can repeat everything that occurred."

Lorena just smiled as they went into the dining room for lunch. They dined on onion soup, a salad of fresh greens, and pepper loin steak sandwiches with fries. It was delicious. The cook explained that she got the recipe for the steak from a restaurant in Collinsville, IL and always receives rave reviews when she makes it. Conversation over lunch was light and breezy. Lorena spoke of growing up across the river in Rockland County. Lorena was 40 years old and never married. She said she graduated with a journalism degree from NYU; tried to get into broadcast journalism in NYC; got tired of the constant pressure and competition; met Tommy about 12 years ago, and worked for him ever since. During those 12 years, she had met all kinds of famous people. A few were down to earth and real, more were self-centered and shallow, and the rest were lightweights intellectually and morally. All in all, they made for a fascinating mix.

After lunch, they went outside and sat on the veranda and enjoyed the spectacular view. Cook served iced tea and lemonade and left the three alone. Tommy started by saying that he felt that she was at the point where she needed to make some decisions as to what she wanted the future to look like.

Abigail interrupted him. "Two acquaintances dropped by yesterday. They aren't what I would call friends. I've run into them several times, or I should say they have run into me. They suggested that I charge for curing people. They also suggested that I take some time off, get away, and do some serious thinking."

"I see," said Sullivan. "What do you think?"

"I hate the idea of asking people to pay for something I really have not earned. I don't know why I have this gift, where it came from, or how long it will last. On the other hand, I can't live for however long as a charity case. I'm going to need some independence no matter how miserable it might turn out to be."

She looked at Lorena, "Ms. Mason, I don't know what you know about me. I've lived a very solitary life so far. I have a job which I like, but I don't socialize with anyone at the office. Heck, I don't socialize with anyone. I say 'Hi' to the neighbors, clerks at the store, and that's about it. When this curing stuff started, I was thrown out of my comfort zone. I've met some wonderful people, like Tommy here and Doug. They are easy to talk to, and they don't appear to judge me. They take me as I am. The thought of going back to my safe former life terrifies me. I want to expand my horizons. Does that make sense?"

Lorena smiled and nodded her head. "It makes perfect sense. The one thing I will tell you is that the world is full of not-so-nice people. There are some real sharks out there. These people would sell their mothers for a nickel and not have a second thought about it. Be careful who you place your trust in."

Tommy said, "Abigail, Lorena is right. You have to be careful. Look, I have a full load of clients. I make more money than I can reasonably expect to spend. Do you know why? I'll tell you why. My clients trust me. They know I will never give them bad advice to make a quick buck. As Lorena said, some of these people are real creeps, but I give them my best efforts. I always have, and I always will. The fact that I have to take a shower after being with them is my problem. Having said that, I never have been and never will be a part of anything that is the least bit shady or questionable. My clients know if they want to go down that path, they will go alone without me."

Sullivan paused and gave a short laugh. "Would you listen to me? Talk about running amuck. It's just that I am passionate about my self-respect and honor. If I can't look at myself in the mirror each morning in a brightly lit room and have no regrets, then I have failed myself as a human being. One of my favorite lines of poetry was written by Richard Lovelace in 1649. He was one of the Cavalier Poets in England during the reign of King Charles I. In his poem *To Lucasta, Going to the Warres*, he wrote, 'I could not love thee, Dear, so much, Lov'd I not Honour more.' That line has always been my guiding light."

He laughed again and said, "There I go again. It sounds like I'm giving you a sales pitch. Well, in a way, I guess I am. I am offering my services to you to protect your best interests and to guide you through the perils you will undoubtedly encounter as you move ahead. Now I'm going to sound like I'm giving you the sales pitch again, but I'm not. Agents normally make between 10 and 20 percent of what their clients earn. I normally charge my clients closer to the

20 percent number. I want to help you. You are special. If you agree, I will represent you for two-and-a-half percent of what you earn."

Lorena uttered a gasp of surprise. Seeing the shocked look on her face, Tommy asked, "Is there a problem?" She shook her head, 'No.'

Sullivan looked at Abigail again and said, "I know you have some people who have helped you thus far. They are the reason you are sitting in this mansion. What I would like you to do is contact them and run this by them. You also need to let them know about what we discovered about your powers at West Point two days ago, as well as your thoughts about what you would like to do in the future in so far as you know them. I'd be happy to meet them face-to-face or perhaps on a t-con. If you think it is worthwhile, I'll bet Doug Keenan would be willing to attend. Whatever you want and are comfortable with. From now on, this is all about Abigail Williams. Doing what is best for her, keeping her safe, keeping her happy, and allowing her to reach her goals. OK?"

Abigail smiled and nodded her head. "You've given me a lot to think about. My head is spinning. I will contact my friend, Rafi, and tell him what you said. He is the one who rescued me when this all first started. I trust him."

Sullivan said, "That's good. See what he has to say. Promise me you won't do anything without first talking it over with him or with me. As I said, there are sharks out there. They look and act like the rest of the fish, then when you least expect it, they attack."

A few minutes, later Abigail showed her guests to the door. She was a troubled lady who needed to gather her wits. She would call Raphael first thing tomorrow.

As they drove away, Lorena said to Tommy, "Two and a half percent. You might as well work for free. You are going to take a loss on this one."

"Hell, I don't need the money. That girl is special. You saw it for yourself. I think she can make an impact on the world if we can keep the dregs from soiling her. I don't have time for another client, but for her, I'll make an exception. I'm going to need to get her to sign a contract with me. For this to be legal, each side has to promise something. She's promising me two-and-a-half percent. Some might argue it is not nearly enough, but I'll fight that battle if I have to."

PLANNING

Several days later, Abigail was incredibly bored. She had walked a beaten path in the lush lawn going back and forth. Abby realized she was traveling between tedium and uselessness and hated every moment of the journey. She remembered a phrase an old soldier once told her, "Patience my ass. I'm going to kill someone." She found herself being rude and curt with the two members of the household staff who were doing everything in their power to mitigate her circumstances. She looked forward to the scam phone calls so she could engage in a battle of wits with the poor souls who daily traded their dignity and self-respect to try to steal from the clueless and vulnerable. She became quite adept at castigating these creatures and grew to enjoy it.

At last, the phone rang and Raphael's friendly and familiar voice was on the line. As promised, she had called him as soon as Sullivan and Mason left the mansion. At that time, Melek promised her that he would make some calls and get back to her.

His tone was upbeat but not giddy. He said that tomorrow, he, Michael Angelo, and Angelina Gabriella would arrive at the mansion around 1 p.m. Joining them would be Drs. Stanton and

Barr, Marguerite Camp, Doug Keenan, Tommy Sullivan, and Lorena Mason. In other words, everyone who had positively affected her since this entire adventure began. Melek promised that they would remain there until they had a viable plan of action. They exchanged small talk for a few moments then he hung up.

Fortunately, the mansion was large. It could easily accommodate Abigail as well as the nine visitors. She went into the kitchen and asked the cook and her husband to please open up and prepare nine bedrooms for use starting tomorrow, and to also buy enough food to feed them for at least four meals. All of a sudden, it appeared as if Abigail had found a purpose, and she was excited. Her excitement was contagious, and the couple cheerfully hastened to obey.

The guests started to arrive around 11:30 the following morning. By 2 o'clock, the final guest, Gabriella, arrived by car from Portsmouth, NH. Introductions were made, lunch was served, and the group, united by a common purpose, got comfortable with each other. The cook and her husband showed each guest to his or her room, advising that everyone was going to gather together on the back porch at 4:00 p.m. for drinks and hors d'oeuvres.

Once everyone was settled on the veranda, Doug Keenan brought everyone up-to-date on the trial at West Point. They now knew what the range of Abigail's healing power was. Thus far, no mission had been set, but if and when it was, they could devise a plan.

Melek went next. He reminded everyone of Abigail's escape from Washington and the riot outside the house in Springfield. She could have very easily been injured or worse. Also, in today's age, there was always the question of crazies, people like Revray and his group. God only knows what they are capable of.

Dr. Stanton spoke after Raphael. He reviewed the success at the hospitals in Philadelphia and St. Louis, as well as the disaster in Ohio, and emphasized that the key to success was secrecy. No one in the general public knew she was visiting the first two cities. However, word leaked about the Ohio visit, and everyone seated there knew the results. He agreed with Keenan that no mission had been set.

Angelina mentioned that, thus far, politics had not entered the picture but was certain that that would change. Politicians would try to use Abigail's powers to leverage their political position. The current president has no interest in anything that does not benefit him personally. He is a loose cannon that could put her in jeopardy. The others on the porch nodded their agreement at this statement.

Melek stared at Abigail and smiled. "Well, kid, on that happy note, I guess the ball is in your court. You have a gift. Where and how you acquired the gift is irrelevant. You have it. The question now is, 'How do you use it." We can advise, but we cannot dictate. It is totally up to you. What do you see yourself doing?"

"I'll be honest with you. I have been giving it a lot of thought. Yes, I know I have a gift. I know I am helping people. But do you want to know something? When I was in the hospitals and on the field at West Point, I have never been happier. I know it sounds selfish, but I really got enjoyment and happiness watching the faces of the people when they realized they were better. If there were some way I could continue to do that without risking people getting hurt, I would jump at the chance. On the other hand, I told Tommy and Lorena the other day that I need to start earning money. I can't depend on the charity of others."

Tommy Sullivan spoke for the first time. "I'm not so sure I would worry about money at this point, and I think I speak for everyone here. I know several of us sitting here would be honored to bankroll you for a while."

Angelina added, "Jimmy Halvorson agrees. He told me to tell you that this place is yours for as long as you want or need it."

Abigail smiled, "You all are too kind. I appreciate the thoughts, I really do. If it is OK with you, I'll continue here for a bit, but down the road, I want to be independent. Pay my own way, if you will."

The discussion continued for the next several hours. Sitting on the veranda, having drinks while watching the scenic view of the river, the Academy, and the mountains put everyone in a sanguine and mellow mood. There was no clear goal in sight, so the conversations drifted like a branch floating in the river. It flowed but had no clear direction or purpose.

The group reconvened on the porch after dinner. Sullivan stood up and took charge. "If it is acceptable to everyone, please let me summarize where we are. If I am wrong in my assessment, stop me. First and foremost, Abigail's safety and wellbeing have to be guaranteed. If we can't do that, it is pointless to go on."

There were no objections from the group, so Sullivan continued. "Next on the list is taking care of the helpless, the critical, and the very sick. To me, that means the hospitals. If I understood Abby correctly, she loves healing children, but she does not want to do that to the exclusion of others in need." He paused and looked at Abigail, who nodded her head violently in agreement. "That means all hospitals, not just children's hospitals. It opens up VA hospitals, mental hospitals, and even nursing homes. We'll need to figure out a way to prioritize all of the possible facilities throughout the country. We also need to establish a protocol that can be used at most, if not all, of the venues. We have only one little lady, and we have to make the very best use of her time and her power. I know this is being presumptive of me, but would Drs. Barr and Stanton and their staff take this on? You have contacts in the medical communities throughout the country. Can you mobilize them?"

Speaking for Stanton and Marguerite, Barr said, "It will be our honor and pleasure to try."

Tommy continued, "Raphael, can you lend a hand with the medical side of things? You know the ins and outs of DC. Perhaps you can grease the skids at the VA, Health and Human Services, and any of the other departments and agencies that may be able to facilitate Abigail's efforts. Heck, you may be able to elicit help from the DoD[3]."

Melek replied, "Of course I will. I'll do anything I can to help."

"That leaves us with how to best get Abigail safely in front of the great, unwashed American public. Doug has a lot of expertise in this area. I have a lot of experience representing 'talent' or lack thereof. What I propose is that Abigail and I enter into an exclusive representation contract, voidable by either party upon written notice, for the commission of two-and-a-half percent of the gross that she brings in.

"Before you all go nuts, hear me out. The industry standard is closer to 20 percent." He then went on to explain the rationale for the contract. The others slowly nodded their assent. Michael said, "Yeah, it makes sense to me. I'm in." There was no dissension from the others. Abigail just sat there emotionless.

Sullivan continued, "How about if Mike, Angelina, Lorena, Doug, and I take a crack at security and ways to deliver Abigail's power to the general public. Everyone is spending the night here tonight. Let's split into subgroups tomorrow morning for a working breakfast. Each group will establish ground rules and a preliminary timeline. We'll plan on leaving here right after lunch and head home. Is everyone OK with this?" Again there were no objections.

The following morning was overcast and rainy. Gray is not a good color in the Hudson Valley. The sky is gray, the river is gray,

---

3. Department of Defense

the mountains are gray, and at West Point, even the buildings are gray. The interval between Christmas and spring is called Gloom Period by the cadets and is a fitting label. At the mansion, the mood inspired by the weather was gloomy. The two groups met until around 11 o'clock. There was no banter or frivolity. Everything was strictly business. Even Michael was subdued. Angelina was facing a four-hour drive back to Portsmouth, so she eschewed lunch, grabbed a soda, bid farewell to everyone, and got on the road. The others followed immediately after lunch.

Before they left, Sullivan and Melek met with Abigail. She was a bit despondent at being left alone again. They tried to cheer her up, both promising to stay in touch. For her part, Abigail tried to put on a brave face. She said she wished she could get away for a while, but realized that was almost impossible. Hugs were exchanged with both of the men, and they departed, leaving her standing in the doorway waving goodbye.

The next morning was the antithesis of the previous one. The sky was clear. The sun was warm. Birds were singing. It was a great day to savor being alive. Abigail woke early and, throwing all caution to the wind, decided to go for a long walk outside of the grounds. She was confident that she would be safe. There were enough back roads in the area that she would not have to walk along Highway 9 or The Bear Mountain-Beacon Highway. She dressed hurriedly in a sweatshirt, jeans, and tennis shoes and quietly let herself out the front door. She unlocked the gate and luxuriated in the sense of freedom. For the next few hours, she had no one to answer to and no one to fear. She walked for several miles up and down the hills enjoying the squirrels climbing the trees and walking on the telephone wires. She marveled at the peace and tranquility of it all. As she was heading back to the mansion, she heard a car behind her give a short toot of its horn. Turning, she saw Barney and Polina in the Maserati waving at her with huge smile on their faces. She thought to herself, "I knew it was too good to last."

The car pulled up and Barney cheerfully said, "Polina had a conference at the Bear Mountain Inn. It just ended, we were in the neighborhood, and you know, thought we would drop in and say 'hi.' Hi!" He laughed at his humor. Abigail just smiled politely. Barney said, "Come on, hop in. Sit on Polina's lap, and I'll drive us back to your place." Abigail was stuck. There was no way she could gracefully decline. It was a short drive, but Abby mentioned how nice the car was. Barney pulled up to the gate and said, "Well, you're in luck. Polina, get out and I'll give Abigail a short demonstration of what perfection feels like."

Polina did as instructed, and Abigail belted herself in the passenger's seat. Barney said, "All right. Here we go." He dropped the car into gear and shot off like a flash. He spent the next 15 minutes or so driving on the curvy roads overlooking West Point. Abigail was thrilled and marveled at how the car clung to the curves and accelerated when on the straightaways. When he returned to the mansion, Polina was waiting. Abigail expected her to be upset at being made to stand there, but she was wrong. Polina was all smiles. "Did you enjoy the ride?'

"It was absolutely fantastic! I have never been in a car like that. I've got goosebumps all over."

Both of her visitors smiled knowing smiles as they headed to the house. Once inside, both the cook and her husband gave Abigail furious looks. Barney asked, "Are they angry at us for dropping in again unannounced?"

"No. They are angry at me. I am not supposed to leave the grounds without an escort. They were worried about me, and angry because I kind of snuck out." Abigail smiled an impish smile of triumph. The married couple just glowered at her.

The three of them found seats at the kitchen table and the cook offered coffee, juice and freshly baked, homemade cinnamon buns. Their aroma was out of this world. Surprisingly, both Polina and Barney refused with thanks, saying they had just eaten an enormous breakfast and couldn't hold another bite.

After some small talk about politics, the weather and such, Abigail mentioned the meeting that she had over the previous few days with her friends to discuss where to go next with her powers. They were searching for a solution that benefited the most people while keeping her secure and safe.

Polina reminded her of the conversation they had with her the last time they visited her. "Abigail, remember Barney mentioned a friend of ours who owns a boat. Barney thought that he may allow you to take a short cruise on it to get away and clear your brain. Have you given that any more thought? I called him a few days ago, and he said he would be happy to entertain both you and a guest if you wanted to bring someone along. Actually, he is a boating enthusiast. He owns four boats. This one is docked right now at Long Island and is the smallest of the four."

Abigail answered, "With all that has been going on in my life, I really have not given it much thought. I do know that I need to get away. I feel like I am jumping right out of my skin, I'm so restless. Maybe this would be what the doctor ordered. I hate to impose on a stranger whom I have never met, though."

Barney smoothly answered, "Abdul was very excited about your taking a short cruise on his boat. I explained your circumstances to him. He said the boat is just sitting there and he is paying to keep it tied to the dock, a total waste of money. It needs to go out and get the engines running."

Polina, the ever-reliable deal closer, jumped in, "Abigail, this is too good to be true. This will give you a rest, a break from the reality that has been closing in on you for months now. It will give Abdul a legitimate excuse to have his boat out on open water. I'll bet he will invite several others to join you. You'll meet new people who have no idea who you are. Meet new people, get some sun, and relax. I'd jump at it if I were you."

Abigail closed her eyes, and the others could tell she was seriously thinking about it. When she opened them, she smiled and nodded, "I agree. I would be foolish not to accept. I need to make a few calls first. Any idea when I would go?"

Barney answered, "I'll call Abdul right after we leave here and let him know that he will have at least one passenger. We'll get back to you as soon as we can firm things up."

After they left and Abigail was walking through the kitchen, she heard the cook say to her husband, "There is something about those two that I just don't like. I don't know what it is, but they make me uneasy. I don't trust them." Her husband just shrugged in reply.

Abigail's first call was to Tommy Sullivan. Instead of being happy and excited for her, he was skeptical. "Abigail, do you know what you are getting yourself into? You know nothing about this Abdul or his boat. He could be a white slaver, a kidnapper, or a pervert for all you know."

"Barney and Polina trust him, Tommy, and they like him. I trust them and like them. What's the big deal?"

"What do you know about them? They just show up from time to time. You know nothing about them."

Abigail started getting mad. "Listen, I didn't know anything about you at first other than you were a friend of Douglas Keenan, who, by the way, was recommended by Barney and Polina. I don't think you are, but you could be just a con man with no morals or scruples. You have to start trusting someone or you'll wither and die."

Somewhat chastened, Tommy replied, "I'll tell you what. They offered to let you take a companion. Let me send Lorena with you. You two seem to like each other. She's smart as a whip, is a good judge of people, and is tough as nails. I think that you will both have a good time together. What do you think?"

Several minutes later, an ecstatic Abigail made her second call. This one to Raphael Melek. She relayed the details of the trip, as well as the fact that Lorena Mason would accompany her. She was not surprised when Rafi was not enthusiastic about the trip. He voiced strong concerns about Polina and Barney, although he had never met them. Then he did a replay of Tommy's concerns about Abdul. Abigail patiently listened. It was only when she again reminded Melek that Lorena would be accompanying her that he relented.

When the two phone calls to her friends were finished, Abigail called Barney. She accepted and told him that Lorena Mason would be joining her. Barney told her that she was making the right decision. He said that he and Polina had contacted Abdul, and if acceptable with the two ladies, Abdul would send his boat up the Hudson and pick them up at the boat landing in Garrison, NY, less than a mile from the mansion, the day after tomorrow.

Abigail excitedly asked, "He is picking us up here? That's great. I was kind of wondering what size boat he had. It can't be too big if it is going to travel up the Hudson." Barney did not reply.

THE YACHT

The following evening Lorena arrived from New York. She had a backpack and one bag. "Are you sure you heard right? We only need a couple of dresses, jeans, blouses, shorts, and bathing suits. They actually have an onboard laundry?"

"That's what Barney said. He said Abdul told him that we would be spending most of the time on deck, weather permitting. He suggested we bring several bathing suits. I only have one, and it is old. It looks like something out of the 1950s. Growing up, we never went to the Jersey Shore or any other beach. I think I was only at a swimming pool once or twice. I don't know how to swim."

Lorena answered, "Well, I think you will be in for a treat. How much money are you bringing? I have about $200 in cash, plus plastic. I hope that's enough. If not, there should be ATM's on-shore."

"Barney said that we won't need money unless we want to buy souvenirs or something. Everything will be taken care of. Oh, and look at this." Abigail displayed a brand new passport. "I don't know how they did it, but they got me a passport overnight. I didn't think that was possible, but they did it."

Lorena said, "That is amazing. They must be miracle workers."

The next morning the two ladies sat in the kitchen, drinking coffee. Their bags were already loaded in the mansion's car, and they were waiting for a call from the boat telling them that it was nearing Garrison. At about 9:30, the call came. They said goodbye to the cook, and her husband drove them down the hill to the dock. As they approached the dock, they could not see the boat. There was, however, a huge 200-foot long yacht at anchor in the middle of the river. It was gleaming white. Abigail said to Lorena, "Would you look at that? Why, I have never seen anything like it in my life. It's beautiful."

Lorena agreed. "It is that. I wonder where our boat is."

Just then, a young man with a killer tan wearing a white naval uniform came up to them. "Ms. Williams?" he asked. Abigail nodded. "My name is Richard. I am the Boson[4] of the *Soul Searcher*. I have come to fetch the two of you." He pointed to another young man also in whites. "Bruce here will get your bags loaded on the boat while I'll help you aboard."

Lorena was the first to regain her senses, "Where is the *Soul Searcher*? I don't see a boat." Richard and Bruce both laughed. Richard pointed to the yacht, "That is the *Soul Searcher*. She's a beauty, isn't she?"

He started to lead the way to a 15-foot open motorboat, but neither of the women's legs would move. They were in total shock. They just stared at the yacht.

Lorena stammered, "She is gorgeous. She looks like she is big enough to land a helicopter on her."

More laughter from the two sailors. Bruce replied, "She has a

---

4. Leading deckhand on a yacht

helipad up near the bow. We use it all of the time." Lorena noted that Bruce spoke with a British accent.

Richard helped the two women get in the boat, then turned his attention to help Bruce and the chauffeur load the luggage. When all was set, they cast off. The chauffeur waved and wished them bon voyage. As they approached the massive yacht, a door resembling a garage door opened at water level amidships. Richard carefully maneuvered the boat into the cavernous opening and cut the engine. Another sailor in a white officer's uniform with two stripes on his shoulder boards caught the rope and tied the boat off to a stanchion. He then gave his hand to the ladies and helped them exit the boat. He introduced himself as Hans. Hans had a German accent and told them that he was the Engineering Officer. He led them up a stairway, which was easily wide enough for two people to climb side-by-side. They went up two flights of stairs and came out onto the main deck. There were two more men there in officer's uniforms. One had four stripes on his shoulder boards and the other three. Hans introduced them as Captain Sven Sorenson and First Officer Olaf Karlsson. Both men were obviously from Scandinavia, both by their Nordic facial features and their accents. He went on to introduce Monica and Suzette each in white uniforms adorned with three and two stripes, respectively. Monica was the Executive Chef, while Suzette served a dual function of Sous Chef and Head of Guest Services. Standing next to them were three of the most beautiful women Abigail had ever seen. They were introduced as Brittany, Tiffany, and Janice. They served as onboard stewardesses. All three were identically clad in tight black golf shirts with red trim and incredibly short tan skirts. Like the rest of the crew, all three had killer tans. Collectively, the crew was a dermatologist's nightmare

The captain gave them a hearty welcome and pointed to his feet. He was barefoot, as were all of the rest of the crew. He explained that the main deck was very tough, costly to maintain, and scratched very easily. He went on to explain that while shoes were optional in the rest of the yacht, they were not permitted on the main deck. He also asked that if the two ladies needed objects like deck chairs moved or repositioned that they ask a crewmember to perform the task. Again, he said this was to avoid scratching the finish on the deck. With a big smile, he said he hoped that the ladies would have a wonderful time on board and that he and his crew were there to do everything in their power to make it so. All the women had to do was ask. With that, he gave orders to make ready to get under weigh.

When the captain departed for the bridge, Suzette told the ladies that Bruce had carried their luggage to their cabins. The stewardesses would show the ladies around the boat a little later, but she was quite sure that they would want to stay on deck, barefoot, to watch the sights as they sailed south on the Hudson to New York City and beyond. "Make yourselves at home. Can we bring you a snack? How about tea, coffee, lemonade, or something a little stronger?"

Lorena giggled and said, "I feel daring with all this excitement. I'd like a Bloody Mary, please."

Everyone looked at Abigail. Her cheeks were crimson. "I've never had a Bloody Mary before. Do you mind if I try one?"

Suzette laughed and touched Abigail's hand, "Of course I don't mind. The captain said that he wanted you to have the time of your life. That's why we are here." Suzette nodded to Janice, who went to the bar on deck and started to make the drinks. Brittany came out with a tray of delicious looking snacks, while Tiffany led them to two deck chairs. She said, "As we head down the river, the captain will point out some of the interesting sights, so don't hesitate to get up and move from side to side on the boat."

Sure enough, as the boat proceeded downriver, the captain pointed out the Bear Mountain Bridge, Bear Mountain, and other scenic sights. Further down the river, they passed the town of Ossining with the infamous Sing Sing Prison lurking on the water's edge. Then came the village of Sleepy Hollow made famous by Washington Irving and his lovable character, Ichabod Crane. The boat finally made its way past Manhattan, sailing leisurely by Ellis Island and the Statue of Liberty.

By this time, the ladies had imbibed two Bloody Marys' each and were feeling mellow. They were sitting on deck chairs on the starboard side, enjoying the view of the two islands and Jersey City, when Brittany came by and offered to give them a tour of the boat and then take them to their cabins.

Both ladies were amazed by the luxury and opulence they encountered on the tour. They had never imagined that a vessel like this even existed, let alone that they would be cruising on it. The time spent on the bridge was fascinating. Captain Sorenson was fully engaged piloting the boat through the harbor, but First Officer Karlsson provided a detailed description of what they were observing. By the time they arrived at their cabins, Brittany was smiling broadly. "Well, what do you think? It's some boat, isn't it?"

Between the alcohol, the excitement, and the tour, Abigail was too dazed to answer. Lorena answered for both of them, "I'll say it is. I've been around a bit, but nothing to compare to this. Who owns it?"

Brittany said in reply, "The owner is a man named Abdul Shaytan. He is a fabulously wealthy real estate magnate from Dubai. I think he owns half of the Middle East. I've never met him. Actually, I don't know anyone who has. Between you and me, this job is a dream come true. The pay is beyond belief. We see exotic and beautiful places, and we meet exciting and diverse people. I graduated from Smith College with a degree in French Literature. I was going to go back and maybe try law or even post-grad work in French Literature, so that I could teach at a college or university somewhere when this job came up. That was over two years ago. I have not regretted a second of it. I think if you ask Tiffany and Janice that they will tell you the same thing. Tiffany graduated from Stanford and Janice from Brown. They could be doing anything they want, but they are happy here. In fact, Janice is in the process of writing a book about her adventures on board."

Lorena answered, "It sounds like a lot of fun. Are you going to make a career in this industry?"

Brittany laughed. "I hardly think so. Maybe another year for me, two at the most. By then, I think I will be ready to get on with my life and I should have plenty saved. My grades in school were excellent. I think I just have to decide what I want to be when I grow up." Both Brittany and Lorena laughed at this. Abigail just smiled. It was as if Brittany were speaking a foreign language. She could not relate to any of it.

Tiffany and Janice walked by. Brittany told them the details of their conversation and both girls readily agreed.

A few minutes later, Abigail was in her cabin with the door open putting her clothes away. Lorena was standing in the doorway of her cabin. Tiffany asked, "If you don't mind my asking, what connections do you have to get invited on the *Soul Searcher*? If I do say so, you both seem so serious and nice. A lot of our guests are just the opposite."

Before Abigail could form an answer, Lorena answered, "I work for an agent. One of his clients was grateful for the work we did for him. He is the one who has connections to the boat. He offered, and Abigail and I took him up on the offer. End of story."

No one could see Abigail in her cabin as she silently mouthed the words "thank you." She wanted to travel incognito and Lorena knew this. Lorena knew her way around.

Lorena asked, "OK, we've had the tour. What's next? By the way, where are we going? No one told us our destination."

Janice answered, "We are heading to Montauk on the eastern tip of Long Island to pick up several more passengers."

Tiffany asked, "Any idea who they are?"

Janice looked at the clipboard she carried. "A Mr. and Mrs. Lionel Simms. I have not met them. It says here that he is a hedge fund manager, and she is a philanthropist."

Janice then frowned as she continued, "We are also picking up Dexter van Allen and Sylvester Berkshire. We have sailed with those two before. They can be a handful. Van Allen is in real estate. I'm not sure what Berkshire does, other than he is the son of the Senator from Wyoming who is the probable nominee of his party for president."

Brittany said, "Well, there go our tops." By this time, Abigail had finished unpacking and had come out into the passage-way. Lorena was still in her doorway. Both women exchanged looks and shrugs at this.

"Oh, listen up. You all will like this. We are also picking up Antonio Spiga in Montauk."

The other two stewardesses smiled broadly at this news. Abigail glanced at Lorena, and to her surprise, she was wearing a lecherous smile. "I wonder who he is," Abigail thought to herself.

After the stewardesses departed, Lorena decided she would change into shorts and go up on deck. Abigail said she would join her later. She sat on her bed, took a deep breath, and tried to gather her wits. It was hard to believe she was on a yacht sailing to the tip of Long Island. The apartment in Upper Darby seemed a long way off. Where was this adventure going?

Abigail changed into shorts and a t-shirt, combed her hair, and went to the main deck. It was a beautiful day, a little windy, but all in all, not bad. They watched Long Island pass by far off to the port side. They passed large vessels heading to the piers in New York and New Jersey. Abigail waved to the sailors on deck and most waved back at her. Well past mid-afternoon, they rounded the Montauk Point Lighthouse and headed to the north shore of the island to the marina and Coast Guard Station. Abigail noted that *Soul Searcher* must have been expected since there was a large, empty berth waiting for them. It took no time for Captain Sorenson to turn his vessel to the harbor's entrance and sail it into position. Richard and Bruce threw lines fore and aft to men standing on the dock, and the boat was secured.

Abigail was standing at the rail just forward of amidships watching the activity on the dock when Lorena approached and handed her a Bloody Mary. Abby gasped. "Are you trying to get me drunk?" she asked.

Lorena laughed, "Oh, loosen up and relax. You're here to have fun."

As they watched, a couple walked down the dock towards the boat. They were each carrying a bag and rolling a suitcase. Richard and Bruce hurried towards them and took the bags. The man appeared to be in his early fifties with dark brown hair beginning to show signs of gray. He was well-dressed, but nothing fancy. He looked exactly like what someone going on a pleasure cruise should look like. The lady accompanying him was in her late forties. Abigail thought the color of her hair was not the color she was born with. She also was casually dressed, wore a modest amount of jewelry, and enormous sunglasses. They boarded the vessel and were greeted by Captain Sorenson and the entire crew, much the same as she and Lorena were welcomed.

The couple started to follow Janice down to their cabin when they saw Abigail and Lorena. Janice stopped and brought the couple over. She introduced them as Lionel Simms and his wife, Dorothy. Everyone shook hands, made some polite small talk, and then they followed Janice down the staircase. Abigail felt like they were down-to-earth people. There was no pretentiousness at all from either of them.

The welcoming ceremony was repeated a short while later as two men came on board. This time it was Tiffany who was detailed to guide the new passengers to their cabins. As they passed by, the two men were introduced as Dexter van Allen and Sylvester Berkshire. Abigail was not impressed. First, neither paid any attention to either girl. Their greetings were impersonal and perfunctory. Clearly, they had better ways to spend their time. Also, Berkshire's handshake was weak, cold, and clammy. It was like shaking hands with a wet, slimy dish rag. Abigail wanted to wipe her hand on her shorts as the two men departed. It was a big boat and she hoped they could avoid 'Jethro and Jughead.'

A short while later, there was a commotion on the dock. Looking down, Abigail and Lorena saw why. Striding towards the boat pursued by several autograph seekers was a tall, well-tanned man in a white suit, white shirt, and white shoes. He had a heavy gold chain around his neck, a gold bracelet on his right wrist, and an expensive-looking watch on his left. He had jet black hair and pearly white teeth, which he flashed early and often. Abby knew immediately that this must be Antonio, and she realized why the three stewardesses smiled at the mention of his name. Lorena told her that Spiga was a very successful recording and movie star, as well as a producer. One of his films had been recently nominated for an Academy Award. He boarded the vessel, met the crew, and this time it was Brittany who led him to his cabin. She stopped and introduced him to Lorena and Abigail. Instead of shaking hands, he took each girl's hand and kissed it while saying something soothing and soft in Italian. It was an over-the-top performance, almost bordering on being a parody. The male members of the crew each rolled their eyes in disgust. The females on deck were a totally different story.

After the Italian singer went below, Abigail needed to clear her head. The three Bloody Marys' and Antonio's performance had given her a slight buzz. She returned to her cabin and lay down on the bed. She felt the boat begin to move and shortly felt the motion of the seas as it cleared the harbor. Between the comfort of the bed and the slight rolling of the vessel, she fell fast asleep.

A soft tap at the door awakened her. Sitting up, she saw an envelope that someone slid under the door. Glancing at the bedside clock, she saw she had been asleep for just over an hour. She stretched, yawned, and retrieved the envelope. It contained the plan for the remainder of the evening, as well as for tomorrow morning. She looked out the porthole and saw they were approaching land. This surprised her. She reread the itinerary and saw that they were picking up two more passengers in Newport, RI. Rhode Island must be what she was seeing out of the window.

She went up on deck as the boat pulled alongside a dock and two women climbed on board. These two proved to be old pros at sailing as they were barefoot when they stepped on the deck. The crew welcomed them aboard, then Janice led them down to their cabins. The boat reversed course and took up a heading towards Bermuda.

Dinner was at 7:30 that evening and was mostly a pleasant affair. The meal Monica prepared was exquisite in every detail. Abigail and Lorena learned that the two new passengers were Phyllis Greenfield and Rebecca Wagoner. Phyllis was the CEO of a Fortune 500 computer hardware company, while Rebecca headed a very large Wall Street Law Firm. They had been attending a society event in Newport, which they both agreed was part of their jobs, not something either aspired to participate in.

As the conversation progressed, everyone learned that the Simmses were acquaintances of both Phyllis and Rebecca. Dorothy Simms served on several committees with one or the other of them.

Antonio said he spent a very long weekend at a friend's beach house in the Hamptons. He had a concert tour coming up in a month or so starting in Vegas, and was trying to get some quiet time now to recharge his batteries.

The girls learned that Sylvester was busy with his father's presidential campaign, which was incredibly time-consuming. He mentioned that he had just been appointed to the board of directors of Uzbekitherm, an energy company formed by a joint venture between several Uzbek politicians and Abdul Shaytan. Abigail remembered that Shaytan was the owner of this yacht.

Dexter explained to them that he and Sly had known each other for years. He proudly noted that he was involved in real estate in both New York and the Atlantic City area. Later, as Abigail sat having brandy on deck with Phyllis and Rebecca, she learned that Dexter was under investigation by the FBI and the Assistant US Attorney for the Southern District of New York for fraud and conspiracy to commit fraud.

When the dinner conversation progressed to Lorena and Abigail, Lorena took over, informing the group that she worked for a famous agent, and Abigail was a friend. The agent knew someone who was a friend of Mr. Shaytan's, which explained why they received an invitation on the cruise. Captain Sorenson mentioned that he sailed up the Hudson to pick the two ladies up at Garrison, directly across the river from West Point.

The mention of West Point got Sly going. He had had quite a few drinks and was slightly slurring his words. "West Point. That's where that 'miracle girl' did her magic act. Can you believe that people actually believe that crap? It was nothing but hocus pocus and mass hysteria. It's all bullshit if you ask me."

Dorothy Simms replied in a tone that would freeze water, "I don't recall anyone asking you for your opinion." Sly just gave her a filthy stare.

As always, Abigail was ignored at the table. No one addressed her or paid any attention to her. She was invisible to everyone. Everyone, that is, but the captain, first officer, and the rest of the crew. They made sure she was comfortable and that she wanted for nothing during the meal. She received many smiles and winks of encouragement from the stewardesses. Being ignored was routine for Abby. She expected it. She told herself it didn't bother her, and she almost believed it.

Fortunately, the conversation took a turn elsewhere. Lorena and Abigail rolled their eyes at each other and uttered silent sighs of relief. After dinner, Antonio found Lorena and escorted her to the rear of the boat to watch the ocean. Abigail sat with the two other single women on deck for a while and chatted. As always, Abigail was largely ignored. She didn't have much in common with these two successful ladies, but nonetheless, she was happy to be part of a group. The Simmses conversed in the lounge with the captain, and the two wayward lambs staggered to their cabins, having imbibed too much from the fountain of Bacchus[5].

The sun rose the next morning upon a glorious day. The temperature was balmy, the sky was clear, and the sea was as calm

---

5. Bacchus is the Roman god of wine.

as a mirror. The yacht headed in the general direction of Bermuda. Monica and Suzette prepared a delicious continental breakfast with short order service available for eggs, omelets, waffles, and such.

Abby woke at 9:45 a.m. She felt deliciously wicked for having slept so late. The bed was so comfortable and the rocking of the boat so soothing that she slept like a baby. She put on her bathing suit and a terrycloth robe and headed up the staircase. When she walked into the dining area, she was shocked. None of the other passengers were there. She took a seat at one of the tables and Janice came over with a pot of hot coffee. "Would you care for some? This is brewed from beans that Suzette grinds herself. Most people think it is delicious. However, if you prefer decaf or tea, I'll be happy to get it for you."

"No, I'd love a cup of coffee. Straight black. Nothing in it. Am I the first one here or have the others already eaten?"

"You're the first. I'm guessing the others will be here shortly."

Sure enough, the others started to straggle into the room a short while later. Most were wearing smiles, and pleasantries were exchanged. No surprise, 'Jethro and Jughead' were the last to arrive. They looked like hell warmed over. Both were green and unshaven with eyeballs that had roadmaps of the world imprinted upon them in red. Neither was in a jovial mood. Their fellow passengers were hard-pressed not to laugh hysterically at their plight. These two did not win many friends at dinner the previous evening.

They sat at the opposite end of the room from where Abigail was seated. Lorena had joined her. When he made his appearance, Antonio asked if he could also sit there. The two of them must have hit it off the previous evening because they were chatting this morning like long lost friends. Abigail rose to go to the buffet table to get some fruit. As she made her way there, she passed close by the table where Dexter and Sly were tightly grasping coffee cups with their eyes shut tight. As she did so, a miraculous transformation occurred in the two wayward young men. Their eyes opened and they were clear. The green tinge of their skin vanished and a healthy glow returned. Dexter said, "All of a sudden, I feel great. There must be something in this coffee that cures hangovers." He looked at Tiffany and said, "I'd like a Bloody Mary."

Sly added, "Make that two."

The rest of the passengers looked around, nodded, and soon everyone was drinking Bloody Marys'. It was a convivial group, and Abigail was enjoying being around such a diverse group of people. She was also very grateful that no one connected her with the sudden disappearance of the hangovers.

As people finished breakfast, they headed out on deck. Richard and Bruce were there to position the deckchairs wherever the passengers wished. Abigail asked that two be placed together for her and Lorena. When Lorena arrived, she had another deckchair placed with them for Antonio. Lorena took off her robe, revealing a bikini that was on the conservative side. Abigail stood up and removed her robe. Her swimsuit was right out of the 1950s. It even had a skirt. Lorena stared at her, "Is that your only swimsuit?"

"Yes. Why? What's wrong with it?"

Lorena shook her head and said, "Oh, nothing. You probably won't get a sunburn wearing it."

Abigail looked around. Dorothy Simms was wearing a one-piece number that accentuated her figure. Phyllis and Rebecca had on bikinis. Phyllis' was similar in style to the one Lorena was wearing. Rebecca was wearing a swimsuit that would have gotten her arrested in a different decade. She did, however, have the figure to carry it off, and she succeeded.

Abby noticed that the three stewardesses were wearing bikini tops that were at least one size too small and tight boy short bottoms. They looked beautiful and sexy, and she was envious.

Antonio made his entrance in style. He came out in gym shorts and a 'wife beater' t-shirt. He stood by his deck chair and made a show stretching his arms and chest. Then he slowly stripped off the shirt and shorts. Every pair of female eyes was firmly fixed on him in anticipation. Much to the collective disappointment of all of the ladies, he was not wearing tight 'Speedos'. He was wearing normal, everyday variety swim trunks. He sat back on the deckchair with a pair of wraparound sunglasses and started a conversation with Lorena.

Several of the other passengers were reading books while sunning themselves. Lionel Simms was doing laps in the pool. Dex and Sly were standing near the railing, watching the water. All of a sudden, Dexter shouted, "Look over there."

Everyone hurried over and saw a couple of porpoises playfully following the boat. Every so often they would gracefully breach the surface to the delight of the onlookers. Flying fish were also on display. Lorena had never seen one before, and Abigail had never even heard of them before. Both women were thrilled.

Eventually, the passengers grew tired of Mother Nature and headed back to their perches. Abigail had never been in a Jacuzzi before and decided to try it out. The one on the *Soul Searcher* was large, easily accommodating 10 or more people comfortably. She climbed in and lowered herself into the warm water, leaned back, closed her eyes, and let the water work its magic. After a few minutes, she realized she had company in the tub. Dexter and Sylvester had come in and were sitting opposite of her. She smiled and then tried to ignore them. Dexter stood up and looked at the three stewardesses and said, "OK, who is going to be the lucky lady?" He then pointed to Brittany, who shook her head in resignation and sighed. She climbed into the whirlpool. Before she sat down, she surprised the life out of Abigail. She removed her top and sat down next to Abby.

She whispered to Abby, "We've had these two on board several times. This is one of their traditions. In fact, they insist on it. At first, we complained to the captain, but he said they were close with Mr. Shaytan. He said that it wasn't like we were prudes or anything, and thinks it is harmless. Besides, we didn't want to rock the boat with Mr. Shaytan, did we? Well, we didn't like it, but by the second cruise with them, we got used to it. Now it is no big deal. The other two stewardesses will have their tops off shortly, wait and see. In fact, I'll wager you that most of the women will be sunbathing topless or naked before the day is done. That's the European way and most of our women passengers will try it at least once just for the experience."

Abigail was shocked. She had never even imagined that this sort of thing went on. Brittany saw the shock and was somewhat amused. She wanted to try to help. She stood up and called to Janice, "Jan, can you get a rum punch for Ms. Williams?"

Dexter shouted, "Make that three rum punches, will you?"

Janice came over to the Jacuzzi carrying a tray with three tall glasses garnished with tropical fruit. She placed the glasses near each of the passengers. Sylvester asked, "Kind of overdressed, aren't we Janice?" She glared at him but reached behind her back and undid her top.

Abigail whispered to Brittany, "Now I understand the remark you all made when Janice read the passengers' names off the list, 'There go our tops.'"

After a while, Abby returned to the deckchair. Antonio appeared to be napping. Lorena had her top off but was lying on her stomach. Phyllis and Rebecca also had their tops off. One was on her stomach and the other on her back. Abigail was embarrassed. She didn't know where to turn her eyes. She saw the Simmses relaxing and both reading. He was reading a hardcover book while she read a Kindle. She noticed that they each had rum punches on the small table next to their chairs. She also noticed that Dorothy still had her swimsuit on.

Abigail must have dozed off. The next thing she knew was that folks were moving about, putting their clothes back on and gathering their possessions. Lunch was served. Monica and Suzette had prepared a light lunch highlighted by different types of seafood and a New England clam chowder that brought raves. Abby sat at a table with Phyllis and Rebecca. Lorena and Antonio sat at a table by themselves apart from the rest of the passengers.

The two New Yorkers conversed about the stock market, the Fed's likely response to a sluggish economy and the upcoming elections. Abigail knew nothing about the stock market or monetary policy and was intensely interested in the discussion. She asked an occasional question which the two ladies appeared happy to answer. They were very gracious and nice. Abigail liked them.

She did know a bit about the upcoming elections. The incumbent was a loud-mouth bully with an incredible inferiority complex. He won the last election not because people liked, admired, or agreed with him, but because his opponent was thoroughly detested by an overwhelming majority of voters. His likely opponent this time was the father of Sylvester Berkshire. He was the senior senator from Wyoming who had a reputation for being a glad-handing, back-stabbing son-of-a-bitch. Those who knew him joked that they always kept their hands on their wallets when they were around him. Abigail joined in the conversation. She was gratified that her opinions were listened to and respected. Her two tablemates did not always agree with her position, but they were always respectful. She could not ask for more.

After lunch, one of the problems with luxury yachts presented itself. The boat was fully locked into Wi-Fi, internet, and all of the modern methods of communications. Both Phyllis and Rebecca returned to their cabins to answer e-mails, send instructions, and basically tune back into their jobs for a short while. Lorena said she was going back to her cabin for a nap. Looking around, Abigail noticed that Antonio had disappeared. The Simmses were conversing with Monica and Suzette and all were laughing gaily. 'Frick and Frack' were throwing a Frisbee in the pool and doing their best to prevent it from blowing overboard into the sea.

She sat in a deckchair and wondered what was happening on the mainland with regards to the 'miracle girl.' God, she hated that name. She asked herself, not for the first time, how could anything as noble as curing people and trying to do the right thing cause so much trouble and so many problems. As always, she failed to come up with an answer. A shadow appeared over her, bringing Abby out of her thoughts. When she looked up, she saw the smiling face of Janice. Janice brought her what she said was a Mai Tai, a cocktail that she thought Abigail might enjoy. She placed the glass on the table and asked if she could sit down. Of course, Abby agreed.

"Ms. Williams, do you mind if I make a suggestion?"

"Of course not. What is it?"

"Well, Ms. Williams, you seem to be a very nice person, but if I may say so, your bathing suit is somewhat dated. It makes you look like an old lady. Oh, I hope I'm not offending you."

Abigail replied, "No, not at all. Look, I never go swimming. I've had this suit for years. It's the only one I own. I guess I'm stuck with it, and everyone is stuck with seeing me in it."

Janice smiled, "The other girls and I were talking. You and I are close to being the same size."

Abigail looked at Janice's breasts and said, "I don't think so."

Janice laughed, "OK. You got me there. Other than that, we are close. Listen, I'd be happy to lend you one of my swimsuits. You might be more comfortable in it. Stand out less, if you know what I mean."

Abigail laughed, "So you don't like my fashion taste in swimwear. Well, I'll be honest. Neither do I."

"Great. Come below with me and we'll try on some of my suits. OK?"

Abigail followed Janice down the staircase to the crew's quarters. Tiffany came along. The crew slept two to a cabin, and Tiffany shared the space with Janice. She went to a bureau and started to pull out bikinis. Abigail's eyes widened. "Oh my, I couldn't wear one of those. I'd be so embarrassed."

Both of the other girls laughed. Tiffany said, "Of course you can. You'll look spectacular. You only live once. You might as well make the most of it. Try it. If you don't like it after a day or so, you can always go back to your old one. We are only trying to help. I hope you realize that."

"I do realize it and I appreciate it." She thought for a minute and finally said, "OK. Let me try the pink one." Minutes later, she was admiring herself in the mirror. The bikini was the smallest thing she had ever imagined. It made Lorena's bikini look like a tent in comparison, but she had to admit, she liked what she saw. It was something she had never before attempted. It left very little to the imagination, but again, she liked what she saw. The two other girls hooted and hollered and were very free with their compliments. They knew she would 'knock them dead.'

"You go, girl!" shouted Janice.

Abigail smiled, put her robe on over her new swimsuit, and went back to her cabin. She wondered when she would have the nerve to show the new Abigail to the world. She knew it would not be today. Tomorrow perhaps.

Dinner that evening was another masterpiece presentation from Monica and Suzette. The wine chosen to accompany each course was excellent and resulted in most everyone having a bit too much.

Lorena and Antonio sat off by themselves, heads close together, obviously enjoying each other's company. Abigail had never been exposed to sudden romances, or if the truth be told, any romances. She didn't know what, if anything, to do. She wished Lorena well and hoped she didn't get in over her head. It was obvious to everyone, even Abigail, that Antonio was skilled in matters of the heart.

The other seven passengers sat together. Sylvester and Dexter did most of the talking. Sylvester, in particular, waxed eloquent about the sweeping changes his father was planning once he was swept into the White House. Lionel Simms exchanged several pointed glances with Phyllis Greenfield. These two were experts on the economy and both doubted the veracity of Sylvester's words. If they were true, the Berkshire presidency was to be avoided at all costs.

Abigail liked Lionel Simms. He did not say much, but when he did, it was always well-reasoned and well-articulated. If one pressed Lionel as to the reason for his introverted manner, he would explain that he had been married for 25 years, and for 25 years, he had tried to get a word in edgewise. Finally, he admitted defeat and gave up.

Abigail noted that if she excluded 'Beavis and Butthead', her dining companions exuded power, competence, and strength. All four knew how the game was played and each was a master in his or her own way. The more Abigail listened, the more she desired to emulate them. They were all wealthy and successful. Two thoughts occurred to Abigail. The first was that money is the medium with which the score is kept. The second, which is a corollary of the first, is that money is portable power. The accumulation of wealth is the measure of how well one plays the game. Everything else was meaningless. In that moment, Abigail found a goal. She wanted to be spectacularly wealthy and experience all the accouterments that were included. Not the possessions and things money can buy, but the respect and recognition that being wealthy brings.

She joined Phyllis and Rebecca on deck for a nightcap and more conversation. Finally, she realized that she was becoming very tired. She excused herself and went below. As she was entering the passageway leading to her cabin, she saw Lorena and Antonio walking in front of her. They were oblivious to everything but each other. Abigail was shocked when Lorena walked past her own cabin and entered Antonio's. She didn't know if she should be happy or worried about Lorena.

The next morning Abigail awoke with unbridled anticipation. She hurriedly dressed in her new swimsuit and put her robe on over it and went to the dining room. She was not the first one there this morning. The Simmses were there, as was Phyllis Greenfield. Janice came over to offer coffee and juice and gave Abigail a wink and a smile. Abby nervously smiled back and also shrugged her shoulders in a "what the heck" gesture.

Antonio was the next to arrive and Abigail wondered where Lorena might be. Rebecca was next, and was followed in short order by Dexter and Sylvester. Finally, Lorena made her appearance. She looked well-rested and satisfied.

Everyone was lively and cordial at breakfast. Much to everyone's surprise, Lionel Simms even cracked a few jokes. Even more surprising, they were very funny and delivered in a deadpan manner, which only served to make them funnier. The breakfast, combined with absolutely perfect weather, foretold of a wonderful day to come.

Eventually, everybody made their way on deck. "Beavis and Butthead" climbed into the Jacuzzi and the three stewardesses lost their tops without any prompting. Abigail returned to 'her' deckchair and stood there for a moment, making a show of stretching. No one paid any attention to her. Then she lost the robe. Things changed immediately. Every eye on the boat focused on her and only her. If one was listening closely, he would have heard the sounds of jaws dropping. Abby stretched a few more times, trying desperately to keep the terror and the smile of triumph off of her face. This was so alien to her that she was terrified and excited at the same time. Janice and her two co-workers started clapping and cheering. Finally, she sat down and made a show of slathering sunscreen on her. She was like a tenderfoot lost in the wilderness without a map or a compass. She had to improvise. She laid back and took in some sun. Then she got up and went to the whirlpool. Again, every eye followed her every movement.

As soon as she sat down in the whirlpool, the two lost sheep moved over and sat on either side of her. Both tried chatting her up. Brittany came to her rescue with a screwdriver cocktail even though she had not ordered it. Abigail thanked her, took a sip, and then started a conversation with Brittany about how good it tasted. When it was obvious that they were being ignored, Dexter interrupted and sent Brittany to fetch two more screwdrivers.

Sylvester, always the spoiled brat, said, "Don't you think you're a little overdressed?"

Dexter, always willing to play stooge to Syl's lead, chimed in, "You look like you're bundled up for a snowstorm. I think you should sit back and make yourself comfortable."

Before she could answer with an appropriate barb, Lionel and Dorothy climbed into the pool. Evidently, each had previously ordered a Margarita because Tiffany came over carrying a tray with two of the frozen concoctions made famous by Jimmy Buffet. The couple sat back, closed their eyes, and relaxed. The group in the hot tub was silent for a short while, then Lionel Simms opened his eyes and asked Sylvester, "If you don't mind my asking, what can you tell me about Uzbekitherm? I know that they are trying to be an up-and-comer on the Middle East energy scene, and that's about the extent of what I know about them."

Sylvester answered with a self-satisfied smile, "They are a joint venture between Mr. Abdul Shaytan, our host on this cruise, and several current and past members of the Uzbek government. Mr. Shaytan is the president and CEO. There is more than a strong possibility that Uzbekistan is sitting on top of the biggest oil deposit on the planet. My company, Uzbekitherm, is getting in on the ground floor on the exploration, drilling, and, hopefully, transportation of the oil. The profit potential makes my head spin."

"Really, do say? What makes you so sure?"

Sly responded, "Well, for starters, Mr. Shaytan is involved. He has a nose for making money. If he did not think that he could make a bundle, I promise you, he would not waste his time. That was enough for me to sign on."

"What exactly are you going to be doing on the board of directors?"

Sly laughed, "Oh, this and that. My role has not been exactly well-defined. Mr. Shaytan thinks that I will bring a fresh perspective and point of view that the rest of the board desperately needs. He said that he has never met anyone with my common sense before."

Lionel almost choked on his drink. "Sorry, I guess it went down the wrong way."

Oblivious to the sarcasm, Sly continued to march straight ahead. "I'm pretty proud of what I have accomplished so far in my life. I'm not bragging, but I am my dad's closest and most trusted adviser. I wouldn't be surprised if I am appointed to a cabinet post after the election."

Lionel glanced at his wife. He saw her roll her eyes wildly. He thought to himself, "God help us all."

"I'll be traveling to Dubai at least once a quarter for the board meetings. I'm looking forward to it. I don't know that much about that part of the world. Dexter here tells me they are famous for a certain type of whiskey. I love good booze, and I can't wait to try some."

Lionel had another coughing fit, and Dorothy had to pound his back to get it to subside.

Abigail took pity on Lionel, so she jumped in. "Sylvester, you must have a broad science-based educational background and probably a business degree, as well, for you to get such an important job. Not to mention all you do for your father. Where did you go to school?"

"Oh, here and there. I started at Brown, but I really didn't like it. I transferred to a liberal arts school, but I got bored. There was no partying or anything. Most of the kids were nerds who spent most of their time studying. I talked my dad into letting me take a year off to find myself. I really grew up that year. It was marvelous. I then went to a state school, but I didn't find it challenging enough."

He was interrupted by Dorothy's coughing fit. "I'm terribly sorry. There must be something going around. Both Lionel and I are a couple of coughing fools."

Sly just nodded and smiled. Then he continued, "Anyway, there was a community college near the house. They have a terrific general studies program. I ended up transferring there and finished in three years. I've never looked back."

Even poor, sweet, innocent Abigail was astounded by Sylvester's tale. She changed the subject before her head burst by asking Dexter, "Tell me, Dexter. You and Sly have been friends for a long time. Tell us a little about yourself. Did you meet at Brown?"

Dexter was much more reserved than Sylvester. "Hardly. There is no way I could afford an Ivy League school. No, Sly and I met in high school. We both had similar interests, booze and broads."

They both had a chuckle at this remark. "Right on, bro," shouted Sylvester.

Dexter leaned his head back as if recalling a pleasant memory. "I went to an upstate school and studied business. My grades were good but not spectacular. After graduation, I moved to New York and got into real estate. I specialize in property in the five boroughs, Long Island, and Atlantic City. Sly and I kept in touch over the years and get together whenever we can. When he got the invitation from Mr. Shaytan for this cruise, he asked me to come, and of course, I said yes. I'm glad I did. I'm having a great time, and it takes my mind off of my problems in New York."

Lionel said, "Problems? What sort of problems?"

"Oh, nothing serious. Just a slight misunderstanding with the Assistant US Attorney for the Southern District of New York's office. No big deal. But I will say one thing. Those guys don't have much of a sense of humor.

Lionel drolly replied, "You don't say."

Abigail feared that questions might start coming her way. She didn't want to answer any right then, so she told everyone that she was turning into a prune from soaking so much and was going back to her chair for some sun. Abby stood up, having completely forgotten the new swimsuit she was wearing, and immediately became conscious of the stares she was receiving. Instead of trying to cover up or exit the pool quickly, she picked up her glass and made a show of draining it. Then she slowly sauntered to the ladder and climbed out. Heck, if they wanted a show, she would damn well give them one.

When Janice walked by her chair a little while later, Abigail asked her to bring her a strawberry Margarita. Janice returned promptly with the drink. As she handed it to her, she told Abby that she and the other two girls were watching her in the Jacuzzi, and that they were so proud of her for the way she handled herself. She surprised Abigail when she told her that they would be making landfall sometime tomorrow. They were going to dock at Atlantic City and everyone, including the crew, was going to the Darby Clark Show at one of the big hotel casinos on the Boardwalk as guests of Mr. Shaytan. Darby Clark was a sexy brunette with a killer body, deep blue eyes, and a voice that would rival anything in heaven. Janice told her everyone in the crew was 'super excited.' Mr. Shaytan always got the best tables in the house. Abigail smiled broadly. She liked listening to Darby Clark's songs.

Abigail looked around the deck. Lorena was lounging next to Antonio sunbathing topless, as were the other two women. Abby wanted to try it, but she was much too shy. Maybe next time. Lorena and Antonio were becoming quite an item. She wondered what would happen when the cruise ended. His concert tour started in Vegas in a month, and Lorena has this fabulous job in New York. It will be interesting to watch how it plays out.

Early the following afternoon, Abby sighted land off of the port bow. As she watched, the spec became larger and larger, and finally, the tall hotels of Atlantic City came into view. Captain Sorenson maneuvered the yacht alongside the dock in the marina, and in no time Richard and Bruce had her tied off and a gangway put in place. Word was spread throughout the boat that a shuttle bus would pick everyone up and take them to the casino around 5:00 p.m. Everyone was free to explore, try their luck at the tables, go to the bar, whatever they pleased. They would all meet in the lobby outside the casino's theatre at 8:30 p.m., get seated, and order dinner.

Abby went below to get ready at 3 o'clock. She had a nice dress that she planned to wear. Just as she finished dressing, there was a knock at the door. Tiffany looked in and started to say something. Then she stopped. "Are you really planning on wearing that tonight?"

Abigail was crushed. "What's wrong with what I'm wearing? It's the best dress that I own."

"Nothing's wrong with it if you are going to a ladies' club tea. You are going out on the town. You need to dress the part."

"Well, this is the best I have. It will have to do."

"Like hell it will. Come with me." Tiffany led her to Janice's cabin on the next level down and knocked on the door. Janice was wearing a red dress about the size of a postage stamp. She was barefoot and in the process of putting makeup on. Tiffany cocked her head. Janice nodded, took Abigail's arm, and led her into the cabin. She didn't say a word and went to her closet and took out a black dress. This dress looked even skimpier than the one Janice was wearing. "Here, try this on. I think it will fit you just fine."

Completely embarrassed and self-conscious about undressing in front of others, Abby complied. She was right. It was skimpier than Janice's dress. She thought it covered even less than the swimsuit.

Tiffany and Janice both nodded their approval. "Now what about shoes," Tiffany asked. "What size are you?"

Abby told her, and Janice said, "That is the same size Brittany wears. You've worn heels before, haven't you?" Abigail shook her head, "No."

"Well, those flats will never do. It's time you learned."

Tiffany left the cabin and returned a few seconds later with two pairs of high heels. One pair looked high to Abby. The second pair looked like stilts. Janice took the tall pair and said, "Here, put these on." Abby did as she was told. "OK, now take a couple of steps to see how they feel." She was as wobbly as a new-born giraffe and almost fell over. Both girls laughed.

Tiffany said, "They take some getting used to and a lot of practice. Let's try the other pair." Abby repeated the process and this time was much steadier, but she yearned for her comfortable flats.

The two girls then sat her down at a mirror and proceeded to redo her hair and put makeup on her. They oohed and aahed, very proud of their efforts. Poor Abigail thought that she looked like a tart.

Then Tiffany said, "I just remembered why I went to your cabin in the first place. Bruce will be your escort tonight. He is a great guy, single, a great dancer, and a lot of fun."

"Oh, I wouldn't want to be a burden on him."

Tiffany replied, "You won't be. Look, the other passengers are paired up: the Simmses, Sylvester and Dexter, Phyllis and Rebecca, and Lorena and Antonio. You will both have a great time. We do this all of the time when we have singles. With men, one of us will serve as their escort. There's never any monkey business, just good company. And don't worry about money tonight. Everything is covered by Mr. Shaytan. If Bruce picks up a check, he'll turn in an expense account. So your job tonight is to just enjoy and have fun."

Eventually, it was time to leave the yacht. Abigail wobbled to the gangway where Bruce was waiting for her. He was wearing a navy blue blazer, a starched white shirt, and white trousers. With his tanned face, he looked great. Abigail walked down the gangway and tried to gracefully climb into the private shuttle bus without exposing all of her charms for the world to see. She had no idea how other girls did it. Bruce helped her into the bus and sat beside her. He was very nice and she liked his British accent. He told her he graduated in hospitality management from the University of Manchester and decided to use his degree in the big yacht industry. He planned to take the Boson exam next year and, after that, he would need to decide if he wanted a career as an engineering officer or as a bridge officer. Abigail was fascinated. She had no idea that this industry even existed.

When they arrived at the casino, everyone went inside to try their luck. Abby followed Bruce to a blackjack table and the two of them watched the action. Bruce explained the rules of the game to her, but she declined to play. She was too shy. Then they went to the craps tables. Again Bruce tried to explain the rules to her, but they seemed incomprehensible. Finally, he took her hand, pointed at a spot on the table, and told her to put a chip there. A man rolled the dice, and Bruce smiled broadly. Then a man dressed in a gold vest put another chip next to her chip. Bruce said, "You won. Just leave both of them there and see what happens." Abigail couldn't believe it. Every time someone rolled the dice, the nice man in the gold vest put more chips on top of hers. Much too soon for Abigail, Bruce said, "OK, let's pick them up and go somewhere else."

"Oh, do we have to? I'm having so much fun. I like winning."

Bruce laughed, "I'm sure you do. Look pick them all up but one. Leave that and see what happens." This time after the dice were rolled, the nice man in the gold vest did not put another chip on top of her chip. He used a cane and scooped her chip away. She looked at Bruce, who smiled and said, "You lost. You never know when it is going to happen, so I never try to press my luck too far."

They walked around the casino for a while, and finally, Bruce took her over to a slot machine. He had purchased several rolls of quarters and handed them to her. He explained how the machine worked and watched her as she played. At one point she was winning big, but at last, she was down to her last quarter. When that was gone, he said, "It's time. Let's go meet the others in the lobby."

As they walked to their tables, Abigail noticed that the eye of every male was fixed firmly on the three stewardesses. They were gorgeous and they knew how to play it to the maximum: a hair flip here, a wiggle there, a coy smile, and occasionally a wink. She also noticed that quite a few female elbows were directed at their partners' ribs. Surprisingly, she received considerable notice which thrilled and unnerved her at the same time.

Just as their dishes were cleared and coffee and brandy served, it was time for Darby Clark. She came out in a low-cut silver, sparkling gown that fit her like a second skin. She sang for about 45 minutes, told some stories, and bonded with the crowd. Then she said, "Ladies and gentlemen, I don't normally do this, but tonight I'm happy to make an exception. Sitting right over there (she pointed at Antonio) is the famous recording and movie star, Mr. Antonio Spiga." There were some gasps from several women as the spotlight shone upon Antonio and Lorena. "Antonio, can I ask you to come up and sing a number with me?" There was hearty applause, and Antonio rose from his chair, smiled, and walked to the stage. The two embraced, said a few words, and Darby then turned and said something to the orchestra leader. The music started, and the audience recognized it as a very romantic duet where both singers each had solo parts plus the duet parts. It was a challenging song to begin with, but was more so without rehearsal. The two started singing and their voices blended into one glorious sound. When it was time for Darby's solo part, Antonio gazed deeply into her warm blue eyes. She became like a fly hypnotized by a spider just before becoming entangled in its web. Her voice faltered just a bit. He took her hand and kissed it, walked behind her, kissed her bare shoulder, her neck and finally her ear. Her voice noticeably faltered and her legs grew rubbery. He held her tight. At the perfect moment of this embrace, Darby's solo part ended, and, without a hitch, Antonio began his solo. Words cannot describe the beauty and sensuality of his performance. When the song was over and the two embraced to a thunderous standing ovation and cheers, a smiling Antonio returned to his seat. Darby, still obviously on rubbery legs, said into the mike, "I think I need a cold shower after that."

When the show ended, Captain Sorenson told everyone that they should meet at the bus in an hour-and-a-half. Until then, they were free to do whatever they wished. She had never been to Atlantic City and wanted to walk along the famous Boardwalk. Bruce was happy to oblige. The pair walked a good distance on it, and then Abby asked if she could walk on the beach and wade in the surf. She took off her shoes and skipped in the sand like a little girl and then darted into the water and let the surf lick her feet. She told Bruce that this was the first time she had ever done this, even though she always wanted to. Bruce shook his head in disbelief and said he was happy she finally got her wish. They returned to the bus and found everyone to be in high spirits. The captain informed them that they would depart at 9:00 the next morning bound for Nassau and wished everyone a good night.

Abigail had a wonderful sleep that night. It had been a magical evening. She even got used to the dress. The shoes were another thing. They probably were an acquired taste. She put on her swimsuit and robe and headed up to watch the departure. When she arrived on deck, she got the surprise of her life. Sitting on deckchairs were Polina and Barney. They smiled and waved when they saw her.

"What are you two doing here?"

Barney answered, "Things were slow back there. We contacted Mr. Shaytan to ask if we could come along. He said that there was still plenty of room and that we were more than welcome to come. He is such a nice man."

Brittany passed by wearing the tight shorts and small bikini top. She smiled when she saw the two new arrivals. "Well, hello there. It's good to see you again. When did you come aboard?"

"About an hour or so ago. Our bags are still in the main dining area. We just came out here to get out of everyone's way while you all work for a living."

"Welcome aboard. What can I get you to drink?"

Barney and Polina declined anything. Abigail ordered a mimosa. "I'm becoming quite the expert on cocktails since I've been on board," she joked.

Bruce came by and told Polina and Barney that he would take their luggage below to their cabins if they would follow him. He looked at Abigail and smiled, "I really enjoyed last night. You looked terrific and were such a pleasure to be with."

Abigail thanked him for a wonderful evening. Then Bruce left with Barney and Polina following. Brittany returned with the mimosa. She asked, "Did you have a good time last night?"

"I did. I really did. Once I got used to the dress and the shoes, I relaxed and had fun. You all were right about Bruce. He is a truly nice man. What did you think of Antonio and Darby's number?"

Brittany replied, "I'll tell you what, he got her so hot she could boil water right on the stage. Heck, he got me hot. I hope Lorena had a good night. I see they haven't come up on deck yet."

Abigail finished her mimosa and decided to go inside for breakfast. Everything on board was excellent. Monica and Suzette made an incredible culinary team. As Abigail was sipping her coffee, the others started to straggle in. Most looked wide awake and ready to go. 'Heckle and Jeckle' came in looking a bit worse for wear and tear, but nothing to rival the first morning at sea. Finally, Antonio and Lorena came in. Antonio looked ready to run a marathon. Lorena looked as if a slow 100-meter stroll would do her in, but she did have a huge smile on her face under her glassy eyes. Everyone had a silent laugh at her expense. Conversation was lively, with everyone congratulating Antonio for his performance with Darby Clark. He graciously accepted and politely reacted to each compliment.

All of the passengers migrated en masse to their normal deckchairs and cocktail orders were immediately taken. When the stewardesses came back with the drinks, they did so without their tops. Abigail was still wearing her robe. She looked around and three of the other women had also removed their tops. Dorothy Simms was wearing a conservative two-piece suit. To Abigail's shocked amazement, Mrs. Simms reached around and unhooked her top. Lionel immediately coated her back with sunscreen. That left Abby as the only 'fully dressed' female on deck. She shuddered. She just couldn't.

Barney and Polina came up and took the two chairs next to hers. Since they were new arrivals to the yacht, Janice called for everyone's attention and introduced them to the group. Everyone smiled, waved, or nodded a welcome to the newcomers. Barney was wearing a swim shirt, presumably to protect him from the sun. Polina stood and made a show of removing her robe. She was tall and incredibly thin. She was wearing a Brazilian bikini and when she removed her top, it was easy to mistake her for a tall boy. Abigail got up and, still wearing her robe, made her way to the Jacuzzi. Doffing her robe, she climbed in, closed her eyes, and put her head against the wall. Abby sensed others climbing in, but how many she didn't know. Much to her disappointment, she heard Sylvester's nasal voice. "Abigail, my dear, do you realize that you and the new guy are the only people on deck wearing tops. Don't you think it is time for you to relax and enjoy life like the rest of us?"

To her relief, she heard Dorothy Simms' cultured voice reply, "Don't you think it is time for you to stop annoying this young woman? She will do whatever she damn well pleases."

Abigail opened her eyes and saw Dorothy smile at her and give a violent nod as is to say, "Take that." Abigail returned the nod. Dexter thankfully had nothing more to say.

Later after lunch, Abigail was sitting in the dining room alone with Polina and Barney. "Tell me, has anything interesting been happening since I've been gone?"

Barney laughed, "You have only been gone for a little over three days. The world is still the same. Occasionally somebody on TV will wonder where you are. They would love to find you."

"I'll bet they would. I've been doing a lot of thinking about myself and what I want to do. I don't have a plan yet, just a lot of random thoughts I'm wrestling with."

"Let's hear them," said Polina.

"Well, first I want to continue to help people. I want to figure out a way to do it safely. I don't want any more riots. I realize that I won't be able to go back to work at the doctors' office, so I need to be able to make enough money to support myself. I want to be independent. I don't want to depend on the generosity of others. I enjoyed going through the hallways of the different children's hospitals, seeing the faces and their parents' faces when they realized they were better. It made me feel really good. Curing the folks at West Point was also very good, but I just didn't get the same feeling. Am I making any sense, or am I just rambling away?"

"I think that you are making perfect sense," said Polina. "Nobody wants to see suffering, especially in a child." A pause, "Abigail, in a perfect world, how do you see this playing out?"

"I know this sounds weird, but I'd like to have two or preferably three options. The first would be hospital visits. If I can figure out a way to do them safely, I'd love to resume them. Of course, there would not be a charge for that. The next option or options would have a fee. In the short time I have been on board, I've seen that money is important. Without it, a person is largely ignored until it is election season. I don't want to sound selfish or greedy, but I want to earn money, a lot of money. The more I can make, the more I can do. I also need a secluded place where I can hide from the world. Can you imagine if I just showed up at a hospital in London or Dublin or wherever? The happiness I could bring. 'Veni, vidi, vici.' I don't know the 'Latin' for cured, but I would replace 'vici' with that. 'I came, I saw, I cured.' I'd cure and then slip away.

"I have two ideas for making money. I don't know if either is feasible. The first would be to get a large arena or stadium and have lanes put in it. People would stand on either side of the lane, and I would ride through on a Segway. We know my power is good for six feet. If the lanes were seven or eight feet wide, I would only be about four feet from each side. That should be plenty close to the people. I have no idea of the cost involved with doing this, but I think it is worth looking into. There is the rental of the facility, security, insurance, I suppose, and then the business side. You know, accountants, tickets, and things like that.

"The third idea is to open an office or a series of offices around the country. People would make an appointment, go into a private room, meet me, and walk away cured. If I spent a minute a person, given changeover and expected delays, I could see 30 to 40 people in an hour. Of course, I would charge more for this option. What do you think?"

Barney and Polina looked at each other with shocked expressions on their faces. Barney said, "You certainly have been giving this some thought. I think you may be on to something. If I were you, I would get back in touch with Douglas Keenan. He does big productions all of the time. He would certainly have some ideas. I'd start with him."

"I agree with Barney," said Polina. I would add that I would not be the least bit hesitant to charge a lot for your services. It's easier to reduce prices than it is to raise them. I would also say to start on a small scale, say just 10 or 20 thousand people. If you charged

$100 per person, you would gross one to two million dollars. Not a bad day's work.

Polina continued, "I'll tell you one other thing. From what I know of you, you have a very soft heart. That's not necessarily a good thing. People are going to try to get something for nothing. You will get a lot of sob stories about how tough life is for them. Once you start giving cures for free, you won't be able to stop. Your dreams of being able to help a huge number of people will dwindle to just being able to help a few. You have to be strong."

Abigail went back on deck while her companions went below, Barney to make a call and Polina to take a nap out of the sun. Abby sat there deep in thought. It was time to get back in the saddle. After much thought, she decided to leave the yacht at Nassau and fly back to the United States. A rough plan began to develop in her mind. She would fly to BWI Airport outside of Baltimore, rent a car and, pay surreptitious visits to Walter Reed Medical Center in Bethesda, MD, and then visit Johns Hopkins Hospital in Baltimore.

When Tiffany came by to check on her, she asked Tiffany if there was any way to make plane and rental car reservations while on board. Tiffany laughed, "Of course you can. We have better links on this boat than what you can find anywhere on dry land. Let me know when you are ready and I'll set it up with First Officer Karlsson."

Sailing time from Atlantic City to Nassau took four days. By the last day, everyone was ready for dry land. Abby had no trouble at all booking her flight and rental car. She texted Rafi that she would be returning shortly and certainly did not tell him of her planned visits to the two hospitals. He said he was looking forward to seeing her and would let all of the others know. He had been worried about her and was relieved to learn she was all right.

When landfall was made, she left the yacht with mixed emotions. She liked the three stewardesses. They had been very kind to her.

They had brought her out of her shell and showed her that she was more than one dimensional. She tried to return the swimsuit and clothes to Janice and Brittany, but neither girl would hear of it. She would miss them, their joy de vivre, and their camaraderie. While she never became friends with any of the passengers, she liked and respected the Simmses and the two ladies from New York. Antonio was a nice guy, and Abigail hoped he would be gentle with Lorena. Sylvester and Dexter, well, they were a different story. Her first impression of them as slime-balls when they first boarded the yacht was dead-on. If she never saw them again, it would be too soon.

Lorena was somewhat taken aback when Abigail told her that she would be leaving in Nassau. Lorena said, "I was sent on this trip to take care of you. I didn't do much of that, did I?" I'm going to stay on board with Antonio. Tommy will be madder than hell, but he'll get over it. If not, I'll try some other line of work." Abby was pretty sure that Lorena would come back at some point, and when she did, Tommy would take her back. They were a good team, and both knew it.

WALTER REED

Abigail pulled into the main parking area at Walter Reed and went into the main lobby. There was an information desk, but she didn't know who or what to ask for. She stood there looking lost when she saw a young officer walking by. He was wearing an Army uniform, but she did not know what the insignia with two parallel silver bars meant. He also had a brass insignia with wings coming from a center rod with a snake around it. It was all a mystery to her. She stopped him, "Excuse me. I need some help. I'm looking for whoever is in charge here."

His jaw dropped and he said, "Say that again." When she did so, he laughed and said, "Do you have an appointment?"

"No, but I do need to talk to him. It's very important."

He answered, "I'm sure it is, but you can't just pop in and say that you want to see the General. General Tillis is a very busy man."

"I'm sure he is, but I'll guarantee that he really would like to see me." She read the man's name tag. "Mr. Spencer."

"That's Captain Spencer or Doctor Spencer. I'm sorry, ma'am, but I don't know what to tell you."

"Let me show you something, Doctor." She walked towards a bank of elevators. Before Spencer could say a word, the elevator doors opened, and a young man in a wheelchair and an orderly dressed in scrubs exited it. Abigail looked the young man in the eye and smiled at him. She then stood aside. The orderly started to push the wheelchair, but suddenly the young man called for him to stop. He looked down and started moving his feet and then his legs. "My God. Look at this. Quick, help me up." The orderly balked at this request, saying that the young man would hurt himself. The young man decided to take matters into his own hands and put his feet on the floor and tried to stand.

Spencer hurried over. "I'm Dr. Spencer. What seems to be the problem?"

"Doctor, I'm Sergeant Murphy. I was hit by an IED[6] in Afghanistan and paralyzed from the waist down. I couldn't move a thing. Now look."

The orderly added, "That's true, Doctor. He was paralyzed. Now look at him."

Spencer said, "OK. Let's not get too excited. Raise the footrests and lock the wheels." Once the orderly complied, Spencer stood in front of Murphy and, taking each of his hands, helped him to his feet. The orderly was standing right next to Murphy in case of an accident. Smiling broadly, Sergeant Murphy took one tenuous step. Then another. Before anyone could react, he had covered over 20 feet, turned around, and returned.

Dr. Spencer asked the orderly what ward Murphy was on. Once he got the answer, he said, "OK, take us there."

They got off of the elevator and saw too many brave souls in

------

6. Improvised Explosive Device

wheelchairs. Some were able to push themselves while others looked like they had no use of their hands and arms. The orderly explained to Abigail that the latter were quadriplegics and the former were paraplegics. Spencer saw a physician in a white lab coat and approached him. "Excuse me, Sir. I'm Dr. Spencer. I'm an internist on staff here. Do you have a minute to speak to me in private?" The senior man nodded and the two went off by themselves a few feet away. Abigail saw Spencer point to her and then to Murphy. The senior man looked incredulous. They then came to Abigail and SGT Murphy.

"Dr. Spencer has told me an unbelievable story. By the way, I am Dr. Marks. I am the Chief Attending Physician on this ward. All of the patients are under my care. Would you mind telling me who you are?"

Spencer interjected, "I am so sorry. That should have been my first question to you when we first met."

"My name is Abigail Williams. I am from a small suburb of Philadelphia."

Marks nodded and said, "Now that we have those formalities behind us, what is going on? I know SGT Murphy. He has been with us for what, two or three months?"

Murphy answered, "Going on three months now, Sir." He paused, "If I may, Sir?" He started to get up out of the chair.

Marks exclaimed in a loud voice, "Wait a minute. Are you trying to kill yourself?"

Murphy just smiled. The orderly locked the wheels and raised the footrests, and suddenly Murphy was on his feet. He was just a bit wobbly, but happy as a lark. He walked to the nurses' station and back. All of the staff in and around the station looked upon the scene at first with stunned expressions, which rapidly changed to big smiles. Marks took Murphy into a room and examined his back. There were no scars or marks from any of the surgeries. He then ordered a complete workup from the radiology department.

While they were waiting, Abigail excused herself to go to the restroom. As she wandered the floor, she went into as many rooms as possible. She would just go in, smile, say hello, and leave. A flood of yells and screams followed in her wake. Nurses and other doctors ran to see what the problem was. They all came out of the rooms smiling and shaking their heads.

Abigail saw an orderly in the hallway and asked her where the burn ward was located. She then took the staircase up several floors and entered an area to find a lot of suffering. As she passed patients in the hall and walked into the rooms of other burn victims, 'She came, she saw, and she cured.' Horribly scarred and disfigured human beings were now totally unmarked. Their skin was as fresh as the day they were born. There was stunned silence in the ward. One nurse walked into a room to change the dressing on a particularly serious burn injury. When she gently took the old dressing off and saw beautiful, unmarked, fresh skin looking back at her, she fainted. The shocked patient had to call for help.

Abigail looked at a clock and decided she needed to leave. Things were going to start getting crazy. She slipped back into the stairwell and hurried down the stairs to the ground level. She caught the shuttle bus to the parking lot and soon was on the interstate heading north towards Baltimore. She counted her visit to Walter Reed as a success. She was unsure what the reaction of the Army would be towards her. Would they arrest her for trespassing? Would they take her to some secret facility like she had read about in one of the tabloids? She was able to cure a large number of injured service members. These were men and women who risked everything for their country. She made a start. She hoped she would be allowed to return one day to do even more, but she would only do it on her terms.

She pulled off of the interstate just south of BWI Airport and called Rafael Melek. From his previous text she knew he was worried about her. When he heard that she went to Walter Reed unannounced, he became upset. Did she realize what could have possibly happened to her? He confirmed the fears she had when she left the hospital. She said she was going to get a hotel room for that evening near the airport and then call her old medical office. She hoped one of the doctors there knew someone at Hopkins. Rafael told her to let him know what hotel she was staying in, and he would drive up and take her to dinner. They could discuss further plans then.

Neither of them was aware of the havoc she caused at Walter Reed. Once the commanding general was informed of the 'miracle girl's' visit and subsequent departure, he called in Drs. Marks and Spencer and read them the riot act. He questioned their judgment, their common sense, and just about anything else he could think of to question. Unfortunately for the general, while he was discussing their failings with the two doctors, word got out about all of the cures. The media went into a frenzy. The White House Press Office was asked about it. "No comment" was the official response. The unofficial response was the president calling the Secretary of Defense and screaming at him. Sec Def returned the favor by screaming at the Secretary of the Army, the Chairman of the Joint Chiefs, and the Chief of Staff of the Army. These gentlemen, in turn, lined up to voice their displeasure with the CG of WRMC[7]. Things really turned sour when the president learned that this girl was the same girl the Philadelphia Police Commissioner, his old fraternity brother, had given him a heads up about. He contacted the Director of National Intelligence, the heads of the FBI and Homeland Security, the Secretary of Defense,

---

7. Commanding General of Walter Reed Medical Center

and the Director of the CIA and asked why they had failed to keep track of her as he had directed. When a satisfactory answer was not forthcoming, the volcano erupted.

A news conference was held later in the day. As expected, the president received questions about what took place at Walter Reed earlier in the day. He started by downplaying the event. When that did not satisfy the press, he attacked them for spreading 'fake news.' He then called that girl, "a weak, unpatriotic individual. If she really cared about the country and its brave warriors, she would have stayed and finished the job. She is a very nasty person." When asked about her whereabouts, the president said that she was under surveillance and would be apprehended if she tried anything like this again. The reporters left scratching their heads. "Like what? Like trying to cure wounded soldiers?" It was beyond preposterous. One thing was clear, 'that girl' had made an enemy of a very powerful, petty and vindictive individual. No one envied her.

Abigail and Raphael watched the news conference in her hotel room. When it was over, she was in shock. "Why would he say such things? I didn't do anything wrong? I was only trying to help."

Raphael replied, "We lawyers have a saying, 'No good deed goes unpunished.' The longer I live, the truer that statement becomes. Sad but true."

On the television, Senator James Berkshire, the presumptive presidential candidate from the opposition party, was being interviewed by a journalist. "Senator Berkshire, you heard President Diamond's comments about what occurred at Walter Reed this afternoon. What's your take on it?"

"Well, I'll tell you this would never have happened during my administration. A facility such as Walter Reed needs to be secured. People can't just wander in and out. I'll guarantee that something like this will not happen on my watch."

The reporter continued undaunted, "Senator, what do you have to say about the young woman who reportedly cured or caused the recovery of over 100 wounded or injured servicemen and women?"

For a minute, the Senator looked like a deer in the headlights. Then he said, "I don't know who she thinks she is. It's the doctors' job to cure people, not hers." He nodded his head with a smug smile on his face, and that was that.

Raphael sadly shook his head and said, "And thus begins the battle of the morons. God help us all."

CONCLAVE

Raphael and Abigail discussed the next step. Neither thought going to Baltimore and visiting Hopkins was a prudent move given the reaction from the White House and government. It was best to let the sleeping dog lie. They got on their phones and called Dr. Stanton's office, Michael Angelo, Angelina Gabriella, Douglas Keenan, and Tommy Sullivan. Angelina checked and the mansion near Garrison, NY was still available, so they all agreed to meet there the day after next to collectively plot their next move, if any.

Abigail returned her rental car to the airport since she planned to travel with Raphael the next day. She was toying with the idea of swinging by Philadelphia and perhaps dropping in at the office. Abby also considered contacting Diana Chan, the television reporter at CNB. Diana had proven that she wasn't a typical media hack when the story first broke. She was fair and presented the facts in an unbiased manner. Raphael surprised her when he didn't offer any objection. In particular, he thought reaching out to Diana Chan was a good idea. It would allow Abigail the opportunity to explain her side of the visits to Walter Reed, West Point, and the hospital in Ohio. He cautioned her firmly, in the event she granted an interview to Diana Chan, against mentioning President Diamond, the Army, or anyone or anything who might take offense. She should stick exclusively to what she had done and not to the perceptions or opinions of others.

With some hesitancy, Abby dialed Diana Chan's cell number. When the phone was answered, Abigail identified herself as Abigail Williams. Chan was very gracious when she inquired if they had ever met before. Somewhat taken aback by the question, Abigail reminded her of their meeting in the bar in Philadelphia and then going to Jimmy G's Cheesesteaks. Chan then exclaimed, "Now I remember. You are the scorekeeper."

Abby smiled "I was the scorekeeper. Now I'm not sure what I am. Look, the reason I called is that I would like to talk to you. Off the record, if possible."

"Off the record. Now I am intrigued. Yeah, I guess we can meet. Where and when?"

"I think that bar we met in earlier serves lunch. How about one o'clock?

"Done. See you then."

The following morning Abigail and Rafi drove to Philadelphia. It is an easy drive if one doesn't mind the traffic and the quaint manners of Philadelphia drivers. Abigail observed more salutes than she could count. Raphael parked in the garage near the doctors' office. They entered the front door, passing several patients as they did so. They approached the reception desk, and sure enough, there sat 'Attila the Honey' in all of her glory. She looked up without a smile and said, "May I help you?"

Abigail was shocked. "May you help me? I work here."

Thoroughly puzzled, the woman looked Abigail up and down. Finally, recognition set in. "Oh, yes. Hi. How are you? How have you been?"

Seething Abigail snapped, "Never mind. Hit the switch."

The receptionist did as she was instructed, and Abigail and Raphael went through into the main area. Abigail led him to Marguerite Camp's office. The office manager looked up, then jumped up and came around her desk to give Abigail a big hug. Greatly relieved, Abigail told her that they were just passing through Philadelphia and thought she would swing by to say hello to her co-workers. Marguerite told her that they were closing the office tomorrow and that she and the three doctors were heading up to meet with her in New York. She then ran out and gathered all of the people who worked in the practice. They were all excited to see her. Abigail didn't go into details about her adventures but did say that she had taken a few days off and got a little sun.

Later they left the building and crossed the street to the bar. They found a booth in the corner where they would not readily be observed. Rafael ordered iced tea; Abigail a Bloody Mary. He looked at her questioningly. She shrugged and said it was five o'clock somewhere. They both laughed. "I'm afraid I've been somewhat corrupted recently. Come to think of it, this place is where I had my first drink ever. It was when I first met Diana Chan. It was a whiskey sour. That seems so very long ago."

She looked up and saw Diana enter the bar. She waved at her, and Diana approached the table. Raphael stood up and Abigail introduced them. Just after taking her seat, the waitress approached with Rafi's iced tea and Abby's Bloody Mary. Diana ordered iced tea. "That Bloody Mary looks good. They do a nice job here. Anyway, I'm on the clock, and they frown on reporters getting toasted before the evening newscast."

"I was just telling Raphael here that this is where I had my first taste of alcohol, and you were the one who tempted me."

Diana snorted, "I hardly think that was the case." She paused, "OK, what's up? What do you have to tell me that is so secret that it is off the record?"

Abigail took a sip of her drink and said, "Oh, you are sooo right. This is delicious. OK, before I answer you, you tell me something. What is going on with the girl who was doing all of the curing?"

Diana thought for a minute then answered, "Well, you're familiar with Children's Hospital in town here. Then there were the two hospitals in St. Louis, which from all reports were magnificent. Then there was the problem in Ohio.

"A little over two weeks ago she did that healing event at West Point. That made all of the headlines. Then poof. She was gone. Disappeared. This 24-hour news cycle is maddening. The media lost interest and the public forgot about her.

"Then yesterday a woman shows up at Walter Reed, of all places. No one is sure if this is the same woman who disappeared, but most assume it is. Anyway, she wants to see the head of the place. The Army got all wrapped up in its underwear. While they were trying to figure out what to do, she just up and walks around the place, curing wounded and injured patients. Evidently, some of the patients were in pretty rough shape. After she worked her magic, there was no sign that they had ever been wounded. One doctor reportedly spoke with her and said that he thought she told him that her name was Amber Something, but he couldn't be sure. Believe it or not, there is not a single person there who can describe her.

"Of course, the president got involved. Reporters at his news conference yesterday afternoon pulled his chain, and he went off. There were reports that when he got back to the Oval Office, he was almost violent.

"That's all I can tell you. That's all I know. As a profession, we in the media dropped the ball when she disappeared that we didn't try harder to find her. If she really has these powers, think what it will mean to the world."

Her two companions shared a glance. Abigail sighed and said, "I feel sorry for her. Look at the mayhem that has followed her. It's like that quote I read in high school by Shakespeare, 'Cry havoc, and let slip the dogs of war.' If we assume that her motives are pure, she is the victim in all of this. The president hates her. He'd probably like to put her in jail or Gitmo[8]. Desperate people will try anything to get close to her to get cured. People are probably going to get hurt. Look at what happened outside of that house in Springfield. What kind of a life will she have?"

Diana replied with a smile, "That Blood Mary makes you wax eloquent, my dear. Unfortunately, you are probably correct. Something has to be put in place to protect her, as well as her 'adoring fans.' I don't have a clue how to do that, but until she appears again, it is a moot point."

Abigail spoke very quietly, "It's not a moot point. I was the 'scorekeeper' when this began, but ironically I am the reason it started. I am the 'miracle girl.' Somehow, I have been given the power to cure people. Don't ask me how or why or even when. I do not know. It just all of a sudden happened."

Diana was thunderstruck. She sat there with her mouth wide-open. Then she became alive. "Of course! When you and I first met, you were sitting in the park across the street. A mother with two autistic sons walked passed you, and suddenly they were normal. I became so excited about the kids being cured that I totally ignored the real story in front of me. How could I be so stupid?"

Abigail looked her directly in the eyes and said, "I'm easy to overlook. Everyone has been doing it all of my life. Things are

---

8. Guantanamo Bay detention camp

about to change. When we first encountered each other, you threatened that you would sensationalize the healings and make life miserable for all concerned if I didn't agree to meet you. Now trust me, I am not threatening you, but I am making a serious promise. We can sit here and I can tell you off the record what I am thinking of doing, but if you go public with it, I can make sure you are excluded from just about everything. Your call."

Diana noted the firmness that came into Abigail's voice. She was no longer a mousy little girl. She was a strong woman. "Go on. I'm listening ... off the record."

Abigail visibly relaxed. "OK. The first part is on the record. You can go public with it, but do not mention my name. For now, it's Mary Doe, OK? Look I realize some people know that Abigail Williams is the 'miracle girl,' but that knowledge is not widespread. I'd like to keep it that way for now." Diana nodded and gestured to a recorder, silently asking for permission to use it. Abigail nodded and then proceeded to very clearly recount without emotion or embellishment what had transpired from Philadelphia Children's Hospital to Walter Reed. She omitted any mention of the mansion in New York or her adventures on *Soul Searcher*. She emphasized that at Walter Reed, all she did was ask to see the person in charge. It was a chance encounter with a paralyzed soldier that set off the chain reaction. When she finished, she made a motion for Diana to kill the machine.

"Ms. Williams, that is some story. Let me ask you this. Where have you been staying all of this time?"

"A friend has a place in the woods north of New York City, which he loaned me. It is isolated and perfect to get away from everything and everyone."

"It must be. Everyone has been looking for you. For a while, you were every network's lead story. Then you faded away. That is, until yesterday." She paused, then continued, "All right, you told me you were going to share your upcoming plans with me. Off the record. Go ahead, shoot."

"What I am about to tell you is a work in progress. It is by no means a final plan. In fact, I have not spoken a word about it to Raphael here or any of my other friends."

A very surprised Raphael said, "I thought your intention right now was just to get your side of the story in front of Ms. Chan. I didn't know you had a plan or were even working on a plan. Isn't that what we were going to start doing tomorrow?"

'Well, it's never too early to start. Here is where I am so far." She went on to describe the three-prong plan she discussed with Polina and Barney. She said that she needed a source of income; thus she would charge a nominal amount at the stadium events and a larger amount for the smaller, more intimate encounters. The money per se was not important, but she did need to survive. She said that she was telling this to Diana in advance so that Diana would be ready when Abigail decided to break the story. She told Diana that when she reported Abigail's side of the healings, including Walter Reed, that she should start preparing the public for more hospital visits. Diana should emphasize that mobs and riots would be of absolutely no help to anyone and could result in Abigail going into seclusion.

Diana listened. She was not happy. She knew there was a lot more to the story, but if she didn't behave and play her cards right, she would be cut off from it. Here she had a potential inside track, and she did not want to jeopardize it. "All right, Mary Doe, I promise to hold your plans in confidence. I assume you will tell me when to go public. I'll work with the management of my station about getting your side of past events out to the public."

On the drive to New York, Raphael was mostly silent. Abigail was sure that he was irritated with her. Too bad. She had to get on with her life.

By noon the next day, everyone had assembled at the mansion and were chatting on the veranda. Abigail did not disclose any of the details of her time aboard the *Soul Searcher* other than to say that she had a great time, relaxed a lot, got a lot of sun, and the food was to die for. As to Lorena, all she said was that Lorena was having a great time and needed a little more time to unwind. Abigail expected her to return shortly.

Then Abigail got down to business. Everyone was shocked by her sudden confidence and assertiveness. She asked the three doctors and Marguerite if they would put together a plan for hospitals. Her visits to Philly Children's and the two St. Louis hospitals were great successes. They should serve as the model. Secrecy, speed, security, and an exit plan were the keys. She was confident that the three doctors here and their associates in **The Practice** had close contacts at just about every major medical facility in the nation. Dr. Lucas promised to contact **The Group of Five** to get the ball rolling and get back to Ms. Williams as soon as possible. His three associates all rolled their eyes at the use of 'Ms. Williams.' They figured Lucas could not remember Abigail's first name.

Abigail next turned to Doug and Tommy. "I'm going to call this section 'mass healing'. I've been doing a lot of thinking about this. I want to rent the Indianapolis Speedway for my trial." The looks on the faces of all present were precious. There were gasps, groans, and a multitude of other sounds.

Ashen-faced, Doug stammered, "You what?"

"Hear me out now. I've been doing a lot of thinking about this. If we were to set up lanes along the straightaways, we could do 10,000 cures at a time. Each straight is 3,300 feet long and 50 feet wide. If we assume a four-foot by four-foot space per person, we can easily get three lanes with people on each side of the lane. That's six rows of people. Each row will hold 825 people. Six times

825 is 4,950 people. That's only one side of the speedway. You have to multiply it by two to get the total number. Now what I am envisioning is filling both sides of the speedway with 10,000 people. I would get on a Segway and go up and down the three lanes on one side of the speedway. Then I would go over and do the other side. While I am doing the other side, the people on the first side would leave and be replaced by a new group of people. Think about it. If we did three or four sessions in a day, 30 to 40 thousand people could be cured. If we charged $2,000 each, we could gross between 60 and 80 million dollars in a single day." She paused for a while with a smug smile to let this all sink in.

Tommy Sullivan summarized what everyone else was thinking when he said, "What were you drinking or smoking while you were away? This is crazy."

Abigail replied, "What's crazy about it? Is the scale too big? Do we need to make it smaller? Tell me what's wrong with it?"

Doug jumped into the fray. "Think of the logistics. You have to print tickets, rent the speedway, get insurance, retain attorneys, hire security, pay city license fees, figure out how to handle parking, and a thousand other things. Also, why do you think you can charge so much?"

Abigail shrugged her soldiers. "Sick people will pay. We just have to figure out how much. Maybe $2,000 is not enough to charge. Also, Indy is big. Most of the other venues will be smaller. I can't charge different prices based on the location's size. I need to charge enough to make it worth my while.

"Doug, you were billed to me as a big-time producer and promoter. You should be jumping at this opportunity."

Before Doug could even respond, Abigail said, "Let me tell you about the last part of my plan. I think a large number of wealthy people would abhor standing with a group of sick people for an hour or two, especially if it is too hot or too cold or rainy. That is for the common folk. Also, some patients may be too infirm to withstand the stadium route, but not sick enough to be hospitalized. To cater to these groups, I am proposing opening a group of offices around the country. I would visit these offices on a rotating basis and meet with the patients individually. I think one or two minutes should be adequate for each patient. They don't care about me. They just want to feel better. For this class of patient, $20,000 might be appropriate. It would all be handled by appointments with a very short window between appointments. I would ask for cash in advance and charge a hefty percent cancellation fee. We would need to rent the office space and staff for each. Maybe we just hire one set of staff, and they travel from office to office with me. That's an idea. It cuts down on overhead."

She paused and looked around at the group of shocked expressions. She smiled, "You know, the more I talk about it and think about it, the better I like it. I am hoping Raphael can handle this side of the operation as well as acting as my chief legal officer. Maybe Michael and Angelina will have time to help. Now before we go on, I don't expect any of you to do this for free. I will get with each of you a little later to discuss compensation packages." She looked at Dr. Lucas and said, "I'm looking forward to that." This elicited muffled laughs from Marguerite and the other two doctors.

Doug Keenan exclaimed, "Abigail, I have to say I am disappointed in you. This looks to me like you are trying to take advantage of a windfall at the cost of innocent and helpless people. I don't want any part of it."

Doug started to stand up when Abigail stopped him. "Doug, you are a good person. I think in your line of work you see a lot of people who aren't so nice. Tommy, am I right?" Tommy nodded, and so did Doug. "I am counting on both of you to make sure we act honorably in this. I know I can go out and get some hacks who will get the job done and won't give a damn who they step on to do it. I don't want to do that. I want and I need you. Please think about that before you make a decision. You all are the closest thing I have to a family. I don't want to lose you. For now, I suggest that we all sit back, relax, and enjoy Mr. Halvorson's hospitality. We will continue this tomorrow morning."

Abigail left the veranda and the others gathered into their subgroups. The medical group was confident that they could get things started with a few phone calls. "What's gotten into Abigail?" Marguerite asked. "I admit I don't know her that well, my fault not hers, but I have never seen her like this. I'm not sure I like it."

"I don't see anything wrong," commented Lucas. "Everyone is entitled to make a living."

Stanton snapped, "Knock it off, Jim. Something happened to that girl, and I'll bet it was more than Lucius Diamond's attack the other day." Dr. Barr nodded his agreement.

The 'mass healing' group just looked at each other in stunned silence. Finally, Sullivan spoke, "I don't like this one little bit. Something stinks, but I can't put my finger on it. From the way she described it, I don't see anything illegal. Do you?"

Keenan answered, "Illegal, no. Immoral, yes. There is no heart, no compassion, and no feeling in this. It is pure money-grubbing."

Sullivan laughed, "Look at us. We are supposed to be heartless. I'm an agent and you are a promoter. Money is supposed to be everything. If we are not careful, we might be drummed out of Hollywood for actually caring." Keenan just shook his head.

In the third group, Michael Angelo was boiling mad. "I am ready to kick some ass. I don't know where to start. Something happened to her."

Angelina said, "I'm going to find out." She got up and followed Abigail into the house. She caught up to her as she was climbing the stairs. Angelina said, "Hold up. Let's talk."

Abigail innocently asked, "About what?"

"Let's start with your trip aboard the yacht. You haven't mentioned it, and I am curious about it. How did you get to be invited aboard it?"

"I have two friends, Barney and Polina. They know an incredibly rich man from the Middle East who has more money than he knows what to do with. In fact, he has four mega yachts. This one, *Soul Searcher*, is the smallest of the four, and it is gigantic. Well, he invited them to go out on it, but they had a previous engagement. They knew I needed to get away and stay out of sight. They asked him and he was nice enough to invite me. He also graciously didn't mind that Lorena joined me. You should see this boat. It is beautiful."

Angelina hid her shock at the mention of Barney and Polina and smiled patiently, "I'm sure it is really something. Do you know who owns it?"

"Oh, yes. His name is Abdul Shaytan. He is from Dubai."

Click. Alarm bells went off in Angelina's head. "Well, I'll let you get to your room. Maybe after dinner tonight you can tell us all about the cruise. I know Rafi and Mike are dying to hear all about it."

Abigail smiled, "That sounds like fun. See you at dinner."

A very shaken Angelina returned to her group on the veranda. "What's the matter?" asked Mike.

Angelina repeated what she had learned from Abigail. At the mention of Barney and Polina's names, Mike went ballistic. "Those slimy bastards. I said I wanted to kick some ass, now I know where to start."

Raphael and Angelina looked at each other and let Mike calm down. Once he was under control, Mike asked, "What did you say the boat's owner's name was." Angelina told him. Mike threw up his hands and said, "Shit, not him!"

Rafi nodded, "I'm afraid so. In Arabic, Shaytan means Satan."

CURTAIN UP

At dinner that evening, the conversation was about Abigail's adventures on the high seas. She described the opulence of the yacht in great detail as well as the professionalism of the crew. She raved about the food and the excellent service. She talked about the Simmses, as well as Phyllis Greenfield and Rebecca Wagoner. Both Doug and Tommy said that they knew Lionel Simms and Rebecca Wagoner and had good things to say about both of them.

Abigail went into great detail describing Antonio Spiga. She was graphic in her description of him, as well as the reaction of every female on board. When she told the story of Antonio on stage at Atlantic City with Darby Clark, everyone howled with laughter.

Abigail saved Dexter and Sylvester for last. As she recounted their antics and lack of civility on board, the group looked on in disbelief and stunned silence.

She then told them about two friends of hers, the ones who arranged for her invitation to join the cruise, Barney and Polina. She mentioned that they joined the cruise just before *Soul Searcher* departed Atlantic City. They were a relatively quiet couple with whom she spent time chatting and relaxing, and were the first people to hear of her plans and were supportive of them, which made her happy. Abigail missed the eye rolls and looks that Michael, Angelina, and Raphael exchanged over this remark.

In her narrative, Abigail did not mention the dress attire, or more precisely, the lack of dress attire on the boat. Some things are better left unmentioned. She also did not speak much about Lorena other than to say she needed a rest and was unwinding. She expected her to return shorty. Tommy did not look impressed. In fact, he seemed pretty irritated.

Abigail was the first to retire for the evening. After she left, there were many comments about the Abigail of today being markedly different from the Abigail who boarded the boat several weeks earlier. A consensus had not formed as to whether the changes were positive or negative. The jury was still out.

Very early the next morning, Marguerite and the three doctors returned to Philadelphia. They thought that their task was relatively straightforward and should be reasonably easy to put together once **The Group of Five** and **The Practice** were brought in. They could get back to their office, treat patients, and start making calls that very morning.

After breakfast, Douglas and Tommy also departed. They promised that they would start the process of putting together a large scale trial, hopefully at Indy or some other suitable locale. They hoped to have something to report later in the week.

Over coffee, the four remaining associates sat at the kitchen table. The television was on and they had watched Diana Chan present Abigail's side of the story. The local CNB affiliate in NYC picked up Diana's piece, which was broadcast on the Philadelphia affiliate yesterday evening. As promised, Diana reported that she had met with Mary Doe. She went into each episode of Mary's story from Springfield to Walter Reed. With each one, Diana fairly presented Mary's side of the story. The debacle in Ohio and the knee-jerk reaction concerning Walter Reed received just the right amount of scorn from Diana. Good intentions were blowing up in poor Mary's face. Diana closed by saying while Mary was disappointed, she was still committed to helping people in need. She and some associates were working on a plan that would provide for the security and safety of all concerned, yet provide maximum opportunity for those in need to have access to her. She closed by saying, "Speaking for people all over the country, we are all looking forward to Mary's return. We are also counting on calmness and reason to be the order of the day for those turning towards her. This is Diana Chan reporting from Philadelphia."

Abigail excitedly exclaimed, "Perfect!"

Raphael nodded his head in agreement. "She did a good job," he admitted. "She got your side out to the public and left a tease out there to keep them interested. Very good, indeed."

The four discussed the office concept. Raphael lobbied for a small, conservative start. He proposed opening one office and staffing it with an office manager/usher, a receptionist, an accountant, and a clerk. The receptionist would book the appointments. The office manager/usher would ensure the office was always the epitome of cleanliness, neatness, and efficiency. He/she would fetch the patients from the waiting room and take them to the room where they would encounter Abigail. When Abigail left the room after the encounter, he/she would escort the patient to the exit door. Three or four treatment rooms should be sufficient at the beginning. Depending on the success of this single office, decisions could be made about expanding to other cities.

Angelina inquired about the possibility of enrolling the office with Medicare and/or Medicaid. None of the other three thought they were qualified to answer those questions. Then Abigail mentioned that she was adamant about charging at least $20,000 a patient. No exceptions. "When I worked at the doctors' office in Philadelphia, I worked as a records and billing clerk. The discounts the government negotiates are mindboggling. I don't want any part of them. My fee is non-negotiable. They can take it or leave it. It is all the same to me." There was ice in her voice when she said this. The other three looked at each other with disappointment in their eyes.

Abigail continued, "One other path that I am considering pursuing actually came to me at West Point. Remember how excited the athletes, the Superintendent, and everyone else became when I cured the injured athletes? What do you think of me charging an annual retainer fee to any sports team that might want to use my services? Of course, West Point would be gratis, but every other team, amateur or professional, would pay me a retainer. I would stagger the fees based on the team's ability to pay. The Yankees, Cowboys, Lakers, and the alike would be several million a year. Teams in smaller markets would pay less, say two million. The big-name universities would be in the 2 to 3 million range. Smaller schools would pay somewhere between $500,000 and a million. For that retainer, the team would get priority for their injured players to get an appointment." The more Abigail spoke, the more animated she became. She did not notice the total lack of enthusiasm from the other three.

Michael finally asked, "How do you propose going about all this? Are you going to put up bill-boards? I could just see them now, 'Sick? Injured? Contact Abigail Williams. She'll make you better.' Heck, you could get some of the sleaze ball-lawyers whose signs are everywhere to give you pointers. Are you planning on TV commercials? How are you going to pay for all of this? Speaking for myself, I have nowhere close to the amount of money that you are going to need."

Abigail was stumped for a minute. Then she replied, "I haven't gotten that far in my planning. Just thinking about it, I can try to get a loan from a bank to get started. I could offer all of you a percentage of the business for investing in it. I could contact Lionel Simms from the yacht. He is a hedge fund manager and is probably loaded. I could contact Barney and Polina; they might be able to help. After all, Barney drives a Maserati. Those are not cheap." At this, Raphael choked on his coffee. Abigail continued, "I'll bet if they contacted their friend, Mr. Shaytan, he would be interested."

Mike's face was so red it looked as if he might be having a coronary. Raphael was blotting coffee off of his tie. Angelina, ever the voice of reason, said, "There's no need to make any decision right now. I agree you have a lot of possibilities. Let's stay calm and see how things begin to play out with the hospitals and the mass curing event. Abigail, promise me you won't do anything by yourself. I think we are all in this together. All right? Also, I think the fewer people who know about this, the better. I wouldn't mention this to anyone. OK?"

Abigail nodded her assent. "I'm OK. I won't mention this to anyone. I did discuss all of this with Barney and Polina on the yacht. They are the ones who told me not to make exceptions to the charges. They told me to be strong."

The meeting adjourned, and the three visitors got ready to depart. Raphael said he would put together a plan for an office and staffing. Abigail was to do nothing other than wait for things to develop. Raphael said that the hospital visits would probably be the best place to start, as they would generate a lot of publicity with very little investment. In most cases, the hospitals would take care of the security and even the helicopter charges.

As the three were walking towards their cars, Michael told Raphael and Angelina that he would make the call. As he was heading south on Route 9W, Michael placed the call. A male voice answered the phone, "Hello. Michael?"

"Yes, it is I. How are you doing?"

"I am well. And you?"

Michael told the gentleman on the line about Abigail. The man said that he was familiar with her. He had followed the story on TV. Michael then told him about Barney and Polina.

The man on the line responded, "Such a shame. Those two can really muck things up."

Michael then told him about the mysterious Mr. Shaytan and how Abigail thought he might loan her the necessary funds.

"Oh, that will never do. We can't allow that to happen. This whole thing could be incredibly important. Spend whatever you need to. Just keep those creatures away from Abigail. Understand?"

Michael replied, "I thought that that might be your answer. I'll take care of it and make certain that she has what she needs. I'll tell you, the change in her is frightening. She has become self-centered and somewhat ruthless. I can only imagine what happened on that boat."

"Don't be so sure that something happened. You have a young girl who has been in a shell all of her life. She is suddenly exposed to sophisticated, worldly people who have worked hard, achieved a lot, and are now used to the finer things in life. I might add, a life that Ms. Williams never knew existed. She realizes that through no fault of hers, she has missed out on a lot. She now has an opportunity to make up for the lost time, and she is doing so the only way she knows. Be patient with her. I'll wager that she will make us all proud."

With that, the call ended. Michael then placed two more calls to Raphael and Angelina. The calls were concise. He just told each of them that funding was in place. They knew what he meant and just responded, "Good."

A week later, Dr. Stanton called. He was excited. Through his contacts, he had arranged a multi-day blitz through Boston. The first stop would be Boston Children's Hospital, followed by the famous Mass General Hospital, and ending with the Dana-Farber Cancer Institute. He recommended setting aside three days for this visit. Each of the hospitals promised air-tight security while she was on site. The problem was where to go in the evenings that would be secure. Abigail said that she would make some calls and get back to him ASAP.

Since this trip would be in New England, she called Angelina. Angelina lived and worked in southern New Hampshire, about an hour's drive from downtown Boston. She would know what to do. Sure enough, Angelina had the solution. Arrangements would be made for Abigail to fly into Portsmouth International Airport located at the former Pease Air Force Base. A helicopter would take her to the rooftop helipads at each of the hospitals. In the evening, the same helicopter would take her to the Isles of Shoals located off of the coast from Portsmouth. Here she could stay at the Oceanic Hotel on Star Island. The isles are fairly remote and relatively easy to secure. At the end of the visit, the helicopter would return her to the airport at Pease.

A week later, Abigail departed from Stewart International Airport by private jet to Portsmouth International Airport. A short helicopter ride then found her on the rooftop of Boston Children's Hospital. As promised, security was extremely tight. No news of the impending visit leaked. The hospital was immense, and Abigail committed to covering every floor and every ward. At 8:00 p.m. and three Segways later, she had completed her tour. She was exhausted and exhilarated at the same time. The chief executive of the hospital accompanied her to the roof and was effusive in his gratitude. While Abigail appreciated his thanks, she was more gratified by the faces on the children as she passed by.

This scene was repeated the next two days at the other two hospitals. Finally, an emotionally drained and exhausted Abigail departed New England for the mansion in New York. Before getting on the plane at Pease, Angelina came up to her with a man in his forties. "Abigail, I want to introduce Jimmy Halvorson to you. Jimmy is my boss, and he is also your host. You have been staying at his place in New York."

"It's a pleasure to meet you, Mr. Halvorson. I want to thank you for your incredible hospitality. I can't tell you how much I appreciate it."

Jimmy replied, "Think nothing of it. I am thrilled to be able to help, to be a small part of this incredible miracle you are working. You are changing so many lives."

When Abigail turned on the television after she returned to New York, she was pleased to see all of the positive coverage of her three hospital visits. The press ran countless interviews with patients and family members, many of whom were very emotional, expressing profound thanks and gratitude for what Abigail did.

She called William Stanton after breakfast the next morning. He told Abby that his phone had not stopped ringing with congratulatory calls from all of his colleagues in Philadelphia, as well as around the country. Hospitals all over the world were clamoring for a visit. "Just say the word, tell me where you want to go, and I'll make it happen. By the way, every hospital has agreed to pay all of your expenses, including a private jet and secured lodgings. Most have also offered to pay you an honorarium. From my experience in dealing with these large institutions, you won't get rich on what they will pay, but you will be able to live comfortably."

She told him she would wait for the other two groups to report in and then get back to him.

Two weeks passed by and Abby was ready to climb the walls. She was going stir crazy. She was determined to call Stanton and set up another hospital visit if she didn't hear from one or the other groups by noon. At 11 o'clock, the intercom from the front gate announced a visitor. The cook listened for a moment and then pressed the button, causing the gate to swing open. Abby walked to the kitchen door and looked on in surprise as Lorena Mason exited her car. Abby went out and the two women embraced.

Later, while sitting at the kitchen table drinking lemonade, Lorena recounted her adventures on *Soul Searcher* après-Abigail. To no surprise of Abigail's, Lorena admitted that Antonio was not head-over-heels in love with her. She said he felt deeply about her, treated her wonderfully, and was never anything less than charming. When *Soul Searcher* made port in Miami, things started to deteriorate. Antonio's agent, as well as Antonio's personal assistant, a spectacular brunette a la Sophia Loren complete with an Italian accent, came on board. The three went to Antonio's cabin, where they remained for an hour, after which the visitors departed the boat amid much waving, blowing kisses, and calling 'ciao.' Antonio told her that the pair came to update him on his upcoming tour. There was an immediate opening that just came up at the WinStar Casino in Oklahoma. The act that was initially booked had to cancel due to some personal crisis. The casino's management was desperate to fill the slot and offered it to Antonio at a very attractive fee. If he accepted, it would give him extra rehearsal time, which always helps when going out on an extended tour. He could not pass up an opportunity like this. She admitted to Abigail that she hoped he would ask her to join him, but that thought did not cross his mind. His focus totally changed from her to the casino in Oklahoma and the international tour following.

She told Abigail that she left the yacht in Miami and caught a plane to New York. She went to Tommy's office, very much the prodigal daughter, and he took her back without making her grovel too much. She was sent to the mansion today to brief Abigail on the progress he and Doug were making.

"I can't believe you asked them to book the Indy Speedway. That is totally so unlike you. Were you drunk or on drugs when you made the request?"

Abigail answered, "Of course not. You know me better than that."

Lorena replied, "Yeah, I thought I knew myself better than that, too." She went on to say that Doug had looked into Indy, but decided that it was too complicated for an initial trial. He was able to get the Pocono Raceway in northeast Pennsylvania for one day. She told Abby that this location was within two hours of both Philadelphia and New York City. It is not in an urban area and has plenty of parking. The management there can provide security, concessions, and whatever else is needed. Both Tommy and Doug recommended starting in a location like this. It is plenty big, so she will get noticed; it is not so big that it will be impossible to control.

Abigail asked her how many people could be accommodated. Lorena told her 10,000 to 25,000 was in the realm of possibility. Abigail then asked how much it was going to cost to rent the raceway. Lorena told her. Abigail gasped. "There is no way I can afford that."

Lorena replied, "Tommy knew that the price was going to make you blink. But that's not all. You have insurance, security, printing tickets, advertising, and a whole lot more."

A very pale Abigail asked, "What is the total cost going to be?" Lorena told her. Abigail was crushed. She knew that if she could get this event off of the ground that she would have enough working capital to fund future events and start putting money in the bank. Mentally Abigail reviewed the possible sources that she previously thought of. Before she could say anything, Lorena ventured that Tommy thought getting the group together again was the way to go. They were resourceful and had a lot of contacts, including Lionel Simms and Phyllis Greenfield.

Abby called all of her associates. They were all pleased to hear from her and promised that they would be at the mansion the following morning before noon. Dr. Stanton and Marguerite were the only ones from the medical practice planning to attend. The other two physicians were seeing patients.

When the group assembled on the following morning, Doug told everyone of his success in booking the Pocono Raceway. There was genuine excitement in the group. Doug and Tommy reviewed the estimate of the costs involved. To Abigail's surprise, there were few expressions of shock and dismay. Dr. Stanton and Marguerite looked mildly concerned but did not say anything. Raphael, Angelina, and Michael almost looked bored, as if such a paltry amount was not even worth discussing. Abigail almost said something, but before she uttered a word, Michael said, "I have some friends. I told them about Abigail and what she wanted to do. They told me to tell her not to worry about money. They would finance her."

Lorena exclaimed, "How wonderful. Do you mind my asking who the people are?"

Michael replied cryptically, "Let's just say that they are old associates of mine." The general consensus at the table was that Michael must have ties with the Mafia and called them in. No matter. Funding was secure, and after all, it was for a good cause.

Abigail announced that she thought bringing Diana Chan in on the story now was the right thing to do. She would do a live interview with Diana and announce details of the Pocono event, including how to purchase tickets. She shocked her guests when she said that the price of the tickets was going to be $200 each.

Dr. Stanton asked, "Don't you think that is a little steep?"

"Not at all. We have a huge overhead to cover. We need to get funds for the next event. Plus, I want to start earning money. On second thought, maybe $200 is not enough. What do you all think of $250 or even $300? We set a price and see who comes."

Raphael answered, "I agree with William on $200 being steep. I definitely would not go higher than $200."

Abigail called Diana and told her that she was willing to do a live interview. Diana was thrilled. They agreed to meet at the Visitor Center at Valley Forge National Park and then find a private and scenic spot to conduct the interview.

The weather the next day was glorious, a lot of sunshine, deep blue sky, a few very white clouds, and a slight breeze. Conditions were perfect. The technical crew directed the two women to positions that accentuated their features. With Raphael standing off to the side out of camera view, Diana opened the interview by saying, "I am at the Valley Forge National Park and am joined by Mary Doe. Mary has recently made headlines with her uncanny gift of curing people. She has been the target of several disturbances when crowds became unruly, and in some cases, violent. Through it all, she has acted with bravery and kindness."

Abbey cut in, "Ms. Chan, we all know that my real name is not Mary Doe. It is Abigail Williams. I am from Upper Darby and have lived in this area my entire life."

Somewhat surprised by this revelation, Diana continued the interview with questions about her past adventures. Then she asked about her future plans. Abigail told her she wanted to continue with the hospital visits. She spoke about planning to open a series of offices throughout the country for personal visits. Finally, Abigail announced the upcoming event at the Pocono Raceway. She described how it would operate, that tickets were available for purchase, and finally how to purchase the tickets. She that they were selling tickets to this event to control the size of the crowd, to defray the cost of renting the raceway, and cover the expenses of running the event. From the look on Diana's face, Abigail knew that Diana was aware that she had just participated in a commercial.

When the tickets went on sale, the results were mind-boggling. Over 50,000 tickets were sold on the first day. An additional 10,000 parking passes were also purchased. Promoters bought multiple tickets and put together excursion packages, which included bus transportation.

Crowds swarmed the raceway early in the morning of the event. Traffic was jammed for miles on both I-80 and I-476. The mood was festive, even though there was a slight chill in the air. Pocono is known as 'The Tricky Triangle' because it is in the shape of a triangle. Lanes were set up on each of the three straights, and each ticket indicated the straight that the ticket holder was assigned. Abbey would stand in a modified golf cart that almost resembled the Popemobile without windows or walls. She would go up and down each row of a straightaway and then move to the next straight and repeat the process. Once people were cured, they would exit the raceway and be replaced by people holding tickets for the next 'seating.'

Abigail was elated. She would gross well over ten million dollars. She arrived by helicopter to a staging area in pit row. As she was walking to her dressing room, she passed a very young boy who was standing all alone and crying. She stopped and asked him what was wrong. He said that his mother was outside. They wouldn't let her come inside. She is very, very sick, but she can't afford a ticket. He said that he ran through security to see the 'magic lady', but now he is lost and wants his mother. He is afraid she is going to die and he is frightened. Abigail's first inclination was to give the boy a hug, have his mother brought in, and cure her. Then she remembered Polina's warning about hearing a lot of sob stories and the need for being tough. She looked around and saw a policeman. "Officer, this boy is lost. His mother is outside. Would you please bring him back to her?" The officer took the boy, and Abigail turned in the direction of the dressing room. Several times she had the urge to turn and call to the officer, but each time she fought the urge down. Feeling like subhuman slime, she finally arrived at the dressing room, closed the door, and gulped down some champagne from a freshly opened bottle that Lorena had brought in.

"What's the matter with you?" Lorena asked.

"Oh, nothing." Then she told Lorena all about the little boy. When she was finished, she saw the look of disappointment in Lorena's eyes. It was disappointment. It was not disgust or disapproval. She could have handled those. It was a look of disappointment. If possible, Abigail felt slimier than she had a few minutes before.

When Abigail entered the track standing up in the 'Abbymobile', the crowd erupted in a huge cheer. Abigail waved and wore a bright, wide smile. As she was driven up and down the lanes, she tried to make eye contact with as many people as she could. As she passed by, she heard many shouts of 'Oh my God,' 'Thank you, Lord,' and 'I can't believe it.' As the cart turned to go down the next lane, Abigail saw people standing, smiling, walking, and even a few jogging a few steps. There was jubilation. This process continued for several hours until all of the tickets holders were cared for. Abigail was torn with mixed emotions. She was elated at being able to help so many. She hated herself for being so selfish and shallow with that little boy. Yes, Lorena was disappointed in Abigail, but Lorena's disappointment was dwarfed by Abigail's disappointment in herself.

The next few months were like a symphony orchestra building to a crescendo. The big healing events kept getting larger and grander in scale. The intimate office visits at $20,000 each were booked out for six months. Obviously, money was no object for some. The hospital visits were becoming fewer and farther between them. There was no money and plenty of personal risk involved.

Abigail bought a secluded estate in the Great Smokey Mountains right on the Tennessee – North Carolina border. The very secluded estate had high walls, a magnificent main house, and a state of the art security system. It was almost impossible to find. It was perfect.

Then the orchestra finally reached the climax. It came in the form of Michael Angelo arriving unannounced at the main gate of the compound on a blustery winter's day. He came in, took a seat by the fire, and sipped on a cup of hot cocoa that Abigail ordered from the cook.

He looked at her. "How's it going?"

"Oh, OK, I guess."

"Well, I don't think it is going so well. I don't think you are at all happy."

"What do you mean?"

"Look at you. It's noon and you aren't even dressed. From what I hear, you go days on end without getting dressed or going outside. You've got the world by its tail and you're letting it get away. Come on. Get up. Go upstairs, get dressed, and pack a bag. You're going to be gone for three or four days. Nothing fancy. Jeans and comfortable casual clothes are what you need."

"Why? Where are we going?"

Big Mike stood up. Mike was a very large man, a very imposing man. When he stood up and looked down at someone, he commanded their utmost respect. "Girl, you ask too many questions. For once, do as you are told. Now get your butt in gear, go upstairs, get dressed, pack a bag and be back down here ready to go in half an hour. Now move."

A quick 45 minutes later, they were in Michael's car heading south towards Georgia.

THE MONASTERY

They drove for about six hours, mostly in silence. Michael would stop every so often for a break or a bite to eat. Abigail wondered if they were heading to Florida. She had realized early on that Michael was in no mood for questions and idle chatter, so she remained silent unless he said something to her.

They drove about three hours south of Atlanta through the Georgia countryside. There wasn't much to see along the way. It was a pretty boring drive. Michael finally reached the exit and turned off of the interstate. Abigail found herself on a narrow two-lane road. It did not have shoulders and was hilly and winding in places. She kept worrying that they would meet a good old boy in a pickup truck that was heading towards them in their lane while attempting to pass a little old lady who was traveling well below the posted limit in her lane. Thankfully, that did not come to pass.

They eventually came to a very unobtrusive sign that directed all visitors to the Monastery of St. Mary and the Martyrs to turn to the right. The two-lane road became a one-lane affair that Abigail was hard-pressed to call an improved road. It was like one continuous pothole with ruts added to give it character. She had no clue as to what happened when it rained.

After a mile or so, they arrived back in civilization. The monastery was a series of attractive, modern, single-story buildings set in and around the tall Georgia pines. It was very peaceful. The sense of tranquility was almost palpable.

Michael pulled into a parking space in front of the central single-story building. There was no sign on the structure or any indication of what its function was, but it was apparent to Abigail that this was not Michael's first visit to this place. He motioned for her to follow him. Once inside, he walked to an office with an open door. He knocked softly, and she heard, "Michael. Welcome back. It's great to see you again." The speaker was a monk. He was the first monk Abigail had ever seen in person, and was dressed the way Friar Tuck dressed in the movies. He was short in stature, about five-foot two-inches tall. His habit was made of coarse woolen cloth. He had a pectoral cross on his chest and a large rosary clipped to his belt. This monk was in his late fifties and was mostly bald. He had an infectious grin and a permanent twinkle in his eyes. The monk rose from his desk, came around and gave Michael a big hug. Abigail noted that Michael was careful not to crush the smaller man with his embrace.

Michael sincerely replied, "Father Jubal. It is my pleasure to see you. You are looking great." He paused a moment and then said, "Father Jubal, may I present Abigail Williams? Abigail is the lady I presume you have heard about that is going around the country curing people."

Father Jubal shook Abigail's hand, "My, yes. This is a real pleasure, young lady. You have a unique gift, and from what I have heard on the news, you are mostly using it wisely."

"Thank you, Father. It is nice to meet you, too." Abigail wondered what the 'mostly' in 'using it wisely' meant.

"Come in. Come in. Let's find Father Buchanan. I think he is in the great room relaxing by the fire. They entered a lavishly decorated room with a huge fireplace with a warm, inviting fire blazing. Sitting in an easy chair near the fireplace reading a book, was a monk who appeared to be in his early to mid-seventies. He stood when the visitors entered the room and greeted Michael warmly. He had distinguished silver hair, bright blue eyes, and a very warm smile. He was very gracious when Father Jubal introduced him to Abigail.

Father Buchanan invited them to join him near the fire. They made small talk about the weather and such, as well as the drive down from Abigail's home. It was apparent that they were trying to put her at ease, and she appreciated it.

Finally, Father Buchanan said, "I'm sure you are wondering why you are here. First, let me tell you about his place and this order of monks. I'll start by giving you a thumbnail history our order and this monastery

"We formed as an order about forty years ago. I was one of the founders. I was a hedge fund manager on Wall Street. I received a bachelor's degree from Harvard and my master's from Wharton. Long story short, I made a bundle on the Street, more than I could begin to spend. I had a huge house in Westchester County, a beach house in the Hamptons, and a loft in Manhattan not far from my office. I had it all, but one day I realized I had nothing. If money were the points in a game, I was one of the all-time champions. No question about it. The reality was that the game was meaningless. It was as if I was the world champion of Solitaire. By the way, I wasn't married or even dating anyone. It was just me, and I just kept racking up the score. One Sunday, as I was leaving St. Patrick's after Mass, I bumped into several acquaintances also leaving Mass. Someone suggested going to brunch at the Waldorf, and we all agreed that was a capital idea. It seems that I was not the only one at the table dissatisfied with what he was doing. There had to be more to life than money. That got me thinking. I did some research, made some phone calls, and presto, the vision was hatched. What if a group of us who knew how the game was played and were masters of the game, got together with the sole purpose of making as much money, legally of course, as was physically possible? The object of making this money was not to accumulate wealth but to use the wealth to systematically combat poverty and corruption worldwide.

"About two weeks after the brunch at the Waldorf, I called the other guys and sprung my idea on them. The other three friends were similarly Catholic and never married. They were hesitant at first, but the more we talked, the more animated they became. Someone even mentioned that we would be modern-day Knights Templar. We all chuckled over this. Over the next few months, we would meet weekly and refine our plan. Finally, we were ready. There was a bishop we were aware of who needed money, real money. His diocese was in the midst of the clergy sex scandal and was hemorrhaging vast amounts of money for legal fees, as well as compensation for the victims. He was in a real hurt. This was years before the story broke nationwide. He was desperate to keep the story quiet. I phoned him and requested an appointment.

"I won't bore you with the details, but we reached an agreement. My three friends and I would enter the seminary for a crash course, and we would be ordained priests in three years. In return, we would work our magic and make this bishop a pot full of money on the QT to allow him to be able to handle the mess he had created. He did, and we did. We were ordained, and he had enough money to keep the scandal under wraps. We also had the clout to operate autonomously.

"Once we were ordained, we requested another audience with the bishop. This time we discussed our hope to form an order of monks with the sole mission of actively fighting poverty and corruption. We explained that this new order of monks would be a very select, very secretive group. All we needed the bishop to do was enroll the candidates whom we would send to him in the seminary and ordain them after they completed their studies. We, of course, would cover the cost of their studies, as well as endow certain facilities and projects that the bishop favored.

"As you can imagine, his Excellency was hooked on the horns of a dilemma. He told us that to create a new order of priests would require the approval of the Vatican. I mentioned earlier that we knew how the game was played on Wall Street. Well, the bishop was a master of the Vatican game. He knew how to navigate the rocks and shoals of the Curia. Somehow he arranged for us to have a very private audience with the new Pope, John Paul I.

Our audience with His Holiness was the epitome of sub rosa. I don't know what the bishop said or whom he said it to when he arranged the audience, but we were taken after normal business hours to a dark alley behind one of the buildings in the Vatican and let out of the car near an unlighted doorway. The car drove off, and simultaneously the door opened. A middle-aged monsignor in a cassock motioned us to enter. After we did so, he turned on the hall light. He led us through a maze of richly decorated halls and rooms and up a flight of stairs. We finally arrived at a closed door, and our guide gently knocked on the door. A soft voice told us in Italian to enter. The monsignor left us at this point. In a very richly decorated office, sitting behind an ornate, antique desk sat His Holiness, John Paul I. He rose and came around the desk to greet us. No one else besides the pope and we two American priests were in the room, which was very surprising to me. The pope was a short man of five-foot five-inches, and he had the warmest, most engaging smile I have ever seen. He bade us sit in two chairs opposite his desk. After we all settled in, he said that our bishop had given him an outline of our plan. He told us he was intrigued. Starting a religious order with the sole purpose of making money to use as a tool for doing good works was a novel approach. He said that the plan was fraught with dangers and risks. If it were not handled correctly, it could cause a scandal that made the Vatican Bank's and the Curia's escapades seem benevolent. He paused for a few seconds and then asked us several questions. After another pause, he said he thought our proposal had merit and should proceed. He promised he would contact the bishop. He told us this was to be held in the deepest confidence. With that, he gave us his blessing, and we departed. Two weeks later, Pope John Paul I was dead.

"The pope had been good to his word. He did contact the bishop before he died. He outlined briefly what he envisioned and told the bishop more work was needed to flesh out the details. He asked the bishop to prepare a full proposal and to present it privately to him in six months. After we returned from Rome, we were exuberant. The bishop was excited. We were excited. And then the pope died. We assumed our dream died with him. The four of us were summoned to the bishop's residence shortly after the installation of John Paul II. He told us that only the five of us sitting in his office knew of the plan or the tacit approval of the pope. He proposed that we carry on. He told us to go forth and make as much money as we legally could under the name of our new religious order, Friars of St. Mary and the Martyrs.

"That's how we started. The four of us moved into my house in Westchester County. We each sold everything we owned and put all of our assets into the order's name. We bought the latest and greatest IT gear and the fastest internet connections possible. We were not limited by corporate short-term goals or politics.

We had one mission: make a lot of money. We did not advertise or publicize. We did not recruit. Some of the more astute traders took notice of our little enterprise, and a few made contact with us. To all inquiries, we responded that we were not hiring. To the more persistent callers, we would pose certain questions: religion, marital status, age, etc. Yes, we knew these questions were illegal, but we were not a business, nor were we hiring. To those few who sounded promising, we extended an invitation to visit the house over a weekend. After about two years as an order, we passed the one billion mark in assets, and we haven't looked back. By far, the hardest part of what we do is finding meaningful ways to use money as a tool to positively affect global justice and prosperity. Sure, we can throw money and feed a few people, but at the end of the day, we still have the same people hungry tomorrow. We face the same problems overseas. We keep praying and searching, and someday we will have a comprehensive plan that will improve lives all over the globe. We will certainly have the assets in place to allow this to happen."

Abigail had been listening intently. "Father, that is a fascinating story. I enjoyed hearing it very much, but it doesn't answer why I am here."

Abigail heard and sensed motion in the far corner. An easy chair had been turned toward the corner. Evidently, a previously unnoticed person had been taking a nap. The person stood up. It was a young man dressed as a stereotypical prep school student from the sweater and button-down shirt to his loafers. Abigail almost fainted. She was staring at the same young man who had been her savior in high school and stopped that bully, Craig, dead in his tracks. Father Buchanan said, "I believe you two are already acquainted, but just for formality sake, Abigail Williams, may I present Cedrik Balthazar?"

Cedrik was grinning like a Cheshire cat. "I can't tell you how much I have been looking forward to this day. Meeting you again. My lord, you have been busy making a name for yourself with all of the folks you have cured. You are really something."

Abigail was totally flustered and stammered, "You look great. You haven't changed a bit. You look exactly like you did that day in high school. You haven't aged a day."

Cedrik smiled, "It's a family trait. We always look pretty much the same."

Abigail was in shock. She just stood there. Cedrik took her hand and said, "Here, grab a seat. We need to talk." He led her to one of the chairs near the fireplace and sat down facing her.

Michael and the two priests sat on either side. Father Buchanan opened with, "Cedrik just returned from Africa. He has a tale to tell you."

Cedrik began, "You know how you woke up one morning and could cure people? You had nothing to do with it. It just happened. Well, something like that happened to me a long, long time ago. I know what I'm about to tell you is beyond belief, but please listen and try to believe. I was born many centuries ago in what is now Germany. I came from a family of warriors, great warriors. Back then, Germany was nothing but wilderness, with tribes constantly fighting each other. Then a Roman general named Julius Caesar led an army of Roman Legions to conquer the Germanic tribes. The tribes united and gave the Romans a run for their money. There were some terrible battles. They took a toll on my family. My uncles, father, and both brothers were killed. To their credit, they took an awful lot of Romans with them.

"One day, I was leading a scouting party of four other warriors, and we saw a group of Roman soldiers attacking a peaceful village. They killed all of the men and boys and were trying to do the vilest of deeds to the women and girls. We were greatly outnumbered, but we could not just ignore their plight and ride by. We attacked the superior force and, even though we were outnumbered four or five to one, we prevailed. We killed every Roman while none of us sustained any injuries.

"After the battle, we helped the women burn the bodies. If Caesar found out what happened, he would have turned his wrath on the survivors of the village. Once we had done everything we could, we mounted our horses and proceeded on our mission. We were traveling through a dense forest and encountered fog. This fog was unlike anything I had ever seen before. It was thick and dense. I can't really describe it. It was like cold, tasteless whip cream without the density. I am not sure how far we traveled or how long, but eventually we came out of it into the sunshine. There was a clearing and in the middle of the clearing stood a man in shining armor. We approached him in peace, but honestly, we were wary. The man was very large but appeared to be friendly. He congratulated us on our victory and told us that we would never be the same again.

"From that moment on, we have lived in a very pleasant state. Every so often, we are suddenly thrust into conflicts where a helpless person or persons are in peril from a bully or bullies. It can be something like a monastery being invaded by barbarians, a village being attacked by Nazis, or a young girl being brutalized by a bully. We never know who, what, when, or why, but periodically we find ourselves called upon to help the helpless. We have no idea why we are asked to fight some fights, but not others. We don't get a vote." He looked at Michael, who just shrugged his shoulders.

Abigail just looked at Cedrik in shocked amazement. The others were nonchalant about the incredible tale. She asked, "You mean you just showed up in the hallway in my high school?"

Cedrik chuckled, "Yup, that's about it. I found myself dressed like one of the preppie kids and placed in a hallway of some school. I saw what was happening, and that no one was helping you. It was a no brainer for me. In fact, I enjoyed it. That little snot deserved everything I gave him and more. And those other jackasses just standing there watching, I'll wager they will never do that again."

"That was the first time in my life that anyone ever stood up for me, was really kind to me, really saw me as a person with value. I have never forgotten it, and I never will. Thank you."

"No need to thank me. It was my pleasure."

Then he continued, "Now you are probably wondering why you are in a monastery in Georgia listening to a fairy tale told by someone you encountered in a hallway in a high school in Upper Darby, PA. Am I right?"

Abigail nodded.

"Have you ever heard of a country in Africa called Loala?"

Abigail shook her head.

"I thought so. Almost no one has ever heard of it. It is located in the very heart of Africa. It is a very tiny country, only 200 miles long and 150 miles wide. It has no access to the ocean. What it does have are deposits of most of the precious metals and minerals in the world: gold, diamonds, uranium, platinum, and palladium. Unlike other places on the globe, these deposits are found in locations that are easily mined. Some gold mines in Africa are miles deep into the earth. Not so here. In fact, it is just the opposite.

"Its people are very hard-working, industrious, kind, generous, and unassuming. Almost every single one of them would share his or her last meal with you if they thought you needed it. It has been such throughout their long history. Neighboring tribes and countries would attack and plunder Loala and carry Loalans off to slavery. Because of their gentle nature, Loalans were prized as slaves.

"Loala was colonized by Europeans in the late 18th century. Like most of Europe's efforts in colonization in Africa, they mucked it up. Loala finally gained its independence in 1962. Since then, its neighbors and other foreign powers, such as Russia and China, have literally lusted after Loala. The UN and African Union have, thus far, been successful in keeping the wolf from the door, barely. China and Russia are very active in Loala's two northern neighbors in trying to destabilize Loala's duly-elected government. With all of its riches, it's hard to believe that there is little or no corruption in the government.

"The major threat is currently coming from Loala's neighbor to the east, Kilnmari. Its leader, Francois Obutu, is resorting to bioterrorism. He is using the Ebola virus to 'sanitize' the population. That's his term, not mine. He is importing the virus into Loala. He is sending in special action squads to exterminate medical aid workers, and is blocking imports of medicine. He thinks he is close to complete victory.

"That's where my band and I have been for the last six months. We have been able to kill many of Obutu's special action people, but we are helpless against the virus. It is a terrible, terrible disease. It causes an excruciating and agonizing death. Several experimental drugs appear to be promising in treating the disease, but Obutu has cut off the supply of them and is killing the people who could administer them.

"We need help. Specifically, we need your help. You cure without medicine. You cure by being near people. What I propose is that you accompany me back to Africa. You will travel around this tiny country, curing the victims. With you there, we can cure at a much faster rate than Obutu can infect. Eventually, I hope to turn the disease on his country and eventually him. My men and I can keep you safe, but keep in mind that 'safe' is a relative term."

Abigail exploded, "What! You are asking me to leave the US, travel half-way around the world to some back-water little country that I have never even heard of, and risk getting killed?"

Cedrik smiled, "Yup, that's about it. What do you say?"

He turned all of his boyish charms on her, and she had to smile. She said, "I'd say you were certifiably crazy." The others in the room just sat there with stone faces watching the debate.

Before Cedrik could say a word, Abigail's cell phone rang. This was highly unusual as no one ever called her. She looked at the caller ID but did not recognize the number. She looked up helplessly, and Father Buchanan told her to go ahead and take it.

"Hello?"

A somewhat familiar voice answered, "Ms. Williams, this is President Lucius Diamond. How are you today?"

Abigail almost dropped the phone. "I'm fine, Mr. President. How are you? Are you still upset about Walter Reed? Believe me, I was only trying to help those poor soldiers." She was so nervous she kept running sentences together. The president couldn't get a word in. Finally, she paused for a breath. As she did, she looked around and saw that she had the undivided attention of all four men in the room.

"No, I'm not mad. I'm sorry if I gave you that impression. I know you meant well."

"That's a relief. How can I help you?" Abigail thought that he was probably going to ask her to go back to Walter Reed with media coverage. Perhaps accompany him there, making it a mega-media event. His reply sent chill down her spine.

"Ms. Williams, the country is facing a national security crisis. We need the help only you can provide. You are familiar with Kim Jong Un?"

"Yes, he is the leader of North Korea. One of my employers calls him the 'little phat phocker.' He is not a nice person, is he?"

The president answered, "Oh, I don't know about that. I've met him and he seems very nice. Anyway, he is very ill right now. He has cancer and, from what I have been told, it is a very aggressive form of the disease. He knows it is terminal. We don't know how he will act. Will he decide to go out in a blaze of glory carrying North Korea's destiny with him? Will he just fade into oblivion? If so, who will replace him? What will he, or she, be like? The Politburo is a snake pit. There is bound to be a power struggle."

"That's very interesting, Mr. President, but how does that concern me?"

The president sighed an exasperated sigh. Clearly, he thought he would get an offer of cooperation. "Ms. Williams, I am asking you to fly to North Korea and cure Kim Jong Un. The benefit to your country would be staggering. North Korea would be in our debt. Think about the positive impact you will have not only on this generation but future generations. This is a tremendous opportunity for you. It will make you a star.

"Right now, I believe you are near Knoxville, Tennessee, right? I'll have an Air Force plane at the airport there in an hour to fly you to Seoul. From there, you'll take a smaller jet across the border to Pyongyang. What do you say? Your country is counting on you. I'm counting on you."

Abigail was shocked. The President of the United States was asking her for a favor. She looked at the four men who were still staring at her. "Gee, Mr. President, I don't know what to say."

"Ms. Williams, say yes."

"Look, Mr. President, I'm not comfortable with this. I don't like the idea of flying to a country like North Korea. From what I understand, it is like a big prison camp. Also, I am really reluctant to fly all that way to cure someone who is a cold-blooded killer. I wonder if the world would be better off without him. Addition by subtraction, if you will."

The president snapped back, "Now you listen to me, young lady. No one cares what you wonder or what you think. I decided it is the right thing to do, and your duty as an American is to do what I order. That's pretty easy to understand, isn't it? You pulled that crap at Walter Reed and I let you get away with it. I should have had you arrested for trespassing."

Abigail murmured, "I knew you were mad about that."

The president got control of himself, and in a calm voice said, "No, I'm not mad. I just don't want to lose an opportunity like this with North Korea. I'll tell you what. I'm going to send that plane to Knoxville. If you are not there, I will send the FBI to detain you as a national security threat and bring you to Washington. Do I make myself clear?"

"Yes, sir, I understand." With that, the president ended the call. The Secretary of State, the Vice President, and the White House Chief of Staff looked at him. The Chief of Staff said, "I think you may have problems. I doubt if the FBI Director will arrest her for refusing to fly to a hostile country to cure someone that most of the world loathes."

The president responded, "Well, I'll get the AG to order him. Damn it, she is going to do what I order her to do or else." Silence followed. He looked at his Chief of Staff and said, "Call the Secretary of Defense and have him send a plane from Andrews to pick her up. Call the AG and tell him to be prepared."

Back in the monastery, Abigail related the substance of the call to the others. "He thinks I am still at my house. Can't they track a cell phone?"

Father Jubal replied, "Father Buchanan mentioned that we have made a lot of money. That is a gross misstatement. Our assets are more than the GDP of many industrialized countries.

"There are a lot of keys in business, and we pride ourselves in possessing most of them. We have an intelligence section that rivals the CIA and NSA. Our IT branch is on the cutting edge of technology and has developed some specialized software and operating systems that are at least two generations ahead of anything currently available. With intelligence comes counterintelligence and security. Again, we have the best. If the president is trying to track your cell phone, he is getting reports it is in Russia, Australia, and the Hay-Adams hotel right across the street from the White House, all at the same time." He chuckled, "I'd love to be a fly on the wall in the Oval Office right now. I think you are safe for the time being."

Cedrik spoke up, "You were saying that I was certifiably crazy right before you were interrupted by President Diamond. Now what do you say? You have the opportunity to visit the world's biggest prison camp or the opportunity to travel to the heart of Africa where you can fight an insidious disease that is being used as a weapon by a ruthless dictator hell-bent on stealing an entire country. What's your pleasure?"

Abigail replied, "I just want to go home. I didn't sign up to be the next Mata Hari. I don't want to be involved in political intrigue. I want nothing to do with extending Kim Jong Un's life. To me, the sooner he is gone, the better, so there is no way I will voluntarily get on an airplane to go to North Korea."

Cedrik said in a soft voice, "I understand, and I completely agree with you about what you said about Kim Jong Un. What about Loala? They really need help. They really need you."

"I also didn't sign up to be the next Mother Theresa. Look, I'm finally being successful. People notice me. I'm no longer ignored. I really don't want to jeopardize that. Most people don't even get one shot at the golden ring. I was lucky. I got a shot, and I'm going to take it."

Father Buchanan smiled ruefully and said, "I think I can understand how you feel. I told you about how, when I was a young man, I was one of the most gifted money makers on the planet. Well, I still am. If you think about what we have here, you will have to admit this place is full of people who have had their shot at the prize and, for the most part, grabbed it. We had the ring in our possession and found it was hollow. There is more to life than money. We want to improve the condition of as many of our fellow human beings as we can. We have come to realize that we can't just throw money at the problems. We have to travel to the source of the problems and try to correct them from there. No matter what the problems are. Be they disintegration of the family, illiteracy, crime and violence, lack of clean running water, or drug abuse." He paused for effect. "Or a warlord who is using bioterrorism to conquer a good and noble people.

"You, Abigail, have grabbed the ring. It's yours. Now that you have it, what are your feelings? Victory? Elation? Satisfaction? Superiority? If you are honest with yourself, and I believe you to be a very honest person, you feel a little bit of each of these emotions. And more! Don't be ashamed. You've earned it.

"But ask yourself, what comes next. Are you going to continue being the 'miracle girl' raking in the dough? How long will it last? If it were to end tomorrow and your powers were to suddenly disappear, how will you be remembered? As someone who started with a vision of helping people only to be sidetracked by wealth and power? Do you want that? Is that you?

"Admit it, you started with the hospital visits, and you loved them. Then you added the big stadium events. You made a lot of money, but you lost contact with the people who you were helping. They were mere droplets in the sea of humanity that you passed in your 'Abbymobile.' You got little or no satisfaction in curing people. To make matters worse, I've heard that you have been unkind to people who cannot afford your fees. I certainly hope that those reports are false."

Abigail was silent. She lowered her eyes. She could not make eye contact with Buchanan.

He continued, "Then you have your private clinics. You dash in, collect an exorbitant fee, and then dash out. Do you honestly like doing them?"

In a quiet voice, Abigail replied, "No, even though they are one-on-one, they are too impersonal, too rushed. I hate doing them, but the money is so good. On the other hand, I really like working with the athletes of the teams who have put me on retainer. Most of them are fun to be around and grateful that I am giving them a chance to continue playing. Besides, the teams pay me enough that I can spend time with each of the players."

Father Buchanan smiled and nodded. "I think Michael is planning on staying here this evening. We certainly have plenty of room since no spiritual retreats are currently in progress. Before we go to dinner, I want to leave you with a quote from Robert E. Lee. 'Do your duty in all things. You can never do more, you should never wish to do less.' I want you to take time and reflect on what he said. The first thing you have to do is decide where your duty lies. Is it to President Diamond? Is it to yourself? Or is it to a little country in Africa that no one in America has ever heard of? Be prepared to defend your answer." He paused for a second as a surprised look crossed Abigail's face. Then he continued, "Certainly not to me or anyone gathered here. You have to be able to defend it to yourself now, and to the woman you will become in 5 or 10 years. In the end, it is just you and what you did or failed to do that will be your epitaph. You are unique in that yours will be written exactly how you want it, by what you choose to do.

He said with a smile, "Well now, that's enough of this deep thought. I think it is time for us to go to dinner. Louis, our chef here, takes it as a personal insult if we keep his culinary masterpieces waiting. These Frenchmen can be real drama queens."

That evening was a tough one for Abigail. The ability to sleep deserted her. She tossed and turned all night. Father Buchanan's quote from Robert E. Lee kept reverberating in her mind. What was her duty? She kept reviewing the three options the priest had laid out. Were there more? Why her? Why was she being forced to choose? Answers eluded her.

She got out of bed and paced around the room. Finally, she put her robe on and started marching up and down the long corridor. She hoped that she would not encounter anyone. As she walked, a smile came to her face. The snoring coming from one of the rooms, even with the door closed, was deafening. This had to be Big Mike's room.

After hours of pacing, things began to come into focus. The first was to utterly and completely dismiss North Korea. She didn't trust the president. She did not think his motives were altruistic. His record is pretty clear that all of his actions have been focused on doing what is best personally for Lucius Diamond. She was sure the president thought that by creating a peaceful climate between the US and North Korea, he would be seen as a great statesman and that, in turn, would translate into his re-election. He might even be able to parlay that into a Nobel Peace Prize. She remembered how he acted about her visit to Walter Reed. No, a visit to North Korea was out.

That left her with two options remaining. Abigail thought she knew the definition of duty. After all, she took history courses in high school. The more Abby pondered her choices, the more she became convinced that she only knew the surface definition of the word. She was too tired to attempt to peel away all of the layers of the word 'duty', but she finally arrived that 'self' was not one of them, at least in this case. There was a moral obligation to face evil head-on, to look it right in the eye, and dare it to give you its best shot.

She looked at her watch. It was 4 a.m. She went back to her room, again smiling at the racket emanating from behind Mike's door. She climbed into bed and fell fast asleep. In what seemed like moments, she was awakened by someone knocking at her door. The time was 6:30 a.m. Father Jubal told her she needed to hurry if she wanted breakfast. Surprisingly, she was refreshed. She was also famished. Dinner the previous evening had been spectacular. Chef Louis had stopped by her table and clearly relished the praise she heaped upon his culinary skills. She couldn't wait to see what delights breakfast would bring.

After breakfast, the five of them gathered back together in the great room and pleasantries were exchanged. Michael voiced the only note of discord. "For some reason, I couldn't sleep. I was awake all night." Abigail stared at him like he had sprouted horns.

Cedrik laughed uncontrollably. "Michael, you really need to re-evaluate and revise that statement. I was in the next room, remember? I thought I was in the middle of a saw-mill."

Looking totally mystified, Mike said, "Really?" To which everyone started laughing.

Father Buchanan looked expectantly at Abigail. "Did you think at all about Robert E. Lee last night?

"I did. In fact, I thought about nothing else." She then related to the group the gist of her deliberations. She noted the collective approval of the group when she dismissed North Korea. When she announced that her travel plans included a tiny country in central Africa, she thought she saw pride and respect in the group. Big Mike came over, pulled her to her feet, and gave her a big hug. He whispered, "I'm proud of you, girl."

Cedrik did not stand on ceremony. He announced that they needed to get moving quickly. Father Buchanan offered anything Abigail needed in the way of inoculations, visas, clothing, and transportation. He told her that when he wanted something expedited, it was.

True to his word, a man in a business suit appeared that afternoon with a valise. He identified himself as being from the Center for Disease Control (CDC) and was here to administer the shots that Abigail would need to keep her safe. Each time he injected her, he told her what it was for. It made her shudder to realize that she had never heard of over half of the diseases before. When he left, Cedrik told her that the man was the head of the Infectious Disease branch of the CDC.

A short time later, a woman appeared with all of the necessary paperwork, including the visa that she needed to enter Loala. Cedrick told her that she was an Under Secretary of State, a person very high up in the State Department.

Finally, a lady appeared and took Abigail aside. She took her measurement, checked her foot size and hand size, and then made a phone call. Within an hour, a helicopter appeared. The woman met the chopper and returned fully loaded down with bags, as well as a backpack that appeared to already be fully loaded. She handed the bags to Abigail. "Here, take these and get changed. Let's see how they fit." Abigail returned in a few minutes fully dressed in camouflaged utilities and a floppy hat of the type favored by the military. She was also wearing a very heavy-duty pair of boots. "How does all of the fit?" Abigail replied that everything was fine. The lady nodded, turned, and got into the waiting helicopter.

Almost immediately after its departure, a second chopper appeared. This one was entirely black and had the crest of the monastery on its sides. It was piloted by two men dressed in black flight suits. The chopper landed, and the pilots shut down the engines. Cedrik ran up to the helicopter ducking under its turning blades, shook hands, and said something to the pilot. He then returned and told Abigail that they would be leaving immediately.

Abigail went inside and came out with all of her new gear. She was scared and also trembling with excitement. As she departed the building, she stopped dead in her tracks at an astounding sight. Almost 200 monks in their habits were gathered. Fathers Buchanan and Jubal were closest to the helicopter, standing next to Michael Angelo. Abigail was not a Catholic. In fact, she was not much of anything. Her parents never spoke of religion or exposed her to it as a child. If pressed, she would have said that there was a God or some sort of Supreme Being, but she never paid any attention to it. Father Buchanan raised his voice so that all could hear. "Abigail and Cedrik, you are departing from our presence to go forth and defeat a terrible evil, to restore hope to a downtrodden people, and to demonstrate to the entire world that good always triumphs over evil. Before you depart from us, we all want to give you a communal blessing. Please bow your heads." Each of the monks raised both of their arms with palms extended as Father Buchanan intoned the blessing. At the end, he made the Sign of the Cross over them. Abigail noticed that both Michael and Cedrik blessed themselves. Then Fathers Buchanan and Jubal came forward and embraced the two travelers and wished them a safe journey. Michael shook hands with Cedrik, then turned to Abigail and almost crushed her in an embrace. He whispered, "You come back safe. You hear?" She nodded, and he loaded her gear in the helicopter. Three minutes later, they were airborne over the woods of Georgia, heading into the vast unknown.

LOALA

Lounging in the boss's luxurious New York City office with a killer view of lower Manhattan and the Hudson River were Polina and Barney. They were relaxing like they owned the place. And well they should.

There were outcries every day against Abigail. Some said she was heartless. Some said she was just a money-grubber. Some said that she discriminated against blacks and other minority groups since you needed $200 to get into a stadium event. Not only that, the patient first had to travel to the event. Then the patient had to figure on staying at least one night in a hotel and probably two. Unless the person happened to live in a city where the event was occurring, they were easily going to spend $1,000 or more. Most folks don't have that kind of money just sitting around. The fact that Abigail never would drop the price or make exceptions for desperate cases only increased their fury. When word got out about the private cures, the outcry became deafening. The late-night comics, as-well-as *Saturday Night Live*, had a field day lampooning her.

Never willing to let an opportunity pass, two out of the three anchors of the more liberal networks' evening news broadcasts called on her to visit areas such as the South Bronx, East St. Louis, and the south side of Chicago. They were inflammatory in their comments, and this was seized upon by a couple of anarchist groups and a firebrand minister. They called upon their people to come out and protest against the 'racist white girl.'

Barney said, "You have to love those news bureaus. They are too easy to manipulate. All it took was one angry phone call followed up by a nasty letter, and off they went. The funny thing is that they firmly believe that what they decree is almost like a command from God, and they will keep beating the drum until it comes to fruition. I don't know where I'd be without them."

Polina looked at Barney and gloated, "Do you realize people hate her more than anyone that I can recall? Back in the good old days when men were men and they burned witches at the stake, she would have been a crispy critter for sure."

Barney just nodded and smiled. He was sure the boss was going to be pleased.

At that moment, in stormed the boss. She was wearing an incredibly short, incredibly tight black skirt, incredibly high-heeled shoes, and an incredibly low cut white blouse. She topped the outfit off with a goat's head pendant on a gold chain. She looked incredibly dangerous, incredibly professional, and incredibly sexy all at once. She walked to her desk, grabbed a paperweight, and threw it across the room. Barney and Polina had seen her mad before, but they had never seen this level of fury and rage.

She glared at both of them. "What are you two doing here? Why aren't you out trying to fix the mess you created?"

Barney and Polina exchanged glances. Finally, Polina asked, "Boss, what is the problem? Things are going marvelously. The Williams girl is making money hand over fist. As a result, people all over the world think she is using them and hate her guts. People are fighting each other over tickets to her events. A couple of people were murdered over their tickets. Barney and I convinced her to turn a blind eye to all of this nonsense and outrage, and she has. She has completely ignored the public, and that only makes the people more furious. To top it all off, President Diamond publicly attacked her. She is definitely persona non grata with his supporters. I don't know what more you could want. This is a self-sustaining chain reaction. It's perfect."

That set her off. "Do you two blathering idiots by any chance know where she is right now?"

Barney ventured in a voice that was more question than answer, "At her house in the Smokey Mountains?"

"Wrong, you fool. She is with that Cedrik Balthazar fellow and his gang of misfits in Loala."

Barney and Polina jumped to their feet. "That can't be true," exclaimed Barney. He paused and then meekly asked, "How did she get there?"

"While you two rockets scientists were patting each other's backs, that big oaf, Michael Angelo, drove her to that Monastery in Georgia. I'm sure you remember that place, Barney. Those monks there kicked your ass last time you tangled with them. They caused you to take that little sabbatical to Afghanistan. By the way, you know whom you are dealing with in Michael Angelo, don't you?" Both Polina and Barney nodded their heads in affirmation. "All we can do now is to wait and see how this plays out. We still have the North Korea situation that we could use as a wild card."

As the boss was speaking, a little over 7,000 miles to the east, Abigail gazed upon a beautiful but foreign scene. She was looking at lush jungle foliage. There was a two-lane road heading into the vegetation where it soon became invisible. She was sitting in the passenger seat of an ancient jeep. Suleiman, one of Cedrik's four associates, was in the driver's seat with an M-16 assault rifle on his lap. Cedrik and the other three associates had dismounted and were looking at something through a break in the foliage. Using hand signals, Cedrik directed the three men to spread out. He raised his right hand into the air with fingers spread apart. He then started counting down from five using his fingers. When only his fist remained raised, the jungle reverberated with gunfire. The five of them charged. A short while later, there was silence.

Abigail heard what she thought was a bird call. Suleiman must have also heard it since he started the engine and drove the jeep around a bend into a clearing. Cedrik and his three men were standing over the bodies of four men in military uniforms. Before Abigail could express shock over the violence, she saw a crude tin hut. Red crosses were painted on each side of the building and on the roof. Cedrik motioned for her to come with him to the hut.

Inside she saw a scene right out of a horror film. At least 20 bodies were lying on filthy cots or on the dirt floor. Flies were everywhere. The stench from bodily wastes was overpowering. A couple of kerosene lanterns provided the only light. Her senses were overwhelmed and all she wanted was to flee. Just as she started to turn, she saw motion. One of the bodies was somehow alive. She went over to find a woman staring up at her. Abigail smiled at the woman and touched her arm. Immediately life came flooding back into the pathetic creature. Abigail turned to fetch some water for the woman, and as she did, she became aware of others moving in the hut. She quickly went around, laying hands on each of the victims. Surprisingly, all but one were still alive, barely.

The five warriors quickly started moving the survivors out of the hut into the fresh air. They all appeared to be making miraculous recoveries. Two of the survivors were white, female nurses from France. They explained that this was a hospital set up by a humanitarian group to specifically treat Ebola patients. The doctors and the majority of nurses had been ordered out of Loala by their parent organization two weeks ago. They had no medicine and conditions were becoming increasingly dangerous. These two nurses had refused to leave. A few days ago, they were attacked by four men they presumed to be soldiers sent by Francois Obutu as part of his attack on Loala. One nurse related how the invaders pulled off all of the PPE[9] of the aid workers exposing them to the virus. In no time at all, everyone was stricken. They described the horrors of the disease in excruciating detail. When the two nurses saw the bodies of the four soldiers, they smiled grimly. One nurse said, "These are the four who attacked us and tried to kill us. I thought they had gone away. I guess they stayed to make sure we were all dead."

Leif, another of Cedrik's colleagues, came up and said, "I wouldn't be so sure that was why they stayed. We found their camp about half a mile away. They had all kinds of equipment that appear to be for collecting and storing blood. I think that they were going to harvest blood and other body parts to take to other villages to infect the people who lived there."

The other nurse asked, "How much equipment?"

Leif replied, "They have a deuce and a half[10] loaded with crates of bottles, vials, and insulated containers.

The nurse asked, "Were the containers empty or full?"

"From what I could tell, they are all empty."

She exclaimed, "My God, they were just starting out. We are on the northwest corner of Loala. I'll bet they were planning to head

---

9. Personal Protective Equipment: Protective clothing, masks, helmets, goggles, etc. designed to protect the wearer from injury or infection

10. Deuce and a Half: 2.5 ton military cargo truck

east and infect every town and village they came to. I wonder how many more of these squads are operating."

Cedrik answered, "There are a bunch of them. We have encountered and killed dozens. However, this is the first time we have seen a mobile harvesting operation. Typically they find some poor soul who is dying or already dead and move the body into a populated area. The results are the same, but this operation we stopped today is much more efficient.

"Now tell us about your organization and the other medical efforts in Loala."

Janelle, the first nurse, answered, "There are very few medical personnel in this country. Most of the doctors and nurses have already left or were savagely executed or otherwise killed. On top of that, the clinics don't have medicine. Francois Obutu has cut off all imports. I'm surprised that you were able to evade his troops at the border crossings. All food, medicine, and other basic necessities end up going to him. They never seem to reach the people who desperately need them. Those who are not dying from the disease are perishing from malnutrition."

Suleiman whispered, "Who said anything about using border crossings?" This brought smiles from both Leif and Alexander.

Abigail asked, "What about the United Nations? Can't they do something?"

The second nurse's name was Claudette. She answered, "They tried, but both China and Russia vetoed any real aid. The African Union has imposed sanctions on Obutu, but thus far, they have been ineffective. To me, this is like the games in the ancient Colosseum in Rome, with all of the spectators sitting there watching a poor wretch get thrown to the lions."

Cedrik interrupted. "We are going to destroy all of the cargo in the truck. As far as I am concerned, the truck is yours to do with as you see fit. Same with the supplies at their camp. They are yours. Ebola is one of the diseases that you can catch only once. Once you have had it, you are immune to a repeat." He looked around at the patients. Most were up and about. A few were smiling. "How are you two feeling?"

Janelle replied, "I feel fine. I'm a little weak and very hungry. I also want something to drink." Her colleague nodded in agreement.

Cedrik clapped his hands, "OK. Eric and Alexander will fetch the truck and supplies. Suleiman will get a fire going and see if he can find something to cook. Leif and I are going to try to find a village nearby and get some help and any food they can spare."

The five warriors set out, leaving Abigail at the clinic. She went about checking on the survivors and found them to be doing remarkably well. She motioned to several of the men that the body of the deceased man needed to be buried before any outsiders came to the clinic. The dead from Ebola are highly contagious.

Eric and Alexander were the first to reappear. They had the rations that the dead soldiers brought with them on the mission as well as several five-gallon water cans. Abigail joined them in serving the food to the patients. By this time, it was impossible to tell that a few hours ago these people had been on death's doorstep. They all look healthy and happy.

The two nurses and several of the men examined the cargo in the truck. Then Janelle noted that while these containers were intended for a vile deed, they had intrinsic value. The natives could put them to good use. Eric nodded, and he and Alexander unloaded the truck and stacked the crates neatly at the edge of the clearing.

Leif and Cedrik arrived at the clinic just as everyone had finished eating. Accompanying them were about 10 men from a nearby village. They were overjoyed to find so many survivors, many of whom came from their village.

The men told stories of horrors they had heard from other villages. The preferred modus operandi of Obutu's special action squads was for a team of four, all wearing PPE, to arrive in a village before dawn along with several bodies of people who had recently succumbed to the disease. The team would place the bodies in locations where people congregated, such as the village well and the market. The bodies would have to be moved, and by so doing, the unprotected people who moved them stood an excellent chance of catching the virus. As one person was felled by the virus, those who tended him also stood a chance of catching it. In no time, it would decimate the village. The team would observe the carnage from a safe distance. If trained medical personnel arrived, or for that matter, anyone who looked the least bit competent, they would be shot and killed by a high-powered rifle.

Cedrik brought over an empty container from one of the crates. He noted the nozzle and the fittings on the lid. "It appears as if their tactics are changing. I'll wager that this is what these bastards were planning. First, they planned to kill all of you. Then as a person died, they would drain all of the blood from the body into the insulated containers. Once all of these things were full, they would head out to a village or maybe even to Loalaville." There were gasps from the nurses. Loalaville was the capital and largest city in the country. It had about 100,000 inhabitants. "Once they were close to their objective, they would pour some of the blood into these things." He indicated the container in his hand and pointed at the fittings on the lid. "Using this fitting, they would pressurize the vessel with air. After that, it works like a paint sprayer. They could run through a village, spraying the slop directly on the villagers. In no time they could infect an entire village or even a city like Loalaville. It's brilliant."

Abigail listened in horror. She was invisible again. As the nurses, villagers, and warriors conversed about the situation at hand, Abby sank back into the shadows. No one noticed her. She was in her comfort zone.

With no order issued or signal given, Cedrik and his four colleagues started packing their gear. Clearly, they were preparing to head out. Cedrik caught Abigail's eye and motioned for her to join him. "It's time to leave. We have done all we can do here. Let's see if we can hunt down some more of these bastards."

Claudette said, "Can we join you? There is not much else we can do here. The Loalans will take care of their own."

Cedrik shrugged, "You are most welcome, but we only have two jeeps. Four people in each jeep will uncomfortable, but if you don't mind, then we don't mind."

Janelle asked, "What about the truck? We could take that. You never know, it might come in handy in the future."

Cedrik replied, "Good thinking. Let's get moving."

The two jeeps and the truck headed off. They traveled from village to village. At some, they were on time, and Abigail could cure anyone still alive. At some, they were early. The squads had not yet visited. They promised the elders there that they would return. Unfortunately, at one village they were late. There were no survivors.

One evening they were driving under blackout conditions. It was a clear night and the moon provided adequate illumination. Suddenly the lead jeep stopped. Cedrik got out with his binoculars and looked at the edge of a clearing. There was a fire burning, and a dozen or so men dressed in Obutu's fatigue uniforms were sitting around it. They were drinking beer and what looked like whiskey from a bottle passed from one to the other. Cedrik motioned for Eric to stay with the three women. Then he and the others spread out to reconnoiter the area. Ten minutes later, they returned. Abigail was amazed. They didn't make a sound going or returning. They were as stealthy as ghosts.

In whispers, Cedrik said that there were 12 men. If they were organized the same as the squad at the first village, that would make three squads of four each. Cedrik laid out the attack plan. He emphasized that at least one of these men was to be taken alive for interrogation.

It was not much of a fight. Between the late hour and the booze, these men were truly *The Dirty Dozen* in the worst sense of the phrase. They never knew what hit them. Eleven surrendered at first sight of the attackers. The twelfth reached for his side-arm and was promptly dispatched to greener pastures. Cedrik's men all carried wire ties and immediately used them to secure the eleven prisoners. With his flashlight, Cedrik studied each of them. All were frightened. One, however, was close to panic. His eyes kept darting left, right, up, and down. He was shaking uncontrollably. Cedrik thought that he would make the perfect candidate. He walked up to the man standing next to the candidate and punched him ferociously in the gut. When the man doubled over in pain, Cedrik hit him with an uppercut to the jaw. A head butt followed and the man's nose spurted blood. The man screamed in pain.

Cedrik next walked over to the candidate and looked him directly in the eyes. The man tried to look away, but Cedrik slapped him across the face. He yelped. Cedrik then began trying to find a common language. It so happened that the candidate spoke French, a very good and cultured French. Cedrik wondered who exactly he had here and intended to find out.

The candidate turned out to be the son of Francois Obutu. He was Francois Jr., but his nickname was Frankie. This lad had led a sheltered and pampered existence. He spent the majority of his formative years at the best schools Switzerland had to offer. Many of Frankie's schoolmates were the offspring of dictators and tyrants from all over the globe. The stories he heard from them about grabbing power and, more importantly, retaining power were almost beyond belief. He listened carefully and learned. Now that he had returned to Africa, Francois was in the process of teaching him the family business. He said he was here because Francois wanted the lad to gain some firsthand experience. Cedrik turned quickly away before he shot the little bastard.

Cedrik made short work of securing the prisoners for the night. Suleiman found the rations that these squads brought with them and prepared dinner for the eight of them. After dinner, Cedrik issued the sentry schedule for the night and they all bedded down.

The next morning, Eric and Suleiman went on a reconnaissance patrol, Alexander started searching the documents and equipment that they had captured, and Cedrik and Leif started interrogating each of the prisoners individually.

Each prisoner's story was remarkably similar as to their mission. Cedrik was correct. These were three of the special action squads. They traveled here separately and planned to meet with the squad that Cedrik's band had encountered and eliminated almost a week earlier.

Alexander came running over to Cedrik with a map in his hand, as well as several documents in French. Cedrik spread the map on the hood of the jeep. It was a map of Loala and also included the northwest quadrant of Obutu's country, Kilnmari. Cedrik traced his group's journey from the first encounter with Obutu's forces in the northwest corner of Loala, then due south through five villages, southeast through several more, and finally due east where they encountered this group. Cedrik figured that they were about 75 miles due south of Loalaville.

Once the first squad arrived, the four squads were to divide the containers of blood and bodily waste and the empty spray containers, split up, and head towards Loalaville. At the designated time, the squads would charge through the city from the southwest,

west, northwest, and north, shooting and spraying all that they encountered. Special attention was to be given to wells and markets.

Concurrently, a second force of four squads was mirroring this group, except from the southeast. They would attack Loalaville from the remaining points of the compass. Obutu's plan called for the elimination of a minimum of 80% of the population, or 80,000 people.

Abigail was stunned when she heard the plan. How could people act this way? Cedrik just shook his head. No one could possibly explain this kind of evil.

Each squad was equipped with a modern Range Rover. Each of the vehicles provided comfort for the squad members, as well as room for their equipment. Alexander said, "I didn't see a Range Rover at the aid station."

Leif had come over from interrogating a squad member and heard Alexander's comment. "That's because they had the deuce and a half."

Abigail said, "How can 32 men kill 80,000 people? I assume the second group will be the same as this one. That means they will have two trucks and six Range Rovers. How can they do it?"

Suleiman answered, "Speed and surprise. Keep in mind that the virus will do the killing, not these guys. They are merely delivery boys. They will run into the town, start shooting, and then the passengers dismount with the spray guns and start spraying. They can be in and out in less than half an hour. They throw a few grenades at police stations and government buildings to make the authorities keep their heads down, and they will have virtually no opposition. They will go someplace safe and watch as the city literally withers and dies, and then make sure that no help can get in. They won't try to stop people from leaving, because the chances are that those folks are contaminated. Even if they are not contaminated with the virus, think of the panic they will spread with their stories."

Abigail continued with her questions. "Speaking of government buildings, what about the foreign embassies? I can't imagine the US allowing their embassy to be attacked and not do something about it."

This time Cedrik answered. "Are you kidding me? That has happened many times in the past. If it is not politically expedient, the US will just sit back. In this case, Loala is such a tiny country that very few foreign countries have legations there. Usually, one country will set up an office and will handle the affairs of the region. For example, Costa Rica has an office there and takes care of the interests of North and Central America. For a fee, of course.

"No, in my opinion, they only have to worry about Israel. No one in the Middle East will let Israel play ball with them, so they have to go it alone and operate their own mission. Whatever these guys do, they have to make sure no harm comes to the Israeli legation. As a result, they will keep their attack well away from foreign missions. Somehow they will get word to the staff at these offices to get out of town quickly before the virus can spread. It's a risk for Obutu, but so is killing 80,000 innocent people."

Cedrik continued, "Obutu's kid said that they are supposed to be in position two days from today. The attack is supposed to start at 3:00 in the morning. The four squads will have to rendezvous to divide the coolers and sprayers just like these guys did. Our job will be to find that location and take them out as we did here. Failing that, we spread out and try to get them on the fly as they attack. That is definitely my least preferred option." All of his men nodded their agreement.

Abigail asked, "What about the two nurses and me? We will be of no use to you in an assault. We'll just get in the way."

Cedrik answered, "Abigail, you are the reason that we are here right now. We need you to stop this epidemic. We are up against something that firepower and force cannot defeat." He paused and smiled. An idea had just come to him. "Remember what I said about the Israeli mission? What if we were to show up at their doorstep, explain what was going to happen in a day or so, and ask them to take you three in for safekeeping? We'll bring Frankie along to verify that an attack is coming. That boy is petrified. He won't refuse to answer questions."

Cedrik and Leif loaded the three women and Frankie in two Range Rovers, left the other vehicles and prisoners with the other three warriors, and drove due north towards Loalaville. It was a 75-mile ride over roads that were actually slightly improved trails. By the time the city was in sight, every bone in their bodies had been jostled and shaken. The government area was in the north-central part of the city. The buildings were less than spectacular by western standards but were head and shoulders superior to the other buildings in the city. The mini convoy pulled up in front of the Israeli mission. The building was flying the blue and white Star of David flag on a pole in front of the building. There were no guards outside, but Cedrik had no doubt they were being observed. Leif remained with the two vehicles, with Frankie still secured in the cargo area of one of them, while Cedrik and the three ladies entered the building. They were met by a female soldier sitting behind a desk. She smiled and asked their business in English. Cedrik politely replied that they would like to speak with the head of the mission if possible on a very important matter. "Could you be a bit more specific as to the reason for your visit, sir? Mr. Weinschenk is extremely busy."

"I am sure he is very busy, but I assure you this will not be a waste of his time. Would you please tell him that Cedrik Balthazar is here to see him along with Ms. Abigail Williams? He may have heard the names Abigail Williams or the 'miracle girl' before."

She picked up a phone, and almost immediately a slightly built man in an open collar-shirt and slacks hurried into the reception area. He went directly to Abigail and shook her hand. "Ms. Williams, this is my distinct honor. I am very pleased to meet you. I am Joshua Weinschenk. What can I do for you?"

Abigail introduced Cedrik and the two French nurses. Weinschenk invited them all into his office. About 10 minutes later, two armed Israeli soldiers entered the office. They were in there a very short while before leaving with Cedrik. They left the building and returned with a very frightened Frankie walking stiffly between them.

From then on, the day was a blur for the female soldier/receptionist. She recognized the heads of most of the other foreign missions, the mayor of the city, some government officials, and even the President of Loala as they hurried in to see Weinschenk. This was, to say the least, very unusual.

Once Cedrik explained the purpose of his visit to Weinschenk, and Frankie very reluctantly confirmed it, things started to happen. In all cases, everyone who was briefed was initially incredulous. The incredulity then gave way to fright and then anger.

The first to receive the briefing was the mayor of the city. He immediately called the head of the police force and the Loalan Minister of the Interior. That gentleman, in turn, called the President, Terrence Ngao.

The two Israeli soldiers took Frankie out of the office. Neither Cedrik nor Abigail questioned where they were taking him or why. Another female soldier, Mariam, came and took the two nurses out to 'freshen up' and get some refreshments. In addition to Cedrik and Abigail, there were the Loalans, Weinschenk, and another man who was not introduced to the group. He just listened and observed. Weinschenk looked at him and said, "Abram, did you know anything about this?"

The man shrugged his shoulders. "No, I had no indication that this was being planned. We had an idea that Kilnmari was somehow behind the Ebola outbreak but were not sure how."

The mayor started to speak about different courses of action, but was interrupted by the president who said, "I think we need to discuss this amongst ourselves and then get back to these fine people with what we will do."

Cedrik politely said, "If I may, Mr. President. I know you did not ask for my opinion, and I hesitate to interject it where it is not wanted." The president made a 'come on' gesture, and Cedrik continued. "As you are aware, we have cut the attacking force in half. The force coming in from the east is not aware of that from what I can deduce. They are expecting units to come in from all directions. I never asked, but I'll bet Obutu's son is at least in titular command of the operation. As we did not find any radios or other communications devices on the group we captured, I have no idea how he planned to exercise command and control. This is a simple operation. It may be just 'one-two-three-go' and then escape and evade back to Kilnmari. After all, there is no Loalan force to oppose them."

Terrence Ngao looked impatient, "So?"

"Mr. President, one of the actions I am sure you will contemplate is issuing an order to evacuate the city. I caution against this in the strongest terms possible. Having a stampede of 100,000 panic-stricken people out of the city with no clear destination in mind is a recipe for disaster. There are not nearly enough villages in the immediate area to absorb this flood of refugees. Your people will find themselves cut off. The Kilnmari Action Squads do not present a significant problem. Oh, sure, they will fire upon and kill some of your people. How many I do not know. Keep in mind that killing your people with gunfire is not their objective. It is to cause the spread of Ebola throughout the country. They aren't particularly interested in killing one or two or even six or seven hundred. They want tens of thousands. When they are finished, Obutu wants to walk in and confiscate your nation's riches totally unopposed.

"What I advise is, and I realize this is almost impossible, to quietly issue martial law orders. Tell everyone to pass the word to their neighbors to stock up with enough food and water for three or four days. More would be better than less. Everyone is ordered for the good of the country to stay behind locked doors for at least three days.

"I have a small band of highly-trained warriors. My squad and I will deploy around the eastern edges of the city. As we see the four squads coming, we will move to eliminate them. If you have some men we could borrow to act as scouts, it would be even better. If you could give us a dozen men with radios to warn us when and where they are coming, we can try to stop them before they enter the city.

"Anyway, please consider what I have said. Oh, one thing I neglected. Mr. Weinschenk, may I leave the three ladies here with you for safekeeping? Ms. Williams' safety is of prime importance. We can't afford to have her romping around with us and getting shot at. She should be very safe here under the protection of Israel. Incoming fire always has the right-of-way. If we can keep her out of the line of fire, we should be fine."

He then explained to the assembled Loalans who Abigail was and why she was there. "She has already visited six or seven villages and cured most of the people. I am sorry to say that in one village everyone had already expired from the disease."

Abigail interrupted, "Cedrik, I'm speaking for both of the nurses and myself. We would prefer to go to one of the hospitals. We will be of use there instead of taking up space here in the mission. In fact, I would like to go to a hospital right now and cure as many patients as possible. Mr. President, can you take me to where the most gravely ill patients are located. If you have Ebola cases, I can start there."

The president looked perplexed and somewhat annoyed, "Is this some kind of joke? If it is, I am too busy to be amused. Whoever heard of someone being able to cure people? That kind of thing went out with the witch doctors decades ago."

Abram, the other Israeli in the room, spoke. "Mr. President, I assure you that it is not a joke. This young woman from the United States has made headlines all over the world. She has demonstrated the ability to come near someone, and just by doing that, the person is cured. I would recommend taking her up on her offer. I would also recommend doing everything in your power to keep her and the nurses out of harm's way. What Cedrik said about incoming bullets having the right-of-way is so very true."

Ngao replied, "OK, I'll give her a try. I have nothing to lose. Is Israel prepared to lend me a few of its vaunted military to act as bodyguards?"

Everyone looked at Weinschenk, who nodded. Abram got up and left the room. He returned several minutes later with Janelle and Claudette and half a dozen heavily-armed soldiers, both male and female. The president nodded grimly, and said, "Now if you will excuse us, the mayor, my ministers, and I must leave and get this city ready for an invasion."

Joshua Weinschenk replied, "Of course, Mr. President. If you agree, I will contact all of the legations in Loalaville and explain what is happening and recommend that they shelter in place. Of course, the final decision is up to each of them."

"D'accord," replied the president as he departed the office.

Cedrik then spoke, "Eric and I will take these soldiers and the ladies to whatever hospital you suggest. We'll drop them off and return here. We'll pick up the prisoner and head back to where we left the squad. All of us will head back here tomorrow morning."

One of the men from the Ministry of the Interior said, "I will accompany you to the hospital. It is operated by a Catholic missionary group. It is the larger of the two in this city and has by far the highest number of very sick people."

They all loaded up in the two Range Rovers and the Interior Ministry's well-worn sedan and followed it along narrow crowded streets to the hospital. During the ride, Abigail asked Cedrik, "Who was that other Israeli man, Abram? He seemed to know a lot."

Cedrik answered, "I assume that he is the Mossad[11] resident on site. He is a good ally to make."

The hospital was in a 1980s four-story building, the tallest in the area. The Loalan official, Cedrik, the three women, and the six soldiers went in and met the hospital director. After a brief explanation, Cedrik excused himself and left. The official recounted to the director what was about to happen and urged that confidentiality and calmness be the two watchwords for the immediate future. The director said that they currently had over 500 people on in-patient status, which grossly exceeded the hospital's stated capacity, but that the staff was doing the best they could with the resources available.

Abigail told him that she would like to offer some help. He had read about her but was still very skeptical about her supposed powers. Not having a better alternative available, the director reluctantly agreed to allow her access to the hospital. He called in one of the chief nurses, a Kenyan woman, to act as a guide. The hospital had an entire floor set up for isolation cases such as Ebola

---

11. Mossad: National Intelligence Agency of Israel responsible for intelligence collecting, covert operations and counter terrorism

and malaria, which only exacerbated the overcrowding on the other floors. Abigail suggested that they start there.

When they got off of the elevator, Abigail expected to see a clean, modern, sparsely populated ward. Instead, she encountered a scene right out of Dante's *Inferno*. The staff looked exhausted. The patients were filthy. In a room designed for one or two patients, six or seven languished. Thankfully, she saw no beds in the hallways. Everyone was in a room, at least.

The Kilnmari special action squads that Cedrik and company captured were equipped with state of the art PPE. Abigail and the two nurses were each wearing a set. They offered a set to the chief nurse, who politely declined, advising she had her own set.

The two French nurses appeared blasé by what they observed. It was nothing new to them. Abigail, on the other hand, was horrified. She quickly composed herself and started going from patient to patient. She would take their hand in hers, or touch their foreheads, or even just look them in the eyes with a smile. She told each of the patients that they were going to be all right in just a few minutes. None spoke English, but they all could sense the kindness in her words. As she left one patient to go to another, miracle after miracle occurred. The folks who had been at death's door suddenly started feeling better. Their fevers were gone. The blisters on their skin were suddenly cured. Their eyes were clear. Many sat up. Many cried tears of happiness. All were grateful. The doctors and nurses were astounded. The chief nurse almost fainted. Every single patient was cured. Someone called the hospital director, who came scurrying into the ward. He took one look around and solemnly made the sign of the cross and said a silent prayer.

Abigail and the two nurses spent the rest of the day and a good part of the evening touring the hospital's three other stories. The results were mindboggling to the hospital staff and the two

French nurses. Doctors and nurses worked like slaves to examine patients and release them from the hospital. The martial law order had not yet been officially released, so these patients happily made their way back to their homes. By the time Abigail finished, 250 of the 500 patients had been released. The remainder were kept for further examination or because they were not from Loalaville and had no place to go for the evening. Word quickly spread throughout the city about the miracles happening at the hospital. A massive throng of the ailing and the curious crowded around the building. Witch doctors were not that far in the distant past, and many wanted to see the great healer who was much favored by the gods. The crowd kept increasing in size and stayed in remarkably good humor. There were no fights or angry words. Everyone wanted a glimpse of the great healer.

A 'limousine' pulled into the street with its siren blaring. A police car led the way. The car stopped, and the President of Loala stepped out to a vigorous round of applause and cheers. He was greatly loved by his people and respected for being an honest and selfless leader. Loala and the Loalan people always came first with him. He was fanatical in his insistence that everyone in the government act in a like manner. As he strode towards the hospital's entrance, the multitude parted much like the Red Sea parted for Moses. He smiled and shook hands with many, yet they did not rush towards him. They stayed a respectful distance and allowed him to come to them. The entire scene spoke volumes about respect and civility.

The president and his entourage reached the entrance, where he turned and waved to the crowd and received a huge cheer in return. Some in the crowd yelled, "Ter-RÝ, Ter-RÝ." He went inside, where he was met by the Israeli soldiers and the director of the hospital. Just then, Abigail and the two French nurses stepped from the elevator. The president hurried over to them and warmly embraced them. He turned to the hospital director and gave a terse command. The director bowed and left. While Terrence Ngao was speaking with the three women, the director returned and indicated all was ready. He then led the three women and the president to the elevator and the second floor. At a large open window overlooking the entrance, a microphone and speakers had been set up. The president went to the mike and welcomed the crowd. He told them that today was a day of great joy for the country and the city. It was also a day where everyone would be challenged as they had never been challenged before. He stopped then and introduced the two French nurses. They were greeted with polite applause. When he introduced Abigail, the crowd erupted. The cheering went on for almost five minutes. It was heartfelt cheering and not a theatrical production. Abigail was touched as she had never been touched in her life. The people seemed to adore her.

"Citizens of Loala, I have come here to help in any way possible. I know life has not always been easy, and that you have recently faced some horrific attacks. Ebola is a terrible disease. Those who seek to gain from spreading it deserve a special place in hell. For some reason unknown to me, I can help. I am able to defeat this disease. I promise I will stay and do everything I can to eradicate Ebola from beautiful Loala. God bless you all."

When she finished her short speech, the cheers were deafening. If this had happened in the US, OSHA would have mandated hearing protection. Finally, Ngao came back to the microphone. He told the people gathered that he expected an attack in the next day or so. He asked for them to remain calm. He told them that tonight and tomorrow they should stockpile enough food and water for three or four days. He asked that people share the food and water with their neighbors. He went on to say that starting at dusk tomorrow, he was imposing martial law. Everyone was to stay inside with their doors bolted and windows closed until the all-clear signal was given. Abigail would remain in the city. Tomorrow she was headed to the second hospital and would probably observe the martial law order at the Israeli legation. He promised that she would be here with them the entire time. He closed with, "The next few days will be critical to our country. If we remain calm and do not panic, if we protect each other, if we stare the danger right in the eye, it will get out of the way, and we shall prevail. God bless each of you, and God bless Loala."

The three women spent the night in the hospital. The staff cleaned a room for them to stay in, and they enjoyed a very restful night. The next morning, after a quick and simple breakfast, they departed with their Israeli bodyguards to the second hospital. This one was much smaller, much older, and quite a bit shabbier than the first. It had about 300 patients. Unlike the first hospital, patients were crowded in the hallways on gurneys, as well as packed into rooms. The staff at the first hospital looked exhausted. The staff here were truly on their last legs. Every day they tried to work miracles with fewer and fewer assets. The man from the Interior Ministry said that the burnout rate among the staff was incredibly high. Abigail was shocked by the conditions. Even Janelle and Claudette, who were hardened by life in the rural clinics, were shocked. Their carefully crafted air of Gallic indifference lay shattered at the pathetic sights they were observing.

Abigail went right to work, and by 3:00 in the afternoon, she had seen the last patient. The looks of gratitude she received from the patients, as well as the staff, would remain with her forever and provide strength to her in the future.

The attitude of the Israeli bodyguards metamorphosed from that of being baby-sitters to that of being the guardians of precious objects. They proudly embraced their mission. Anyone or anything seeking to harm these women would have to get past them.

Another large crowd had gathered outside the hospital. When Abigail emerged with her entourage, she was greeted by wild applause and cheers. As with the throng yesterday, respect was the word of the day. Abigail did not go directly to the waiting vehicles. As she did in Springfield, PA, she went into the crowd smiling and touching everyone she could reach. The crowd parted out of her way and embraced her with their deep respect and appreciation. Abby spent over an hour with the multitude of Loalans and relished every second of it. She finally went to her vehicle for the drive to the Israeli mission building. As soon as they arrived, it went on lockdown and assumed a wartime footing. Her six 'keepers' requested and received permission to continue their mission.

While Abigail was at the two hospitals, Cedrik and his band had driven to Loalaville. They deposited their prisoners with the Israelis and accepted their hospitality for the night. The next day, they met the dozen men promised by President Ngao. They showed them how to operate the radios and gave a quick class on radio procedures. There is nothing worse and more frustrating than one or more 'ratchet jawed' radio operators tying up the net with gibberish when bullets are flying. The president also made sure that all 12 of these men were fluent in Parisian French. Although French is the official language of Loala, most of the people speak a dialect unrecognizable by most Frenchmen.

Leaving the 12 observers under the charge of Leif and Suleiman, Cedrik and his other two men got in a Range Rover and toured the eastern outer limits of the city from the 12 o'clock to 6 o'clock positions on the compass, deciding what the likely avenues of advance would be and where they would position the

12 observers. Leif and Suleiman were teaching them the fine art of camouflage, cover, and concealment. Hopefully, they would be invisible to an attacking force.

They had found a large stock of PPE in the captured deuce and a half. It was apparent that Obutu wanted his son and his men safe from the horrific pestilence they transported. Cedrik discussed the pros and cons of issuing PPE to the observers. The consensus among his men, including himself, was that they were better off without it. All of the outer garments were white and would draw attention to the observers. Besides, if they did their job correctly, the Kilnmari force would drive by oblivious to them.

At dusk, they split up with Cedrik and each of his four men, taking a couple of observers to their duty posts. A final radio check, and they were set.

Cedrik's plan had the observers on an arch from north to south about one to one-and-a -half miles from the edge of the city. Cedrik and his men were placed on the same arch, except theirs's was about six blocks inside the city on major roads. They needed to be able to move quickly to intercept the attackers.

The hardest part about an ambush is the waiting. Minutes go by like hours. This was true for Cedrik's band and even truer for the dozen Loalan observers spread in remote solitude. The tension of the waiting causes fatigue. This, coupled with the very early hour of the morning, caused several of the observers to doze off. Radio reports from other observers jolted these sleeping beauties awake, but it was too late. Two of the raiders' vehicles had gotten past them unobserved. The two vehicles that were observed, the deuce and a half and a Range Rover, were heading in from the northeast and east, respectively. These were sectors manned by Alexander and Suleiman. The observers identified the streets they were using, and Alexander and Suleiman moved to intercept.

Alexander maneuvered his vehicle to a point where the deuce and a half was heading down a road right towards him. He pulled a Light Anti-tank Weapon from his vehicle and armed it. He waited until the truck was less than 50 yards from him and fired. It was a direct hit, and the truck exploded, instantly killing the two raiders in the cab. Two more jumped out of the back of the truck and were immediately cut down by Alexander's automatic weapon.

Suleiman watched the Range Rover approach his position. It was traveling at a high rate of speed. Just as it came in front of him, he fired his weapon and blew out two of the tires. The driver lost control of the vehicle and swerved into a building. As the soldiers evacuated the vehicle, Suleiman and his weapon personally welcomed them to the afterlife.

The other two Range Rovers got into the city unopposed. Cedrik, Erik, and Leif were on different streets when the attackers passed. C'est la guerre. Being the consummate professionals that they were, Cedrik hurriedly ordered Alexander and Suleiman into blocking positions to the north and northwest and vectored Eric and Leif to likely objectives of the marauders.

One of the Range Rovers headed to the older hospital. When it got near, three of Obutu's troops exited, threw a few hand grenades, and fired their weapons at buildings and windows. As Suleiman had predicted, they were just trying to keep people's heads down. They had their sprayers out and started spraying the entranceway to the hospital, a drinking fountain, a well, and several benches. They then got back into their vehicle and proceeded towards the market district.

The second Range Rover was not nearly as fortunate. The driver got lost and wandered into the area where the foreign legations were clustered. Big mistake. As he rolled past the Israeli building, Abigail's protectors were waiting. The Range Rover was completely decimated by six machine guns fired by six very serious and very angry soldiers.

The surviving Kilnmari vehicle was intercepted just short of the market by Cedrik and Eric in the front and Leif from the rear. The attackers saw what was happening and quickly exited their vehicle with hands in the air. They were satisfied that they had completed the most critical part of their mission. They were unaware that the remainder of their force had been eliminated.

Cedrik was unaware as to what happened with the fourth vehicle, the one which lost its way. Leaving the prisoners with Leif, he and Eric mounted their vehicles and started to patrol the city. All was quiet. When Eric approached the legation district, he saw the carnage wrought by the Israelis upon those who dared harm Abigail. He called in on the radio and his fellow warriors relaxed.

Proceeding to the main government building where President Ngao, the Mayor, and the ministers were waiting, Cedrik quickly briefed them on the early morning's activities and current status. He urged them to get decontamination teams to the sites where the three wrecked vehicles still smoldered and to the older hospital area. He emphasized that these needed to be rendered safe before people ventured out.

The president quickly grasped the situation and barked orders. HAZMAT teams were dispatched to contain the virus. Vehicles with loudspeakers started to continuously roam the city urging people to remain inside and announcing that the president would deliver an address to the city and the nation later in the day.

Abigail and the nurses were overjoyed when Cedrik and his band arrived. The entire staff of the mission celebrated the victory and the safe return of all of them. Abigail looked at Cedrik and said, "It's time. There are no casualties here. I have done what I could at the hospitals. Maternity wards are functioning. They don't need me. Let's head out to the villages and help those people. They are still fighting Ebola and God knows what else."

Cedrik nodded in agreement. "You're right. We'll head out in an hour or so."

Janelle and Claudette both volunteered to go along. They said they stayed in-country to help, not sit in relative comfort in a city. Now that they had the truck and Range Rovers, as well as the jeeps, transportation was not an issue. Cedrik readily agreed that they could join them.

When the foreign officials were briefed two days earlier about the upcoming attack, the diplomats relayed the information to their respective governments. Several also contacted members of the media to alert them to the situation. Loala is a very remote country; thus travel there is not instantaneous. As a result, there were almost no members of the foreign press in the country when the gunfire erupted. That soon changed. The vehicles were still smoldering when the first reporters arrived. Concurrently, a small convoy of two jeeps, two Range Rovers, and a deuce and a half departed the city heading southeast towards the border with Kilnmari.

EBOLA

I t was no surprise that the reports filed by the press about the events in Loala were grossly sensationalized. Government officials were quick to denounce Obutu and Kilnmari and called on the African Union to take action. Genocide cannot be tolerated. They were also quick to lavish praise upon the brave warriors who conquered the invaders, upon the two heroic French nurses who braved death to help a helpless population, and especially upon the young American woman who cured 'thousands upon thousands' of sick Loalans.

Interviews with people on the street, as well as people who had been in the hospitals reaped even more sensational headlines. Some called her a saint, others called her a miracle worker, while still others compared her to some of the ancient and famous witch doctors. The press had a field day.

However, not everyone reveled in Abigail's accomplishments. A very sick Kim Jong Un castigated his lackeys. "How could President Diamond fail to deliver his promise of sending that girl here to cure me? Was the president a paper lion? How could he allow a mere girl to publicly defy him? Maybe it is time to show Diamond who the boss is." He went on to ask his generals, "When will you be ready to launch some more missiles?"

On the other side of the Pacific Ocean, things were even more tense and uncomfortable. In the boss's office, Polina and Barney stood at rigid attention while she screamed bloody murder at them and threatened them with all kinds of unworldly torment. When Abigail first went to Loala, the boss had a meltdown. That was nothing compared to what she was doing now. "Fix it! Do you hear me? Fix it! I don't care what you have to do, just fix it!"

A little farther to the south, a similar scene was playing. Lucius Diamond was pacing the Oval Office. Sitting ashen-face were most of the key members of his cabinet, as well as the Chief of Staff, the Director of National Intelligence, and the FBI Director. The president was reviewing the collective and individual failures of all who were seated in the room. The fear among them was palpable. The president did not formally adjourn the meeting. He told all present to "get their sorry asses out of his sight."

Located almost halfway between the boss's office and the Oval Office was the cubicle of Diana Chan in the Philadelphia studio of CNB. Diana was closely following the events unfolding in Loala. She liked Abigail and felt sorry for her. Diana had been in the business long enough to realize that scruples and morals were not in the vocabulary of most journalists. She prided herself that they were two of her guiding values, never to be forgotten or overlooked. She was a very astute and savvy journalist, and knew a good story when she saw one. She knew from experience that sensationalism was just camouflage for lack of talent. Without a doubt in her mind, she knew she could and should present Abigail's adventures in Loala to the world. Her problem was she was just a minor reporter in a mid-size television market. She did not have the gravitas to make demands on management. She had to sell them on the idea. She took a deep breath and picked up the phone.

It took a monumental effort on her part to get the station manager to even think about putting her on the story. She was relentless to the point where he actually called her a 'human hemorrhoid' to her face. She was thrilled. She was finally making progress. She was not sure whether he truly believed she was the best for the job or if he just wanted to appease her, but he called the network executives in New York and made a pitch for her. He reminded them that she was the one who originally broke the story and was the only reporter to whom Abigail had granted an exclusive interview. Since there were not a lot of volunteers to get the inoculations required for travel to that part of Africa or who were willing to subject themselves to the rigors of that journey, they acquiesced and granted permission for Diana to take on the story.

A coalition military force from sub-Saharan members of the African Union was dispatched to Loala to assist in fortifying the borders and to investigate Obutu's transgressions. Frankie sang like a canary concerning his father's plans for annexing the riches and resources of Loala while maintaining his own total innocence. He was a victim. He was also a prisoner. He was ordered to appear before The International Court of Justice in The Hague to answer charges of conspiracy to commit genocide, attempted genocide, and murder. He cried like a baby as he was led in chains to the helicopter that would transport him to the nearest international airport for the flight to Europe.

Abigail, Cedrik, and their associates traveled southeast from Loalaville. They stopped at every village that they found. Several were very fortunate. They had not yet been visited by Kilnmari raiders. Unfortunately, most had. The survivors all told similar stories. The raiders would drop off one or more bodies of Ebola victims into the village, usually near the well and or market. The villagers who moved the bodies usually became infected and spread the disease to their family and friends. No one had PPE, so they were helpless. Any medical personnel encountered by the raiders were immediately shot.

Abigail worked tirelessly to help anyone still alive. Some of these poor souls had one foot in the grave and were in the process of putting the other foot in with it. She gently brought these folks back to life, such that it was.

Disease was not the only enemy. Food was almost non-existent. The raiders learned that stealing or destroying food and crops would enhance their evil process. In some villages, they fouled the water supply, making it undrinkable. The nurses did their best scrounging up food. They even took some rations from their supply. They were as generous as possible with their water knowing full well that they would find the same conditions in the next village. After the third or fourth village with the food and water supply destroyed, Cedrik dispatched Leif in a Range Rover back to Loalaville to report on the growing crisis.

After two weeks on their journey, they were exhausted both physically and mentally. The three women were also discouraged. Cedrik and his men, unfortunately, had seen examples of man's inhumanity to his fellow man far too often and in far too many forms to be discouraged. They learned to put their minds in neutral, and just drive on doing the best that they could. By this time, the supplies that they had brought with them in the deuce and a half, including fuel, were getting desperately low.

Leif had been gone five days when Cedrik called all of his people together. He said that they did not have a choice. They needed to return to Loalaville for re-supply. He did not know what happened to Leif, but they could not take a chance. They had to go back.

"Please, let us do at least one more village. I won't be able to face myself if I leave knowing I could have helped." said Abigail. The nurses nodded in agreement.

Cedrik answered, "And then there will be another village and another one after that. We have the potential to save a lot of people, but if we expend all of our resources, we won't be able to help anyone."

Abigail pleaded, "Please, just one more village, and then I won't argue. We will just go back."

Cedrik knew what battles to fight and what battles to run from. He ran from this one. The next day they entered another village. It seemed that conditions in each village they entered were worse than those in the previous village. They were in a downward vortex sucking the soul out of humanity. Abigail wondered aloud about how it was possible that things could get worse, yet they seemed to with each subsequent village. In this village, they encountered a quarter of the population dead. Of the remaining people, half were in the last stages of Ebola. Their suffering was almost over. Those who were spared from the disease were starving. They drove past a pathetic and heartbreaking sight of a woman in her early twenties lying dead along the side of the road, with three young children all under five years of age sitting next to her crying their eyes out. The nurses yelled for their vehicle to stop. They jumped out and Janelle hurriedly gathered up the children. Claudette examined the mother. She did not expire from the virus, so it must have been either some other disease or starvation that killed her. Abigail and the warriors did a quick recon of the village. Abigail picked a starting point and began the process of visiting and curing the sick. She was again able to pull all of the surviving villagers back away from the Grim Reaper, though she was powerless to do anything about the food and water supply, which frustrated her to no end.

Not for the first time, Abigail was impressed and moved by the people of Loala. Even in their misery and suffering, they were patient, kind, and generous. From time to time in her life, she had met one or two people with those qualities. Now she was in a nation where everyone she encountered possessed them. This only drove her to work harder.

Just as the band was finishing up in the village and getting prepared to head back to Loalaville, they saw a dust cloud on the horizon heading in their direction. Cedrik moved his squad to defensive positions where they could intercept the interlopers if they were, in fact, hostile. From the size of the dust cloud, there was more than one vehicle heading their way.

Finally, everyone breathed a sigh of relief. The first vehicle in the convoy was the Range Rover driven by a grinning Leif. He explained that he had a flat tire on the way back to the city which delayed him some. Once in the city, he learned that the African Union dispatched a force to Loala. His report on the Ebola, coupled with efforts to starve anyone the virus spared was met with outrage. In the convoy were five trucks loaded with food and bottled water. Also, each truck was pulling a water trailer filled with clean, potable water. There were two fuel trucks, a couple of ambulances, medics with medical supplies, and a couple of doctors, as well. Leif reported that they visited all the villages that their party visited after leaving Loalaville and dropped off additional food and water, and reported that the survivors in those villages were in good spirits and appeared to be doing well.

Cedrik looked at the map and conferred with Abigail and the commander of the supply convoy. Abigail was the key to the humanitarian effort. They devised a plan where Abigail and the French nurses would head out with the convoy to the next village. Abigail would work her powers and then they would move on to the next. At least one truck with appropriate medical personnel would remain at the village to distribute food and ensure the village was secure. At some point, it would depart to catch up with Abigail, who, by that time, could be three or four villages away. Speed and the leap-frogging of the relief vehicles were the keys to success.

Cedrik was boiling with rage at this point. That bastard, Francois Obutu, could not be permitted to go on and vowed to take him out. He took the commander of the supply column aside and entrusted the safety of the three women to him. He told him that he and his warriors were going to Kilnmari to pay a visit to Obutu.

Before they departed for Kilnmari, Cedrik knew that he and his men needed food. The entire group of the warriors and the women sat down in a clearing and opened their rations. While they were eating, he told them the story of Francois and Annette, Obutu's evil first wife.

It all began when Francois was a private in the army. He was a devious little prick who ingratiated himself to the sergeants and a few junior officers. He kept his ear to the ground and his ass out of the line of fire. No matter what happened, his hands were always clean. Officials were so used to having him around that they took little or no notice of him. They discussed matters in front of him that should never have even been contemplated, let alone uttered. When Francois heard several officers whispering about a coup d'état, he thought he had a golden opportunity.

As always, his top priority was taking care of number one. He 'just happened' to bump into the sitting president's Chief of Security and mentioned that several officers were planning a takeover during the Independence Day parade in two days. He briefed the security chief in detail about the plotters' plan. The security chief devised a plan to ambush the ambushers. He had the grandstands on either side of the president's reviewing box filled with his armed men in civilian clothes.

As the designated assault troops were passing in review in front of the president, they suddenly turned and started firing. The security force was ready and returned fire. The carnage was devastating on both sides. Francois had positioned himself in a very secure position at the back of the reviewing stand. The president dove for cover with his security chief and major cabinet ministers right beside him. As they lay there, Francois came up behind them with a submachine gun and eliminated all of them. He waited until the firing in the parade was finished and saw bodies in the road and in the grandstands. There were very few who were not killed or wounded. He then walked up to the microphone and declared himself to be the ruler of Kilnmari. At this point, the army could have put a stop to the nonsense, but most of its leaders lay dead in front of the stands. Without anyone in charge, Francois was able to fill the void.

His first task was to consolidate power. He was ruthless. He found associates who were more than willing to trade honor for gold. He purchased loyalty. He was brutal with anyone who questioned his authority. Then he pulled off his master-stroke. He married Annette.

Francois was not a deep thinker. He thought about today, and sometimes he thought about tomorrow. Not so Annette. She had been brought up the daughter of a ne'er-do-well. Her family was somewhere between the peasant class and the relatively wealthy merchants and landowners. She did receive an education of sorts, but certainly not at schools in Europe like some of her friends. She was always just lacking, always not quite good enough. She chafed at her station in life and vowed to improve it no matter what price or who paid it. In Francois, she saw a weapon that was potentially deadly, but only if used by a skilled practitioner.

Through her efforts, Francois' hold on power intensified. Enemies and potential enemies were not just neutralized; they were eradicated in the most extreme fashion. If Annette's secret police came for someone, it was a safe bet that person had but a very short and very painful time to live. She used to attend interrogation sessions. Interrogation was a euphemism for torture. Annette would invite guests to watch the festivities and was quick to criticize and chastise interrogators if she judged that the punishment being inflicted was not up to her standards. As a result, they were energetic and creative in their duties. Another result was that her guests came away terrified and with a new appreciation of her depravity.

Francois was inept as a lover. He provided her with a son, and then she refused to have any further relations with him. Naturally, he protested. So as not to cause a scandal or jeopardize her position, she told him to take a second wife. She insisted that he only use this person for sex. Annette was to be the chief wife, while the new girl would be the lesser wife. That is how Marie Justine entered the picture. Marie Justine endured Francois, and she was petrified of Annette. She soon became a refreshing wind in the country. She was friendly to everyone. She took an interest in the welfare of the people. She would often nag her husband to do the right thing and not the politically expedient thing. Annette hated her, but Marie Justine's popularity was growing exponentially. She found herself powerless to remove her. The people would not tolerate it, so Annette had no choice but to 'suffer' in silence.

Having finished with the tale, Cedrik told Abigail and the nurses that he and his men were leaving. He met fierce resistance. This time Cedrik knew this was a battle he had to fight and win. No matter what the women said or threatened, he was intractable. He would not be swayed. All three of the women tearfully embraced each of the men and hugged them tightly.

The men loaded two of the Range Rovers and the deuce and a half. Then they all donned the white PPE coveralls and masks. It was impossible to tell who they were or even what race they were. Cedrik called down from the deuce and a half that they would try to link up with them down the road, or failing that, they would see them back in Loalaville.

When the three vehicles departed the village, they were about 10 miles from the Kilnmari border. Cedrik figured that it was an additional 50 miles to reach the capital and Obutu's palace. A total of 60 miles over roads of questionable quality. He was sure that they would not be high-speed Autobahn quality, but hopefully they would be paved. As always, speed was of paramount importance. They needed to get in and out before people knew they were even there.

They reached the border crossing, a single guard hut with a manually operated crossing barrier. The barrier was just a pole, hinged on one end and free on the other. Its sole purpose was to keep an honest person honest. A determined person would hardly notice it. Such was the case here. The deuce and a half with Cedrik driving just smashed through the pole. The guards recognized the vehicles as Kilnmari military and held their fire. They noted the occupants were wearing PPE. They figured Frankie was in a hurry to get home. One guard got on a landline to report the incident. The bored voice on the other end of the line agreed with his assessment about the return of the prodigal son. They both had a chuckle and then promptly forgot about the incident.

The sun was setting when the three vehicles approached the city. The one word to describe it was shabby. Loalaville was a poor city, but it was evident that people tried to keep it clean, tried to maintain the buildings, tried to show pride in their city. This city was just the opposite. It could have been the poster city for desolation and despair. It was a dirty, run-down cluster of buildings that could easily be mistaken for hovels. The notable exception was a magnificent pink edifice sitting behind high walls.

It was two stories high and had a sturdy tile roof as opposed to the tin roofs of the city's other buildings.

The band of warriors pulled into an open field near the jungle overlooking the city. They noted possible routes of entrance, as well as egress. Surprise, speed, shock, and awe were about to be displayed for Obutu and his men. After deciding on the plan and making sure everyone knew their role in the attack, the deuce and a half led the way down the hill. They stopped at the front gate and were confronted by two heavily armed guards. Still unrecognizable in his PPE, Cedrik, in a very soft voice muttered one word, "Ebola!" The two guards recognized the word but were unsure of the context. The split second that they hesitated cost them their lives. Cedrik in the passenger's seat and Suleiman in the driver's seat brought up a pair of 9 mm Glocks with silencers and shot both of the guards directly between the eyes. They then pulled through the gates and stopped short of the massive doors of the palace. The two Range Rovers entered the compound and turned around so they were facing the gate. Leif stayed with the Range Rovers, while Eric and Alexander joined Cedrik at the door.

Cedrik gave the signal, and Suleiman dropped the truck in gear and hit the accelerator. A deuce and a half is not fast, but it is powerful. It effortlessly crashed through the doors, then backed out. The other three warriors went into the house with guns in hand. A man in uniform came into the hallway with gun drawn. Alexander dispatched him with a burst from his Uzi submachine gun.

Alexander stayed by the stairway as Cedrik and Eric raced to the second floor. Once there, they started kicking in doors. A few bursts of gunfire from their weapons ended any resistance. In one room, they found a very beautiful, graceful woman who exuded dignity. Cedrik thought that she must be Obutu's lesser wife, Marie Justine. From all reports, Marie Justine was totally out of place here. She was well-educated, refined, gentle, generous, and kind. Cedrik had not read an unkind word about her anywhere. He bowed slightly to her. She gave him an imperious nod. There was no hint of fear in her. Cedrik smiled and departed.

In the next room, they found their quarry. Obutu was hiding in the closet. Annette, Obutu's prime wife, was standing in front of the closed closet door with her arms folded, glaring malevolently at the intruders, daring them to try to come in. Eric went into the room and walked up to her. Before she could utter a word, he hit her with a vicious backhand across the face. She yelped and fell over. She started to get up with a pistol in her hand but found that Eric had a serrated hunting knife at her throat. She dropped the gun and Eric kicked it out of the way. In French, Cedrik told whoever was in the closet to come out, unarmed with his hands in the air. When no one appeared, Eric fired a brief bust at the top of the closet door.

Magically, the door started to open. Cedrik, using the door for cover, grasped the handle and pulled it open. Standing there in all of his five-foot two-inch evil splendor was the personification of evil itself, Francois Obutu. He had a bald head, a goatee that ended in a sharp point just below his chin, and a close-cropped mustache. He was wearing his thick, black-rimmed glasses and a splendid dress uniform. Once his eyes became accustomed to the light, he saw Annette sitting on the floor with a huge red welt beginning to form on her cheek. "Who are you?" he demanded.

With a sneer, Cedrik replied, "Your worst frigging nightmare. Now get your ass in gear and help the 'lady' to her feet."

Eric secured both of their hands behind their backs with ties, and Cedrik led them to the door. Standing just outside the door in the hallway was Marie Justine. She ignored Cedrik and Eric and stared at the other two with pure hatred in her eyes. Cedrik was convinced that if he handed her a weapon, she would arrange immediate transportation for these two to a place with a very warm climate. She was a woman who was very slow to rile, but once riled, get out of her path.

"Madam. Would you care to stay here, or would you rather accompany us? I assure you that you will be safe with us."

"Do you think for a minute that I will not be safe here? These are my people, and they love me. They have been terrorized by that jackass and his whore for 20 years." She paused for a moment then continued, "No, I am perfectly safe here. Trust me, there will be celebrations all over the country when these two depart. Now, if you please, get them out of my sight."

Obutu started to say something, but a Judo chop to the neck from Cedrik caused him to take an unexpected nap. Cedrik called for Alexander to come up the stairs and carry Obutu out. Cedrik then turned and bowed again to Marie Justine, who returned the bow along with a smile.

Once outside, they loaded the two prisoners in the cargo sections of each Range Rover. With Suleiman and Leif driving, they headed back to Loala. Somehow word must have gotten out. Standing along the roads were small clusters of people waving the Kilnmari flags and waving at the two vehicles.

They were well inside the Loalan border when Suleiman asked, "What should we do with those two?"

Cedrik replied, "What we should do is turn around and return them to the people of Kilnmari to dispose of as they see fit. We won't do that unless you have a strong disagreement. Vengeance has never been productive. No, I think we should bring them with us to Loalaville and let the bastards join their son and stand before the International Court of Justice. What do you think?"

The other four squad members nodded their agreement, and the decision was ratified. Cedrik then said, "Let's go find Abigail.

They can't be more than three or four villages away.

They embarked on their journey heading in a southerly direction. They were amazed by what they found in each village. The villagers were up and about. They appeared healthy and reasonably happy. The aid workers in every village were working on decontaminating the water supply and helping the inhabitants plant new crops. Those who had died of the virus before Abigail's arrival had been buried in respectful, individual graves. Life in all cases was going on and heading quickly to normalcy.

They found Abigail in the fourth village. She was bending over an elderly lady who was suffering greatly from the virus. Cedrik's blood boiled when he saw this sight. He ordered that the two prisoners be brought immediately to this hut. Leif and Alexander roughly threw the two into the hut. They recoiled in horror at what they witnessed. The men wondered if they were horrified by the havoc that they caused or the fact that they were so close to it that they might become infected. It was probably the latter. Abigail held the old lady's hand and spoke gently to her. Although there was a language barrier, the woman knew that the young girl was there to help and to provide solace. She looked at Abigail with a mixture of hope and gratitude. Abigail smiled at her and stood up. With an awful French accent, she said to the woman, "Bonne chance mon ami."

As Abigail walked over to Cedrik and away from her, the old woman got to her feet, stretched her arms, and took a deep breath. She was alive. Cedrik pointed at the two prisoners and said, "Ms. Williams, may I present Francois and Annette Obutu? These are the two individuals responsible for this disaster."

The withering look that Abigail flashed at the pair was full of contempt, loathing, and disdain. Abigail said not a word. She pointed violently at the door for someone to get these two people out of her sight. As Leif and Alexander roughly manhandled the prisoners in their restraints towards the two vehicles, Francois protested that he and his wife needed to stretch their legs. They had been riding in the cargo areas of the Range Rovers for several hours and needed to move about. Leif grabbed him by the collar and his belt and literally picked him up off his feet and threw him into the vehicle. He then turned to offer the same service to Annette. She was a quick learner and hurried into the cargo hold of the second vehicle without assistance.

They continued their trek of mercy heading due south until they reached the southern border, then they turned west. Each village that they encountered was struggling with the virus, as well as poisoned water and destroyed crops. Abigail brought comfort and healing to the sick and the supply trucks brought sustenance. Unfortunately, the supplies were again almost depleted. Abigail herself looked totally spent. She had been running on nervous energy almost from the day they departed Loalaville.

They finally came upon a village that had armed men out on the road. The weapons were old, and those who held them looked very uncomfortable holding them, but they were there making a defensive stand. Cedrik stopped the convoy and got out of the Range Rover smiling. His squad did the same. They started congratulating each other as if they had just won a victory. The people in the trucks, as well as the defending force, looked at the five warriors like they were escapees from an insane asylum. Cedrik walked calmly to the defenders and somehow made them understand that they were not hostile. They were visiting villages that had been ravaged by Obutu's forces and helping the villagers. The defenders got the message and put up their weapons with bright smiles on their faces.

Abigail and the two nurses watched the scene unfold and had no idea what was happening. Alexander came back to the vehicles and Abby posed the question. He replied, "Don't you understand. Obutu's men didn't make it this far. They stopped or were stopped before they could go any further. I think it is over. These guys must have learned what was happening elsewhere from a survivor and decided to put up a fight. God love them. They would have been massacred, but they would have gone down fighting."

The squad returned to the vehicles and made their way into the village. It was just as Alexander surmised. They heard about the attacks on other villages and decided to put up a fight. Cedrik asked for and received permission for them to remain in the village overnight. Every village and town, in the best of circumstances, has many sick people. Abigail spent several hours curing all who were ailing. That night Abigail, the nurses, and the warriors slept like babies knowing that a grateful village was watching over them.

ABBYVILLE

Diana Chan sat in the lobby of the Grand Hotel, drinking what euphemistically was called coffee. It was liquid, hot, and black. Those were the only things her drink had in common with the coffee she was used to. Same with the hotel. The only thing grand about it was the name. While it was the best in Loalaville, it barely offered the basics of cleanliness and security. Comfort was not on the menu.

The waiting was becoming interminable. Abigail was somewhere out in the boondocks, exact location unknown. The only word from Abigail and her party was when Leif came back to report on the deteriorating conditions that they had encountered and to request additional resources.

When word first broke across the world about Kilnmari's use of Ebola as a weapon of war against its neighbor, civilized nations across the globe recoiled in horror. Their citizens clamored for news about the horrific events unfolding in this tiny African country. A swarm of journalists and reporters descended on Loala and waited. The media is not known for its patience. These people were racking up charges on their expense accounts and were producing nothing. Network executives increased the pressure on the reporters to produce. The result was that many sensational and totally false reports were filed and broadcast.

A reporter for a German network reported that an unnamed but reliable source claimed that Abigail and her entourage had been ambushed by Kilnmari soldiers and killed. Abigail and the two French nurses had been repeatedly raped before having their throats cut.

A correspondent for a British tabloid reported that Cedrik and Abigail had abandoned the group and had run off to parts unknown. With a nod and a wink, the writer ended the story with a line about him assuming that the pair were engaging in some rather intense research.

After a while, even the perpetrators of these tales grew tired of the fiction they spewed. The Loala story quickly became stale. The 24-hour news cycle moved on and most of the reporters left the country. Diana stayed and breathed a sigh of relief that the imbeciles had gone. She was tired of waiting and growing more nervous each day about Abigail's safety.

After days of waiting, she sensed real excitement building in the city. Somehow word had reached Loalaville that they were returning. Throngs lined the streets of the capital, cheering wildly as the convoy came into view. Some waved Loalan flags while a few held signs with one word: MERCI. The crowd was exuberant, but as with everything Loalan, they were respectful and well-mannered.

Cedrik drove to the building housing the Israeli mission. A smiling Joshua Weinschenk was standing outside of the entrance with Abram by his side. Both were waving at the returning heroes. Also with them was the Loalan Minister of the Interior. He walked up to Cedrik's side of the vehicle and asked Cedrik to please drive to the main government office building. Cedrik nodded that he would comply with the request. Before he drove off, he motioned for Weinschenk to approach. When he was close, Cedrik was seen motioning towards the back of the vehicle. Weinschenk appeared to be stunned. He called Abram over and the three of them conversed, along with the Minister of the Interior. Finally, all four men nodded. Abram hurried inside of the mission and returned in just a few minutes with eight heavily armed and very serious looking soldiers. Four went to each vehicle and roughly pulled Francois and Annette out. Both prisoners were still wearing restraints. Two soldiers went to each prisoner and literally dragged them into the building.

Diana was in the crowd, observing what was happening. When the two prisoners appeared, the people around her became highly agitated. Diana was not sure who the man and the woman were, but she was certain that the crowd hated them. When she later learned their identities, she marveled that the Loalan character traits of discipline and restraint prevailed. There were angry words and curses hurled at the two criminals, but nothing that would physically harm them. The two monsters cowered as they were dragged by the soldiers to the front entrance.

The crowd soon forgot about them and turned their attention on Abby, the two nurses, and Cedrik and his men. They cheered and cheered until Abby timidly got out of her vehicle and waved to them. The others followed. Diana was truly moved by the outpouring of affection. She could not recall ever seeing anything like this before. As Abby moved around the vehicles smiling and waving, Diana was able to catch her eye. Abby smiled in delight. In sign language, Diana conveyed that she would like to speak with Abigail later, and Abby nodded her head in agreement.

A short while later, they loaded back up and followed the Interior Minister to the main government building. Standing in front of the building was President Terrence Ngao, as well as the mayor of the city and other high ranking government officials. Handshakes were exchanged all around, and then the party posed for pictures taken by the few photographers still in the country. They all went inside the building where Ngao excused himself as he, the Interior Minister, and the mayor went into an office and closed the door. While they were in the office, refreshments were served to the guests. About 20 minutes later, Joshua Weinschenk and Abram hurried into the building and the office. Cedrik whispered to Abigail, "I'll wager that the president just learned about the two presents we brought him."

Sure enough, in no time, the five men exited the office wearing huge grins. The president was almost giddy with excitement. It is one thing to have your country saved from a disaster, but to have it saved and your mortal enemy removed at the same time was beyond belief. He asked all of the visitors to follow him to the upstairs balcony. When they stepped out onto it, the crowd erupted into cheers, which lasted for minutes. A bank of microphones had been set up, and he stood behind them to address the crowd. Speaking Loalan French in a slow and clear voice, he began by telling the people that the crisis had passed. They were no longer in danger. He related the exploits of the eight crusaders with particular praise going to the two French nurses for staying to help even after they came perilously close to perishing. He expressed undying admiration for and gratitude to the five warriors. He finally came to Abigail. Words failed him for a moment. When he finally composed himself, he said that the number of Loalans who owed their lives directly to her could barely be counted. He borrowed Churchill's famous quote about so much being owed to so few by so many.

After each segment, the crowd erupted in cheers. By far, the loudest and longest came when he spoke about Abigail. When the cheering had almost run its course, Ngao continued, "I have a surprise for the people of Loala. Monsieur Balthazar and his colleagues brought us a present. I should say that they brought us two presents. Sitting right now under guard in the Israeli legation are Francois Obutu and his wife, Annette. They will be turned over to The International Court of Justice in The Hague, where I am confident they will be dealt with appropriately. I will say that whatever the court decides will be infinitely more humane and just than what they did to Loala and Loalans."

The crowd roared for a full five minutes. Diana, standing with the masses, recorded every word. She could hardly wait to transmit this to Philadelphia. If she could follow it up with interviews of all of the participants, she would have the scoop of the century.

Diana found a satellite phone and filed her report on Loala. She did not embellish it or sensationalize it in any way. This was a story that could stand on its own two feet. When it hit the airways of the world, it set off a chain reaction.

First in Washington DC, President Diamond was livid. He kept asking his cabinet and senior officials of the intelligence services and Defense Department how this girl got out of the country, traveled to Loala of all places, and then mounted an invasion of an independent country without their knowledge. No answers were forthcoming. It so happened that as the president was walking back from Marine 1, the presidential helicopter, earlier that morning, reporters started pelting him with questions about Loala and Kilnmari. The president was caught with his pants down. He had never heard of either country. Never wanting to appear weak, out of the loop, or having to admit he did not have the answer, he said he was fully aware of the situation and that the State Department would be issuing an official statement shortly. So that they did not appear weak, the reporters kept pressing him and pressing him.

The president finally turned his back on them and went inside the White House. On just about every broadcast news program later that day, very earnest, serious-looking, knowledgeable, and wise reporters speculated that the president had authorized United States personnel to invade and bring down the government of a sovereign power. Congressmen and senators from the opposition party could not get in front of the media fast enough to denounce the president and call for investigations. One congressman from California called for Diamond's immediate impeachment. Legislators from the president's party called for restraint.

Across town, James Berkshire and his son and chief campaign aide, Sylvester, watched in rapt silence as the story broke and expanded on television. The senator asked, "Where the hell are Loala and Kilnmari? Someplace in Asia? I've never heard of them."

Sylvester answered, "I'm not sure, Dad. Australia, I think."

Berkshire just looked at his son and shook his head in disbelief.

Sylvester went on, "You know, Dad, I think you need to make a statement that you don't condone this sort of action. Something like this would never happen in your administration. You would make certain that the United States respects the sovereignty of every nation." He paused and then continued, "By the way, Dad, do you know that I actually know this Abigail person?"

His father shot up out of his chair. "You what? Tell me about her."

"Well, I met her on Abdul Shaytan's yacht. She's an OK girl. Real quiet. Kind of shy. Decent body, not great. Drinks a little, not a lot. OK face. Definitely not my type."

James Berkshire thought to himself, "That means she can stand up straight, doesn't drag her knuckles when she walks, and she speaks coherently in complete sentences. No, definitely not your type." Instead, he asked his son, "Can you get in touch with her? I'd love to meet her. Perhaps you can ask her out for a date or something."

"I'll think about it." Changing the subject, Sylvester said, "Did you hear that my friend Dexter van Allen got indicted the other day for fraud and conspiracy to commit fraud. It's all a bunch of crap. When you get elected, Dad, I hope you will be able to do something. Dex is a good guy and didn't do anything wrong."

Back in the Oval Office, the president exclaimed, "I received a message from Kim Jong Un's personal representative. It seems that the cancer has metastasized and Kim is in really rough shape. He asks that we get the Williams girl over there right away and for her to make him better." He was met with deafening silence. No one wanted to be the first to enter this pool. Diamond looked around at his minions. "Well, someone say something. How do we get her over there?"

The Secretary of Defense answered, "Well, we know she is in Loala. It's a tiny spec of land right in the center of Africa. It has a few unimproved landing strips, but no airport to speak of. A couple of the strips might be able to handle a C-130[12] with JATO's.[13] Roads lead into the country from all four directions, but at best they are only two-lane and not-well maintained."

A frustrated Diamond snapped, "I don't have time for a lesson on Loala. I want an answer on how we get her to North Korea quickly."

SECDEF answered, "I recommend we move a carrier to the west coast as close as possible to Loala. We get permission from the countries over which we have to fly and send in a chopper. We'll have a good-looking young officer come out of the chopper and persuade her to come with him. He can tell her that you sent him to bring her back for a hero's welcome. If she refuses, we will have some not-so-friendly serious men come out of the chopper

---

12. C-130: Four-engine turboprop military cargo plane

13. JATO: Jet Assisted Take Off, auxiliary rockets mounted on the side of cargo planes to provide extra lift

and snatch her. Once we get her on the carrier, we put her on a transport and send her to Asia. Case closed."

Both the Attorney General and the Secretary of State looked at Defense like he grew two heads. Finally, State said, "Are you nuts? You want to send in a military mission to kidnap a US citizen in a sovereign country? I don't want any part of this. This is the type of crap that the Saudis and Iranians pull. Not the United States."

The president said in a condescending tone, "It's Loala. No one has ever heard of it. Who are they going to protest to? Even more important, who cares? We can keep this quiet and no one will ever know. We get her over to Kim, and he will owe us a big one. Think about what that will do for my campaign. Berkshire won't know what hit him." He looked at the Secretary of Defense and said, "Make it so." The others in the room knew that he would brook no protests and meekly departed.

The next day in Loalaville, Diana and Abigail were having coffee in the lobby of the Belgian mission. Diana had a camera set up and was recording the interview. Abigail started by describing her last few mass events and her refuge in the Smokey Mountains. She did not mention the monastery in Georgia per se, but she did mention President Diamond's phone call about going to North Korea. Very unprofessionally, Diana blurted, "Say what?" Abigail continued with the details of the call and how upset the president became. She then described leaving the country with Cedrik and traveling to Loala. She went into considerable detail about her adventures in Loala, culminating in her sitting in the Belgian mission, drinking coffee, and chatting with Diana. Diana was mostly silent during Abigail's narrative. She would occasionally interject a question or two to clarify something or to get Abigail's emotional involvement in the crisis. As the interview started to come to its conclusion, Diana was congratulating herself on what she considered to be her best interview ever.

Suddenly there was a commotion among the staff of the mission. Diana and Abigail looked up to see a very beautiful and regal woman striding towards them.

"Please excuse my interruption. My name is Marie Justine Obutu. I was Francois's lesser wife until I divorced the bastard yesterday. I am currently the acting president of Kilnmari. I have come to offer my most sincere thanks to you, Ms. Williams, for saving so many innocent souls here in Loala. What my former husband and his wife did is unpardonable. It could have been so much worse without you. In fact, it would still be going on."

Diana had subtly moved the camera to include Marie Justine in the picture. Abigail asked her to please have a seat and make herself comfortable. She did so and explained that she contacted President Terrence Ngao and asked his permission to pay a formal visit to Loala. She went on to say that the purpose of the visit was to apologize for Obutu's actions and to see if there was anything Kilnmari could do in the way of reparations to try to mitigate the damage. She and her staff would be meeting with the Loalans a little later. First, she wanted to thank Abigail and the five soldiers who actually carted the two Obutu's off to justice. She stayed just a few minutes more and then got to her feet and excused herself. After shaking hands with Abigail and Diana, she departed to try to find Cedrik and his squad.

Diana turned off the camera and said to Abigail, "Abby, this is an incredible story and it just keeps getting better. Before you know it, they will change the name of this city to Abbyville."

EXTRACTION

The aircraft carrier USS *Eisenhower* had been operating in the Mediterranean Sea based out of Naples. Thus far, it had been a very uneventful and sometimes pleasant cruise. No aircraft had been lost. There had been few incidents when the crew had liberty ashore. The task force had performed well in joint maneuvers with other NATO forces. All in all, the captain was happy with the way things were progressing. In three months, he would relinquish command of 'The Ike,' and he fully expected to be on the next promotion list to flag rank. However, he had been in the Navy long enough to always be wary of the fickle finger of fate. One never knew when it would turn on him.

Sure enough, he received a flash message to head to a location off of the west coast of Africa. When he approached Gibraltar, he was to be prepared to receive an inbound helicopter and to follow the orders that an officer/courier carried. The captain grinned ruefully. Things had been going too well, and now the fickle finger was beginning to turn.

Just after passing Gibraltar and entering the Atlantic, the officer of the deck reported that a helicopter was requesting permission to land. After it had powered down, a lieutenant commander (LCDR) deplaned, followed by four heavily-armed men. The captain thought to himself, "SEALs, great. What next?"

The LCDR came to the bridge and reported to the captain. The captain was surprised to see that he was not a SEAL. He was a Naval aviator. His name tag said "Dawson." "Sir, I'm LCDR Trevor Dawson. Here are the orders I am to deliver to you."

The captain read the orders and shrugged. "Well, these seem simple enough. Are there any hidden surprises in these?"

"Not that I am aware of, Sir. They seem pretty cut-and-dry to me, also."

"I assume that you will be using the chopper that just brought you here for this mission and not one of mine."

"That is correct, Sir."

"Who are those men who came with you? SEALs?"

"That is correct, Sir."

That was about the extent of the conversation. The captain ordered a course change and the ship, plus her escorts, turned south. Dawson was an aviator, so he knew his way around an aircraft carrier. The SEALs also knew their way around, having deployed from them on several missions. An orderly took Dawson to his quarters. The SEALs, being enterprising go-getters, had already staked out bunks in the Chiefs' quarters.

After Dawson left the bridge, the executive officer (XO) came over to the captain. "So that is the famous Trevor Dawson, God's gift to the Navy, Naval Aviation, and women everywhere. He looks OK."

The captain growled, "I'm not taking any chances. I want every female on board, both officer and enlisted, confined to their quarters when they are not standing watch. Pass the word very discreetly. I don't want any EEOC or sexual harassment complaints. It's for their own good. From what I hear, anytime a woman comes into close proximity with that son-of-a-bitch, she starts taking off her clothes. It's a wonder he has the energy left to climb into the cockpit of an F-18."

The XO laughed and said, "Aye, aye, Sir." For the next three days, until they reached their destination, anywhere that Dawson went on the ship, at least three pairs of female eyes were surreptitiously on him. If he noticed, he did not let on.

For the three days that Trevor and company were at sea, Abigail would travel with an escort, usually Cedrik and one or more of his men, to outlying villages where she cared for the sick. As always, the appreciation of the people was priceless.

The day after they returned to Loalaville and a thunderous reception, Janette and Claudette departed for France. The French government sent a helicopter to pick them up. France was waiting with unbridled excitement to celebrate their return and welcome them back as heroes. A parade up the Champs-Élysées was planned upon their arrival. No delay or excuses would be tolerated. They hugged their traveling companions and wished them well. The people of Loalaville gathered to watch the helicopter depart with waves and blown kisses. Diana Chan asked for and received permission to accompany the nurses to Paris, where she would board a flight with her precious interview recoding. CNB promised the French government they would reimburse it for Diana's trip and they agreed. There was no good reason not to.

On day four, Abigail and her mates were sitting in a park near the Israeli mission building when a US Navy CH-53E Super Stallion helicopter hovered overhead and then landed in the park. A crowd of curious Loalans gathered to watch. Two helicopters landing within a week of each other was almost unheard of, let alone two days. When the rotors stopped turning, a door opened and out walked a very large man. He looked like a stereotypical California surfer: deep tan, blond hair, sun-glasses, perfect teeth, and radiant smile. He wore the Navy patterned blue camouflage utility uniform. The major difference is that the uniform typically is baggy on all who wear it. On surfer god, it was different. The uniform looked like it was sprayed on him. It displayed all of his muscles.

LCDR Trevor Dawson was a defensive tackle at Annapolis. A big defensive tackle. His muscles had muscles. He was drafted by an NFL team, but he wanted to fly and see the world. He became a very good Naval aviator. He was a valued member of whatever squadron to which he was assigned. The initial reaction of many who met him was that this guy was too good to be true. He was probably a real jerk. That reaction never lasted long. He was a real person, one of the guys. He was such a good aviator that he had flown a tour with the famed *Blue Angels*. What the captain of the *Eisenhower* said about him was also true. He was a real babe magnet. They flocked to him. It got to the point where one of his commanding officers 'advised' him not to go to the officer's club unless he was with a group of male officers. There were too many women, single and married, who would love to do the wild thing with him. His 'talent' did not go unnoticed by certain admirals, and not in a negative sense. Oh sure, they hid their wives and their daughters as a precautionary move, but when missions such as this came up, he was their man. This type of mission happened more than most people would imagine.

As he strode towards Abigail, he wore his radiant smile and offered a wave. Abigail was a female and had never seen anyone like this. The closest she had ever come was Antonio Spiga on *Soul Searcher*, but Antonio wasn't in this guy's class. As he walked up from the chopper, he exuded confidence. He reached Abigail and said, "Ms. Abigail Williams?" Abby nodded. He thrust out his hand while showing off his pearly whites, "Hi. My name is Trevor Dawson. Is there any place quiet we can go and talk?"

Abigail pointed at an empty park bench. As they walked over to it, she noticed that Cedrik's squad had drifted over to their vehicles and were going through the motions of getting their gear ready. Once they were seated, Dawson began, "Ms. Williams, I was sent here at the direction of the president. He wants you to come home. You have done a marvelous job here. The entire country is proud of you. He is proud of you. He wants to officially welcome you home."

"Mr. Dawson, when the president and I last spoke, he was not a happy man. In fact, he was quite irritated with me. He wanted me to go to North Korea and see its leader who is dying of cancer. I refused, and that infuriated him. I can't imagine that he would suddenly have such a change in his opinion of me."

"Please call me Trevor. All of my friends do. No one calls me mister. I can't speak for the president as to why he changed his mind. I do know that he desperately wants you to come with me. The plan is for you and me to fly in that chopper to an aircraft carrier. From there, we will fly together on a Navy jet to Ramstein Air Base in Germany and then on to our final destination."

Abigail noticed that Dawson did not specify where the final destination was. "Where is the final destination? Washington?"

Dawson was honest, "I'm not sure. I assume that it is DC. My orders did not specify the destination. They just ordered me to come and fetch you at the direction of the president."

Abigail shook her head and sighed. "Trevor, I'm afraid I am going to decline your kind offer. I'll take care of getting myself back when it suits me."

"Ms. Williams, I don't understand your hesitation. Believe me, it will be so much easier for both of us if you accept the hospitality of the US Navy and fly with me."

Abigail shook her head, no. Unhappily, Dawson nodded his understanding and waved to the helicopter. At his signal, four lightly-armed men dressed all in black came rushing towards the bench. They had barely taken a dozen steps when a loud voice called out, "**YOU MEN, HALT!**" The four SEALs stopped and looked around. The voice emanated from a very angry looking Cedrik Balthazar who was holding a submachine gun. The SEALs also noticed four other men standing near some Range Rovers and jeeps. Three of the men were also holding submachine guns. One was holding a Light Anti-tank Weapon pointed in the general direction of the helicopter. Cedrik called out, "Fellas, it's a long walk back to your carrier. I suggest that you stop and drop your weapons."

Dawson asked, "May I ask who you are? We are US Navy personnel on an official mission."

"Commander, who we are is not important. What is important is that we are companions of Ms. Williams, and you are on a hostile mission in a sovereign country. I hate to think about how many international laws you have broken by being here. I really hate to think about how this will play out in the media. I suggest that you and your men get back on the copter and head out of here immediately. Suleiman there has a nervous finger and he loves to see things go BOOM when he fires the LAW. I'll guarantee that the crew of the chopper would prefer it that way. They don't relish the fact that they would be crispy critters if his finger suddenly tenses up."

Trevor Dawson was a proud man. He hated to lose. He was also a wise man. He knew he was outgunned and in a no-win situation. He was also a moral man. He thought something smelled about this mission from the start. His orders did not specify where the final destination would be, but he strongly suspected it was not Washington DC. He stood up and motioned for his men to withdraw back into the Sea Stallion. He turned to Abigail and took her hand. He gallantly bowed and kissed it, gave her a wink, and climbed aboard the chopper. The pilots started the engines and soon it was airborne heading back to the carrier.

No sooner had the naval aircraft cleared Loala airspace than a second copter landed. This one was a sleek executive model painted black. It had the crest of the monastery in Georgia on its sides. Once the blades stopped rotating, the door opened, and a figure emerged wearing a black flight suit and a Roman collar. Abigail was surprised and delighted to see the smiling face of Father Jubal. She rushed to him, followed close behind by Cedrik, and gave him a warm embrace. "Oh, Father, it is so good to see you."

"You, as well, Abigail, and, of course, Cedrik here. Has he been taking good care of you?" He saw Cedrik's squad standing nearby and walked over to shake hands. It was evident that he knew them as they traded jokes and insults back and forth. He returned to Abigail and Cedrik after a short while and suggested that they go somewhere and grab lunch.

While seated at a table in a small café, Abigail brought Father Jubal up-to-date on everything that transpired from the time she left Georgia until the Navy helicopter departed. He expressed wonder and joy when they told him about helping the population and about defeating Frankie and his men. He was outraged by Obutu's excesses. He was shocked by the attempt to kidnap Abigail by members of the US Navy. He looked at Cedrik and said with a smile, "This is the second time you were able to defeat an assault on an Abby. You're getting good at it."

Father Jubal excitedly told them of the impact of Diana Chan's story and video of the interview. He said that no one in America knew where either Loala or Kilnmari were before this. Now everyone knew. The three Obutu's were probably the most loathed people on the planet. Just about everyone was anticipating the trial and punishment at The International Court of Justice in The Hague.

Father Jubal noted that President Diamond did not appear to be overly impressed with her efforts. When peppered with questions, he answered that it looks like things worked out OK. He just wished that 'that Williams person' was more patriotic and put her country's interests first. Evidently, the media had a field day with that quote.

He went on to tell them that when Senator Berkshire was asked for a comment about Loala, he said that he was proud that an American was able to do such a heroic feat. He also said that his son, Sylvester, is a close personal friend of Ms. Williams and was looking forward to seeing her again. Both men noticed Abigail shudder when the priest said that.

Abigail asked him if he would like to meet President Terrence Ngao if she could arrange a meeting, and he quickly accepted. She was surprised when she learned that President Ngao could meet with them that afternoon. At the appointed time, the three of them were shown into the president's office. Father Jubal was still wearing his flight suit and clerical collar. She was further surprised to see that Marie Justine Obutu was there, as well. Ngao explained that she had remained in Loalaville for several days and the two of them were discussing possible areas of cooperation that would benefit both countries. A joint venture in a new power plant had already been agreed upon.

As always, Marie Justine was gracious and regal. She warmly greeted Father Jubal and appeared positively delighted to see Cedrik again. Cedrik said, "Madam President, it is good to see you under better circumstances. We have not yet been formally introduced. My name is Cedrik Balthazar."

"Mr. Balthazar, I tried to find you the other day without success. It is a pleasure to make your acquaintance. Forgive me if I was somewhat curt in Kilnmari. I had a lot on my mind."

"That, madam, is a gross understatement. No apologies are necessary."

The five of them sat around a coffee table and had an enjoyable conversation. Most of it was focused on where these two presidents saw their respective countries progressing. There was no doubt in the minds of Abigail, Cedrik, and Father Jubal that both countries would progress and prosper with the hands of these two on the tillers of their respective ships of state. Finally, it was time to depart. Abigail announced that she was leaving Loala and Loalaville. Ngao was shocked. "My dear young lady, I knew this day had to come, but it saddens me greatly that it has arrived. You and your companions saved my country. We are in your debt forever."

Back at the helicopter, a huge crowd had gathered. President Ngao had released a statement about Abigail's upcoming departure and encouraged as many people as possible to say goodbye, thank you, and God speed. The people responded. As always, respect permeated everything Loalan. They crowded around her, but kept some distance, and parted to make a path for her as she walked. Abigail realized that she was truly beginning to love these people.

When they arrived at the helicopter, Cedrik took her aside. "Look, Abigail, I think we make a great team. I'd like you to join us. Join me. As I told you in Georgia, the five of us live in a very pleasant state. I can't describe it, but it is wonderful. From time to time, we are called upon to help someone in need. When that task is done, we go back. Please come with me."

While he was speaking, his four companions gathered around them. Leif echoed Cedrik's words and the others nodded in agreement. Their eyes pleaded with her like a puppy begging for food. Her heart was breaking. She had shared so much with these warriors and had grown fond of each and every one, yet she knew she had to go back to the US. Duty had brought her to Loala, and duty will bring her back to the states. Sadly, she shook her head and told them her answer. They understood. They didn't like it, but they understood. She embraced all of them and kissed them on the cheek. Cedrik was the last and the hardest to say goodbye to. The embrace lasted a good while and, when it was done, he climbed into one of the jeeps and both vehicles proceeded out of the city. Abigail noticed a dense fog in the distance. She thought this was strange as the weather was warm and dry. The jeeps drove into the fog and disappeared.

Abigail then turned and followed Father Jubal into the helicopter, stopping at the door for one last wave to the crowd. The chopper took off and made a final, slow pass around the city before heading into distant lands.

HOMECOMING

ather Jubal looked at her and smiled. "Well now, what are your plans?"

"Oh, I don't know. I think I would like to make some changes. I'd like to concentrate more on hospitals. I'll still do a limited number of mass healings, but I won't charge for them. I've done a lot of thinking, and I think I received some bad advice. It is totally my fault that I followed it. I should have known better. I made a small fortune charging for the mass healings. I'll use that money now to finance future healings. Renting stadiums and racetracks is not cheap."

Father Jubal patted her hand and said, "That sounds wonderful."

Abigail continued, "I think I will still do the private appointments. I'm going to change the scope of them. I love dealing with athletes, so I am going to continue the retainers to the teams. This would give me a revenue stream. I'll fill the other appointment slots with people who are truly sick and desperate. I won't charge them. In fact, in extreme cases, I will pay their expenses to come to me, or perhaps I'll go to them. It depends. I expect that, eventually, I'll go overseas to work there. I haven't figured that out yet."

She then changed the subject, "Am I going to have problems

re-entering the country? I imagine that the president has an alert out for me when I return."

Jubal replied, "I'm sure he does. That boy doesn't forgive or forget. No, I expect that every border crossing has your picture prominently displayed and all agents are on the lookout for you." Then he smiled, "You're forgetting whom you are traveling with. Lucius Diamond doesn't play in our league. But to answer your question, no, you will not have any problems. You will be back at our monastery in Georgia before he even knows you left Loala."

Several days later in the Oval Office, the Secretary of Defense; the Chairman of the Joint Chiefs of Staff, a Marine Corps General; and the Chief of Naval Operations, a Navy Admiral, were standing at rigid attention in the middle of the room. The remainder of the cabinet and the president's close advisors were cowering along the walls, silently praying that they would remain out of the line of fire. The president's invective was impressive. He was using words few had heard before. He was even inventing words. Some of what he was saying were personal insults to the three victims. The Chief of Naval Operations' lips were quivering, he was so mad. Neither flag officer had ever been spoken to that way, even during their plebe year at Annapolis. Finally, the president said, "Get that sorry ass officer who commanded the extraction team in here."

All three of the targets spoke at once, noting that bringing the team's commander in for a presidential reprimand was inappropriate and flat-out wrong. He made a command decision, and from all indications, he made the correct one. More than one of them worried what Dawson might actually do if he got pissed enough. The president ignored them, "Bring him in. NOW!"

The Chief of Staff moved with his back along the wall to the door and summoned LCDR Trevor Dawson. While the door was open, the president saw the first lady deep in conversation with

Dawson. She seemed fascinated by his every word. She played with her hair like a teenage girl, smiled coyly, and crossed and uncrossed her gorgeous legs several times to draw attention to them. When Dawson got up to enter the Oval Office, she made the international sign for "Call me." The president erupted. His blood pressure was probably off of the chart.

Wearing his dress blue uniform, he marched smartly up to the president and reported as ordered. The president had to look up at him. Way up. That made the president even madder. He hated being looked down to. Very calmly in a very professional tone, Dawson recounted every detail of the mission, and he was honest. He recounted that Abigail had asked him where the final destination was and he told her he assumed it was Washington, but his orders did not specify a final destination.

"Why didn't you just tell her it was definitely DC?"

"Mr. President, because I was not sure where it was. It was not specified. I would expect that on a mission like this, the final destination of Washington would have been clearly spelled out."

"Why didn't you just lie?'

Dawson just looked down at him with a withering look of contempt and loathing. He did not dignify the question with a response.

Finally, the Chief of Naval Operations exclaimed, "That's it. I am done. I cannot in good conscience listen to this crap anymore. Mr. President, you will have my letter of resignation first thing tomorrow morning." He started to storm out of the office.

"You ingrate. You can't resign. You're fired. Now get the hell out of here and take this Casanova with you."

When they were in the hall, the chief said to Dawson, "Well, Commander, that was fun. Oh well, I was looking for an excuse to get out. That guy really wears you down. He truly is a moron.

Don't worry about it. I'll have orders cut today transferring you to CINCPAC.[14] He'll protect you and keep you out of harm's way. And for God's sake, don't take any calls from the first lady." They both laughed, shook hands went their separate ways.

Barney and Polina were, for the most part, content as to where things stood. For one thing, and most importantly, the boss was off of their backs. They thought that the most logical target of their attention should be the Berkshire campaign. 'Jethro and Jughead', a.k.a. Sylvester Berkshire and Dexter van Allen, were the openings into the campaign that Barney and Polina were looking for. The two young men were sitting at a bar in mid-town Manhattan when Barney and Polina 'just happened' to walk by. Barney stopped in pretended shock and exclaimed to Polina, "Talk about a small world. These two gentlemen were on the *Soul Searcher* with us. Polina and I were just talking about how great a time that was."

It took a few seconds for the two lads to connect that they did, in fact, know these two outgoing and friendly people. Sylvester got to his feet and extended his hand. "I remember you. You joined the cruise late. You got that right. It was a blast. I'd love to go back out on it, but I'm too busy with my dad's campaign. Here, sit down and join us."

Both Polina and Barney dove into the empty seats before Dexter could oppose. He had not said a word and barely acknowledged them when they came to the table. It was obvious that he was not happy about something. Barney quickly started the conversation, "We know that you are Sylvester and Dexter. In case you forgot, my beautiful companion is Polina, and I am Barney. So, how have you two been? How's the campaign going?"

---

14. Commander in Chief Pacific Fleet

That's all it took. Sylvester was off and running, talking about his favorite subject, himself. The campaign was fine, followed by detail after detail. Barney and Polina were dazzled by Sylvester's responsibilities and his input into major decisions. Uzbekitherm was doing splendidly. Money just kept pouring in.

Polina inquired, "That's wonderful. You must have found a huge deposit of gas and oil."

"No. Not yet, but things really look promising. Mr. Shaytan and I spoke just yesterday, and he thinks it is just a very short time before the drillers strike the big reservoir down there."

Polina asked, "Where is the money pouring in from if you haven't found oil yet."

In a very condescending tone, Sylvester explained, "Oh, you would be surprised. Dealing with the Uzbeks is wonderful. They appreciate the development that we could potentially bring to the land and are not bashful about showing it."

Barney looked at Dexter, who was staring into his drink. "And what about you Dexter? How are things going?"

"Just peachy! I just got off of the phone with my lawyer. That grand jury indicted me. It's just a bunch of crap. I didn't do anything wrong. The damn FBI and the Deputy US Attorney for the Southern District of New York are both out to get me. They promised one of my partners a plea deal if he would turn on me. The son-of-a-bitch took the deal and is lying his ass off to protect himself. The dirty bastard."

Barney responded in a solicitous tone, "I'm awfully sorry to hear that, Dex. You are such a stand-up guy. I'll bet it will all blow over shortly."

Polina asked, "Do you hear from any of the others on the cruise? I ran into Abigail before she went to Africa. I had no idea she was the 'miracle girl' when we were on the yacht. Did you?"

Sylvester perked up. "Do you know how to contact her? I'd love to see her again. I really liked her on the yacht. She was so much fun to be with. Boy, could she tell some stories."

Even Barney, who never was surprised by anything, choked up on this. Polina almost died laughing at his discomfort. She finally was composed enough to answer Sylvester's question, "When she returns, we're supposed to have lunch. Give me your cell phone number and I'll send you her contact info after I get it from her."

In Georgia, Abigail felt that something was somehow different. She first noticed it on the helicopter while leaving Loala when Father Jubal had patted her hand. She couldn't put her finger on it, but she felt different.

The priest did not lie. They had no trouble getting back to Georgia. The helicopter took them to an airstrip in South Africa, where they boarded a sleek executive jet that also had the crest of the monastery on its sides. She was exhausted when she got on board the jet and fell fast asleep. The next thing she knew, they were taxiing to a hangar at a small private airport. She recognized it as the one the helicopter from the monastery dropped her and Cedrik off at for the flight to Africa. Waiting for them was the black helicopter with the monastery crest on each side.

When the helicopter touched down at the monastery, 200 monks were waiting to greet her. Father Buchannan came forward and warmly embraced her. Behind him stood the imposing figure of Michael Angelo. After he embraced her, he said, "Well, you've been a busy girl. I can't wait to hear the stories. Neither can the others. You and I are going to drive to Philly where everyone will be waiting. We are going to have a reunion with the entire group."

At dinner that evening, Abigail mentioned that she felt a little different. She shrugged it off as being the difference in climate between Africa and Georgia. Also the food. The chef at the monastery had created an exceptional masterpiece that evening to celebrate her return. She remarked that she had certainly not eaten anything so delicious in Loala. Fathers Buchanan and Jubal, as well as Michael, exchanged pointed glances but remained silent.

Back in Washington, the Secretary of the Navy held a press conference to announce the firing of the Chief of Naval Operations. He thanked the admiral for his service but claimed that he had recently lost confidence in him. He closed by saying that eventually everyone gets stale and needs a change. The press went wild. There were rumors of a rift between the president and certain members of the military. SECNAV would not confirm these rumors. One reporter mentioned that there was a rumor that the 'miracle girl' had returned from Africa and asked if the secretary had any information about this. Of course, the SECNAV denied any knowledge. At any rate, rumors were flying. The media was on high alert. The White House was in lockdown mode. Situation normal.

While driving back to Philadelphia with Mike, Abigail suggested that they stop at a hospital she saw signs for just off of the interstate in North Carolina. She just wanted to go in unannounced, walk around and cure as many people as she could before everyone got excited. Michael told her he didn't think it was a good idea, but she would not take no for an answer. Reluctantly he pulled into the hospital's parking lot, and they went inside. As Abigail walked around the lobby, waiting area, and ER on the first floor, she passed many obviously sick and injured people. There was no reaction. There were no euphoric cries of "I've been healed." Abigail made a point of getting as close as possible to some of the patients without invading their personal space. Again there was no reaction. Eventually, she headed to the doors, and they got back on the road.

They drove for an hour or so in absolute silence. Finally, she turned to Michael and said, "Did you see that back in the hospital?

I didn't cure anyone. What's going on? Did I lose my power?" She was really upset.

Michael looked very concerned. "I don't know. I saw what you tried to do in the hospital back there and saw that it didn't work this time. Has that ever happened before?"

"No. Not ever."

They continued on mostly in silence to Philadelphia, each deep in their own thoughts. When they arrived at the five-star Rittenhouse Hotel, the entire gang was there: Drs. Stanton, Lucas and Barr, Marguerite Camp, Raphael Melek, Angelina Gabriella, Tommy Sullivan, Douglas Keenan, and Lorena Mason. These were the folks who were with her on her incredible journey. They were like family. Heck, they were family. The closest she had ever known. They dined that evening at Lacroix Restaurant at the Rittenhouse, the site of many meetings of **The Practice**. Miracle of miracles, Dr. Lucas picked up the check. It was a wonderful evening. Abigail told story after story about her adventure in Africa. She described the nobility of the Loalan people, the ruthlessness of the Obutu's, the heroism of the French nurses, the grace of Marie Justine and the potential of Terrence Ngao. She said little about Cedrik and his warriors. She missed all five of them terribly and could not speak of them without shedding tears. She told them her plans for the future were up in the air, but she would like to get together with them in a week or so to discuss options.

The next morning while having breakfast at the coffee shop off of the lobby, who should arrive but Barney and Polina? "Hello, old friend," Barney said as they grabbed two chairs at her table. "Welcome home. How have you been?"

Before she could, answer Polina said, "Are you staying at the Rittenhouse? It has always been one of my favorites?"

Abigail said, "It is a lovely hotel. Everyone is so friendly."

Polina asked, "Now that you're back, what are your plans?"

"I really don't have any right now. I think I'm going to concentrate on hospitals right now and leave the mass healings alone, at least for the time being." They chatted for a while, then Barney and Polina excused themselves.

Abigail went shopping later that morning. Most of her things were still in her house in the Smokey Mountains, so she needed some clothes and necessities. When she returned to the hotel, she grabbed lunch and went to her room and took a nap. She was woken from a deep sleep by the ringing of the hotel phone. When she answered it, much to her surprise and chagrin, it was Sylvester Berkshire.

He spoke to her as if they were old, close friends. Abby was too polite to tell him to get lost, so she listened and answered when appropriate. Sylvester said that his father, the senator and presidential candidate, found out that they were close friends and wanted to meet her. At this, Abigail pulled the phone from her ear and looked at it like it was a snake. Sylvester went on that it would be great if he could drive to Philadelphia tomorrow, pick her up, and take her to meet his father. After that, he wanted to take her to the trendiest restaurant in DC for dinner, then back to Philly. Abigail thought to herself that she would rather have all of her teeth extracted without Novocain than spend time with this scumbag, but she couldn't think of a good excuse. Reluctantly, she accepted.

Sylvester picked her up the next morning in his BMW SUV. She was shocked to see Dexter van Allen sitting in the back seat. Sylvester told her that once Dex found out she was going to DC with him, he insisted that he come along for old time's sake. The two goofballs chatted nonstop like a couple of magpies. Abigail would have killed for a pair of noise-canceling headphones.

When they arrived at Senator Berkshire's campaign headquarters located in Alexandria, Virginia, Abigail was shocked to see a large crowd around the entrance of the building. When they saw her, they mobbed the vehicle. With the aid of several policemen, Sly and Dex led her into the building. Once inside, Abigail straightened her clothes and asked, "What was that all about?"

Sylvester responded, "I guess once they found out that you would be here today, they wanted to come and see you?"

"How did they find out that I would be here this morning?"

"Well, I guess I kind of put the word out. I hope you don't mind." Abby wanted to strangle the little weasel but restrained herself with great difficulty.

They went in and met with Senator Berkshire. The senator was very charming and gracious, but also shallow and hollow. His bonhomie was a well-rehearsed act. They chatted a while and she posed with the senator for the obligatory photographs. She could only imagine where those would turn up. After a polite period of small talk, the senator indicated that he had a pressing appointment and had to excuse himself.

As Abigail and her two knights in shining armor exited the building, she immediately saw a difference in the crowd. Before, they were almost desperate to get close to her. Now they demonstrated pure hostility. At first, she was baffled, then she was stunned. These people came here expecting to be cured and became irate when no cures were forthcoming. The three of them quickly ducked into the Beamer and raced out of Virginia. No words were spoken until they reached Maryland.

"Sylvester, those people were mad as hell. Did you promise them that I would cure them?"

He was adamant in his denial. "No way. Of course not. I would never do anything like that."

She told them that she would take a rain check on dinner and to please take her back to the hotel. Once safely in her room, she turned on the television to the evening newscast. She was horrified to see images of herself and the crowd at the Berkshire headquarters building. It was a riot, all right. The reporter on the spot said that the Berkshire campaign had sold tickets for $200, each promising a cure. When it was obvious that that was not going to happen, the crowd became incensed.

The Berkshire campaign issued a statement that they were not behind this 'unfortunate incident.' Unfortunately for them, the horse was already out of the barn. An enterprising reporter was able to produce printed tickets that proudly proclaimed, "Senator James Berkshire Proudly Presents Abigail Williams." The price of $200 was prominent on the ticket. In small print, it read, "Contribution to the Campaign of Berkshire for President."

The president had a field day. He called Berkshire a scammer, a con man, a cheat, a villain of the worse sort to prey upon desperate people, and everything else he could think of. The media loved it. "Cheatin' Berky" was the presidential nickname for his opponent. "If he would do this to his supporters, think what he would do to this country" was the slogan he used whenever he could on the campaign trail.

Senator Berkshire fought this with a counterattack about Diamond unilaterally invading Loala and trying to kidnap a US citizen to travel to cure a tyrant of the worst sort. His campaign came up with the slogan, "He's like a fake diamond: pretty on the outside, but worthless inside." They gave him the nickname of "Worthless Lucius."

Shortly after the newscast ended, the phone rang. It was Diana Chan. Diana asked how it was going. When Abby told her, they both decided they needed a drink. They met at the bar across from her old office where they had met in what seemed like so long ago. They laughed, got totally hammered, and then took a cab to Jimmy G's Cheesesteaks.

EPILOGUE

Abigail lost her power to cure, but her story did not end there. In a large part, it only began there. She sold her mansion in the Smokey Mountains and moved into her father's house in Springfield, PA. Father Jubal flew up to Philadelphia and spoke with her about her powers and Cedrik. He told her that she had had no powers prior to her first encounter with him at the high school. She really had no idea when she was granted the powers or who granted them to her. It was only after she was out in the real world that they manifested themselves, and they did so in a very quiet and unassuming way. At first, she didn't even know she had them.

Father Jubal laid out a possible scenario for her to consider. When Cedrik rescued her from the bully in high school, he was scouting her. He liked what he saw. She had potential. The powers were granted to her, but she needed to learn how to use them. There was going to be a fight in the future, and he wanted her ready for it. Thus began the journey that eventually led her to Loala and the massive humanitarian feat she accomplished along with Cedrik and his warriors. When they had defeated the enemy and the assault on Abby, Cedrik offered her the chance to join them. Up to that point, everything she did was her duty. She had powers, and she did her duty in using them. The choice Cedrik offered her in Loala had nothing to do with duty. It was purely about her personal preference. It was like, "Did she want to be a doctor or a lawyer?" When she chose to go back, she had no pressing need for the power. She was going to live as normal a life as possible. It was as simple as that.

She asked, "What about Cedrik and his men?"

Father Jubal replied, "He told you while you were at the monastery. For some reason, they were selected thousands of years ago after doing a brave and noble deed to become timeless. They are sent out by some unknown power from time to time to rescue someone in dire need of rescuing. He and his men do what our order of monks try to do. They try to do noble deeds and make the world a better place."

She promised the priest that she would think long and hard about what he had said. After he took his leave, she decided what she wanted. She loved healing people. The two French nurses inspired her. She wanted to become a doctor. She knew that academically she was deficient, particularly in math and lab sciences. She approached her three doctors and told them what she wanted. They were thrilled. They arranged for her to get tutored to the point where she could pass the SAT's with a high enough score to get into a college. All three of them were graduates of Penn and were able to pull some strings. They were also very generous contributors to the university, which helped. She was admitted to the University of Pennsylvania and was able to graduate in 18 months. She was then admitted to Penn's Medical School. After she graduated, she chose Pediatric Oncology as her specialty. After several residencies and fellowships, she returned to Philadelphia and joined her three doctors in their practice. Coincidently she accepted an invitation to join **The Practice**. Along the way, she found time for romance. She married and moved to a large house in Gladwyne, PA, and filled it with three children.

Tommy Sullivan continued to prosper. His reputation for honesty and scruples carried him to the top of the profession. Lorena Mason joined him as a full partner in his firm.

Doug Keenan also prospered until he was killed in a traffic accident while on the way home by a drunk driver. Tommy gave the eulogy at the funeral Mass.

Michael Angelo's pizza business in Brooklyn continued as the cornerstone of the neighborhood. The restaurant that he helped his wife's cousin start did not fare so well. The cousin was incompetent. Michael bought him out, put his nephew in charge, and now business is booming.

Angelina Gabriella continued to work for Jimmy Halvorson in Portsmouth. He promoted her to president of the company, while he retained the title of chairman and chief operating officer.

Raphael Melek continued to fight the Battle of Washington as a lobbyist. He always seemed to be on the side of good. That meant that most congressmen and senators were wary of him.

Diana Chan won a Pulitzer Prize and an Emmy for her work on the story. She also received acclaim for her reporting on the Uzbekitherm scandal. She was looked upon by many as being in the same league as Walter Cronkite, David Brinkley, Chet Huntley, and Cokie Roberts.

Dexter van Allen was tried and convicted of multiple counts of fraud and conspiracy. The government wanted to make an example of him to deter others. He was sentenced to 25 years in a medium-security prison. It was not a nice place. Among other things, Dexter was often the subject of beatings and rapes.

As to the election battle between Diamond and Berkshire, the country got exactly what it deserved for allowing two dullards like them to compete for the position of the most powerful person on earth.

ABOUT THE AUTHOR

Thomas O. P. Sweeney graduated from the United States Military Academy at West Point and received an MBA from Southern Illinois University Edwardsville. He served in the U.S. Army as an Armor officer with postings in Germany and the United States. He then worked in the chemical industry for 37 years, both in production as well as supply chain management. He has been married to Jennifer for 45 years and resides in Frisco, TX. He has published two previous books, *My Dearest Christina – A Father Remembers his Daughter and her Battle with Lupus* and *Barney–The Likeable Demon*. Both are available on Amazon. Visit topsweeney.com for more information.